W9-AXY-498

Praise for *New York Times* bestselling author Tawny Weber

"Tawny Weber's characters generate enough heat to melt the polar ice cap! I double-dare you to pick up this book."
—*New York Times* bestselling author
Vicki Lewis Thompson on *Double Dare*

"Fiery hot sex scenes, strong characters and exciting action make this one of the best stories in the Uniformly Hot! miniseries—and one of the best Blaze reads."
—*RT Book Reviews* on *A SEAL's Seduction*

"*A SEAL's Secret* is captivating, compelling and very sensual.... A truly exceptional book, Tawny Weber's best ever."
—*Fresh Fiction*

"Forget the hot chocolate, the wool socks and the space heater—Tawny Weber's *Sex, Lies and Mistletoe* will keep you plenty warm this season!"
—*USA TODAY*

"Tawny Weber has a gift when it comes to writing about hot SEALs and the women they fall for."
—*Lush Book Reviews*

"The story is well constructed, solid, believable, very deftly written, featuring the author's trademark humor, and the dialogue is spot-on... Tawny Weber remains THE class act when it comes to contemporary romance."
—*Fresh Fiction* on *A SEAL's Fantasy*

"Deliciously blending sexual tension, heartfelt emotions, misunderstandings, humor and love, talented author Tawny Weber has penned a story you do not want to miss!"
—*Romance Junkies* on *Just for the Night*

MAR – 2017

Coming soon from Tawny Weber and HQN Books

A SEAL Brotherhood Novel

Call to Engage
Call to Redemption

Other titles by Tawny Weber

Uniformly Hot!

A SEAL's Seduction
A SEAL's Surrender
A SEAL's Salvation
A SEAL's Kiss
A SEAL's Fantasy
Christmas with a SEAL
A SEAL's Secret
A SEAL's Pleasure
A SEAL's Temptation
A SEAL's Touch
A SEAL's Desire

To see the complete list of titles available from
Tawny Weber, please visit tawnyweber.com.

TAWNY WEBER

CALL TO HONOR

Free Public Library of Audubon
239 Oakland Avenue
Audubon, NJ 08106

HQN™

If you purchased this book without a cover you should be aware that this book is stolen property. It was reported as "unsold and destroyed" to the publisher, and neither the author nor the publisher has received any payment for this "stripped book."

HQN™

ISBN-13: 978-0-373-79928-2

Call to Honor

Copyright © 2017 by Tawny Weber

The publisher acknowledges the copyright holder of the additional work:

Night Maneuvers
Copyright © 2017 by Tawny Weber

All rights reserved. Except for use in any review, the reproduction or utilization of this work in whole or in part in any form by any electronic, mechanical or other means, now known or hereinafter invented, including xerography, photocopying and recording, or in any information storage or retrieval system, is forbidden without the written permission of the publisher, HQN Books, 225 Duncan Mill Road, Don Mills, Ontario M3B 3K9, Canada.

This is a work of fiction. Names, characters, places and incidents are either the product of the author's imagination or are used fictitiously, and any resemblance to actual persons, living or dead, business establishments, events or locales is entirely coincidental.

This edition published by arrangement with Harlequin Books S.A.

For questions and comments about the quality of this book, please contact us at CustomerService@Harlequin.com.

® and TM are trademarks of Harlequin Enterprises Limited or its corporate affiliates. Trademarks indicated with ® are registered in the United States Patent and Trademark Office, the Canadian Intellectual Property Office and in other countries.

www.HQNBooks.com

Printed in U.S.A.

Recycling programs for this product may not exist in your area.

CONTENTS

To my family.
For always being there.

CALL TO HONOR

CHAPTER ONE

IT PAYS TO be a winner.

And Diego Torres was a big believer in winning.

But it was *the winning* that he liked.

The competition.

The thrill of testing his skills, pushing his limits. Of knowing he was better than his adversary.

Yeah. He liked knowing he was the best.

He didn't do it for reward.

Especially not when the reward came by way of the pomp and pageantry of a ceremony like today. Standing onstage in front of the various platoons that made up SEAL Team 7, listening to Admiral Cree pontificate was a pain in the ass. What made it worse wasn't the couple hundred sets of eyes inspecting him or the discomfort of his dress whites, too tight across the shoulders.

It was the damned shoes. Diego's toes pinched in the mirror-bright black patent leather, begging him to flex. He didn't, of course. Not while standing at attention. But damn. Give him a pair of combat boots any day.

As the sun baked through his cap and the heat of the morning swirled around, he wondered what yahoo had decided to hold this ceremony outdoors. And why it felt so much hotter standing in the San Diego sun in whites than it did in the Afghan desert in full combat gear. Probably because combat gear fit him better.

Diego had spent a large portion of his life fighting over the wrong things. He'd fought over turf. He'd fought over gang colors. Hell, if the mood struck, he'd have fought over just how blue the sky was. It'd taken a bullet barely missing his heart to clue him in to the fact that maybe the things he was fighting over simply weren't worth dying for.

He'd figured that out when he woke in a hospital bed, his mother's careworn face wet with tears. Wondering if he'd see his eighteenth birthday, Diego had taken stock of his situation. He'd started out a street thug, worked his way up to gangbanger, then into the powerful role of First Lieutenant of the Marauders, an East LA gang determined to claw its way to the top of the food chain.

It wasn't the bullet that had made him reconsider his chosen lifestyle. Nor, he was still ashamed to admit, was it his mother's misery. It was the fact that his gang, his sworn brothers, had left him in that filthy alley to bleed out while they ran to save their own asses.

That'd made Diego rethink his definition of brotherhood. Of honor.

Now that he was a Lieutenant in the United States Navy he still fought. But he fought for his country. He was still a badass. But he was a badass SEAL. And if he got shot now, he knew his team would lay their lives on the line to get him out.

And that was key for a man who put loyalty above all else.

As the admiral's voice boomed out his pride in the elite power of Special Forces, Diego didn't look toward his superiors on the left, even though he stood shoulder to shoulder with Lieutenant Commander Ty Louden, who stood with Commander Nic Savino on his other side. Diego didn't look to the right toward his teammate,

Lieutenant Elijah Prescott, or beyond him to Petty Officer Aaron Ward.

But in his mind's eye, he could see them all standing as he did, eyes forward, shoulders back. Basking somewhere between pride and misery at such focused attention, their faces were as familiar to him as his own. Brothers in every way but blood, Diego would—and had—put his life on the line for every one of them and knew they'd do the same for him.

With his mother dead three years past, these men were Diego's family. They'd helped form him into the man he'd become. They'd been part of shaping him into a SEAL he could be proud of.

And these here onstage? They'd led a raid to capture three high-level militants, doing so in the dead of night without detection. Proving, once again, that Poseidon kicked ass.

Which was pretty much why they were standing up here being recognized.

As SEALs, they were trained to be the best.

As members of Poseidon, they were expected to be better than the best. Twelve men had come out of BUD/S together, each earning his trident a decade ago. Thanks to Admiral Cree, all twelve served among SEAL Team 7's various platoons, allowing them to continue to train together, to study together, to excel together. And, when called up, to serve together. Team Leader Savino's doing, Diego knew. The man had had a vision in BUD/S of an elite force of warriors, all focused on one purpose. They trained longer, they pushed further, they fought harder than most.

They made their mark.

And now they were getting awarded for it.

Diego damn near rolled his eyes as the speech eulogizing that award droned on. And on and on and on.

But, thankfully, years of Navy discipline stepped in and kept his eyes still and his discomfort at bay.

Finally, the admiral wound up the ceremony by personally pinning a commendation to each man's chest. The weight of the man's congratulations was twice the honor of the bronze Expeditionary Medal.

There was one final salute, a few words of thanks from Captain Jarrett, then the band played, the color guard stepped in and the team was dismissed.

Thank God.

Diego didn't let his grin show, but he sure felt good as he stepped off the stage. He didn't rip off his hat, but he mentally tossed it in the air and, hell, why not, did a fist-pumping victory dance in his mind.

Oh, yeah. It paid to win.

"You looked good up there, my friend." Chief Petty Officer Jared Lansky grinned, his boyish expression pure glee as he met Diego at the bottom of the platform.

"Why the hell wasn't your pretty face up there, too? The entire Poseidon team was being honored."

"Special assignment in Sudan. Plane got in late, so I didn't get here until Cree was winding down. I'll have to pick my medal up in private." Lansky pulled a face of fake regret, then grinned again. "But let's talk about what this is really about. Dude, we are so going to get laid. Nothing like a commendation to impress the ladies."

"Thanks for the perspective. Is there anything you don't bring down to sex?"

"Hmm, let me think." The other man tugged on his bottom lip, looking as if he were considering the weight of the world, before shaking his head. "Nope. I'm pretty sure the day I'm not thinking about sex will be the day you're tossing dirt on my grave."

Since the man hadn't shifted focus in the ten years he'd known him, Diego had to figure Lansky was in no danger of imminent burial.

"You look like a combination of choirboy and Boy Scout. It always blows me away to realize what a complete horndog you are."

"My looks are my secret weapon." Lansky beamed his pearly whites, those baby blues pure innocence. "A woman looks at you, all dark and brooding, and she knows she's looking at trouble. Me, I'm—"

"What?" Diego interrupted. "Stealth trouble?"

"Yes, sir. That I am." Jared tapped his knuckle on the brim of his cap, then tilted his head toward the Officers' Club. "Celebration time. On base or off?"

"Off, for sure." But as Diego's gaze swept over the dispersing crowd, he knew the team leader, Commander Savino, would want to offer up thanks to those who hadn't been onstage. The rest of the team—the ones who weren't a part of Poseidon, the support personnel. He'd give a little speech, buy a round of drinks. Public relations, Savino would call it. Pure hell, in Diego's opinion.

"We've got a meeting first." Diego jerked his head toward the long white building that held the offices of command.

Jared's gaze swept over Savino's back as he and a few others accompanied Admiral Cree in that general direction.

"Good times." Jared watched two more COs join the group and muttered, "Wish the plane had been a little later."

They headed for duty, making their way toward the

low-slung offices instead of joining the crowd heading toward the freedom of the O Club. Diego loved what he did. Every damned thing about it. Except the politics. Meetings like this, with all the glad-handing and posturing, they ranked right up there with dress shoes on his list of things that sucked.

But twenty minutes later he had to admit that politics went down pretty easy when served with whiskey.

"To Poseidon." The admiral lifted his glass, light gleaming in his steady blue gaze as it swept around the circle of men crowded into the pomp and polish of his office. "You do justice to my vision."

They were all well trained enough to keep from smirking as they lifted their glasses in response.

"And to Lieutenant Torres for leading the latest mission to prove Poseidon's might," Savino added, his dark eyes assessing, his expression satisfied. Which was about as close to a grin as he got while in uniform.

A little weirded out at being toasted, Diego knocked back the rest of his drink. As the heat slid down his throat, he realized that while this might not be the pinnacle of his career, it was a pretty high peak.

As if cementing that realization, Savino aimed a finger at Diego. The admiral nodded, setting his glass on the desk before giving Diego a sharp look.

"Torres. My office, oh-seven-hundred tomorrow morning. You'll be leading Operation Hammerhead."

With that, the admiral headed for the door, apparently leaving his office—and his bottle of Jameson—to the men.

"Gentlemen," he said in dismissal as he swung through the door, his two aides trailing in his wake.

"Check you," Elijah Prescott said, tossing his cap aside now that the brass had cleared out. Green eyes amused, the man leaned one hip on the desk while lifting the decanter to offer refills. "Leading another mission. A big one, from the sound of it. Hot damn, El Gato. Way to kiss brass ass."

El Gato. The cat. That was the call sign his BUD/S team had given Diego back in Basic Underwater Demolition/SEAL training because he moved with stealth and grace. Prescott was called Rembrandt owing to his habit of sketching his way through every spare minute. Lansky's skills had earned him the name MacGyver. The rest of the team was similarly nicknamed, with Savino in the lead as Kahuna.

"Brass-kissing is Savino's job," Diego reminded them, giving his commander a grin. The man carried enough weight to put Diego in charge of higher-ranking SEALs on his recommendation alone. Fast-tracking him, Diego knew, toward that pinnacle. "Thanks, man."

"You've led plenty of missions." Savino refilled his glass, then passed the bottle to the left. "But this one can make your career."

Diego's gut clenched. Nerves or anticipation, one or the other. He was silent as they all waited until the bottle made it back to Savino.

"Some things in life are worth fighting for." The commander raised his glass.

"Some things in life are worth dying for." Lansky raised his.

"And some things," Prescott said, giving his glass a frown before raising it high, "are better to simply walk away from."

"The trick, of course, is knowing which is which," Savino pointed out before jerking his chin to indicate that Diego drink up.

Formalities over, the seven men relaxed. Some refilled their glass; others said their goodbyes. Diego couldn't get his curiosity about the upcoming mission out of his head. Knowing he'd get no details from Savino before the briefing, he decided to find a few distractions in the form of a crowd and, taking his cue from Lansky, a willing woman.

"Heading out," he said. "Thanks for the recommendation."

Savino simply nodded, his dark eyes inscrutable.

"Next step, DEVGRU." Lansky smacked Diego on the back.

"Next step is leading Operation Hammerhead," Diego corrected. But damned if that wouldn't be sweet. DEVGRU, the Navy's Special Warfare Development Group, was the stuff of legends—like SEAL Team 6. Serving on the highest elite Special Ops team in the country was Diego's dream. Each mission, each operation, each commendation was a step in that direction.

And he was getting closer.

"One step at a time," Savino said as if reading his thoughts. The light bounced off his silver oak leaf as he gestured toward the door. "C'mon. We'll buy the rest of the team a round before you all head out to debauch in the name of celebrating."

That it was only fourteen-thirty hours didn't much matter. The team, SEALs, sailors, were skilled at many things, including drinking at any time, day or night. And the support crew, the rest of SEAL Team 7, deserved a drink.

They headed for the O Club by way of the barracks, where they ditched the misery of dress whites. Diego, Jared and the others went for digies—blue tees and camouflage fatigues—while Savino kept to his khaki uniform.

The whole time all Diego could think was that he'd come a long way. Riding the wave of success, he barely held back his grin as he followed Nic through the crowded O Club, taking the shouted praise and ribbing with equal grace.

When he reached the front of the room, he stood to Savino's right, legs braced and hands clasped behind his back. Like a wave, the conversation rose, then settled as each man gave Savino their full attention. With a few simple words, he thanked everyone for their hard work and contribution. Even though Savino made it look easy, Diego hoped like hell that whatever future pinnacles he climbed didn't include giving speeches.

"So that's that," Savino wrapped up. "And since you've all listened so kindly, the next round of drinks is on me."

A few of the men laughed. A handful cheered. The rest raised their glasses in thanks. Lansky tossed his back, then turned to give Savino a fist bump.

"Nice speech. Short, to the point, rounded out with booze. You're the man." After Savino's nod of thanks, Lansky turned the fist bump toward Diego. "And here's another man. King o' the hill, if you ask me. El Gato, the badass kitty cat."

"All hail the king," Savino said with a quiet smile before he slid out of the conversation like smoke from a flue. Quick, silent and barely noticeable. Diego knew he'd leave the room the same way. Hero worship was a sad and pathetic thing in a grown man, but admiring class wasn't. Nor was appreciation. Everything Diego was he figured was due to Savino. To his drive, his vision and his unswerving loyalty to those he believed in.

"Dude." Diego laid a hand on Savino's shoulder, waiting for the other man to meet his eyes. "Thanks."

Savino's eyes lit with appreciation.

"Don't party too hard" was all he said. "You're going to want to be one hundred percent for the briefing."

That was all the warning Diego needed to know he'd be nursing a single beer tonight and heading to bed early. The only thing more important than his gratitude to Savino was the success of his career.

"C'mon, Kitty Cat," Lansky said to Diego when Savino turned to leave. "Let's blow this joint. Find a place where we can be people instead of military machines."

"You mean a place where you're fawned over by civilians who'll be impressed when you tell them you are a military machine."

"Curvy civilians. Sexy ones in short skirts and high heels." Lansky's Boy Scout smile flashed, a little blurry around the edges from the back-to-back whiskeys. "Gotta love them all, right?"

"Couple more drinks and the only thing you're gonna be loving is the toilet seat." Shaking his head, Diego headed for the door.

"Yo, Torres," a voice beckoned before he'd made the exit.

Diego glanced over to see Prescott waving from a prime table next to the dart board. As usual when he wasn't on duty, the man had a pencil in hand and that engrossed look in his eyes.

Seated with Prescott was another SEAL and one of the team's support members. Petty Officer Dane Adams kicked back with his feet on the table and gestured with a dart, making as if he were aiming it at Diego. Next to him, Lieutenant Brandon Ramsey just smiled and murmured something under his breath that made the other man laugh.

Both IP officers, or Information Professionals, they

specialized in tech. Adams had a solid rep as a Special Warfare Combatant Crewman, while Ramsey was on his third tour as a SEAL. They'd transferred to Coronado eight or so months ago after deployment in Afghanistan. It hadn't taken more than a couple of weeks to realize that Ramsey was used to being top dog and not only expected to stay on top but expected everyone to kiss his ass while he was there. Since SEALs didn't kiss ass, he'd had a little trouble adjusting at first. But Prescott had taken the guy under his wing, showed him the ropes. And made him one of the team.

"How about a few games of pool," Ramsey suggested with a wink as Diego and Lansky drew near. "We'll play for shots."

"I hear you're good with the cue," Diego said.

"I hear the same about you," Ramsey acknowledged with an assessing look. Even in digies, the guy came across as a movie star with his blond hair spiked in casual disarray, intense blue eyes and his perfect smile. "Why don't we see who's better?"

"Ego still bruised over Torres busting up your record on the range?" Lansky asked, a sneer creasing his face. "I warned you he would."

Something ugly flashed over Ramsey's eyes, but it was gone just as fast. As a man with a temper of his own, Diego had to respect a guy who could reel it back that quickly.

"Then it's only right that you give me a shot at redeeming my rep," Ramsey suggested mildly, his hands spread wide in invitation. "What do you say, Torres? You willing to go head-to-head on a universal field? Say, a pool table?"

The taunt "Or are you afraid?" went unspoken, but they all heard it. Insults like that went hand in hand with the dog tags the men all wore. Years of training, both as a SEAL and as a man, had taught Diego to think before he reacted.

"You think I need to stack the deck to win, you don't know me." Diego rocked back on his heels to offer a smile. A very small, very effective smile that mocked the idea. And, of course, the man asking it.

From the way his face tightened, Ramsey understood just fine. Not surprising. He was a smart guy. He was also after Diego's spot on Poseidon. A useless goal, since it was known that Poseidon was made up entirely of graduates of BUD/S class 260. But like everything else, Ramsey apparently figured that he'd be the exception to that rule. It had to be the rich boy in him, used to being number one, always the top of everything. From his rich parents to his perfect son, according to Brandon Ramsey, he had it all and expected more.

Not a problem for Diego, since he respected someone who aimed high. Except Ramsey was going to have to get whatever he was looking for from someone else. Because Diego was keeping his share.

"I've already got plans, so pool is out. But I'm happy to buy you a beer instead." Diego ignored Lansky's look of disgust. Ramsey wasn't all that bad. And any time spent with Prescott was time well spent. Besides, for all they knew, it was Ramsey's relentless focus on competition that'd pushed Diego to step it up and do better. To be better. He definitely had to push past 100 percent to beat the guy. As far as Diego was concerned, that made Ramsey a good man to have on the team.

"You'd rather share a beer than go head-to-head?" Ramsey laughed. "Sure. Why not? You might as well toast my success, too."

"Success?" Diego waited until Lansky was through

rolling his eyes before waving a hand toward the bartender. He circled his finger, indicating another round, then grabbed his own chair. "You finally score with that pretty little redhead you were hitting on so hard?"

"Dude, have you seen pictures of Ramsey's old lady?" Adams blew on his fingers as if they were on fire, then shook his head. "You'd be so lucky if a woman that hot even turned you down."

"Can't say as I have," Diego said with a shrug. Looking at other guys' wives had never been a favorite pastime of his.

"Show him that picture you just got, Brandon." Adams let out a low whistle. "The one where she's wearing the bikini."

"You're a sad, sad man," Ramsey told his friend with a laugh, even as he pulled his cell phone from his pocket and swiped through the screen. He shot Diego a look. "You want to see?"

Not really. He figured if you'd seen one guy's old lady, you'd seen them all. But Diego was trying to build a bridge here. So he was already trying to think up polite comments as he took the phone.

Hellooo.

Diego was pretty sure there was an ocean in that shot somewhere. He was vaguely aware of a kid on the screen, but only because he was blocking the view of the blonde.

The woman was stunning. Hair more gold than blond blew in the breeze, the long strands covering part of a perfectly sculpted face. Full lips smiled wide, accented by cheekbones sharp enough to cut glass. But it was her eyes that grabbed him. Too dark to tell the color in the photo, they were round with an exotic tilt echoed by the dusky gold of her skin. And oh, man, that skin. It covered a body meant for hot fantasies. She was made up of long, lean lines and lush curves.

For the first time, he envied a man his woman.

"She's a looker" was all he said, though, as he handed the phone back.

"I'd do her in watercolor. She's got that mermaid thing going there," Prescott murmured, his attention on the paper he was scrawling on. It took a second for the silence to hit him, then another for him to realize what he'd said. "I meant I'd paint her. Not, you know…"

They shared a good-natured laugh as Prescott grimaced.

"I just do her," Ramsey joked, slapping Prescott on the shoulder. His smile turned possessive as he looked at the picture again before tucking his phone into his pocket.

"Thought she was your ex," Jared chimed in, taking his beer from the server without taking his eyes off Ramsey. "Isn't that the way of it? She took your kid and split? Dumped you, right?"

Really? Diego's attention perked up at that bit of news, his body doing a happy salute to the idea of a woman that hot being free and clear. Except she wasn't, he reminded himself. As much as it might suck— and oh, boy, did it—Ramsey had staked prior claim. Whether he and the gorgeous blonde were a couple or not, she was still his.

Ramsey clearly thought so, too. His blue eyes chilled to lethal ice, his sneer blade sharp.

"As usual, Lansky, you've got your details wrong. I left Harper because my career had to be a priority, not the other way around. And given that I can't take my kid with me while I'm out saving the world—and because I'm a hell of a nice guy—I let her take care of him. She appreciates that, and is pretty damned good at showing just how much on my visitations."

"Is that how you want to tell it?" Jared's expression called bullshit.

"That's how it is."

Jared leaned forward, that schoolboy face looking for all the world as if he were about to call out what he saw as a lie.

"So what particular success are we toasting?" Diego interjected, wanting to end this before Jared escalated the conversation into something that required everyone to drop their fatigues to prove who had the biggest dick.

"Nominations for DEVGRU are coming up, pal. And I'm going to be on that list." Ramsey leaned back, crossing his hands behind his head and offering a big smile. "I've got Captain Jarrett's support. And my father's golfing buddy, Senator Glassman, is gonna make sure of it."

He waited a beat.

"You got anyone pulling for you, Torres? You know, someone on the outside with influence?"

His first thought was, *Yeah, right.*

His second was, *Seriously?* It wasn't that he begrudged Ramsey the success. But did they have to compete for everything? There were only a few slots offered each year.

He felt like a jerk for coveting the nomination, but he couldn't completely shake the feeling. After all, DEVGRU was top of the line. A counterterrorism, special missions unit made up of the most elite operatives in the Navy. Once upon a time, some people had called it SEAL Team 6. It was a unit filled with mystery, power and prestige. And Diego wanted in.

So he tilted his chair onto the back two legs, making as if he were carefully considering the question. He pulled off his cap, rubbed a hand over his short, spiked hair, then tugged the hat back in place. Then, giving Ramsey a look of long-faced regret, he shook his head.

"My old man rolled with the Hells Angels as a Nomad. That'd be king o' the hill to you and me. But he was shot down in '91 during what turned out to be a rather heated discussion," Diego mused, tapping his fingers on his knee as he pretended to think it through. "He did leave behind three brothers, though. The ones that are still alive are serving time, one in Quentin, another in Pelican Bay. They probably have the better access to politicians than a golf course, but I guess we'll see."

Diego barely kept from offering his own sneer when he caught the looks on their faces. Disdain-covered horror with a barely concealed side helping of fear. *Typical*.

"Is your mother doing time, too?" Adams asked, his usual smirk sliding back in place.

"Dude," Prescott protested.

Diego's smile dimmed.

His momma had been shot dead three years back while sweeping the floor in the little bodega where she'd worked. No matter that he'd bought her a house, set her up so she didn't have to slave day and night like she had most of her life, she'd insisted on keeping that job out of loyalty to Manny Cruz.

While Diego didn't mind using his father to get a reaction out of others, he never shared his momma. That'd be disrespectful.

Besides, it was nobody's business.

But Adams's comment required a response. Instead of going with a smart-ass comment, or better yet the brutal slap down he'd prefer, Diego figured he'd channel Savino.

"See, here's the thing." Diego leaned forward, his elbows on his knees and his expression as serious as a howitzer. "I figure you had no say in your upbringing. And maybe it was awesome, or maybe it was pure hell. But whatever it was, whatever you brought with you from your past, it made you the man you are now. A solid officer, an outstanding IP tech and in your case, Ramsey, a damned good SEAL."

Diego took a swallow of beer before continuing.

"Bottom line, we fight for the same thing. We have the same goal, and we serve the same team." He had to dig deep for the rest, but, picturing Savino giving him that impatient, just-bullshit-if-you-have-to look, he managed. "I'm proud to serve with you, man."

It was a toss-up who looked more shocked at Diego's words. Adams, who appeared to have swallowed his tongue. Lansky, whose expression warned that he'd puke at any minute. Or Ramsey, who tried to hide his surprise with a frown but didn't quite succeed.

Prescott simply grinned as he dashed his name over the bottom of the piece of paper before tearing it from the sketchbook. He handed it to Diego with a wink.

Diego snickered. His own face stared back at him, finger pointed like a gun, cocked and ready to rock. The caricature emphasized Diego's dark eyes, his large head teetering on a slender body weighted down with fat muscles.

"You're all right, Torres," Ramsey said, his frown shifting into a grin. "I'm proud to serve with you, too."

Figuring Lansky really would gag if this kept up, Diego stood.

"Congrats on your shot at DEVGRU," he said, offering his hand. "Enjoy the beer. Lansky and I are heading out."

He exchanged the team's hand slap with Prescott. To Adams he gave only a nod. Just as well, seeing as Diego and Lansky didn't get ten steps before they heard the asshole comment, "Bet he's full of shit about his father. He just said that to make himself sound tough."

"Let it go," he muttered to Lansky, who'd started to turn back with his fists ready.

"But—"

"You might want to learn to watch your mouth," they heard Prescott warn, his easy tone not disguising the threat beneath.

"Let it go," Diego said again, shoving open the door and stepping into the sun's heat. He'd come to terms with his history. When he'd first joined the Navy, he'd kept his past under lock and key. Not out of shame— out of concern that he'd be thrown in the brig for giving someone a serious ass kicking over their comments about it.

But after a while, he'd come to realize that his past was as much a part of him as his height or his skill with a knife. It made him who he was.

A success, dammit.

"We'll hit Olive Oyl's, and drinks are on me until ten-hundred hours when I head back to base."

Lansky frowned. "You can't be serious. Things will just be heating up then. The hottest women don't hit the bar until after dark, my friend."

"Yep, totally serious. You want to wait for women who look better in the dark, you're gonna have to get yourself a ride back to base. Me, I've got a briefing in the morning, and I plan to be sharp." Then, because Lansky was a good friend and deserved a little payback, he added, "This operation is going to shoot me to the top, buddy. A dozen of Daddy's senators won't help Ramsey get ahead of me after this."

As his friend whooped and hollered, Diego accepted the fist bump with a laugh.

He was within kissing distance of the high point in his career. No way some blowhard like Adams, or even a rival like Ramsey, were going to mess it up for him.

No way in hell.

CHAPTER TWO

GOOD THINGS CAME to those who focused on what they wanted, then worked their butts off to get it.

That was Harper Maclean's life motto, and she figured that she was living proof it was true. As she sautéed the mushrooms, onions and garlic with an expert hand, she looked around her kitchen with a smile of delight. From the glossy planks on the floor to the custom glass-fronted cabinets to the granite countertops, the kitchen—like the house—screamed luxury.

Holy crap, she was living in luxury. Harper added a giddy two-step as she added a dash of garlic salt to the vegetables. Six months ago, she'd been in an apartment so small, she'd had to put her desk in the coat closet. Now she was cozied up in a house five times as big and ten times as fancy.

It was all she could do to keep from doing a butt-wiggling happy dance as she pulled a golden piecrust from the oven. But butt wigging wasn't ladylike, and Harper had spent the last seven years transforming herself into a lady. So she settled for a tiny shoulder shimmy.

"If I knew making me dinner would give you such a thrill, I'd have hit you up a week ago." Andi Stamos strode into the kitchen in a wave of Black Opium, reaching around Harper to snag a mushroom out of the pan.

Used to greedy fingers trying to sneak food before

it was ready, Harper tilted her head toward the center island. "If you're hungry, eat an apple."

"I'd rather have chocolate," Andi muttered.

Who wouldn't? "After dinner."

"Fine, I'll wait," Andi agreed before snagging another mushroom.

"Hey," Harper warned with a laugh, automatically shifting the springform pan out of reach.

Most people wouldn't recognize the untidy waif with her black hair in a messy ponytail and her jeans ripped at the knees as Andrianna Stamos, thrice-divorced estranged daughter of Greek tycoon Maximillian Stamos, society darling and trust-fund baby. Andrianna wore leather and silk, spoke five languages and had a reputation for starting her day with a martini instead of coffee. Whereas Andi was happy wearing jeans to eat in a friend's kitchen, handed out hundreds to the homeless and adored a small boy named Nathan.

They'd met three years before when Harper worked for Lalique & Lalique as an interior designer and had decorated the house for Andi and her new husband, Matt Wallace. Since Harper had had an easier time melding the Spanish architecture with Andi's modern tastes and Matt's preference for Louis XIV and rococo than the couple had in combining their lifestyles, she hadn't been surprised when their marriage ended before she'd fluffed the last pillow.

By the time Harper had helped Andi get through the packing of Matt's stuff, the redecorating and the heartbreak, their friendship was as solid as the gold-toned granite countertop Andi was currently leaning against doing her impression of a *Vogue* ad for wealthy bohemians.

In contrast to Andi, Harper's gold-streaked blond

hair swept straight and choppy to just above her shoulders. Her silk tank was the color of peonies and her linen Capris wrinkle-free. And she was pretty sure her entire outfit, right down to the diamond studs in her ears, hadn't cost as much as the other woman's threadbare denim.

"Drink?" Harper offered, moving to the refrigerator. "I've got a nice Pinot Grigio."

"Water's fine."

Uh-oh. Harper gathered what she needed from the fridge, including a bottle of water. She set it, eggs and cream on the counter, then grabbed a lemon.

She sliced it and added a squeeze and a twist to a cobalt-blue glass before pouring in chilled water.

"I take it last night's party wasn't as much fun as you'd hoped," she guessed as she handed her friend the drink.

"It was a deadly bore. Same people, same drama. I'm pretty sure it was even the same food as Monique's last gala. The woman is tapping people for a thousand dollars a plate—you'd think she'd try a new recipe or two."

While Harper shredded sharp cheddar over the golden crust for the quiche, Andi regaled her with wickedly disparaging tales of the rich and famous.

"So there he is, this big shot banking CEO, in the coat closet with his pants around his ankles and his hands down the front of this woman's dress. His sister-in-law, it turns out. But does Monique care about the scandal? About a dozen guests seeing her closet used for an upright quickie? Of course not." Andi paused to sip her water, then gave Harper an eye roll. "Monique's only concern was whether they'd wrinkled the coats they were doing it against. To which the CEO responded in a dismissive tone, if her guests didn't have enough class to wear quality, they deserved a few wrinkles."

"He didn't." Harper laughed, entertained as always by the adventures of the rich and spoiled.

"He did," Andi assured her as she helped herself to more water. "And even that couldn't liven up that snoozefest of a party."

"You sound so jaded."

"Sweetie, I *am* jaded."

"No. You're bored. You need a project. Actually, you need a career. But since you won't do that, you really should find a project."

"Not won't. Can't," Andi corrected meticulously, her fingers tapping a quick beat on the counter. "Any income I bring in will impact my divorce settlement. That weasel cheated on me enough while we were married. I refuse to allow him to cheat me out of anything else."

Harper couldn't blame her. Matt was a complete dog. The jerk had been caught with his pants down twice in less than a year of saying his vows. Harper wasn't sure if that betrayal had damaged Andi's heart, but she knew it'd done serious damage to her confidence. For that alone, Harper believed he should pay.

Something Andi was doing her best to ensure. But it'd already been eight months and was looking like it'd be at least a year more before they settled. Doing nothing for that long would drive Harper crazy.

Still, Harper couldn't complain. Not when the divorce settlement was the reason she was living in this gorgeous house with a huge kitchen.

Since she'd gained control of the California properties three months ago, Andi had rented the place to Harper for a quarter of its worth. If not for that, there was no way Harper could have afforded a house in the exclusive Santa Barbara neighborhood.

Oh, sure, over the last three years, Harper had made a strong name for herself as a visionary interior designer. But last year she'd risked it all—her savings, her security and, sometimes she thought, her sanity—when she'd left Lalique to go it alone. But she was making it work. Homes by Harper had an exclusive client list, a sterling reputation and a solid portfolio.

Most people had no idea that beneath her sophisticated demeanor, Harper was obsessed with saving for her son's college fund, worried about being a year behind on her career goals and often frantic trying to be a good mom, raise her son to be a better man than what he'd come from and still find time to polish her nails.

Whenever she thought about trying to juggle it all, she remembered living on welfare, wearing church-donated hand-me-downs because her mom couldn't afford to both feed *and* clothe her only child, and finding the safest route home from school in a neighborhood where drive-by shootings were simply shrugged off.

And that, she decided as she sprinkled more cheese over the vegetable mixture, was the only use she had for her past. As a yardstick for how far she'd come.

"I'm pretty sure you're the first person to actually cook in this kitchen," Andi observed, her words muffled through a mouthful of the apple she'd finally given in to.

"Now, that's a crime against kitchens." Harper broke a dozen or so eggs into a thick pottery bowl, added cream, then with a careless shake of a few spices, whipped it together. "I can't believe you lived in this house for two years and never cooked."

"I'd lived in various other places twenty-six years before that and didn't cook in any of them, either." Andi looked around the rich, airy space with its touches of red pottery, midnight-blue fabrics and cozy eating nook. Three low-backed stools bellied up to the sleek island with its prep sink and marble top. When Andi had lived here, that island was often decorated with fresh flowers or, more often, caterers' supplies. Now it held a blown glass bowl in bleeding greens that contrasted sharply with the bright red apples.

"You suit the kitchen, this house, much better than I ever did," Andi said with an easy shrug. "Not only because you decorated it. For all your sophistication, you fit in suburbia. As much as I tried, I never could."

"You're definitely more comfortable downtown than you were here. And your penthouse is a better showcase for your personal style."

"The penthouse is closer to the dating scene," Andi corrected with another casual shrug at odds with the discontented look in her eyes. "Speaking of dating…"

"We were talking about decorating, not dating."

"Then let's change the subject." Andi leaned her elbows on the counter and propped her chin in her hand, still munching the apple. "You need to start dating."

"I've dated."

"When was the last time?" Andi challenged.

Harper had to think about that.

"Sometime late last year, since I wore my black knee-length boots and that gorgeous three-quarter-length peacoat I got on sale at Nordstrom."

That Andi didn't question that Harper filed her memories according to outfits was just one of the reasons they were such good friends.

"Did that date end in sex?" Andi inquired.

"No. It ended in the stomach flu."

"The guy gave you the flu on a date?"

Laughing at Andi's confused expression, Harper shook her head.

"Not quite. The babysitter called while we were finishing the entrée to tell me that Nathan was throwing up. End of date."

Nothing came before her son. Not men, not work, not even her own memories.

"Obviously it's time to step up your dating life. I've got some ideas on that."

"Why don't we work on your dating life instead? Or better yet, what do you think about adding a fountain to your foyer? Something in metal. I saw a gorgeous piece last week at one of the art galleries."

"Really? What form? Colored metal or brass? No, wait." She threw up one hand and scowled. "Don't do that. Don't distract me with pretties."

"But if we talk about decorating, we're both happy and both get something we want," Harper pointed out, getting cranberry and passion fruit juices and the seltzer out of the fridge. "If we talk about dating, you end up frustrated and I get a headache. Why should we do that to ourselves?"

"The real question is, why would you do this to yourself? At least I'm trying to get back out there. But you? You're a gorgeous, vital, interesting woman. And you're cutting yourself off from the opposite sex. You need to get out there, live it up."

"I've hardly cut myself off from the opposite sex. I date when I feel like it. I have a member of the male species living with me. And I deal with male clients, designers and contractors all the time."

"Your son doesn't count, nor do business relationships. I'm talking about the possibility of sex, Harper.

Something every woman needs in order to be healthy, energized and sane."

Harper's lips twitched. Poor thing sounded as frustrated as if it were *she* who was going on eight years without doing the deed. She probably shouldn't have shared that sad little truth, but she'd been trying to comfort her friend over a bottle of wine while Andi lamented her eight sexless months. If nothing else, the revelation had shocked Andi out of her funk and into a frenzy to ensure she didn't end up in the same dry spell.

"I'm doing okay without it." Before Andi could argue that okay wasn't enough—after all, they'd had this conversation so many times, Harper could recite it in her sleep—she gave her friend a sad shrug. "I really am. I've heard that some people simply aren't very sexual. Maybe I'm one of them."

Pretending her best friend wasn't looking as if she'd just punched her in her perfectly toned belly, Harper set the ingredients aside and leaned her own elbows on the bar, resting her chin on her fists.

"I don't miss it. The few times I have wondered if maybe I should, I think about everything that'd have to be done to actually have sex. And it's just not worth it."

"What's to be done? Find a hot guy. Do the deed."

Harper rolled her eyes.

"Sex requires knowing the guy, which requires more than three dates, which means being away from Nathan. That requires a babysitter, which until recently, was a luxury I couldn't justify. Now that I can, I find I don't really want to." Harper straightened. "It's just not worth the trouble. Or the risks."

Andi opened her mouth, then closed it again. "I'm not trying to psychoanalyze or anything. Believe me. But do you think that's the reason you aren't interested in sex? That the last guy you had it with got you pregnant, then walked out?"

Harper didn't physically move, but she did withdraw. She could actually feel herself pulling away, closing in. She didn't talk about that time in her life. Partly because there wasn't a whole lot to brag about when it came to teenage pregnancy. And partly because she hated talking about her past. She hated even thinking about it.

But mostly she kept quiet because she was afraid. The last thing Brandon had said to her after she'd told him she was pregnant was goodbye.

Right before he'd uttered that word, though, he'd warned her that if she didn't get an abortion, his parents would take the baby. If they knew they had a grandchild, they'd insist on raising it to be a proper Ramsey, and there was nothing she'd be able to do to stop them.

Harper had believed him.

She hadn't obeyed him, of course.

But she'd definitely believed.

She'd kept her pregnancy a secret from everyone she knew, cleaned out the college savings she'd been hoarding since she was eleven, stuffed her clothes in a backpack and ran. She'd changed her life. She'd become the opposite of where she'd come from. And she'd kept quiet. Because she had no doubts about the reality of Brandon's threat. If his parents knew about Nathan, they'd try to take him.

She had built a life that would be hard for them to challenge if it went to court. She was an upstanding citizen with a thriving career; her son was happy and healthy and attended one of the best private schools in Santa Barbara. Their lifestyle wasn't as affluent as the Ramseys', but it was good. Solid. No custody court would say otherwise. If it ever came down to it, nobody could justify taking Nathan from her.

It wasn't until she felt Andi's hand close over hers that Harper realized she'd been silent for way too long. And that her hand was trembling.

"Sorry," she said, dismissing her anxiety with a laugh.

"I'm the one who's sorry. I shouldn't have pried."

"It's been a long time. It'd be pretty stupid of me to let him control my choices after all these years, wouldn't it?"

"I don't know, Harper. Maybe leaving you high and dry, never contributing a penny to help raise his child and never once contacting either one of you is a good enough reason to avoid sex."

Harper frowned.

"If he's the reason I'm avoiding it, maybe it's time to reconsider," she murmured, half to herself. At Andi's whoop of delight, she shook her head and rushed to add, "I said reconsider. Not run out and have tons of wild, sweaty sex. Just, you know, maybe consider keeping a guy around for a third date."

"That's the only opening I need," Andi all but sang. As she patted Harper's hand in support, she asked, "So, what's your preference? Dark hair or light? Working class or businessman? Butt or biceps?"

"Butt or biceps?"

"Yeah, which is your trigger? I'm going to find you the perfect man," Andi vowed with the fervency of an evangelical minister on cable television.

Harper was rescued from having to decide by the back door swinging open. In swirled her very own seven-year-old tornado.

Her heart melted just a little at the sight of her son

dancing into the room. His elegant features were alive with delight, smudges of dirt on his chin and cheek and his hair, the same burnished gold as her own, tumbling over his brow.

"Mom, guess what. Louie Dryden's cat had kittens. Five of them. She had 'em on his bed, too. He got pictures on his iPhone and it was, like, so gross." He stopped talking long enough to drop his prized baseball onto the counter next to the bowl of apples.

He threw his arms around his mother for a quick hug, grabbing his ball again before remembering to offer the same to the other woman. "Hey, Andi. Do you want a kitten? Now that all the gross is off them, they're really cute. Tiny, with lots of black hair. Kinda like you."

"Aren't you the charmer?" Laughing, Andi squeezed him tight before ruffling Nathan's hair. "And what am I supposed to do with a kitten?"

"Love it, of course," Nathan said in the same tone he'd use to remind her the sky was blue. "You'd have to take care of it and give it food and stuff, like Mom does me. You pet it a lot and maybe let it sleep on your pillow next to you. Then you'll have something to play with, and you won't get lonely."

He turned guileless brown eyes on his mother, his wide smile all the more enchanting for its missing teeth.

"If Andi gets one, you should, too, Mom. It could keep you company if I went to summer camp."

The pitch for a kitten had been going for several weeks now, with Harper standing firm on her no. But camp was new. Ever since he'd found out a few days ago that his best pal, Jeremy, was going, Nathan had been begging to attend. But it was two weeks away, on an island, with strangers. Three strikes, no camp.

"Nice try," Harper murmured, shaking her head both

at his ploy and at her quite possibly overprotective concerns. "Dinner is in a little less than an hour. Why don't you go play until then?"

She knew his face as well as she did her own—better, actually. So Harper could easily read the struggle in his eyes as he fought the urge to push.

Then he shrugged.

"I'm seriously starving. Can I have something to eat before dinner?"

"An apple."

"Thanks." Nathan grabbed the apple and his baseball, then headed out of the kitchen. At the arched doorway, he glanced back. "Do you think kittens like stories? I bet I'd get a lot of extra reading done if I had to read to a kitten every day."

Harper smiled as she got the glass pitcher down to mix the juices into Nathan's favorite.

"He's only seven, and he already knows when to push and when he'll get more by simply walking away," Andi murmured with an appreciative shake of her head.

"The rest of the time, he uses charm, guile and a golden tongue," Harper agreed. In that respect he was so like Brandon.

Andi waited until they heard his footsteps fade up the stairs before giving Harper an arch look.

"How long do you think you'll hold out against getting him the kitten?" Andi asked.

"Hopefully another year." Harper blew out a breath. "If not that, then I'd like to at least get through this Little League season before he takes on that big of a responsibility."

That she'd give in was a given. But she figured as long as Nathan didn't realize that, the power balance was exactly where it should be.

"And camp? Why don't you want him going?"

"The longest he's been away from home is a sleepover. This is two weeks. And it's not like it's space camp or baseball camp, which I could understand, given his obsession with those. This is adventure camp. Rafting and climbing and sleeping outdoors." Harper gave a mock shudder. "All of that aside, I can't afford it."

There. That sounded perfectly reasonable.

"He'd have fun. And wouldn't it do him good to explore other interests?" Andi gave her a look that said she saw right through all that reasoning. "You always say you want to give Nathan as many opportunities as you can. This is an opportunity."

"So is circus school. But that doesn't mean I'll be signing him up for trapeze lessons."

"Mmm-hmm."

"What's that supposed to mean?"

"You're in tiger mode." At Harper's blank look, Andi curled her fingers into claws on either side of her chin. "You're like a momma tiger protecting her cub from danger."

Before Harper could ask what was wrong with that, Andi straightened one hand to wag her finger in the air.

"Except this isn't danger. It's camp. Singing around the campfire and learning to tie knots. It's swimming and tire swings and hikes. It'd be a great learning experience. After all, education isn't found only in the classroom."

"What'd you do, swallow their brochure?" Harper muttered, her words lost in the refrigerator as she pulled out berries for dessert. But Andi still heard.

"I served on a board for underprivileged kids a couple of years ago. We had to provide a study of the benefits of programs like this in order to get funding. It really does make a difference for some kids. The independence, the skills and the friendships can be priceless."

Harper's scowl was hot enough to rot the glossy strawberries, but she couldn't argue any of those points.

"Besides, if you don't start letting go, you're going to end up with a wimpy momma's boy." She paused for effect before adding, "Like Matt. You know, the man who wanted to bring his mother along on our vacations, whose mother still bought his underwear and who after being kicked to the curb for cheating, moved home with Mommy, who now makes him breakfast every day."

Cute at seven, iffy at seventeen. And at thirty-two it was definitely pathetic. Even as they shared a grimace, Harper knew she'd be poking through her bank account later to see if she could juggle the registration costs. Not that she was totally convinced. But she was teetering.

"I'll cover the fee," Andi offered, giving her that last push over the edge. "Call it my contribution to loosening your inhibitions."

"What does one have to do with the other?"

"If Nathan's safely away at camp, you can do more than reconsider having sex. You can have it."

And that was supposed to convince her?

The doorbell chimed before Harper could do more than shake her head in dismay.

"I'll get that—you start reconsidering. When I get back, we'll find that perfect third-date guy."

"I'd put money on Nathan getting a kitten sooner than that happening," she murmured as Andi swept from the room.

"I heard that," the other woman sang out, her words echoing down the hall.

Harper's frown intensified. All of this dating and sex

talk was stupid. All it did was stir up thoughts of Brandon, bad memories and hurt feelings. And like anything to do with Brandon Ramsey, the second one thought occurred, a million followed. He was the poster boy for taking a mile when an inch was all she'd offered.

No more, she ordered herself. He wasn't a part of her now, and her past was over.

"Registered letter for one Mr. Nathan Ramsey, care of Harper Maclean," Andi said, coming back waving a large envelope. "Who'd get his name wrong?"

The bowl of cleaned berries suddenly shaking in her hands, Harper set it on the bar with care and stared. Her chest hurt. She couldn't think for the buzzing in her ears.

Ramsey.

Harper's heart raced so fast, it tripped over itself. How was that possible? Why whould Brandon contact Nathan? As far as he knew, she'd followed his instructions to end the pregnancy. How did he know she'd had the baby? How did he know Nathan's name? Had he always known?

The air locked in Harper's chest, vicious and tight, cutting off her breath, sending shards of pain knifing through her.

Why was he contacting her? Contacting Nathan? Was he going to try to get custody?

Or had his parents gotten wind of unaccounted Ramsey DNA and tracked down their heir apparent?

Harper looked toward the stairs with a desperate gaze. She should get Nathan. They should go. Now.

As soon as she thought that, Harper squared her shoulders.

To hell with that. Nathan was her son. This was her

home. She'd be damned if Brandon or his rich parents were going to screw with either.

Still, her hand trembled so much as she took the letter that she dropped it onto the marble countertop as if it were on fire.

"Aren't you going to open it?" Andi poked at the letter with one perfectly manicured nail. "It's from a Dane Adams, US Navy, registered mail. It's gotta be important."

Dane Adams? The Navy?

Relief poured through her so fast, so strong, that her legs almost gave out. Irritation followed fast, because it was still all about Brandon. So Harper eyed the envelope with intense distaste.

"Harper," Andi moaned. "You're killing me. Open. Open. Open."

Knowing Andi would keep it up until she did, she huffed out a hot breath. Sliding her thumbnail under the flap, Harper reluctantly tugged the paper out.

She noted the official-looking insignia and the fancy lettering denoting it to be from Admiral H. M. Cree, Special Ops commander.

Her brow creased as she read.

The room narrowed, and all the air disappeared. The words spun into a swirling blur of black on white. She needed to sit down. But she managed only a single step before her legs gave out and she sank to the floor, the letter clutched in her hands.

"What is it?" Instead of pulling her back up, Andi dropped down next to her, gathering Harper into her arms. She tried to read the paper, but Harper couldn't let it go. "Sweetie, what does it say?"

"He's dead," Harper murmured, her voice sounding as if it were coming from the other end of a long tunnel. "Brandon is dead."

CHAPTER THREE

MOURNING THE LOSS of a brother was never easy.

SEALs, support personnel and civilians gathered in the backroom at Olive Oyl's bar to toast the memory of a warrior and to share their grief. Lieutenant Brandon Ramsey was memorialized with words like *honor* and *skill* and *dedication*. Captain Jarrett had choked giving his toast, and a visibly grieving Petty Officer Dane Adams had to be led out after delivering a eulogy so heartfelt that it was hard to hear over the audience's sobs.

But when it came time for the men who'd served on that ill-fated mission, the core team, to say goodbye to their brother, they kept it private and took it off the beaten path. Savino chose a bar in Lemon Grove, far enough from base for them to mourn freely. The place was just a few steps up from a dive, and seedy enough that nobody would feel constrained by good behavior.

"Kinda crap that they won't offer a military funeral for the guy. Decorated SEAL and all that, he'd have liked the fancy send-off."

"Bet he'd like being alive even more."

"Shame that none of his family showed. Not even his kid."

"Sometimes civilians can't handle it."

"Dude isn't officially declared dead—chances are they're holding on to hope."

"No point. Even if they didn't find enough of him to declare him dead, he's gone. Still, the Navy'll tie it up in red tape, drag it out as long as they can to avoid paying survivor benefits."

"I hear he had an in to DEVGRU. Guy went down before he got a chance to snag an elite spot."

"Poseidon is the real elite."

"He didn't get a shot at that, either."

"Yeah. Totally crap if you ask me."

All excellent points. Conversation floated around him as Diego kicked back in the corner. Boots propped on the table and his chair tilted back, he considered his next shot of whiskey.

"You'd think I'd be drunk by now," he said, the words slurring in his ears.

"Dude, you are shit-faced," Lansky corrected, his bloodshot eyes as round as dinner plates.

"Yeah?" Not sure why he didn't trust Lansky's word—after all the guy spent half his time drinking— Diego looked toward Savino. "You think I'm drunk?"

"I think Lansky might be a few ahead of you, but you're well on your way."

"I'd better catch up, then."

"Yo, Torres. There's a pool table back here. I figure you being three sheets to the wind is the best chance I've got to beat you."

Diego pulled his eyes off his glass to look at Aaron Ward. He tried to return the guy's smile, but found he could only shake his head.

"You go ahead. It'll take another fifth before I'm drunk enough for you to beat me."

Amid laughter and a few crude suggestions, everyone headed for the poolroom except Diego and Lansky. His cell phone chiming, Savino stepped away, too.

Diego felt like a jerk, but a part of him was glad to see them go.

"The last guy to ask me to play pool was Ramsey," Diego realized, feeling like shit all over again. "This sucks."

Images of the mission played through his head like a movie reel. They'd fast roped from the helo, landing just over the hill from the enemy base. Powers, Lansky and Ward had headed into the compound to rescue the hostage while Ramsey, Prescott and Lee secured the control center to begin downloading secret files. Everyone had been in place; everything had run exactly as planned.

Until it hadn't.

The explosion had come just as Lee had signaled the all clear. Lee and Prescott both moved with their usual stealth as they exited the building, Diego provided cover. Then it had all blown to hell. The explosion had taken out half the building, the fire burning too hot for any survivors.

Diego had been faced with the choice of going into the flames in search of Ramsey's remains or getting an injured Prescott, the rest of the team and the extracted hostage the hell out of there.

He'd chosen the unthinkable.

He'd left a man behind.

Eyes hot, he poured more whiskey, knocking it back before pouring again.

"You didn't fuck it up," Lansky said quietly.

"Listen to MacGyver," Savino ordered as he rejoined them from wherever he'd gone to take his call. The guy spent more time on the phone than a teenage girl. Diego figured he'd mention that when he was a little more numb.

"Why should I listen to him?" he muttered.

"Because you didn't fuck it up. There was no way to retrieve Ramsey. The fire was too intense. When support hit the site the next day, there wasn't even enough of him to ID. Your orders were explicit. Your first duty was to the hostage. You got him out of there and Prescott to medical care so he didn't die. That's enough."

It wasn't, though.

It'd never be enough.

"He was a damned good SEAL," Diego said quietly.

"He was a strong officer," Savino murmured, his eyes scanning the room.

"He was an asshole."

"What?" Lansky's eyes widened when Diego glared at him. "I'm supposed to lie? Like getting himself blown to hell suddenly makes the guy less of an asshole?"

"You never liked him."

"And he never liked you. The guy wanted to take you down in a bad way. He'd have done anything to screw you over."

"Would he?" Savino asked. His voice didn't change. Nor did his expression. So Diego couldn't tell why Savino's tone pierced through the alcohol hazing his brain.

"What are you thinking?" he asked his commander, studying Savino's face. He had to blink a few times to bring it into focus.

"That things aren't always what they seem."

Even well on his way to drunk, Diego could see the dots Savino was laying out. But they didn't connect.

"Ramsey is dead. We saw him go up in flames when that command center blew."

His throat dry as the images pounded through his brain again, Diego grabbed his glass.

Savino laid a hand on his arm before he could drink.

"What?" His gut clenched when he looked at the other man's face. Serious as a heart attack didn't come close.

"Sober up" was all Savino said before glancing at Lansky. "Make your excuses. Then the two of you take a room nearby. Don't return to base until you hear from me."

"What—"

"Sober up," Savino said again as he got to his feet. Diego was drunk, but not so drunk he didn't see the flash of concern on his commander's face as he glanced toward the other room, where their team played a loud game of pool. Diego's buzz starting to fade, he lowered his feet to the floor, unconsciously coming to attention.

"Let me know where you land. Just me." He waited until Diego and Lansky nodded. "I'll be in touch tomorrow."

He left, calling a friendly goodbye to the rest of the team as he went. Then Lansky looked at Diego. Diego frowned back.

"What the hell?" Lansky muttered.

"I don't know, but I guess we're calling it a night."

His head swimming in whiskey and confusion, Diego could pinpoint only two things.

One, they had their orders.

And two, Savino was worried. So whatever those orders led to, it was going to get ugly.

TWENTY HOURS LATER, Nic Savino strode through the night-drenched parking lot like a man on a mission.

Which, of course, he was.

The run-down motel was lit by one stingy streetlight; the others looked like they'd been shot out. Trash heaped against the cyclone fence as if it were trying to climb free, and the air smelled of the ocean on a bender, week-old fish, rotten eggs and rust. A bored-looking hooker leaned against the graffitied wall three buildings down, and the sound of an argument heading toward violent rang out over the desperate plea of a car alarm.

He noticed it all.

He gave none of it his attention.

His entire focus was on reeling in the fury pounding through his head before he reached room 207. He was a man known for his control, and he was going to need every shred of it to deal with this situation.

Situation, he thought bitterly. That's what the admiral was calling it. Savino's SEAL team was under investigation. Or as the directive from Naval Intelligence had put it, a duly authorized official had been assigned to look into Operation Hammerhead, which had resulted in the death of one team member, the hospitalization of another and the dissemination of classified information to the enemy, possibly for profit.

It hadn't taken much to read between the lines.

They were looking at his team for treason.

His men.

Him.

Savino climbed the cement stairs to the second floor, stepping around the bum sleeping under a pile of rags in the corner of the landing, breathing through his teeth to avoid the stench.

Three doors down the concrete walkway, he knocked once, then walked in.

"Lansky, you have crap taste in motels," he said by way of a greeting. The room was wood veneer and orange polyester coated with a thin layer of grilled onions.

"You told me to find a place close to the bar. This is close." Lansky shrugged from his spot on the floor. His back against the flowered bedspread, he had a notebook on one side of him, a bag of chips on the other and a computer in his lap.

"How'd you get a laptop?"

"Guy on the corner was selling them." Lansky flashed a boyish grin. "You didn't think I was just going to sit here watching Kitty Cat work off his drunk, did you?"

In other words, Lansky was trying to figure out what was going on. *Good.* Savino considered the shiny new MacBook Air. He knew it was hot. But it shouldn't be traceable.

His gaze shifted to Torres.

He'd installed a rod in the bathroom doorway about three-quarters of the way up from the floor. Shirtless and with one hand tucked behind his back, he used the other to pull himself up, lowered and did it again. And again. His unshaven face was set, blank. Sweat poured and his breath huffed, telling Savino he'd been at it for a while.

Savino took in the man's mood with a single glance. An IED was less dangerous than Torres right now.

"You get the pull-up bar from the same guy?"

"Found it by the Dumpster," Lansky said, frowning as he peered at the laptop. "Mood this one's in, he'd have ripped a pipe from the wall if I hadn't come up with something."

Torres's only response was a grunt as he switched arms.

"He been at it long?"

That got Lansky's attention. His frown didn't fade, but he did look from Torres to Savino before shrugging.

"We been here, what? Almost a day, give or take?

He's clocked about two weeks PT in that time, and about two hours sleep."

The team generally spent between ten and twenty hours a week on physical training, depending on their status. Torres had put that in already? It didn't bode well.

Savino raked his hand through his hair. Giving in to the stress pounding in his head, he gripped the back of his neck as if he could squeeze the pain away.

Torres was a SEAL. He'd step up and do the duty when Savino assigned it. But the weight of it would be a lot easier to dump on the guy if he wasn't in a pisser of a mood.

It was rare that Savino worried about that sort of thing. But this was a rare situation. And the duty would be more in the lines of a favor.

"You want a beer?" Lansky offered.

"Thought you were sobering up."

"I've only had three. That is sober." He tilted his head toward Torres, who'd flipped himself around so his knees were anchored over the bar and his head toward the floor, doing sit-ups. "He's the one who was drunk anyway."

"Right." Though procrastination wasn't in his nature, Savino had a desperate urge to put this conversation off for a month or five. But the betrayal gnawing at his gut wasn't going to go away. And this situation was only going to get worse. So...

"Fall in, men."

As expected, the quiet command had instant results. Lansky closed the laptop, got to his feet and waited with his hands clasped behind his back. Torres grabbed the bar with one hand to free his legs, then flipped to the floor. He didn't bother to grab a towel but stepped over to match Lansky's stance, pausing only to wipe a rivulet of sweat from his eyes before coming to parade rest.

"Word has come down through sources I trust that we're being investigated on the QT. The team in general, Poseidon in particular."

Lansky's minuscule flinch made it clear that he hadn't ferreted that much out yet. *Good.* He was one of the slickest hackers around. If he couldn't find it, others wouldn't, either.

"Let me make this clear. I consider this a bogus investigation. But some of the brass are taking it seriously because, if my intel is correct, it's happening at the behest of the CIA."

That got a frown from both of them.

Savino gave a satisfied nod. He wouldn't have to explain just how potentially FUBAR this situation was. The CIA digging its sticky fingers into Navy business was never good. But into Special Ops and the SEALs? Poking at the DOD's classified protocols? That had the potential to be beyond fucked up.

"It's been determined that classified information has been sold to the enemy. Information believed to be available only to those participating in Operation Hammerhead."

"Believed to be?" Lansky asked, his eyes sliding toward his notebook. At Savino's nod, he leaned over to grab it and started taking notes.

"The information they intercepted could only have come from the compound in Kunar," he said quietly, referring to the base they'd infiltrated during Operation Hammerhead. "The scientist you rescued had been close to a breakthrough on the formula for a particularly lethal chemical weapon when he was grabbed. Because he is also a member of the Russian government, every piece of information, every byte of data he produced during his capture, he covertly tagged."

He waited for both men to nod their understanding. Tagging the data didn't make it traceable. But it did pinpoint and time-stamp its source.

"The chemical weapon formula was discovered in the hands of jihad militants." He named the faction, a particularly violent extremist group who'd claimed responsibility for three European bombings the previous year, including an amusement park.

"One of the militants could have sold it," Lansky pointed out, although he didn't sound very confident.

"The electronic signature pins the data to a specific time frame." He ignored the clutch in his gut and continued. "The CIA believes it's unlikely to be one of them given that the militants themselves were under attack and their compound in flames at that time."

He waited a beat, then arched his brow.

The two men looked at each other, and he could see the messages pass between them. In just a look, they replayed the mission, they explored the options, they reached the same conclusion.

When their gazes met his again, Lansky seemed as if he were going to explode. Torres simply stared.

"You think someone from our team stole the formula? That they betrayed the team, the country, by selling?" Lansky asked, his words two shades from livid. "You think one of us is dirty?"

"No. He's telling us the damned CIA thinks that," Torres corrected, speaking for the first time since Savino had entered. There was no surprise in his words, making it clear he'd been expecting something ugly. But the look in his eyes said he hadn't thought it'd be quite this ugly.

"I think that we have to consider every possibility, no matter how impossible it seems," Savino said slowly. "It could be that whoever did this targeted this specific information. They could have targeted this specific mission. Or there was no target and it was simply opportunistic."

"Which is it?" Lansky asked.

Savino arched a brow at Torres. The other man rubbed his thumb over his forehead, took a long breath, then blew it out before meeting Savino's blank gaze.

"He thinks it was mission specific. That's why we're rooming with roaches here in Hotel California. He had us lay low in case he needed us off base and off duty, so whoever is looking can't tag us if he sends us on special assignment."

And that was why he'd groomed Torres for higher things. The man was good. Excellent even. That this could take him down, ruin his career, was fucking unreal. Fury reared its head for just a second before Savino slammed the lid again. It didn't matter. He prided himself on never letting his thoughts show. So his words were calm and his expression neutral.

"In light of various pieces of information that have been filtered my way, I think this mission was targeted for a reason. I just don't know what it is. Yet. Neither does the CIA."

"Are they looking at me specifically because I led the mission?" Torres asked quietly. Savino had served with the guy for ten years. He recognized the pain and fury beneath the words.

"The quickest way to put this to bed is to find out who is behind it," Savino answered. "Who had the most to gain, and how would they pull it off."

"Ramsey," Lansky said, the words coming almost

faster than Savino finished talking. "That dude thought he was so much better than everyone else on the team— he never tried to fit in. He was Cyber, so he knows computers and could have pulled that formula before the place blew. And he had a major hard-on to take Diego down in any way he could."

Torres shook his head.

"You're reaching, man. You just want the guy to be dirty."

"And you refuse to see reality because you believe in a code of honor that says a SEAL *can't* be dirty. Doesn't mean other SEALs follow that same code."

"The guy is dead. What'd he do, sell the formula from the great beyond?"

"The guy was slimy as hell. He probably staged that explosion and snuck out of there like the snake he is. Was. Is."

"Can't decide?" Torres asked with a smirk.

"Is," Lansky shot back, his boyish features grim.

"And this is what we have to find out," Savino interrupted. "Word came down this morning that a large sum of money was deposited in an account attached to Ramsey's name."

"That son of a bitch got paid?"

"I didn't say that," Savino corrected Lansky. "The account is attached to his name. His and his kid's, with the mother as guardian. But she's not a signatory on it, and there's no record that she's ever used it. It could be a smoke screen."

"Whoever did the deed had the money put in Ramsey's account in case eyes were cast, they'd be cast his way," Diego summed up.

"Yes."

Lansky rubbed his fingers over bloodshot eyes, then shook his head.

"So you're saying it was someone besides Ramsey?" He sounded like a kid who'd just been told Santa had been arrested on Christmas Eve.

"No," Torres said in a toneless voice before Savino could answer. "He's saying that's how the CIA is looking at it. They're gunning for one of us."

"The CIA and NI," Savino confirmed, letting them know that Naval Intelligence was involved.

"You have a plan, right?" Lansky pressed his hands together. "Tell me you have a plan."

"I have a plan." He nodded toward the chairs. It was going to take a while and they might as well be comfortable.

"Brilliant," Lansky said an hour later, his pen tapping a quick beat on his notebook. "Except for one thing."

"You want the woman," Torres said from the floor, where he was doing push-ups.

"I want the woman."

"Nope." Now that he'd outlined the situation and given the orders, Savino was finally comfortable enough to step out of command mode. "You're volatile, MacGyver."

"Me?" Lansky pressed his hand to his chest and tried for offended. "Kitty Cat is the one with the temper. He's the one with the rep. I'm the guy next door."

"Your specialty is tech. We need you on the computer researching, digging. Prescott is our expert in information warfare, but he's still in the hospital, recovering. Torres trained under him for two years, he's got solid IW skills. He's our best bet."

Savino considered the stakes. A chemical formula in the hands of militants whose mission was mass terrorism spelled every kind of ugly in the book of possibilities. The threat to US security abroad was high. The threat to the SEAL team, and especially Poseidon, was even higher. If they didn't reel this in and reel it fast, there was going to be blood on the floor. Too much blood to mop up.

So Savino added, "Besides, you're biased."

He didn't add that Lansky was hitting the bottle a little too heavy these days.

"Ramsey was an asshole," Lansky argued. "He had a grudge against Torres because our boy is the best. Add means and opportunity, and that's realism. Not bias."

"Right. You want him to be guilty."

"So? Better him than one of us."

"And that's your bias." Savino leaned back in his chair. "Torres here is coming from the opposite end. Not neutral, but opposite."

"Come again?"

"You believe Ramsey's dirty, so you'll work to find facts to support that premise. Torres wants Ramsey to be clean. He'll work to prove the man's innocence so he can clear the team's name. The truth lies somewhere in between, and by coming from opposite ends, the two of you will find it."

"Yeah, but Kitty Cat gets to work his end with a great view chatting up a sexy broad in a fancy zip code. Me? You're gonna stick me here, aren't you. In bumfuck nowhere with orange drapes." Lansky gave the motel room a sneering look. Ignoring them both, Torres switched from push-ups to sit-ups.

"Nobody knows you're here, so this is as good as any until we have a direction," Savino agreed with a nod. The bone-deep tension finally starting to loosen now that he knew things would be handled, he rested one booted foot on the opposite knee.

"Bottom line, Torres is the one whose head is gonna roll farthest if we don't figure it out. He's the one I want staking out the ex."

"You think he'll go to her?"

Savino glanced at Torres, who'd finally hit his wall and sat, arms draped over his knees, trying to catch a breath.

"Everything I've seen indicates that if Ramsey's our guy, dead or alive, he'd involve her."

"The way he talked, they were a pretty hot item," Lansky agreed. "Maybe that's why she didn't bring the kid to the memorial. She knew Ramsey wasn't dead and didn't want the boy blowing their cover."

"Or maybe she simply didn't want to bring her kid to a bar to meet a bunch of strangers for the first time while they share stories of his old man going up in flames," Torres muttered.

Exactly. Savino knew Torres's history, knew where the guy had come from. Just another reason he wanted him leading this mission.

If Ramsey was dirty and his girlfriend complicit, the kid's life was going to be blown all to hell. Torres had been there himself; he'd felt the betrayal of a selfish father who'd put corruption ahead of his family. Who'd put his personal vision of glory over his son.

Torres would take care not to point the finger and put another boy on the same painful path he'd walked.

Which was something Savino was counting on. Not so much to protect the kid, although he wasn't indifferent. But because that care, that meticulous focus on detail, was what they needed if they were going to present a clean case to NI and clear Poseidon's name.

Of course, if Ramsey was truly dead and they confirmed that he was whistle clean, SEAL Team 7 was up a creek. That would mean there was a traitor in their midst. That kind of thing was a black mark against the entire team. It could be a major blow to Torres, who'd led the mission. It could result in loss of rank, loss of command, dishonorable discharge and quite possibly imprisonment.

At odds with Savino's usual cool, fury flamed hot and livid in his gut. NI already had it in for Poseidon, disliking their air of exclusivity and admiral's auspices. This was all they'd need to disband and destroy the Special Ops group.

Savino wanted to lay that all out. To underscore the severity of this situation.

For each one of the team personally.

But that'd be indulgent.

Stating the obvious would show a lack of faith in his men. And it'd waste time.

"Your orders are to watch, engage if engaged, but don't give any hint that you believe Ramsey might be alive."

Mid-sit-up, Torres paused to give Savino a look that was clearly a pledge.

"Watch, engage only if engaged? I specialize in recon and counterterrorism. That sounds like babysitting."

Distaste and discomfort were both evident in the man's voice. Sitting and watching, not acting, it was the antithesis of what they were trained for. And a man like Torres, who, as he said, specialized in action, probably thought an assignment like this was next to impossible. But that's what they were trained to do. The impossible.

"Observe, blend, engage if engaged. Play nice and, if possible, earn their trust. Consider yourself undercover as a nice guy." Savino almost grinned at Lansky's snorted amusement. He couldn't stop himself from adding, "Nailing this guy will put an end to this investigation. Otherwise…"

The end of Poseidon.

"We're clean. We fight the good fight. We fight the clean fight. Until we have to fight dirty." Elbows on his knees now, Torres shrugged. "Poseidon is clean. Nothing they find can prove it any other way. But we'll do their job for them and prove it our way. Prove we're crystal."

Exactly what he'd wanted to hear.

And that was why Torres was the best man for the job.

CHAPTER FOUR

DIEGO HAD BEEN to a lot of places. Stinking slums and baking beaches, crowded cities and ice-crusted mountains. He'd served with people from all walks of life and had gone through most of the states in the union. But he couldn't recall ever actually bunking down anywhere he fit in less than the exclusive Riviera Enclave in Santa Barbara.

Throttling his Harley back from a roar to a grumbling purr, he prepared to stop as he neared the guardhouse. But for the first time in the three days he'd been here, the orange-and-white-striped gate rose at his approach.

Well, well. How about that, he mused as he rolled right on through. Maybe it was a sign.

His first day he'd had to register both himself and his bike. When he'd come through a couple of hours later with his gear, the same guard had made him show his ID all over again. Same the next day, and the one after that.

A hint of satisfaction worked its way through the fury-filled frustration that had fueled his every waking moment for the last four days.

He'd be happier if it stemmed from, oh, say, hearing that Jared had made a breakthrough in hacking Ramsey's email accounts. Or better yet, seeing Ramsey himself stroll up the sidewalk, as alive as can be. He'd even settle for the extraction team finding DNA in the dust they'd scooped up from the mission site and proving that Ramsey was well and truly dead.

But Diego had served on enough missions to know that success was built one small triumph at a time. And that he needed to take what he could get.

He kept his speed under twenty. There weren't any of those signs posted warning that children were playing, probably because they weren't allowed to. It was *that* kind of neighborhood. Rich, upscale and exclusive, the lawns were all perfectly maintained, the birds chirped in sync and the few people he'd actually seen looked like something off a movie set. *Pretty and Perfect*, he decided the film would be titled as he slowed his bike to a crawl.

He didn't turn his head, but his eyes locked on his target as he pulled into the driveway next door. Sun-pinked adobe and gleaming rod iron were accented by arched windows, a covered front patio and fat clay pots overflowing with jewel-toned flowers. The green sweep of lawn was intersected by a curving walkway decorated with pebbles the same color as the house. Next to the sidewalk and at odds with the picture-perfect landscape a little blue wagon tilted drunkenly to the side, its front wheel missing.

So far Diego's recon hadn't done more than confirm the information they had. Ramsey's ex lived in the house with their son. She worked from home, led a supposedly quiet life and drove an aged Camry.

He needed more.

And he wasn't going to get it watching from the outside. He just hadn't found his way in.

Not yet.

His orders were specific.

Watch and wait; engage only if engaged.

Damned if following orders wasn't a pain in the ass sometimes.

But then, as if someone had decided to cut him a break, a movement swept up the sidewalk in the form of a kid pushing his bicycle.

Diego let himself smile. *Why not?* He might have just found his angle.

He'd been watching the house and occupants for three days, so he knew at a glance that the slight figure with tousled blond hair and scuffed orange high-tops belonged to Ramsey's kid, Nathan. This could be it. His entry to Ramsey's woman.

Taking it slow, Diego parked his bike and removed his helmet before swinging his leg over the seat. All the while, he kept his eyes on the kid and tried to figure his opening. By the time he removed the keys, he knew the drizzle of sweat skating down his spine had nothing to do with wearing a leather jacket in hotter than usual May sunshine.

Approach an admiral? He had that down pat. He knew the protocol on engaging a working girl on the docks of a foreign country, a militant with a nervous expression or a snitch in the Afghan mountains.

But a kid?

Diego grimaced. He didn't like to admit that he was totally clueless. But reality was reality. And yeah, he was clueless. He ran a hand through his sweat-dampened hair as he watched the boy push his bike closer.

The kid raised his hand to shield his eyes. Even from a dozen yards away, it was easy to see him slide a glance toward his front door, then back Diego's way.

Giving the door a considering look himself, Diego

had a brief vision of Lansky's theory being true. That Ramsey was inside there, alive and well, kicking back with a beer. Would he be flashing that shit-eating grin of his, looking as if he owned the world? Or would he take one look at Diego and shoot him dead, destroying yet another piece of the brotherhood that the team honored so highly?

Diego's teeth clenched tight and hard as he turned toward the door of his current abode instead of kicking in the neighbor's door to find out.

"Hey, mister," the young voice called.

"Yeah?" Shoulders braced, he froze halfway between the sidewalk and the door. After a long moment, he turned his head to look. That's when he noticed the bicycle's chain dangling, its greasy loop of metal scraping along the sidewalk.

"You know anything about bikes?" The kid jerked his chin toward the Harley. "That's yours, right? So you probably know how to fix 'em and stuff, maybe?"

"You need help fixing your bike?"

The kid looked at him, then at the chain drooping sadly on the sidewalk. Didn't need to be a mind reader or have jack worth of experience with kids to hear the unspoken "duh" loud and clear.

Diego snorted, amused at his previous hesitation.

"Sure. I can help." He strode over to take the bike in hand. His gaze tracked the larger sprocket the chain was hanging from, noting the damage to the smaller one behind it.

"This is supposed to be hooked over here," he pointed out, poking at the chain. He noted the broken teeth, figuring that's why the chain had slipped.

"I keep putting it there, but it won't stay." The kid

nudged the chain with a worn tennis shoe, but his eyes stayed on Diego. "I thought you knew bikes."

"I know how to fix that one." Diego tilted his head toward the Harley. "We'll have to see what I can do with yours."

He dropped into a crouch, flipping the bike to rest upside down on the cement. A couple of tweaks of his fingers had the chain in place.

"It's not going to stay there," he noted. "You need to replace this part."

"Can't you fix that, too?" The boy's eyes slid toward his house and whatever he saw there had his bottom lip poking out. "Can't you try?"

"Why?" Diego followed his gaze, then gave the kid a closer look. He was clean, well-dressed and had an open, easy expression. None of that said abuse to Diego. But, again, what did he know about kids? "You gonna get in trouble over it?"

"Maybe." One of those sneakers scuffed at the sidewalk as the kid wrinkled his nose. "Can you tell how it got broke just looking at it? Could it have just sorta, you know, fell off?"

"Could these teeth on this sprocket have just sorta fell off?" he repeated, tapping the part in question.

"Yeah. Could it?" His brows drawn tight enough to furrow his freckles, the kid fingered the sprocket. Testing the other teeth, probably.

"Your parents stupid?"

"My mom's not stupid." The kids eyes shot back up, flashing with a protective kind of heat that Diego recognized, having felt it often enough over his own mom.

"Didn't say she was. But it's gonna take stupid to believe that pieces of metal just sorta fall off."

"Oh." The kid frowned at the sprocket again, then at

his house. Then he gave Diego an easy smile. "Okay. Why don't you show me how to fix it, maybe? Then I can do it myself if it falls off again."

"Better plan," Diego agreed, skimming a finger under the chain to dislodge it. "Here's what you do."

He proceeded to take the kid through the steps, then walked him through how to replace the sprocket.

"Your dad should be able to replace it, no problem," he added, tossing out a line. "But this way you know how, too."

The kid wasn't biting. His eyes stayed locked on the chain for a few seconds; then he shrugged.

"It wouldn't do any good to take it apart unless I had the new, what'd you call it?" He raised clear blue eyes.

"Sprocket."

"Yeah." After contemplating for another second, he shook his head. "Even if I had enough money, I'd still have to ask Mom for a ride to the store. So she'd know."

"Moms usually do."

"Yeah." The kid tossed off his gloomy expression. "Still, thanks for the help, mister."

Damn.

"Hang on. Maybe I can tweak it a little." Telling himself it was just a way to keep the kid talking until he mentioned his father, Diego unlatched the saddlebag on his Hog and pulled out a few tools.

"You're cool. Thanks tons. You got any kids?"

"I'm not married," Diego answered automatically, watching the kid out of the corner of his eye to gauge his reaction.

"Okay." The expectant expression didn't change. After a second, his blue eyes flashed with impatience. "So? You got any kids?"

Laughing under his breath, Diego shook his head.

"So you live here alone?" The boy glanced toward the house, a small line creasing his freckled brow.

"For now." Diego tilted his head toward the kid's house. "You live there alone?"

"'Course not," the boy said with a laugh, shaking his head at what was obviously a stupid question. "It's me and my mom living there."

"Just the two of you, hmm?" Was it wrong to lead a kid on? Diego knew his motives were solid. Still, the boy was so open and, well, sweet, that Diego had to twitch his shoulders to shake off the sudden discomfort.

"Just us now. Used to be Andi and Matt, but we were here a lot cuz mom was decorating things. Then Matt moved out cuz he had issues and it was us and Andi. Then Andi went to live the high life, so it's me and Mom."

Andy *and* Matt? Two guys? Diego blinked and rocked back on his heels. He wasn't sure if he was more impressed that the kid had blurted that all on a single breath or at the insight into Ramsey's ex's sexual habits. Remembering the photo of the blonde on the beach, he pursed his lips.

"'Course Andi's still here all the time. Except for trips to Greece for obligation visits. My friend Jeremy is going on a trip, too. He's going to camp. Have you ever gone to camp, mister?"

Camping, was it? After indulging the image of an oil-coated threesome in his imagination for another second, Diego gave the kid a nod.

"Sure. I've camped." Sleeping in a tent in the Afghan desert counted, right? "So you're going camping?" *With who? Maybe your late, not-so-great father?*

"Nah. I can't go. I want to, cuz Jaermy is my best friend and it'd be fun. And his dad's gonna chap'rone, too, cuz his mom's paranoid. That's what his dad said. That his mom won't let him go unless his dad is there to make sure he doesn't fall out of a tree or drown or something. That'd be cool, huh?" The kid looked pretty excited about those possibilities. "Do you got any pets? You know, like a dog or a cat or even a bird? If you've got a cat, it could have kittens, right?"

Blinking as the kid jumped tracks, Diego shook his head.

"No pets. But your bike is set." Diego rose. With a quick flip of one hand, he righted the bike, then gave it a little shake for good measure. When everything stayed in place, he nudged the kickstand down and let the bike rest on it. "That should hold it for a while."

"You're the best, mister." The kid had to get his smile from his mother, Diego decided. Because not once could Diego remember Ramsey's smile making him want to offer one in return.

"Diego," he said after a second, figuring talking was better than standing here on the sidewalk, grinning like an idiot. "You can call me Diego."

"Cool. I'm Nathan. I'm seven. I'm gonna be a stuntman when I grow up. Or a veterinarian. I'd rather be a Jedi warrior, but Mom says we'll see about that one. She says that about a lot of stuff. We'll see. What are you?"

Huh? Was that a question? The kid's expression said it was, so Diego did a mental replay.

"I'm in security," he said, using the cover Savino had decided on.

"Bet you're good at it." Grabbing the bike by the handles, the kid gave it a good shake, then grinned when the chain stayed in place. "You're good at fixing things, too. Maybe you could teach me to fix some things?"

Diego didn't have much experience with kids—hell,

he didn't have any experience. Despite that, he had to figure this one was something special.

Before he could answer him, a delivery truck rumbled its way to a stop in front of the kid's house. Something he'd noticed was a regular occurrence. At least once, sometimes twice a day.

"You sure get a lot of deliveries," he observed, watching a guy in shorts carry a stack of boxes toward the door.

"Yeah. Mom gets tons of stuff. She decorates for people's houses. She orders pillows and bowls and things like that. Sometimes she gets material and things to help her decide colors."

Convenient. Or it would be if Ramsey were running drugs or stolen goods—that'd be a solid cover. But unless he'd shipped himself home in an ash can, it probably wasn't pertinent. Lansky would claim otherwise, though, so Diego made a note to mention it in his next report.

He caught a flash of something out of the corner of his eye. All it took was a casual glance toward the house to send him rocking back on his heels.

Damn.

Not even signing for a slew of packages and fending off the flirtations of the delivery guy were enough to keep Harper Maclean from sending her son a protective frown.

So far his glimpses of her had been at a longer distance than the twenty feet currently separating them. Her photos didn't do her justice. He'd known she was a looker, but no way he'd have thought fully dressed in person could trump that bikini shot, even if that bikini shot had been kind of blurry.

He'd have been wrong.

Even glaring at him, as if she thought he'd get greasy cooties all over her sweet little boy, she was gorgeous.

From the tip of her tousled blond hair to the toes of her strappy high-heeled sandals, she screamed California girl. She was too far away to see many details, but he knew from the file Lansky had compiled that she had strong features. A wide mouth with its generous bottom lip and dark brows that arched over big blue eyes.

Diego wasn't sure why he felt as if he'd just taken a kick to the solar plexus. He'd never gone for the good-girl look, and there was nothing particularly sexy about what she was wearing. The turquoise pleated skirt flared in a way that made her waist look miniscule and her cream-colored top looked like a silky T-shirt, but both were a little too generous with the fabric for his tastes.

Which didn't matter, he reminded himself as the woman walked from the front door to her courtyard's arch. Sexy or dog ugly, she was a means to an end. And that end had nothing to do with getting her naked, more's the pity.

"Hey there," he called in what he figured was a friendly manner.

From the way she frowned and hugged one of the delivery boxes to her chest, she didn't seem to agree.

"Hello," she responded after a moment. "Nathan, you need to come inside."

"But, Mom—"

"Now, please."

With that uncompromising edict and one final stare at Diego, she was gone. Leaving an open front door and a whole lot of curiosity bouncing through Diego's head. Only some of it having to do with his mission.

"Guess your mom's not much on being neighborly," he murmured.

"She's not mad. She's just, you know, suspicious about me talking to strangers. I had to call when I left Jeremy's house, and she times it, you know? She's probably watching now through the window." The boy rolled his eyes. "It's the paranoia. That's what Jeremy's dad says. Moms are paranoid about stuff happening to their kids. He says you gotta indulge the paranoia sometimes."

Wrinkling his nose, the kid grabbed the bike by the handlebars. "What's that mean? Do you know?"

It meant that Jeremy's dad better watch out or one of those moms was gonna kick his patronizing ass.

"What do you think it means?" Diego asked instead of sharing that opinion.

"I dunno. I asked my mom, and all she said was that even Neanderthals had their uses. What's that mean?" Never taking his eyes off Diego, he straddled his bike. "Isn't a Neanderthal a guy who rides dinosaurs?"

Diego grinned at the image of a caveman saddling a T. rex for a ride through lava flow.

"I suppose your mom meant that some people's attitudes are stuck in the dark ages. That their brains haven't grown much since the caveman days." After half a second, Diego added, "Maybe you shouldn't say that to this guy, though. People who think that way tend to dislike being called on it."

"Okay." The boy shrugged. "I'll see you again, right? Cuz we're neighbors now."

"Yeah. We'll see each other again."

The boy flashed a bright smile and waved one grubby hand before riding away.

Diego watched the boy drop the bike against the side of the house in clattering disregard before running toward the front door, pausing to toss another friendly wave over his shoulder.

The kid had talked more in that ten minutes than Diego had in the last ten days. And that, Diego realized, was a certified entry into Ramsey's world.

As he strode toward his fancy new barracks, he assessed the neighborhood's security and debated various means of getting to see that kid again. Another twenty minutes, half hour tops, and he'd get all the intel he needed to clear Ramsey or nail his ass to the wall. And maybe, just maybe, get a little more info on the sexy blonde and who had apparently a very creative sex life.

It wasn't until he stepped through the front door that he realized he was grinning.

HARPER COULDN'T RELAX.

Not even after Nathan was inside, safe and sound.

Feeling like she'd been punched in the gut, she could only stand in her kitchen and stare at the box from Petty Officer Dane Adams. Apparently the man thought she, or rather, Nathan, would want some of Brandon's effects.

Why?

They'd done just fine without a single thing from him—other than DNA. Why would that change because he was dead? She'd figured it didn't matter. Even after she'd received notice of Brandon's death, she'd decided she'd set it aside to tell Nathan later, when he was older and might better understand.

She glared at the box, hating it and everything it represented. She wanted to ignore it. Her gut told her to ignore everything, to continue to pretend that it didn't exist. That he didn't exist. But she couldn't. Not anymore.

Once, when he'd been four, her sweet little boy had

asked why he didn't have a dad like some of the other kids in his preschool class. All she'd been able to come up with was that the man had made a choice and gone away. That must have been enough for Nathan, because he'd never asked again, and she'd been happy to leave it that way.

Harper pressed her hand against the churning misery in her belly. She'd told herself she was waiting for the right time to tell him. Really, she'd been ignoring it, and quite nicely, too. And it had been working just fine.

A part of her wanted to continue ignoring it, to throw the box in the trash and be done with the entire issue. Taking a deep breath she tore open the plastic packing slip envelope. Inside was a simple note.

Ms. Maclean,
Brandon Ramsey was a hero. A man to be proud of. His death is a blow to his friends, to his team and to the country. It's important that we honor our heroes. Please pass on these things to his son, so he can honor his father.
Dane Adams

So not only had Brandon known about Nathan, and where to find them, but his friend did, too. Which meant she couldn't ignore this. Not until she was sure that the Ramseys with their high-powered attorneys weren't going to show up next. She forced herself to cut through the packing tape. She unfolded the flaps and, cringing only a little, lifted aside the neatly folded tissue paper.

On top was a large envelope with her name on it, and beneath that what looked like a small leather-bound book or photo album. She didn't open it. Couldn't. Not yet. She set it aside to look at the rest. A rosewood box of ribbons and medals. At least a dozen bound certifications for things like marksmanship and diving. Even a cap, the white fabric and black plastic formal and stiff.

She didn't know this world. She didn't know the man who'd belonged in it. Why was she bringing it into her son's life?

Because she didn't have a choice, she realized with a sigh. Eyes burning with tears she refused to shed, Harper tucked the box under the kitchen desk, then tossed the note and large envelope addressed to her on the built-in kitchen desk to deal with later. She wanted to toss the box out the door but refrained.

Did she need this right now? She stormed through dinner prep like a woman riding a tornado. Oil heated, lettuce ripped and—screw it—the oven door slammed on frozen French fries.

Wasn't it enough to have to deal with Nathan going away on his first trip longer than an overnight sleepover? Not only away, but away at camp on a tiny island in the middle of the freaking ocean. Okay, not quite the middle, but it was an island and it was surrounded by Pacific waters.

She was handling that, wasn't she? Granted, she hadn't told him that he was going yet. Once she did, she wouldn't be able to change her mind. This morning Andi, with her usual efficiency, had forwarded the email showing the camp registration fee paid in full. Now Harper had no choice. But she hadn't had a tantrum about that, had she?

Had she climbed onto the roof, yanked at her hair and screamed her throat raw yet over Brandon's dramatic reentry into her life? Leave it to him to force his presence into Nathan's life in a way she couldn't stop. He would have known she'd tell him to take a flying leap if he'd contacted her about meeting Nathan, about being a part of her son's life. He'd had his chance. He'd made his choice.

Now he'd never get to change his mind, or try to change hers. Her gaze slid to the red-and-blue-striped priority shipping box that'd been delivered an hour ago. She'd shoved it under the small kitchen desk, half-hidden but all too visible.

Harper grabbed her drink. Her teeth clenched tight on the straw as she sucked down a long sip of lemon-infused water and tried to settle the flood of emotions pouring through her. The water cooled her throat, but it didn't help with the confusion storming through her chest.

Was she supposed to be sad? Was she supposed to grieve? And how did she tell her son that the father she'd never once mentioned was dead? Would he care? By trying to keep him from getting hurt, had hiding Brandon from Nathan actually hurt him?

And how was that for a convoluted guilt trip? Harper closed her eyes to the pain she didn't understand and took a shaky breath. A part of her wanted to gather Nathan and run, hide. The rest wanted to climb in bed, pull the covers over her head and pretend that none of this was happening.

Since Harper was made of stronger stuff than that, she did neither.

Instead she finished dinner preparations.

"Mom, I'm starving. Like, I could eat a whole Tauntaun," Nathan announced as he ran into the kitchen.

"I didn't have time to stop by the planet Hoth for Tauntaun, so we're having chicken instead." Harper forced a smile. She had to struggle with some of the *Star Wars* references, but anything from the first three movies, she was solid on. She pointed a finger at her son before he could slide into his chair. "Wash. Then set the table."

"'Kay." He hurried to the kitchen sink, nudging the stool in with his foot and turning the water on before she could remind him of her opinion on kicking the furniture. "Chicken is way better than fish. Jeremy said his mom is making him eat something called hall butt tonight because he's going to adventure camp."

"Halibut." Harper's lips twitched and just like that, the bulk of the stress drained away. "And you hate eating fish."

"I'd eat it if I went to adventure camp. It'd be different there, cuz I'd be catching it and all that stuff. Jeremy says they go fishing and hiking and all sorts of cool things. They even learn how to tie knots." Nathan jumped down, not bothering to move the stool aside before hopping over to gather the dishes she'd already set out on the island. "Do you think they tell ghost stories around a campfire, too? That'd be cool. I know some good stories."

Harper let the questions roll over her as she tried to figure out how to tell Nathan that his father was dead. Did she explain that before she told him he was going to camp? Or did she start with the camp news and let him revel for a while before she burst his happy little bubble?

"Mom?"

"Hmm?" Forcing herself to shake off the what-ifs and focus on what mattered—Nathan—Harper brought the salad to the table.

"Those are guy things, aren't they?"

Guy things? She replayed the conversation as she handed Nathan a bowl of salad, then arched one brow.

"Are you trying to say that a woman couldn't hike

or fish or sail?" she asked, dishing up her own salad while giving her son a narrow look.

"Sure. Girls can if they want." He stabbed a chunk of cucumber, then shot her a wicked smile. "Not you, cuz you don't like anything that's dirty or slimy. After we tried camping last summer, I heard you tell Andi that you'd rather eat slugs than sleep on the ground again. But I suppose some girls prob'ly like dirt and slime. It's okay that you don't."

"Smart boy," she murmured. Andi was right. She couldn't be enough for Nathan. Not by herself, she admitted as a wave of guilt washed over her. This guilt was as familiar as her own skin. It'd come with the pregnancy hormones and never left.

"Eat your salad" was all she said.

"I met the guy who's living at Mr. Lowenstein's house."

"So I saw."

Oh, yeah. She'd seen the guy. A muscle-bound, Harley-riding guy with an intimidating stare, and most likely an IQ lower than he could bench-press. Starting on her own salad, Harper told herself to relax. She was sure he wasn't dangerous. The Riviera Enclave was an exclusive gated community and the Lowensteins were vigilant in their screening. Added to that, the longest they ever sublet was a month. So the man might be a little intimidating, but he wasn't likely to have any real impact on their lives.

"His name is Diego. He fixes things and secures stuff. He doesn't got a kid, but he likes pets." With the look of wide-eyed guile that he'd perfected, Nathan smiled at his mother. "That's a good thing, right? In case we ever had to go on a job that's overnight like the one you did in San Diego last summer for that music lady, there'd be someone next door to feed a pet. If we had one, I mean."

Nicely done, Harper thought, appreciating how many creative ways he could make that pitch. While he rambled on about the care and needs of a kitten and debated the cuteness factor of gray tabbies versus orange, she pulled the warming chicken and finished fries from the oven.

"Chicken fingers?" Nathan exclaimed, pausing in his recital of possible cat names. His excitement slid into a frown as he noted the potatoes she was scooping onto the royal-blue Fiesta platter. "And fries? Why're we having Saturday food? Isn't today Wednesday?"

"Sure it is. But you'll be at camp on Saturday, so we're having Saturday food today instead." Nathan's jaw dropped. He gave a war whoop at the same time he shot out of his chair and launched himself into her arms.

His grateful enthusiasm was almost enough to drown out her concerns.

"You're the best, Mom. The absolute best. Thanks. I'm gonna call Jeremy. Can I? Can I? I want to tell him so we can bunk together."

"After dinner." Harper held on a moment longer. Then because she knew she had to start getting used to it, she slowly let go. She scooped her fingers through the wavy mass of his hair, then tilted her head toward the table. "That way the two of you can talk as long as you like."

That he'd still have words for later was just one of those things that always amazed her about Nathan. He'd talk through the meal about everything from camp to the LEGO project he was working on to baseball and back again. Unlike his mother, he never ran out of words. Never had to search for them.

But she was searching now. For the words, for the right way to tell him what she had to share. As he scooped his last fry through his ketchup, she still hadn't figured it out. But like most of motherhood, she realized she'd have to figure it as she went.

"Leave the dishes for now, Nathan." She laid her hand on his arm to keep him from jumping up from the table. "We need to talk."

"Am I in trouble?" His face creasing, Nathan settled into his chair again.

"No, sweetie," she rushed to say, sliding her hand down to mesh her fingers through his smaller ones.

He was growing so fast. Once, those fingers had been tiny as they'd wrapped around hers, his just-born eyes staring into her face as if she were his world. Those fingers had gripped hers as he'd taken his first teetering steps; that hand had held tight the first day of school.

She'd spent her entire life trying to protect him. To give him the best and keep him as happy as she could. Now she had to hurt him. God help her, she blamed Brandon.

Harper took a deep, shaky breath as she tried to fight back the tears clogging her throat, then gave her son a reassuring smile.

"You're not in trouble. I just need to tell you something."

"Something bad?" he ventured when she bit her lip, trying to gather the words she still hadn't found.

She wanted to assure him that it wasn't bad. She wanted to continue ignoring Brandon's existence. His death shouldn't change that.

Except that she couldn't. And it did.

Once again, Brandon had managed to turn her entire world upside down, and once again, he hadn't stuck around to watch the fallout.

CHAPTER FIVE

So THIS MUST be what it felt like to get run over by a truck.

A very large, dirty truck overloaded with painful regrets and parental guilt.

Sitting on the edge of the bed, head resting in her hands, Harper used her fingers to try to massage away the pain throbbing a tango on her scalp.

He'd taken the news well.

Too well.

She'd told him that the man who'd fathered him was dead, and Nathan had simply nodded. He hadn't asked any questions. He hadn't been interested in Brandon's heroics as a SEAL, or why he'd never been around. He didn't care what was in the box of effects sent to him by the person who claimed to be Brandon's best friend. The first time he'd shown any emotion was when she'd suggested he might want the glass-fronted rosewood case of medals to keep in his room, and that'd been to throw the case back into the packing box with a scowl.

Before she could ask if he wanted to talk about it, or if he had any questions, he'd demanded to know if they were done yet so he could call Jeremy.

Harper hadn't known what else to do other than wave him toward the phone. Maybe he was just too excited about camp to focus on the other. Or maybe he simply didn't care.

She'd spent the rest of the evening watching for signs while pretending not to. She'd done her yoga in the TV room while he chatted on the phone. She'd worked on her laptop in the dining room while he'd tossed his baseball in the backyard. And she'd curled up with him on the couch while he grumbled over his summer reading.

But she hadn't seen a single sign of grief or confusion. He'd been his usual, upbeat self.

Maybe he was repressing something.

Or maybe he simply didn't care.

"Mom?"

Harper jumped to her feet, hurrying down the hall to Nathan's bedroom.

"What do you need, sweetie?"

"I can't find my baseball." In Thor pajamas, wrapped in the bedtime scent of coconut soap and bubblegum toothpaste, Nathan sat in the middle of his floor surrounded by LEGO pieces. "I wanted to use it as the power source, but it's not here."

"Power source, huh?" Harper knelt down next to him, careful to avoid jabbing a tiny plastic block into her knee. "Is this going to be a space station?"

"Yeah. It's gonna be Kylo Ren's hideout." He didn't look at her, but Harper didn't need to see his eyes to conclude he was upset. "He's gotta recover and learn to control his temper and figure out stuff."

Kylo Ren. Harper's breath came slow and painful as she tried to figure out how to ask her little boy if he was suddenly relating to the villain's father issues. She wanted to gather Nathan tight in her arms and rock away any pain, soothe any confusion.

Her eyes burned as she looked at the top of her son's tousled hair as it lay drying in shaggy waves. He wasn't a baby anymore. And while she didn't claim to understand much about the male ego, she knew her little boy was already too much a man to accept either words or hugs until he was ready for them.

She didn't know what it said that she grieved over that more than anything else today. But there it was.

So she did what she always did. She sidestepped the emotional drama and went for the practical.

"You were playing with your ball when you were in the yard. Did you leave it out there?"

"Maybe." His face creased as he continued to snap the tiny gray pieces together. "I think so."

"I'll find it," she said, giving in to the urge to run her hand over his hair before rising.

"Can I listen to a story, too?" he asked before she reached the door.

"Percy Jackson?" Harper asked, reaching for the remote she kept on the spaceship-shaped shelving unit and aiming it for the CD player. Already queued to chapter 7, the narrator's voice filled the room with the adventures of Percy and Grover. Harper waited another moment, but Nathan seemed content.

He wouldn't be in a half hour when she called for lights-out, though. Not without his ball. He'd never had a blankie or teddy bear. Just like he'd never had a father.

He'd had her. And he'd had his baseball.

Since he'd probably left it in the backyard, she started her search there. It wasn't until the evening air cooled her hot cheeks that she realized they were covered in tears.

Harper dried them with an impatient swipe of her hands, bending low to peer under chairs, stretching sideways to check behind the bank of variegated hosta plants and rich purple spikes of salvia.

It took her a few seconds to realize she was hear-

ing more than crickets in the night. Was someone yell-
ing hiyah?

She stepped through the iron fence and froze.

The new neighbor was in his backyard. Barefoot
and shirtless, he wore what looked like black pajama
bottoms. He simply flowed across the moon-drenched
lawn. Kicks, turns, chops and punches flowed in a
seamlessly elegant dance.

Was that martial arts he was doing?

Shirtless.

She couldn't quite get past that one particular point.
It was too delicious.

But instead of licking her lips, Harper clenched her
fists tight at her sides.

Why the hell was a man who looked like that living
next door to her? More to the point, why did her libido
choose now to wake up? Was it some cosmic joke that
she'd remember now, despite her claims to the con-
trary, she was a sexually aware woman who had needs
and desires?

Harper watched him do some sort of flip, feet in the
air and his body resting on one hand. Muscles rippled,
but he wasn't even breathing hard as he executed an elegant somersault to land, feetfirst on the grass, knees
low and arms extended.

Wow.

She'd bet all of her needs and desires could be handled quite nicely by her gorgeous, and quite physically
impressive, new neighbor.

Harper would have growled if she weren't worried the guy would notice the slightest sound and turn
around. The last thing she wanted while she was going
through this personal crisis was attention.

She wanted to blame Andi. Oh, not for the new

neighbor. Arranging for good-looking neighbors wasn't one of Andi's oft-bragged-about skills. But putting the idea of sex and lust and, yes, dammit, craving, into Harper's mind so her imagination ran wild when she looked at the new neighbor? That was totally and completely Andi's fault.

Her stomach tightened with an edgy need she recognized as desire as the guy did a series of kicks, each one higher than the other with the last aimed straight overhead.

Again, wow.

He had tattoos.

A cross riding low on his hip and something tribal circling one bicep.

Who knew tattoos were so sexy?

Harper's mouth went dry. Her libido, eight years in deep freeze, exploded into lusty flames so hot they scorched away all her spit. She couldn't swallow, could barely breathe. She had to try twice to clear the tight knot of lust in her throat.

Wow, she thought for the third time.

Because some things definitely deserved repeating. The man was incredible.

Gorgeous. She was pretty sure he was gorgeous. It was hard to tell, though, because her head was spinning.

He looked like some kind of pagan god—the ones who liked to deflower virgins—with that commanding air, impressive body and golden skin stretched over well-toned muscles.

Short black hair that spiked here and there over a face made for appreciative sighs. Sharp cheekbones rose high, accenting full lips. Thick brows arched over deep-set eyes, and he had a scar on his chin that glowed in the moonlight.

She heard herself gulp before she realized she'd done it.

Wondering where her spit had gone, Harper decided that she'd better get the hell out of there. Before he saw her. Before she did something to make sure he saw her.

But just as she turned to go, she spotted Nathan's baseball sitting on a raised brick flowerbed. It was all she could do not to groan out loud. Her hint of a sigh must have been enough though, because the guy looked her way. Just a glance, not enough to slow the elegant ballet of kicks and punches. But enough to show that he knew she was there. He'd probably known all along.

"You looking for the ball?" His words were lightly accented with a familiar Hispanic lilt. They came low and easy like his smile, which made it all the more irritating that Harper was still too breathless to reply right away.

"Yes, my son lost it." She eyed the distance between her nice, safe spot next to the fence and the ball. It wasn't far, but she'd have to skirt awfully close to the man who was now, what? She narrowed her eyes. Was he praying?

Palms together, eyes closed, he lifted his hands high overhead so that long body stretched toward the moon. Shimmering light danced over a puckered scar riding high on his chest, glistened off the sharp-edged tattoo that circled his bicep like barbed wire before he lowered his hands to chest height. Eyes still closed, he took a deep breath. Wondering if he'd do it again, Harper edged a few inches inside the fence line. Before she'd taken a full step, though, his eyes shot open.

"Good yard for working out," he said with a nod of approval. He moved across the lawn with the same light-footed grace as he'd shown in his martial arts dance. He stopped along the way to grab the ball, then continued until he was a couple of feet from her. There, he simply stood, tossing the ball from hand to hand, staring.

"I should get that to Nathan." She cleared her throat, tried a smile. It failed but she figured she at least got points for trying. "He's very attached to it."

"The kid's a pistol." His eyes were much too intense as he watched her face.

Didn't the man blink?

That's when she realized what she must look like. She'd tossed an oversize tee claiming Just Say Zen atop her green yoga bra and leggings, so unlike some people, she was decently covered. But her hair was pulled into a sloppy ponytail, and she was sure that whatever makeup she hadn't sweated off during her workout had washed away during that first, or maybe the second, crying jag.

The only way this could be any worse was if she threw herself on his chest and started licking her way down his body. And given her reaction to simply thinking about it, she decided she'd better hurry up and get out of there before she did exactly that.

From the look on his face, he knew it, too.

"Thanks for finding it." She held up one hand to indicate that he throw her the ball. But while he tossed it in the air, it was only to catch it again. What was he waiting for? She had to remind herself that this was a friendly neighborhood, and people expected actual conversation from time to time.

"I appreciate you taking the time to fix Nathan's bike," she said, wishing she could clear the nerves out of her throat. But that would just give him proof that he had her all stirred up, and one thing Harper had learned young was to never give a man that kind of upper hand.

"Fix his bike?" he repeated, as if surprised. "You mean out front today? We were just talking."

Despite the shimmying tension in her belly and the tightness in her chest, that attempt at innocence in his voice made Harper laugh.

"Mmm, he's having trouble with the chain. Probably has something to do with jumping his bike when he's not supposed to."

"Wouldn't know about that. Like I said, we just talked for a few minutes. He's a friendly kid."

The compliment smoothed out her frayed nerves just a little. Breathing deep for the first time since he'd stepped through the hedges, Harper glanced up at the second floor of her fancy new house. Nathan's window glowed with friendly cheer.

"He's comfortable with people," she said, half to herself. "Easy with them."

"How about you?" He waited until her eyes met his again, the shadows dancing in wicked angles over his face. "Are you just as at ease and comfortable with strangers?"

She wasn't even that comfortable with friends. But that wasn't any of his business.

"I'm not seven years old, so I see people a little differently than Nathan does" was all she said.

"I guess he gets that easiness with people from his dad, huh?" Even as his lips quirked, that dark gaze seemed to intensify. "Me, all I got from my old man is my height."

His expression was easy, his demeanor mellow. Still, nerves did an edgy cha-cha through her system. Maybe it was the mention of fathers, or just the pointed reminder of Brandon. Whatever it was, Harper didn't like it.

"It's a little soon to tell how tall Nathan will be," she said, her words a chilly sidestep to his question. "Thank you for the help finding the ball. I'll take it in to him now."

His eyes not leaving hers, he moved closer.

Close enough that his scent—fresh male with a hint of earthy sweat and clean soap—wrapped around her.

Close enough to touch. All she had to do was reach out to trail her fingers over that hard flesh. Was he warm and slick after that workout? Or had his skin cooled, sweat sticking like a salty blanket? Her body hummed, nerves shimmering so hard her fingers trembled. She reached for the ball.

What was he looking for? What was he seeing? Finally, he placed the ball in her outstretched hand. Then, as if expecting something more, he stood there, waiting.

For what?

No matter how much her jump-started libido wanted otherwise, she wasn't actually going to lick him.

"Thanks," she murmured, gripping it tight. It was stupid for her heart to speed up now that she was only a moment from safe, but race it did. Harper gave the no-longer-smiling neighbor a brief nod, then turned to duck back through the vine-covered gate.

"Hey."

One hand filled with the soft leaves, the other gripping the ball to her chest, Harper stopped to glance over her shoulder.

"Everything okay?"

No. But since she didn't know why it wasn't, she lied. "Fine." Unable to resist, she added, "Why do you ask?"

Clouds cloaked the moon now, dimming its light so his eyes were cast in night shadows. But Harper could still feel the power of his stare.

"Maybe I just don't like seeing a beautiful woman in a hurry to get away from me." The shadows did nothing to hide the wicked charm of his smile or the hint of sexual heat in that shielded gaze.

It was the same heat Harper felt sizzling deep in her belly. An awareness and a whole slew of promises—all of which were as suited to the dark night as the man himself seemed to be.

Who knew she'd want that so desperately?

Oh, boy, there it was, Harper realized in a flash.

The reason for her nerves. All that masculine energy, all that sensual interest, all the impossible possibilities, they crowded her thoughts, filled her body.

Thankfully, the tiny voice in her mind still had enough control to scream danger.

"I'm hurrying because I don't like to leave my son inside alone," she managed, hoping her words didn't sound as breathless to him as they did to her. "Again, thanks for your help."

And with that, she tossed pride and dignity aside and slipped through the hedge before he could say another word. It wasn't until she was inside the house that she realized she was holding her breath. Releasing it in a harsh whoosh, Harper leaned against the closed door and focused for a moment on getting the air in and out.

What was she doing? Getting lusty over a man just because he had a sexy smile and a gorgeous body? Just because his eyes promised all sorts of delights and his chest made her fingers tingle to touch? Sure, he looked as if he could've posed for Michelangelo's *David* with those sculpted muscles and all that smooth skin. And maybe the hint of an accent and flashes of humor were intriguing. But was that an excuse to picture the man naked? To wonder if he had the kind of talent in bed to make her moan with pleasure?

At that point, Harper had enough breath to laugh at herself. Because if those weren't reasons to get lusty, she couldn't think of what was. Deciding to give herself a break, she peeled herself off the door and, resisting the urge to peek out the window, flipped the lock and turned off the lights.

Wouldn't Andi be proud, Harper thought, grinning and tossing the ball from hand to hand as she climbed the stairs. Not that she would tell her. Andi wouldn't understand. Because as much fun as it was to discover that, yes, indeed, she had a libido, Harper had no intention of doing anything about it.

No matter how lusty the guy made her feel.

AN HOUR LATER, halfway through her nightly bedtime routine, Harper glanced in the bathroom mirror and frowned. Was that a wrinkle?

She rubbed her finger along the faint line scored between her meticulously arched brows.

Her frown deepened. So did the line. It *was* a wrinkle. How could she have a wrinkle? She was only twenty-five. Weren't wrinkles at least a decade away?

What the hell was she thinking, wondering if she should get naked with the hottie next door when her face looked like this? She yanked open the bottom drawer of the floor to ceiling corner cabinet and pawed through the array of bottles and jars and tins. Bubble bath, body lotion, tanning cream. Eye shadows, miracle mascaras, blushers by the dozen. Harper shuffled and dug until, a fistful of samples in hand, she rose to spread the tubes and tins over the bathroom counter.

After squinting her way through the tiny print and

wondering if bifocals were next, she settled on four anti-aging ones that promised to turn back time. A daytime moisturizer with SPF, a hydration-boosting serum, an age-reversing night cream and a mask rich in botanicals.

She'd need to visit one of those skin care counters at the mall, but she figured there wasn't a moment to lose fighting the affects that that bitch, age, was trying to gash into her face. She'd be damned if she'd let her win.

Twenty minutes later, she'd washed, masked, toned and moisturized. She flexed a little, feeling righteous in her fight. *Take that, bitch*, she huffed into the mirror.

Hair pulled back in a tight ponytail and her face glistening with a thick layer that promised dewy youth, she caught sight of herself in the cherry-trimmed cheval mirror.

She had to laugh.

She looked like this, and she was worrying about wrinkles keeping her from hitting on the neighbor?

This was the closest thing to seduction wear she owned. The black nightshirt fit just fine, skimming her breasts and hitting midthigh. But it was roomy rather than revealing, and while the cotton was wonderfully soft, Wonder Woman was so wash-worn that she was more a shadow than an actual image.

She was so not the seduce-the-neighbor-into-a-puddle-of-lust type of woman.

Hoping that little taste of reality would put an end to the crazy thoughts that kept trying to take hold, she headed down the hall. She stopped to take a quick peek at Nathan. In the glow of the star-shaped nightlight, her son slept with his usual exuberant abandon. Blankets kicked this way, arms and legs sprawled. His face buried in the pillow, his hair stuck up in little tufts. Her fingers itched to smooth it down, to straighten his blankets and settle him into the center of the bed. But he'd wake at the lightest touch. So she simply listened to the gentle sound of his breath, watched the easy rise and fall of his chest. After a long moment, she pulled the door three-quarters shut again and went to her own room.

The bulk of the furnishings in the house belonged to Andi, including the four-poster bed. But the bedding, oh, that'd been Harper's single indulgence for herself when they'd moved in. Heavy gold brocade and apricot satin, it was so rich and elegant, it made her feel like a princess. She woke every morning feeling as if she actually belonged in a house this fancy, as if she'd finally earned the right to such sumptuous surroundings. That she'd finally shed the grasping guttersnipe label pinned on her so many years before by Brandon's mother.

With that thought firmly in mind, knowing she'd put it off long enough, Harper reached under the mound of decorative pillows on her bed and pulled out the envelope that had come with today's delivery of a box of memories.

She tapped it on her palm a couple of times, then set it on the nightstand. She pulled back the blankets, climbed beneath the cool sheets and fluffed her pillow a couple of times before leaning back.

Then she lifted the envelope again. With a deep breath, she slid her thumb beneath the flap and carefully tore the seal.

Ms. Maclean,
You don't know me but I served with Brandon Ramsey. He was my mentor, my friend and my roommate. He was a hero who deserves to be honored. But the Navy is tying that honor up in

red tape. They are trying to make him a scape-goat for a team too incompetent to retrieve his body. That means they won't send Brandon's son the benefits he deserves. Instead they're destroying the legacy your son's father left behind. I'm sending a few things so his son can appreciate what a great man he was. But that's not enough. They need to honor Brandon, to show the world what a hero he was. This is a mess. I hope you can help me fix it.

Keep the Spirit Alive!
Dane Adams

Harper read it again, then one more time, then glanced at the rest of the papers. News clippings, write-ups on Brandon's deeds, certificates.

She could only sigh.

This poor guy. Of course the situation was a mess. What else would Brandon leave behind? She didn't understand the part about the Navy making Brandon a scapegoat. More likely it was just red tape and some sort of military rules or regulations that this guy was upset over.

It wasn't until she saw a tear splash onto the paper that Harper realized she was crying. She didn't know why. Brandon had destroyed all of her illusions years ago when he'd crushed her heart.

She shoved the unread documents back into the envelope.

This wasn't her life. It wasn't her problem.

Whatever Brandon had done, whether he'd died a hero or not, it didn't matter.

Not to her.

But tears still came, even as she slowly drifted into sleep.

Not for Brandon this time. Or even for Nathan.

But for the girl she'd been, the one who'd believed in heroes.

CHAPTER SIX

So THAT WAS Ramsey's ex.

Now that he'd seen her up close and personal, all Diego could think was, *Hot damn*.

Ramsey might have had a tendency to be an ass, and he might have had serious issues sharing the spotlight. And Diego wasn't sure if the man had been a good SEAL or a dirty, rotten sonovabitch.

But he had to credit Brandon Ramsey with having good taste in women.

Diego had just finished installing cameras and listening equipment around the exterior of her house when he'd seen her heading out the back door. He'd had his cover handy, jumping right into a tai chi workout. She'd been emotional, but she hadn't acted suspicious. He'd have thought she'd act a little warier if she were dirty. But maybe she was cucumber cool. Maybe Ramsey hadn't shared the extent of how bad his actions were.

Or maybe Ramsey was alive, and she knew just how deep in the ugly her ex swam.

As Diego headed inside his temporary quarters, he brought her image to mind.

Her eyes were a work of art under strongly arched dark brows. Lushly lashed, they were large in her delicate face. Probably because they'd been a little puffy and red.

What had she been crying about? Ramsey?

What little intel they had so far on her showed that she'd lived within her means until about six months ago when she'd moved into the fancy house next door, that her kid attended a pricey private school and that she had a pretty high credit card limit that she charged up and paid in full each month.

None of that, or his own limited observations, pegged her as the overly emotional type. So he doubted an evening of popcorn and chick flicks had leveled her like that.

Alive or dead, he'd figured she was crying over Ramsey. The guy had to be in her head right now. If he was alive and dirty, did she struggle with her part in treason? If he was dead and dirty, was she upset to be holding the bag?

And if he was innocent? Maybe she had simply loved the asshole.

Diego rubbed his hand over his hair, then shook his head.

God, what a thought.

Then again, maybe it wasn't Ramsey who'd put that upset look on her face.

Maybe it had been Diego himself?

He'd kept it friendly, totally nonconfrontational, and the woman had left looking as if he'd punched her in the gut. No accusations, no grilling, not a hint that he was wondering if she was maybe harboring a supposed-to-be-dead, treasonous, backstabbing bastard.

Maybe he'd been too focused on doing all that to hide the fact that he thought she was hot, but he figured she was used to that. She had to be. The woman looked like a cross between a centerfold, a society princess and a sexy Betty Crocker. The kind of woman who'd wear diamonds and one of those cute white aprons while baking homemade cookies…naked.

A man would have to be a month dead and incredibly stupid to ignore a woman like that.

Diego was neither.

He just had to figure out which one Ramsey was.

An hour later, his skin cool from his shower and his stomach comfortably full thanks to a freezer full of take and bake, Diego glanced out the window at the house next door. The lights were off downstairs and faint enough upstairs to give the impression that she and the kid had both hit the sack. Turning away, he flipped through his notes, hoping to find something new that would spark an opening. They had to find Ramsey. Had to confirm dead or alive, then go from there.

And he had jack diddly toward that end. He'd had eyes on the blonde for fifty-six hours now, but he didn't have much to add to his notes. At least, not much that was relevant.

Frustration dogging his mood, Diego tossed the file onto the little table next to the window. Papers slid across the dark wood, a mocking reminder that he had nothing.

Probably because there was nothing to have, dammit.

It was crazy to think Ramsey was alive.

If he was, it meant that the guy had betrayed his country, his vows, his team.

Diego dropped onto the bed, almost sinking into the cloud-soft mattress as he covered his eyes with his forearm. As if shading the light would dim the headache brewing behind them while he tried to shove through his tangled thoughts.

The facts were clear enough. The mission had been compromised, confidential information had been sold and someone was a traitor. Lansky was sure that was Ramsey. Diego still wasn't sure if that belief was fueled by certainty or by Lansky's hate for the guy.

But Savino must believe there was a chance that Lansky was right, or Diego wouldn't be here.

And Savino was never wrong.

So Diego's reluctance to believe they'd been fucked over by one of their own didn't matter. He had his assignment. He might not be wearing his dog tags, but he was on duty. It didn't matter if he was stationed in the baking heat of Afghanistan, diving to the icy depths of the Pacific or watching a sexy blonde from the window of a piece of prime US real estate. And like any other assignment, he wouldn't walk away until his mission was complete.

He pushed himself to his feet. He skirted around the fancy furniture that had come with the sublet. He would be fine with a sleeping bag and a crate to sit on, but if he had to do recon sitting on a cushy chair, hey, he was a SEAL. Trained to handle any conditions.

Any conditions and any situation. The SEALs were trained to kick ass, to do the impossible and to cover one another's butts, no matter what.

No matter what…

Fury, tangled and confused, pounded through his head. He'd spent his entire adult life in the service. He'd gotten off the streets and joined the Navy at eighteen with one goal. To survive. It'd been twelve years since boot camp, and he'd learned that there was more to life than just survival. Oh, survival was still tops on the list. Doing the impossible against all odds would be straight-up stupid otherwise. But he'd learned to excel. He'd grown out of his in-your-face, badass attitude and learned to take—and value—orders. And he'd embraced the concept of brotherhood. Of trusting in others, and knowing without a doubt that his team had his back.

He'd trusted that.

He'd believed in it.

He'd put his life on the line for it, without a moment's hesitation.

And now he was supposed to believe that trust was for naught? That a SEAL would betray his own team?

Diego growled, his chest as tight as his fists. He wanted to beat something, smash it, pummel it to dust. Screw the security deposit. He grabbed the bedside lamp, his fingers gripping the thick metal base. Before he could swing, he heard a buzz. The red haze blurring his vision dimmed, and he heard it again. It took another second before he realized it was his cell phone.

A deep breath, then two, cleared the haze.

"Yeah," he answered, still clutching the lamp.

"Miss me, Kitty Cat?"

Like a smack upside the head, the words knocked Diego right out of his crappy mood. Laughter trumped anger every time. Even if the laughter was coated in bitterness.

"That's El Gato to you, MacGyver," he shot back. "What's your status?"

Let it be an opening. Anything that'd get him the hell out of suburbia and away from the temptation of the blonde.

"Still digging in the dark," Lansky said, his tone a verbal shrug. "Make my job easier. Tell me you saw Ramsey. Tell me you've got something we can take to the NI team."

"First off, you don't know that Ramsey is alive. All of the intel points to him being ash. Second, don't assume that he's the traitor. Assumptions are half-assed work, unworthy of a SEAL."

Diego let the silence roll over him. He didn't need words to hear Lansky's fury, his pain and frustration. Hell, all he had to do was check himself, since he was sporting all those feelings and more. But sloppy intel wasn't going to get them off the hook with the Naval Criminal Investigation team.

"Have you got anything at all?" Lansky finally asked, his words tight. Diego heard the clink of glass against glass and grimaced. The guy wasn't going to have a liver left if they didn't get this put to bed soon.

"I've had eyes on Ramsey's ex. So far, nothing suspicious." *A whole lot of interesting, sure.* But nothing that played into their situation.

He remembered the kid's offhand comment about the two guys who'd lived there. Andy and Matt? But since neither had been Ramsey, it didn't play into the situation. But it did feed a few of Diego's fantasies.

"Ramsey showing his face is a long shot. But Savino's sure if he taps anyone, it'll be her or his parents. Did you see my report about Ramsey's old man being in prison? Just shows you what a liar the guy was, saying his family was rich and powerful."

That report had been a kick in the face. Everything Ramsey had said about his fancy family had been true enough, but a lie.

Diego frowned.

"The guy is doing time for running a Ponzi scheme. Doesn't negate that the family is rich and powerful. Especially since the feds tagged less than a tenth of what they thought he'd scammed."

"Maybe." Lansky hesitated. "Speaking of lies, fact or fiction? Is she as hot as Ramsey always said?"

"Ramsey's mother?"

"His ex, dude. Was he lying about that, too? She's a dog, right?"

"Truth be told, she's even hotter than he said."

Diego stepped over to the window, his brows rising when he saw Blondie through the window of what he'd determined was her bedroom. The light pooled around her for a moment before she pulled the curtains shut. But he could still see her shadow against the white fabric.

She made one hell of a silhouette thanks to a body that was freaking amazing. The kind of body that would take a man a week to show his appreciation for, then inspire him to start all over again.

He puffed out a breath. She was hot.

"And? Observation and opinion only. Is she dirty or not?"

Now that was a question worth exploring, and one that would likely keep him awake well into the night. But given that Lansky wasn't scoping out the hot blonde, Diego knew the guy's question referred to their mission and not her kink preferences.

"It's hard to tell at this point," Diego sidestepped. "She's been in residence the entire time, with company and a kid for most of it."

"So, what? You're saying you've got nothing?"

Yes, dammit. His career, his team, his fucking brotherhood was in the crosshairs and he didn't have a thing. And how was he supposed to find anything sitting here in suburban hell watching a hot blonde and her fancy house? He wasn't built to wait, to watch. He wasn't made for inaction. He clenched his fist. But orders were orders.

. "I'm saying that I'm still doing recon, the target

hasn't been sighted and that I'll notify you as soon as anything changes." He didn't add that his orders had been specific. He wasn't there to haul the woman off and interrogate her.

The phone did nothing to disguise the sound of Lansky grinding his teeth.

"I'll figure this out, man," Diego said in the same tone he'd used when he'd promised Lansky that he wouldn't leave him wounded behind enemy lines. Quiet assurance.

"I'll keep working on the electronics," Lansky said after a couple of seconds. His tone was much less assured, but Diego knew he'd come through. He had to.

Because, yeah...

Their careers were on the line.

Diego hit the off button and tossed his phone onto the bed, watching it sink in the mattress before turning his gaze back to the window.

The moonless sky was a pitch-black backdrop to the lighted window. The curtains hid her features, but couldn't disguise the shape of the woman undressing in her bedroom. Diego could see the curve of her breasts as she stretched her arms over her head, the slenderness of her waist and the fullness of her ass as she bent down to touch her toes.

Diego shifted his weight from one foot to the other, proof of what he had stiff and hard between his legs. The tapping of his fist against the window frame grew harder with each beat. He was here to prove, one way or the other, Ramsey's status. The man had been declared presumed dead by the Navy, but things weren't adding up.

Lusting after Ramsey's ex wasn't a part of the mission. And while it might not be sanctioned by the

Navy—yet—Diego was on a mission. He was going to settle the issue of Ramsey's life or death. Once he did, he could clear his team and his own reputation. And expose a traitor.

So no matter how it shook out, Ramsey's ex was trouble.

Diego glanced back at the darkened window and grimaced.

But there was trouble, and then there was *trouble*. When a man spent most of his life in danger, he became an expert on recognizing it. On knowing how to use it, how to diffuse it, how to make it explode. And how to simply make it go away.

And his current mission was to figure out which kind of trouble Harper Maclean was.

And deal with it.

"WE NEED TO FIND you someone sexy. Maybe intense, but not prison break intense. Not that prison break can't be sexy," Andi mused. "I'd imagine it could be given the right guy."

"You have issues. You might consider talking with a professional."

Harper made the halfhearted suggestion with most of her attention focused on finding just the right shade of blue to complement the yellow color scheme in the Andersons' atrium.

She was working with a design board, three-by-four-feet in size, which was framed in the same wood that would cover the floors. Instead of paper, it was covered in a muscat-toned plaster she planned to use on the wall, and sketches of the furnishings and various swatches. She used digital software when necessary, but preferred a variety of boards. The colors were truer, the textures and contrasts more visibly appealing.

And she liked to touch.

"What sort of professional are we talking about?" Andi asked, her joking tone coming through the speakerphone as clearly as if she'd been sitting right there in Harper's office with a smirk on her face.

"I was thinking a health care one, but given your obsession with sex, maybe other options would be more helpful."

Harper draped a cobalt length of satin over the board and stepped back a couple of feet. Head tilted to the side, she considered the impact of that strong blue against the butter-yellow leather designated for the couches, the rich walnut of the floors and the creamy biscuit hue that would be the cement planters.

Mrs. Anderson wanted the space for friendly luncheons, cozy teas and the occasional intimate dinner party. Why she couldn't use the dining room was beyond Harper, but who was she to question the rich and snobby? Mr. Anderson wanted a place where he could sit down for some peace and quiet and read a damned book, to paraphrase his only request.

She thought she'd achieved that balance with the comfortably stuffed couches, the feminine, curved lines of the chairs and the oval stained glass table for those intimate meals.

"Speaking of sex," Andi said, bringing the conversation back in a direction Harper was trying to avoid. "Let's find you a date."

"I thought I'd made it clear that I'm not in the market for a guy," she murmured under her breath as she switched the cobalt-blue swatch for cornflower and stepped back again.

Hmm, personally she preferred the bolder cobalt, but she was pretty sure the client would go for the softer shade. With that in mind, she began pulling various swatches in the same shade from the cedar box where she stored her fabrics. Cotton, linen, brocade, silk.

"Fine. If you don't want a man, I'll find you a woman. What type do you like?"

"Exotic brunettes who prefer tequila to champagne, sing off-key and sneak chocolate to my kid," Harper reeled off, paying more attention to the play of shantung against the leather than to the conversation. Man or woman, doing either wasn't on her agenda. If it had been, Brandon's abrupt reentry into her life was enough of a reminder of just what stupid looked like. Since she'd already been there, she didn't see any reason to go again.

"Please. We both know I'm not your type."

"I don't have a type." Unless handsome, smooth-talking men with more money than morals were a type. If that were the case, she'd definitely prefer to avoid her type.

"Everyone has a type." Andi dismissed that so easily that Harper's fingers clenched around the silk. Did that mean Brandon was the template for hers? Oh, Lord, what a thought.

"Do you really plan to go another eight years without sex?" Andi asked, the words dangling in the air as if she'd read Harper's mind. "Or forever?"

"Don't be silly." Harper tried to laugh, but the sound stuck in her throat. *Forever?* Sure, her memories of sex were on the vague side, and definitely tinged by the results. And while she was perfectly capable of taking care of the basics herself, suddenly the idea of forever didn't sound very appealing.

With her typical skill for sensing a weakness and pouncing, Andi added, "Are you going to let him win? Forever?"

Was she?

Harper dropped the fabric over the top of the board before she made a mess of the silk. Then, feeling a little sick to her stomach at the idea of Brandon still having that kind of control over her life, she sank into a chair and blew out a long breath.

"I'm only talking about hooking you up with a great guy for one date. It can be during the day—just meet for coffee," Andi wheedled. "You'll like the guy. Whichever one I pick out, I swear, he'll be likable."

"No. No, no, a million times no."

She remembered last night's reaction to her new neighbor. The hot, intense awareness. The instant flood of lust so overwhelming that she'd actually considered licking the man. Her dreams had been a cacophony of images, slick and sweaty and filled with pleasure-drenched moans. She'd actually welcomed the distraction those dreams offered because it had meant she wasn't plagued with thoughts of Brandon. She'd been grateful not to be awake all night, worrying about Nathan being fatherless—again. And, yeah, she'd kind of liked all the sexy fun.

Now that she'd rediscovered her sex drive, was it going to live only in her imagination?

Because of Brandon?

Or because she was afraid?

Neither sat well.

"Okay," she finally said with a sigh. "Maybe a dozen times no."

"You're willing to do it?"

"I'm willing to consider, someday, going out with

a guy past the first date," she hedged. "But I can get that date myself. I don't need you or your professional contacts."

"Oh, sure you'll…"

Harper got to her feet with a soft laugh as Andi's accusation trailed off.

"You have someone in mind. You've already picked a guy. Tell Andi everything," her friend cajoled. "I need details. Who is he? What does he do? Where'd you see him, and have you made first contact?"

"I didn't say there was a particular somebody." As soon as she did, Andi would put her matchmaking into overdrive.

"There's somebody."

Harper tacked the cornflower shantung to the pillow outline before opening the box of notions and trims. Tassels would be too fussy, but maybe fringe? Something with a subtle crocheted edge.

"It can't be anyone you work with. There's nobody new. Besides, most of those men are gay. Your clients are married—that rules them all out." Andi continued her guessing, hitting everyone from the checker at the grocery store to the camp director Harper had met the previous day.

It wasn't until she almost giggled—giggled, for crying out loud, something she never did—that Harper gave in.

"He's subletting the house next door. He told Nathan he's in security and that he's single and childless." Harper figured that covered Andi's initial questions.

"And?"

"And what?"

"Is he hot? Sexy? What's he look like? Did he give you the tingles? Nuh-uh-uh," Andi chided before

Harper could scoff. "Don't pretend you don't know what I mean."

She might, since this was turning out to be a lot of fun. More than she'd had since, oh, maybe high school. But unlike high school, she now knew the meaning of the word *responsible*. Which, she glanced at her watch, meant finishing this up since Nathan would be home any minute now.

"Okay, fine. There were tingles," she admitted. "The guy is gorgeous. He's got a face worthy of the big screen and a body straight out of fantasyland. He was friendly with Nathan, he's well spoken and he rides a Harley."

She was so—admittedly—uptight. Who knew how sexy she'd find a Harley?

"He sounds delicious," Andi decided, her words a purr. "I'm sorry I won't get to meet him before I leave. He'll still be there when I get back, won't he?"

"How would I know?" How did she find out, Harper wondered as she made notes of the fabric and trim she'd chosen. "The Lowensteins' place usually sublets by the week, not the month."

"Well, that's not good," Andi mused, her tone making nerves dance in Harper's stomach. "Maybe I should change my flight."

"Don't be silly," Harper said, starting to feel as if the walls were closing in and cutting off any chance of escape. "I've only seen the man twice. I spoke with him for maybe three minutes. For all I know, he has a girlfriend. Or twenty. Or he likes men. Or he's waiting for his cot to become available at a monastery."

All of which was too depressing to contemplate. Wouldn't it just figure that the first man to spark her fuse was completely off-limits?

"Or he's free and clear and looking for love," she continued, letting her insecurities take a deeper dive into the theme. "But that doesn't mean he'd be interested in me. Maybe he prefers redheads or brunettes or older women. Maybe he's anti-motherhood or hates the way I look or has some issue with my—"

"Harper, stop," Andi interrupted with a laugh. "You're talking yourself out of this before it even has a chance."

Maybe it was better that she did. It wasn't as if pursuing something with this guy would turn her life inside out. Going on a few dates, maybe enjoying an orgasm or two, that was normal, healthy. Nothing wrong with wanting to be normal and healthy. It wasn't as if sex had to come with a heavy price.

Did it?

"This is the first time you've even so much as hinted at interest in a man since I've known you. I've got to check this guy out. Find out how long he's staying. Maybe I should change my flight, head to Greece tomorrow instead of this afternoon."

"Don't be silly. If you're late for your grandmother's birthday kickoff, you'll hurt her feelings. Worse, you'll lose her support," Harper said quickly, trying to keep the desperation out of her voice, but definitely not wanting Andi here, boxing her in. "I'm sure he'll be here when you get back."

And maybe it'd be better to keep the relationship with the neighbor to a few waves, the occasional friendly hello.

Trying to set it aside and focus on the job at hand, she flipped through the catalog images she'd chosen for accent pieces while Andi continued her pitch.

Harper ignored her, but after a few seconds realized

that she hadn't paid attention to any of the photos, so she went through each image again.

"I'm just saying that you should explore the possibilities and see where it goes," Andi finished.

Before Harper could decide if she wanted possibilities that went anywhere, Nathan bounded into the room. The tension that had knotted her stomach eased as she gave him a quick once-over. The knees of his jeans were slicked with green and his blue tee streaked with dirt, proof that he'd had fun playing at the park.

And just like that, sexy times were over. Or in this case, talking about the possibility of sexy times was over.

And that was fine by her.

"HEY, MOM." BOUNCING in his new tennis shoes, Nathan automatically looked toward her desk. As soon as he saw the cell phone lit up in its cradle he grimaced. Turning fast, he checked the two-sided sign that hung from the doorknob. The side that said, "Join Me" faced out. *Whew.* When it said, "Quiet Zone" he had to keep his mouth shut and step lightly.

"It's Andi," his mom murmured. Her smile seemed normal, but she still had that look in her eyes. The one she'd had after dinner yesterday when she'd given him that talk. His stomach started hurting the same way it did when he was going to throw up when he thought about the things she'd said. So he tried really hard not to think about them.

"Is that Nathan? Let me talk to him," Andi's voice called out.

"Hey, Andi," he called back, adding a wave even though she couldn't see him. "Are you coming over?"

That'd be perfectly awesome. She'd keep his mom

busy talking and cooking and stuff and make her laugh. Then mom wouldn't look at him like she was all worried and stuff.

"Nope. No way." Blowing that hope with a shake of her head, his mom tossed a stack of papers on the long table she used as a desk. "Gotta go. Have a safe trip—call when you have a chance."

And there Nathan's hope for escape went. Gone with the push of a button.

"Andi sends her love," his mom said, looking at him like she had lasers for eyes and could see right into his brain. He knew she was searching for hurt feelings or sadness. Time for evasive maneuvers.

"Is Andi in Hercules yet?"

"Heraklion," she corrected with a laugh, tapping her finger on the bill of his hat. "She's flying there tonight."

He liked the sound of Hercules better. Andi looked a little like Meg, Hercules's girlfriend in the cartoon, too. Still, he knew wherever she was, Andi would bring him back a cool gift. She always did.

"I saw Diego's bike out front when Jeremy's mom dropped me off. You said he's the one who found my ball, right, Mom?" Nathan moved it from hand to hand. He knew better than to toss it in here.

Busy zipping her design board in a leather case, his mom froze for a second, then nodded while tucking another pile of papers into the pocket of the case. "Yes, Diego found your ball."

"We should thank him. That's the polite thing to do."

"I thanked him last night."

"Yeah, but it's my ball, so I should say thanks, too. I wasn't born in a barn—I should show I have manners, right?"

Even though she wasn't frowning, that little line dug

in between her eyebrows. He knew that look. It was her no look. Before she could say it, he added his most persuasive smile—the one he saved for Santa visits and major trouble—and added, "Please."

As he'd hoped, she couldn't hold out against his please smile.

"Fine. I have to make a client call—then we can go next door and show off your manners."

Nathan's eyes flashed mischief. "Maybe we should take him a kitten. You know, to show our appreciation and stuff."

He knew a long shot when he threw it out there, but he figured it was worth a try. Sooner or later, she'd take the hint.

"Oh, I don't know about that." Pulling him closer, she wrapped her arm around his neck and gave a gentle squeeze. "How about we make cookies instead?"

"Chocolate chip?"

She hesitated for a second before nodding.

"Go wash up while I make my call. Then we'll see if we have chocolate chips."

"I'll check. I'll get the 'gredients after I wash my hands." With that and a whoop of joy, Nathan charged toward the downstairs bathroom. He almost used the pretty flower soap, but remembered before he got it wet that his mom would grump. He exchanged it for a squirt of liquid soap, then made sure to do a good job. The week was going too well to get in trouble over dirt.

He was going to adventure camp with his best friend. He had a cool new neighbor who looked like a superhero. And now he was getting homemade chocolate chip cookies.

With a quick wipe of his hands over his pants, he was ready for the cookie dough.

He made it only a few feet down the hall when his gaze landed on the red-and-blue-striped box sitting at the bottom of the stairs. He froze.

His mom was all upset and sad because of that stupid box. Because of the jerk whose stuff was in the box.

Nathan was a little scared at how mad he suddenly felt. Like the Hulk with tons of rage wanting to explode with punches and kicks and screams. His fists clenched, and his teeth did, too.

Mom said it was stuff from that man. Like he cared about a guy who'd dumped them before he was even born? Nathan wasn't willing to call the guy a father or dad. He'd talked to Jeremy about it because his best friend actually had a dad, so he knew what was what.

According to Jeremy, a dad read bedtime stories and played ball and yelled and paid for the house and car and stuff. A father pretty much just paid support money but was around once in a while. Mostly on holidays and the summer.

The guy whose stuff was in the box hadn't done any of that, so he wasn't either one.

Besides, the guy was dead. What did Nathan care about a box of his stuff? Mom had told him there were medals and junk the guy's friend said was proof he'd been a hero. But heroes didn't do what that guy did. They didn't walk out and leave their kid alone. They didn't make the lady have a baby by herself, and never help with anything.

Nathan's breath shook, his chest hurting like he couldn't get enough air.

Heroes didn't make his mom cry.

Nathan sniffed. He'd always figured that someday, if the guy came around, he'd tell him all that. And maybe he'd punch him a time or two.

But the guy went and died.

So that was that.

Nathan didn't want his stuff. Not any of it.

He ground his teeth back and forth a few times until his eyes cleared and the threat of tears was gone. He took a big breath, just in case. As soon as he was sure he wasn't going to cry, he yanked open the closet door, then grabbed the box. He pushed it all the way to the back corner and covered it with the picnic blanket. But that wasn't enough. He started to unzip his baseball duffel but stopped. He didn't want that stuff in his bag. Nathan's eyes narrowed on Jeremy's bag, the one he'd left here yesterday. Mom put it in the closet because they wouldn't have practice again until they got back from camp. Sure his friend wouldn't care, Nathan ripped the zipper open and shoved the box inside, then put the blanket and his rain boots on top of it.

There. Shutting the door, Nathan leaned against it for a brief second. He kicked it with the back of his foot for good measure, then, considering it a done deal, ran for the kitchen.

"Cookies," he called, ready to dive in.

CHAPTER SEVEN

HARPER WAS SURE that going next door, deliberately seeking out their neighbor—the man who'd made her think all sorts of naughty things that should be off-limits—was a mistake.

Yet here she was, walking toward the man's front door with Nathan at her side and a Tupperware container in her hand. Trying to ignore her nerves, Harper smoothed the crinkle cotton fabric of her skirt over her hip. She adjusted the wide leather belt, then checked her necklace to be sure the clasp was in the back.

"This'll be fun, huh, Mom? I'll bet Diego lets us inside. I wanna see if he has a pool table like Mr. Lowenstein does."

"We're only staying long enough for you to show off your manners and to say welcome to the neighborhood." And that could be done from the porch. "I'm pretty sure Mr. Lowenstein leaves all of his furniture here when he travels, so unless you saw him carry the pool table with his suitcases, it's still here."

"Bet he could," Nathan stated, dancing backward up the step to the door to offer a gap-toothed grin before ringing the bell. "Mr. Lowenstein is a scientist. I'll bet he comes up with all sorts of cool inventions."

She knew just how disappointed he was that the neighbor's science didn't focus on gamma radiation.

"Do you think he has another car we didn't see?" Nathan asked a few seconds after ringing the bell.

"I think not everyone runs to answer a door like some small boys I can think of."

"If you run, you get there faster."

One of his lifelong priorities, Harper thought with a smile.

A minute later, they were still staring at the wrong side of the door—or the right side, in Harper's opinion—and Nathan looked ready to explode.

"Maybe he's busy or he didn't hear the bell," she said, secretly thrilled even as she soothed Nathan's disappointment. "We can try again later."

Before she could write this off as an A for effort, the door swung open.

He had heard the bell.

He'd failed to put on a shirt, though.

She forgot all about her urgent desire to leave.

"Hey," Diego greeted with a curious smile at odds with the caution in his eyes.

She wasn't paying a lot of attention to his eyes, however.

She was much more interested in that body.

Because oh, my, he was built.

His shoulders were broad and muscular, his arms ripped. A dark sprinkling of hair covered his chest, bisecting his pectorals before leading down abs so flat and hard, she'd bet that she could bounce a quarter off of them.

His skin was a dusky gold, and marred here and there with scars. The tattoo she'd noticed on his arm the night before was actually a series of jagged tribal swirls intersected by a trident. The other, the rose-strewn word *Honor* that sat low on his belly, curving over his navel just above the waistband of his jeans. Harper's fingers tingled as she imagined tracing them over that work of art.

Were the colors as smooth as his skin? Was there significance in the placement of the word? She wet her lips, not sure what it meant, but really, really curious.

Her gaze meandered its way up his chest again with a slow side trip across those shoulders before returning to his face.

The man was gorgeous.

He was also staring at her as if she was a gaping groupie offering door-to-door cherry-flavored hot oil rubs.

A sexual haze wrapped around her, tinting her vision, blurring her judgment. Her thoughts were filled with questions and ideas.

It wasn't realizing that she wouldn't mind getting her hands on that body that pulled her out of the haze. It was the look in his eyes that said he'd like it, too.

She had to call on every inch of poise she possessed to keep her feet glued to the step instead of running and the blush heating her neck from climbing.

"Hi," she managed. That was the only thing she could think of to say, other than yowza. Which was probably inappropriate.

Probably.

Thankfully, Nathan never had a problem finding plenty of words.

"We're like the Welcome Wagon. It'd be cooler if we had a real wagon, wouldn't it? It'd be a lot more fun, too. But sometimes words don't mean what they sound like. That's what Mom says," he said before slanting his mother a look that said he wasn't fully satisfied with her explanation of why they didn't really need to bring his wagon along to deliver the cookies.

"Welcome Wagon?" Diego leaned one shoulder against the doorjamb, letting the door swing wide as he looked from Nathan to her, then back again.

"You know, like saying we're glad you moved to the neighborhood. Mrs. Petrillo brought over a pie and a bunch of papers and maps, and a plant and stuff when we moved here." Nathan took the plastic dish from his mother's hands. "We don't make pie. Not from flour and sugar and stuff."

Diego shifted his gaze to Harper while Nathan described their baking process. Those dark eyes watched, waiting. Like, what? He thought she was going to visually lick him again? Not likely.

Harper lifted her chin, daring him to make something of her temporary insanity.

He just grinned.

She wanted to be irritated but was too busy trying not to smile back.

"So it's not the food that matters on the welcome thing. It's the meaning that counts, right, Mom?"

"Mmm," she agreed, finally tearing her gaze from Diego's to look down and give Nathan a smile. "The meaning, or in this case, the gesture of offering something homemade as a housewarming gift."

With a nod, Nathan held out the covered plastic dish.

"Here. We hope your house is warm and that you like the neighborhood while you're here. We want to be friends. Cuz, you know, friends make the best neighbors."

She thought she saw something uncomfortable flash in those dark eyes before Diego took the offering.

"Thanks." He lifted the dish, trying to peer through

the opaque plastic. "So if this isn't pie, what'd you make?"

"Cookies. Me and Mom are good at those. I got to pick the kind, cuz it's my turn. When it's Mom's turn, she picks things like oatmeal or lemon." Wrinkling his nose at the healthy connotations of those flavors, Nathan shrugged. "They're okay, but I like chocolate chip best. So that's what we made you."

"Get out." Diego's grin was filled with a boyish delight that surprised Harper with its sweetness. "You guys made me chocolate chip cookies? All the way from scratch?"

He peeled off the lid. Not to check, she realized. But to dig one out and pop it into his mouth.

"Good," he declared around a mouthful of cookie. He tilted his head toward the interior of the house. "Come on in."

"Oh, I don't know…"

Nathan scrambled over the threshold and out of sight before Harper could finish her refusal.

"He likes the pool table." She couldn't help but smile when her son's whoops sounded out. "Mark Lowenstein is teaching him to play eight ball."

"Is he any good?"

Harper shrugged. She wasn't much of a judge at games like that.

"We can't stay long." In fact, she should find Nathan now so they could start making their excuses to go. "We simply wanted to offer an official welcome to the neighborhood."

"Uh-huh."

His nod was agreeable and his tone neutral.

And she knew perfectly well that he was laughing at her. What she didn't know was how she felt about it.

While she tried to figure that out, she made a show of looking around the foyer.

She'd seen it plenty of times before, though, so the elegant drop-leaf table, glossy black urn and spray of peacock feathers weren't much of a distraction. There was a light layer of dust in the corners of the oak floor, proving that Diego wasn't much of a housekeeper. There was a pair of polished black boots resting on the bottom step of the wide staircase and a navy blue duffel on the step above.

Was that why he wasn't dressed? Was he on his way somewhere?

"We should go. You're obviously busy." She gestured toward the bag, then turned in the direction of the pool table, ready to call Nathan.

"Stay."

Glancing over her shoulder, her eyes landed on that chest again. The small scar, puckered and wicked looking, accented the perfection of his golden torso. She almost sighed her appreciation before she caught herself with a shake of her head.

"Stay," he said again, reaching into the duffel and pulling out a shirt. As he tugged it on, she had to give him points for sensitivity.

But as soon as the worn gray cotton covered those muscles, she missed the view. And she felt like an idiot.

Before she could repeat her desire to leave, he lifted the plastic container high and waved it in the air.

"I've got cookies," he coaxed, his words filled with a cheerfully naughty innuendo that made Harper want to laugh.

"The question is, do you have milk?" she asked as she moved farther into the house. She ignored the nerves dancing in the pit of her stomach and the warnings clamoring in the back of her mind.

"Milk I have. Glasses might be an issue. I haven't navigated the kitchen yet," he admitted as he shut the door behind him with a thud, leaving the foyer in dusky shadows.

He was a good foot away, and they weren't touching. But Harper felt an intimacy with him that she couldn't remember ever experiencing before. Not with any man.

It was as if nothing she could do or say would surprise him. As if he were looking inside her and knew her deepest secrets, her every wish.

Above that, he seemed to have an air of honor about him. Something he clearly valued, since he'd embedded the word itself in his flesh.

Who knew she'd find that so incredibly sexy?

When they stepped into the kitchen, with a single wave of his hand he invited her to take over.

"Milk's in the fridge. The glasses are a mystery." His eyes were gleaming in the light in a way that made her think of Aztec gold. Rich, compelling, dangerous.

"Since I'd rather Nathan didn't start drinking straight from the carton before he's a teenager, why don't I see what I can do," she murmured.

She stared into those hypnotic eyes for just a second longer, images of pagan dances, bonfires and naked bodies filling her head.

Then she turned away. And just like that, the haze lifted.

But it didn't leave completely.

Even after she'd found the glasses, after she'd called her son, when Harper relaxed on the banquet seat, a soft cushion at her back and the sun warming her arms, it was there.

She couldn't dismiss the sexual awareness that'd sparked between them. She knew it wasn't one-sided. But here, in the sun-drenched kitchen with her son sitting between them, it was tucked away. She could see hints of it every once in a while when Diego glanced her way. She could feel the edges of it deep in her belly.

But it wasn't front and center.

Nathan was.

And he reveled in it.

She'd never considered her son reserved. But he opened up even more with Diego. He talked longer, with more enthusiasm, about a wider variety of things. From baseball to math struggles, Chewbacca to swim lessons. They touched on the monsters in the closet, agreed that wearing ties sucked and debated whether Iron Man could beat the Hulk without Veronica.

She'd fight to the death anyone who claimed that her son was neglected in any way. But watching him with Diego, she had to admit that this was something she'd never given him. Never thought to give him.

A strong male influence.

And Diego was just as into the discussion as Nathan. He was just as interested, just as focused, just as involved.

Now even as her mind worried over the implications, her heart sighed.

RAMSEY WAS DEAD. He had to be.

And Diego was damned tired of sitting around watching for a dead guy. Especially while lusting after his ex. He should be on base, training. Or on a mission, doing. Not lounging around a luxury house in freaking Santa Barbara with nothing to do but peek over the fence or stare at monitors all day.

How long was he supposed to watch a house where nothing was happening? Diego wasn't sure which was going to push him over the edge, frustration or boredom. He was sure that he wasn't suited for inaction, and that suburbia—even wealthy suburbia—was its own sort of hell.

It'd only been yesterday that Harper and the kid had come by with their container of cookies, but the kid had been back a few times. As appealing as he was, it was the mom who filled Diego's thoughts.

Diego paced from one end of the house to the other, each time stopping to check the monitors, to take a look out the window. This was stupid. Crazy. The most useless assignment he'd ever had.

Five days, he'd been in Santa Barbara watching the house next door. And other than cookies and some impressively carnal fantasies about the blonde, he didn't have a damned thing to show for it. He'd talked to the kid, learned that Nathan, while entertaining and fun, had no information on his father to share and didn't seem to care one way or the other. And, sure, he'd had a couple of conversations with Harper. But other than realizing that he enjoyed her company, that they had the same taste in music, that she could make him laugh and that she was one hell of a mom, he hadn't learned anything from them.

Nothing that'd solve a single one of the Ramsey-related questions.

Not a damned thing that'd help get him out of suburbia and back into the action. The sort of action he knew how to handle.

So it was no wonder his mood was pure crap when he heard the doorbell chime. Diego debated ignoring it for about a half second, then shoved his hand through his hair, tugged his worn T-shirt to make sure he was fully covered and headed for the door.

When he threw it open, some of the tension dropped and a wide grin covered his face.

"Hey, there," he greeted.

Guilt? Should he feel guilt? If a teammate's ex was off-limits, what was the rule on falling for the guy's kid? Because as far as Diego could tell, Nathan Maclean was irresistible.

"Hey, Diego. Can I hang out? I told Mom I was gonna come see if you wanted company. She's talking on the phone to some lady in New York, but she said I could hang out with you if you didn't mind." Big blue eyes gazed up at him with an appealing blend of curiosity and laughter. "Do you?"

"Do I what?"

"Want to hang out?" Nathan laughed. He held out his baseball, the worn red laces a contrast to the grass staining the leather. "We can play catch, maybe. Or I can help you if you're working. I help my mom sometimes. She lets me sort things and use her drawing table, and once in a while she lets me use the computer. She has this cool program that has, like, rooms in it and furniture and stuff that you can pick out and color and arrange on the screen. I decorated a houseboat and a castle, and once she made it look like a spaceship, even."

Were his ears ringing? Diego smacked one hand on the side of his head to check his hearing.

"So what do you say?" Nathan prompted.

What could he say? Hey, kid, you're a lot of fun and great to hang out with. By the way, do you have any tips on where your father might be and if he's dead or alive? Oh, and what're your mother's views on treason and one-night stands?

All valid questions, all at the top of his mind.

Unable to answer that, or resist the big-eyed stare, Diego opened the door wide and waved the boy inside.

"Do you want to play pool?" Nathan asked as they crossed the foyer. "I'm pretty good. Mr. Lowenstein said so. Or maybe you wanna help me practice my fastball? Mom's good with regular catch, but not so much with pitching. I really need some help."

"Do ya?"

"Yeah." The small face lost some of its usual animation as Nathan's shoulders drooped. "Some of the kids, they made fun of me for wanting to be pitcher cuz I'm too young. They said I was dumb and didn't stand a chance."

Little jerks. Diego hadn't wanted to beat on a bunch of kids since he'd been one, but he did now. But given that he'd learned the hard way that violence rarely changed anyone's mind, he figured there was a better way to get back at the mouthy brats.

"You just need to practice," he replied. "C'mon. I'll help."

"Really?" Nathan's face lit right back up. "Can you make me good enough for next season, d'ya think?"

Unless it was an explosive, Diego couldn't say he'd had a lot of practice throwing things. But he'd be damned if anyone was going to steal the kid's dreams.

"Let's see what we can do," he said, tilting his head in the direction of the backyard.

"You're good, kid," Diego complimented ten minutes later. The boy had one hell of an arm on him. "Who taught you to pitch?"

There, he thought, crouching low to catch the ball. A normal question that anyone would ask. And given the kid's propensity for running off at the mouth, Diego figured it'd net him all he needed to know about Ramsey's haunts, where the family hung out, possible vacation spots. Enough intel to move on and get the hell out of suburbia.

"My mom mostly plays catch with me, but my friend Jeremy's dad helps, too. He's okay. Not as good as Coach Peabody, though. He can throw a fastball and a curveball and he's got this wicked cool hook ball that I wanna learn so bad. Mom said it takes practice, though. Why does everything take practice?"

The kid had excellent hand-to-mouth coordination, managing to get four pitches into Diego's glove during his recital.

"What about your dad?" Diego asked directly, since the circular route hadn't worked. "I'll bet he's taught you a lot, right?"

The little face closed up.

"I don't have a dad."

"Everyone's got a father," Diego said as he tossed the ball back. When Nathan missed, the ball bounced between his high-tops before rolling across the lawn. The boy's jaw worked as he grabbed it.

"I said I don't have one." Blue eyes swimming as he lifted his trembling chin, Nathan stared at the ball. Struggling for control, Diego realized.

Could he be a bigger asshole? Diego tried to find something that'd clear the tears out of the boy's eyes.

"My dad was a real jerk," he heard himself saying. "He wasn't around much when I was growing up, and when he was, he was pretty useless. He caused a lot of trouble, hurt my mom a lot. To tell you the truth, I was usually glad when he wasn't around. It made life easier."

"Yeah?" Nathan gave a shaky sigh. "Mine was never around. But I'm pretty sure he was a jerk, too."

Past tense. Pretty sure he was lower than the slugs in the flower bed, Diego forced himself to keep pushing.

"Was he mean to you? Or to your mom?"

"I dunno." Narrow shoulders hanging low enough to dim his bright blue shirt, Nathan shrugged. "I never knew him, and he's gone now, so it doesn't matter. I used to wish…"

"What'd you wish?" Diego asked quietly, moving forward to sit on the brick wall so he was closer to eye level with the boy.

"I used to wish I had a dad. I pretended he was a hero who'd gone away to save the planet or fight Baron Zemo or something. But I know better now," Nathan said, wiping the back of his hand under his nose. "I know he was just a jerk. Jeremy's dad says Jeremy is a chip off the whole block. Does that mean I'll be a jerk?"

He should push for facts. Dig deeper. But looking into that crumpled face, Diego couldn't bring himself to make the kid feel worse.

"You know, sometimes people let us down and it's easy to let that disappointment make us feel bad about ourselves. I did that when my dad let me down. I thought I was like him, that I should be like him because it was because of him that I was born, you know?" Diego thought back to the many ways his father had influenced his early choices, and he shook his head.

"I finally learned that I have to do what I think is right for me. Not because it was what I thought my old man would do or even because I figured it was the opposite of what he'd do." With those big blue eyes watching him as if he had all the answers, Diego searched for something wise to offer. "It's easy to be mad, or to think you have to prove something. But the only person you have to prove anything to is yourself. If you think what you're doing is right for you but it's not selfish, if you figure it's the sort of thing a hero would do, that the man you want to grow up to be would do, then I don't think you have to worry about being a jerk."

Nathan seemed to be processing all of that with deep concentration. Then he tilted his head to the side. "Do you think getting a kitten is right for me? Is that selfish? Cuz I think my mom could use the love and cuddles a kitten would give her, too. Is that okay?"

"Not gonna touch that one, kid," Diego said with a laugh, admiring the way the kid stuck to his guns.

"Okay. We can throw the ball a little more, right?" Nathan moved back into his pitching stance, eyes glinting with a hint of his usual spark as he waited for Diego to get into place.

"So you learned all that hard stuff, right?" Nathan asked after they'd tossed it back and forth a few more times. "Are you a hero?"

"Me?" Horrified, Diego shook his head. "No way. I'm just a guy who learned that even when it's not easy, I need to do what's right."

"Like Captain America?"

Diego almost pointed out that Captain America was Army, not Navy. Then he remembered why he was there.

So he carefully steered the conversation back to easy topics like superheroes, comic books and movies.

By the time Harper stepped out her back door twenty minutes later, the boy was back on an even keel. Diego wasn't, though. He should have pushed harder for information on Ramsey. Even if the kid didn't realize he had it, he might still know something.

"Nathan. Dinnertime."

Still in a crouch, Diego looked over his shoulder to

see Harper waving her son home. Her gaze skittered over him as she offered a friendly smile, but she didn't move past the doorway.

Nathan was talking about a mile a minute as he danced around Diego while they walked to the gate between the backyards. The sun was setting, the air cool and soft as the scent of the honeysuckle plant growing over the fence.

"Mom's making homemade pizza tonight. Wanna have some? She doesn't mind when I have friends over for dinner."

Diego's gaze slid to the glass-backed wall of Harper's house, tracking the sexy blonde as she worked in her kitchen. He wanted some, all right. But not pizza. And nothing he could nibble on in front of the kid.

"Nah. I've got work to do."

Diego grinned at the skeptical look in Nathan's eyes as the boy glanced from him to the house to the setting sun. Damned if the kid wasn't too smart for his own good.

"I'm designing a security system. I can do the first part of it here working on my computer," he explained.

"Oh. Kind of like how I decorate a spaceship on my mom's computer?"

"Yeah, kinda like that." Then, ignoring the guilt, Diego added, "We'll have to sit down with your mom's computer soon and check out all of your designs."

With that and a couple more tosses of the ball, the boy skipped and waved his way inside. Diego didn't need a listening device to know he was filling the kitchen with chatter about their visit.

He didn't need a warning, either, that he was stepping over a line here that he had no business touching. If all he was doing was pumping the kid for intel, that'd be fine. It'd mean he was doing his job. His job wasn't to build up the child's confidence or make him feel okay about his father being a jerk.

If all he was feeling for the sexy blonde was lust, he'd be okay. But watching Harper hug her son, watching her face light with laughter and seeing that sweetly curved body, he knew the tightness in his gut was teetering on a lot more than lust.

And it was mixed with a healthy dose of self-contempt.

CHAPTER EIGHT

COVERT OPS, STEALTH and clandestine surveillance were precise skills that merged perfectly together.

And Diego was trained in them all.

Covert Ops, spy craft and upscale suburban neighborhoods?

He was so completely out of his element.

"Come in, Kitty Cat" came Lansky's voice through the communicator.

"Torres here," Diego confirmed. "You got anything new?"

"That'd be an affirmative. Got three phone calls made to the house next door. All three from different numbers registered on the Coronado Naval Base. First two lasted fifteen seconds, third was three minutes."

Shit.

Still...

"You think Ramsey, a man presumed dead who, if he isn't wants us to believe he is, is hanging out on base? Not possible."

"Why don't you tell me what it means, then?"

Diego wished he could, but he had no idea. None. Who on base would call Harper? And why?

"That's your job to figure out," he said, tossing it back at Lansky. "I'm here doing my job."

"You've been there a week and you have jack shit," Lansky said. Since his voice was coming through the pencil-eraser-size mini-communicator tucked in Diego's ear, it was like having the guy's bitching and moaning echoing through his brain.

"You have a better plan? Should I don camo, slick my face with war paint and hop the back freaking fence? You think I need to suit up in body armor, strap on an M67 grenade or two and maybe storm the French doors?"

Yeah, right.

"Better than kicking back in a cushy spread, downing gourmet eats and playing Peeping Tom."

"As opposed to holing up in a dive poking into a few computer files between watching porn and downing the brewskis."

Which Diego knew had to be frustrating as hell for a man who depended on action to keep his demons at bay. Still, even knowing that, Diego didn't manage to get a grip on his irritation before the words snapped out.

Telling himself anger wasn't going to help, he forced a couple of deep, cleansing breaths. He'd worked too hard, too long, to put rigid confines on his temper to let it shred over minor irritation. Especially when he knew Lansky was goading him, pushing for a reaction.

Besides, losing control tended to piss him off. So he took another couple of breaths, then said in a neutral, even tone, "Savino's orders were clear. Until he rescinds or amends my assignment, I'm following it to the letter. Doing otherwise, that's what landed us here."

"A greedy asshole with an aircraft-carrier-sized ego, no loyalty and a dick attitude is what landed us here." The sound of Lansky grinding his teeth came through loud and clear.

Diego got it. He had the same frustration pounding through him. He closed his eyes, rubbing the ache between them, and reminded him that Savino expected him to keep his head. To stay on track.

"Look, NI assumes we're dirty and they feel justified acting on those assumptions. Are we going to do the same thing? Play cop, judge and jury? Aren't we better than that?"

"Who gives a damn about better or worse?" Lansky muttered. "You're stuck believing that crap like honor and brotherhood make a difference. You can't get past a pretty face to see that you're getting fucked over."

Was that what he was doing? Diego stood in the shadows of the front-facing window of his temporary base, watching his target load a duffel, a sleeping bag and a slick-looking backpack into the trunk of her Camry.

For a second—just a brief one—his attention was diverted by the play of sunshine turning the golden strands of her hair silver and highlighting the perfect curve of her cheek.

She did have a pretty face.

Was he letting that influence him? Was that why he was so sure she was innocent? She was a strong woman, and he had no doubt she was smart enough to pull off whatever she wanted. But treason? Aiding and abetting the sale of military secrets, of providing weapons to the enemy, of endangering millions?

Maybe. If she thought she loved Ramsey…yeah, maybe.

But not even for love would she risk her son. That he was sure of. He'd been raised by a woman like Harper.

A woman who would do anything, put up with anything, to make sure her son grew into a man of honor.

"She's clean," he murmured as he watched her wrap around her kid to give him one of those rocking-from-side-to-side hugs. He could see the tears in her eyes from here and knew it was slaying her to let the boy go. But when she straightened, her gaze was clear and her smile bright.

"How d'you figure she's clean? Everything she's got points the other direction. She's got means and opportunity. She's got unaccountable funds. She's got Ramsey's kid." Lansky ticked off reasons why he figured Harper was guilty. "Her kid is attending a pricey camp that she didn't pay freight for. She's getting calls from the base. While she's not done it herself, she meets regularly with various people who do a great deal of traveling outside the US and, helloooo, she's Ramsey's old lady."

"Ramsey's ex," he corrected under his breath.

"You *are* hot for her," Lansky accused. "You're wanting her to be clean because you want to do her."

"Don't be a dumb ass." It was up in the air whether he was talking to Lansky or to himself.

Not that the claim was so wrong. He definitely had plenty of *do her* urges. A man would have to be three months dead and incredibly stupid to ignore a woman like that.

Diego was neither.

"I'm the dumb ass? You're the one making a wild claim that Ramsey's old lady is innocent. What're you basing it on?"

He had a feeling. He had his instincts, his gut. He'd looked her in the eyes; he'd sat with her at a table over cookies and milk. He'd watched her with her kid.

Hell, he'd simply watched her.

"My basis is as circumstantial as the evidence" was all he could say. Because his feelings didn't make for a valid argument. And they were dealing with treason. And he was on a mission, so what he thought was irrelevant. He had a duty to carry out. "I'll take her place apart, search every crevice. If there's proof against her, I'll find it."

"Bottom to top?"

Diego eyed the house next door, calculating the variables. He'd gone through this one inch by inch, and while the layouts weren't the same, there were enough similarities. An attic and four bedrooms upstairs, living room, kitchen, office and great room downstairs.

"Top to bottom," he stated. "You can handle the electronics, right?"

"You turn 'em on, I'll tap 'em out."

Diego watched the taillights flash and Harper pull away. As he watched her drive off, he took a moment to mourn the chance he'd never had with a woman he'd never deserve.

Then, because the clock was ticking, he calculated. "Five minutes."

"Check," Lansky confirmed before signing off.

Diego heard the irritation, figured it was because his friend was chomping at the bit over being left out. About the only thing worse than a clean man being accused of dirt was a man of action being forced to sit on his ass instead of acting. Or maybe that was vice versa.

Either way, Lansky was pissed and feeling put-upon. Throw in the booze the guy was likely sucking up like air, the fact that he hadn't uncovered anything worthwhile yet, and the litany of *I told you sos* that were likely running through his head, and Lansky was a time bomb.

Didn't matter. Not to Diego. Not now.

Like any other possible distraction on a mission, Diego ignored it. He let it roll over him, through him, while he gathered the supplies he'd need to break in and search the house next door.

It felt weird to strap his utility belt on over jeans instead of fatigues. Weirder still to leave behind any weapons. Other than his wits, he thought with a smirk as he slid the electronic devices he'd need into his belt's various pockets.

Instead of rappelling in, he simply walked through the back gate separating the two houses. Instead of blowing the door with electronics, he used the bump key he'd fashioned in the wee hours while the household slept, breaking in through the back door.

Nice to see his gang education pay off.

Diego spared a quick glance around the kitchen, taking one second to appreciate the slick warmth of the house. The clean lines of the glossy wood of the table and chairs were echoed in the cabinetry. Gleaming marble and a pretty blown glass bowl stood welcoming in the center. There wasn't a smudge on the stainless steel appliances, but the fridge was covered in Nathan's art. He was impressed that the place looked like something out of a fancy magazine, yet still screamed comfy home for a kid.

Then, shutting it down, he flicked the button on his comm. "Interior accessed."

"Acknowledged," Lansky responded quietly. "Electronics?"

"Stand by."

Sticking with his plan to start at the top, he climbed the stairs, checking for tech as he went.

"Kid computer." And a spaceship-shaped one at that, which was pretty cool, Diego admitted. He glanced into the spare room, saw nothing, then moved on to Harper's bedroom. As soon as he stepped inside, her scent wrapped around him. It was like being hit by a ballistic missile, exploding his entire system, blowing him straight to hell.

Like the rest of the house, this room was warm elegance. Rich colors and soft fabrics were an invitation to imagine Harper there, on that bed. It was a good-size one, too.

Which meant he could imagine himself right there with her.

Focus, dammit. The mission was the priority. The mission was everything. "There's an iPad, digital photo frame, cell phone charger," he reported after a quick search.

"Put the iPad on a charger, hit Safari and plug in this code." Lansky waited for Diego's grunt before offering the code. As soon as it was in, the tablet took on a life of its own as the tech worked his magic digging into the files.

Diego was happy to use Lansky's expertise without dealing with his judgmental stare to go with it. Like Covert Ops: Suburbia, being on the outs with his teammate wasn't something Diego was comfortable with. Then again, neither was searching the house of a woman he'd been having naked dreams of for intel on a rogue SEAL.

"You're set on the tablet," Diego said, heading for the attic. "While you deal with that, I'm moving on with the search."

He wanted this done. Fast. Thorough. Over.

Not finding proof wouldn't clear Harper in Lansky's eyes, or in Savino's. But it would support Diego's gut feeling. About the situation. About the woman.

He looked around the attic, noting the light sheen of dust coating the space. Boxes were stacked neatly against the walls, bins tucked under the eaves. No footprints, no smudges. Nobody had been up here for a very long time.

Perfect.

If Ramsey had anything stashed here, proof of his presence would be as simple as disturbed dust. Diego would know if he returned. With that in mind, he slipped one of the lozenge-size devices from his belt and attached it to the door frame as backup.

He tapped the side of the mic in his ear, activating communications.

"Attic's clear of recent activity."

"Sloppy searching if you went through it that fast." Lansky's judgmental voice sent a spear of irritation down Diego's spine with enough force to rattle his teeth.

"The space is clear of recent activity," Diego repeated tightly. "Unless Ramsey came in with a dust blower and expertly covered the entire attic with a perfectly even layer of age, nobody's been up here since January."

"You're taking that as proof of the woman's innocence?" No need to see him to know Jared was shaking his head in that condescending way he had.

"Your assignment is to track the unsub via electronics. Mine is to observe, assess and take an action *I* deem necessary. You want to question my abilities, you take it up with Savino."

Fury ricocheting through his system with enough force to make him want to knock someone on their ass, Diego double-tapped the com, cutting off communications.

The anger almost pushed him into searching the attic. Into disturbing the simple monitoring system. Into wasting time searching through Christmas decorations just to prove he was right and Lansky wrong.

Fucker had him second-guessing himself.

Blood pounding a tribal beat in his head, Diego forced himself to breathe. *Level out*, he ordered himself.

Nobody should be able to rattle him. Nothing should be able to push him off balance. Not during a mission.

Too many things about this operation were scraping his nerves raw. Time for that to stop. He had a job to do.

He was doing it. The way he'd been trained. The way Savino expected of him—the way *he* expected of himself.

He'd go through the rest of the house, inch by inch. He'd check every conceivable hiding place; he'd paw through Harper's underwear. Whatever it took.

And if he did find proof that she was dirty? That he was wrong about her? He'd deal with that, too. Bottom line, he needed to know that his instincts were wrong.

Again.

Then he'd have to figure out just exactly what that meant. To him, and to his career.

To his honor.

"GOODBYE," HARPER WHISPERED, the tear-choked word silent in the cool morning air. With burning eyes, she watched the island holding her heart fade into the distance as the ferry made its return trip to the mainland. She had to steel her muscles to stop from diving into the water and swimming back to Nathan.

God, she was pathetic.

She rode on that thought for the rest of the ferry ride, ignoring the other passengers as their chatter was drowned out by the ocean's waves and the raucous seagulls circling overhead. When they reached the dock, Harper was the last to disembark. Rubbing her hands over her arms, she breathed in the salty ocean air and, finally, forced herself to walk away from the boat.

She'd made it about three steps when the cell phone in her jacket pocket buzzed.

"Talk about timing," she said in lieu of a greeting.

"I figured you'd need a hug. Since I can't give you one in person, I'm going to distract you from missing Nathan until you have to get ready to meet your first client." Andi's tone was as determined as it was cheerful. "It was this or send a stripper. I figured you've got enough to look at next door that a half-naked guy was de trop."

"You're the best," Harper murmured with a half laugh, deciding to focus on her friend's cheerfulness instead of thoughts of her neighbor half-naked.

"Of course I'm the best. Because I am, I insist that you talk about it for exactly one minute. Then it'll be out of your system and we can move on to me." She gave a dramatically short pause, then added, "You see what a good friend I am? Anyone else, it'd *all* be about me."

"Since I'm sure you've got tons to tell me about your trip, I know what a sacrifice that is for you."

"I'm glad you appreciate that. Now come on, Harper. The sooner you get your minute started, the sooner I can tell you about the drunken duke and the chocolate soufflé."

It sounded like a bad erotica novel. Harper's smile faded as she glanced over her shoulder toward the no-longer-visible boat.

"I'm a cliché. Overprotective and emotionally obsessive. I cried. I couldn't stop myself. When Nathan hugged me goodbye, he suggested that I might not be quite so lonely if I had a kitten to play with while he was gone. When he got off the boat, it was like my heart was going with him," Harper admitted, feeling like an idiot.

Needing to work off some of the energy in her belly, her heels tapped a quick rat-a-tat on the wood as she headed toward the marina parking area.

"I'd think it's only natural. It's his first time away, and two weeks is a long time. Maybe you can keep your cool mom status if he thinks you were crying because he won't quit with the idea of getting a cat."

"I'm pretty sure I forfeited most of my cool mom points already," Harper said with a grimace, pushing her hair back when the wind sent it tangling over her face. "I packed and repacked his bags four times yesterday. I put my contact information in every one of his pockets and, yes, I admit it, I added a GPS app to the cell phone I purchased specifically for this trip."

"Is that bad? I did the same thing to my ex."

Harper's laugh trailed off on a huff of air as she wended her way around a trio of stroller-pushing moms. She'd never belonged to one of those moms' clubs, with their playgroups and diaper dates. She'd never pushed Nathan in a stroller along the pier for socializing and a side of fresh air.

Of course, she'd never owned a stroller, either. And the few moms she'd met with babies Nathan's age didn't have much interest in hanging out with a seventeen-year-old. Especially when she was single to boot.

"Maybe it's just as well that Nathan's gone for a while," she admitted after casting one last glance over her shoulder at the candy-colored strollers and perky moms in designer yoga pants.

"Ooooh?" Andi filled the drawn-out word with so much naughty allusion that Harper was surprised her phone didn't catch on fire.

"Nothing like that," she said with a laugh. "I had another phone call last night. That friend of Brandon's who sent the package. Apparently he's missing his BFF and wanted to share stories with Nathan about him."

"You have got to be kidding me," Andi snapped. "Where does that son of a bitch get off? Who the hell does he think he is, trying to worm his way into your life like that? Screw him. If he's missing his buddy, he can visit a reptile house. I'm sure there are plenty of worthy replacements there."

"Not quite the words I used, but I had the same reaction."

"How far did you tell him to jump?"

"I didn't," Harper confessed as she stepped off the wooden pier onto the sidewalk. The balmy day was pretty enough to lure a lot of sailors, so she had to make her way through the crowd heading into the marina as she aimed for the parking lot. "I mean, I told him no way, but I could tell he wasn't going to give up."

Unlike Brandon, who hadn't thought twice before giving up on his unborn child.

"So maybe it's best that Nathan's away. He won't answer the phone or overhear any distressing conversations while he's at camp," she continued.

"Right. This will give the idiot time to realize that he's not worming his way into your life or your son's. Meanwhile, Nathan will be having fun. He'll be around other guys, roughing it. Spitting and scratching and making manly noises."

"Good times," Harper agreed, pulling a face.

"Maybe it's time for you to have a great time, too. This is your chance to spend a little time as Harper instead of just Nathan's mom. To figure out what floats your boat, what winds you up. What pops your cork."

"I have too much to do in over the next couple of weeks for floating or winding. And my cork doesn't need popping."

"Oh, please, are we going to go through all of that again?" Andi sounded so aggrieved that Harper burst into delighted laughter.

The sound snagged the attention of a pair of men in trendy sail wear and Versace sunglasses. They started moving toward her with smiles a few steps toward the smarmy side of charming. Rejection was as easy as a practiced tilt of her chin and a chilly frown as she got into her car and drove off.

"You need to stay focused, keep yourself too busy to fret while knocking around in a silent, empty house," Andi advised.

"I'll be fine. I'm booked solid for the next two weeks. I've doubled my usual number of appointments and have interviews with three potential clients. I have Mrs. Walcott planning a supersecret surprise room renovation for her husband's birthday, complete with code words and a burner cellphone. With that much to do, how would I have time to fret?"

"Uh-huh. And the rest of the time? Nighttime?"

She knew Andi didn't mean to make it worse or nag. Well, at least not make it worse. But all of this support and caring concern was starting to give Harper a stomachache.

"Quit worrying so much," she asked quietly. Then, before Andi could ignore the plea, she added, "It's going to be fine. I have a plan."

"To work yourself into a stupor?"

Well, yeah. Was that a bad thing?

Maybe not, but it probably wasn't enough to keep Andi from worrying, or worse, sending strippers.

But she thought she knew what might be.

Harper smiled. A slow, delighted smile filled with an awareness she'd thought she'd long forgotten.

"I've got something a lot more interesting in mind other than work," she murmured.

Something very interesting.

It involved her temporary neighbor, and that sexy body of his. She'd spent a lot of time over the last week thinking about Diego. Fantasizing about his body. Those fantasies had offered distraction from her middle-of-the-night worries about Nathan going to camp and thoughts of her past. Without even realizing it, Diego had helped her get over some of her lingering concerns that Brandon had messed her up.

Why not let him help her get over the rest of those concerns? Why not go all the way?

"Harper?" Andi prompted, drawing the name out in a warning tone.

"I thought I'd get to know Diego a little better and see if we have anything in common besides a fence line. You know, flirt a little."

Her body warmed at the memory of the heat she'd felt each time she'd flirted with Diego. That day over cookies. Once or twice when he'd hung out with Nathan. The man had a way of making her feel special. He had a way of looking at her that brought to mind all sorts of options for cork popping, to use Andi's phrase.

"You're saying you plan to green-light your sexy neighbor? A man that you admitted gave you the tingles?"

"Sure. Why not?"

As Andi processed that, probably deciding whether challenging the blatant lie would push Harper to actually go through with it or if it'd make her run, screaming in terror, Harper pulled into her housing complex. She waited for the gate to rise, waving to the watchman as she drove on.

Harper swallowed hard to get past the knot in her throat. He would make the perfect distraction, though, wouldn't he? And the perfect way to prove to Andi—and more important, to herself—that she wasn't letting her experience with Brandon rule her life. The idea was big enough, scary enough and potentially exciting enough to keep her mind too occupied to miss her son more than, oh, twenty or thirty times a day.

What more could a single mother ask for?

CHAPTER NINE

"TARGET APPROACHING." LANSKY'S warning shot through the comm in Diego's ear, the urgency as loud and clear as if it were right there smacking on his shoulder.

Diego's eyes skipped to the clock on the wall. Had he lost time digging through Harper's undies? Nope. He should still have a good two hours.

"Verify," he ordered.

"Gate watchman logged her license plate in, verified she's the driver. Target approaching," Lansky repeated, irritation clear in his tone. "ETA two minutes."

Even as his body tightened in response, his mind detailing the exits, hiding places and remainder of the house to search, Diego continued his meticulous, page-by-page examination of the leather-bound photo album he'd pulled off Harper's bedroom shelf.

Not a single shot of Ramsey, no photos taken outside the country, hell, there weren't even any pictures that appeared to be taken outside the great state of California.

What the hell?

Less than a dozen shots of Harper pre-Nathan. A couple were obviously school photos, with their generic blue backdrop. She'd been a cute kid, a gorgeous teen. Where were the prom pictures, though? Hell, even he'd had one of those. Where were the big group family shots? He'd come across a handful of Harper with an older woman, the resemblance strong despite the worn, exhausted air of the woman in the pictures. But no grandparents, no cousins, nothing. Unless she'd burned the rest, the photo log of Harper's life really kicked off at Nathan's birth.

Diego carefully replaced the album, checking the room to make sure he'd returned everything to its place.

"You out?" Lansky asked.

"On my way."

Attuned to it, Diego caught the soft purr of a car humming up the street and knew his time was done.

"Engage or avoid?" Lansky asked, not even trying to hide the taunt as Diego headed down the stairs.

"Kiss ass." Diego disengaged, removed the comm and tucked it into his belt. He checked the belt's pockets, ensured nothing was showing and continued through the kitchen and out the back. He closed the door behind him, making sure the lock snicked shut.

Glancing at the backyard of his pseudo-bunker, Diego debated. Since hiding had never been his style, he angled around the side of the house and timed it so he stepped onto his porch as she was focused on turning off her engine.

When Harper looked up, he knew it appeared as if he'd just stepped out of the house. Despite Lansky's suggestion, Diego didn't figure cornering the woman with threats was going to net them much intel, but he did have a job to do.

She was supposed to have taken Nathan to camp. To have gotten him out of the house, away from Santa Barbara for two weeks. The drop-off and goodbye was slated to take four hours, so why was she back so early?

Had Ramsey played into it?

Damn Lansky for putting doubts in Diego's head.

Doubts that were only exacerbated when Diego saw the look that flashed over Harper's face when she caught sight of him. Keys in hand, one sleek leg out of the car, Harper froze. And damned if that wasn't guilt and— Diego narrowed his eyes—desire? Was that desire?

Her gaze didn't leave his as Harper slid from the car; she looked as if she were debating the idea of running as fast as those spiky shoes of hers would carry her. *Adapt and blend*, he told himself, slowing his pace and trying for an innocuous smile. Innocuous would work until he figured out why the guilt and how hot the desire.

"Hey, Harper," he greeted, wandering over. "How's it going?"

She sure had a way of wearing clothes. What he'd taken for a skirt was actually shorts that ended just above sexy knees. Black and cuffed, the narrow tan stripes matched the jacket draped over her arm. Tucked into a woven black leather belt was a silky-looking tank top the color of ripe raspberries that skimmed over full breasts. Other than the do-me heels, there was nothing that could be called sexy about her outfit.

He was turned on anyway, just looking at her.

He was close enough to see those pretty eyes. Huge, blue and heavily lashed, they reminded him of a stormy sky. Quite a contrast to hair the color of burnished gold and creamy smooth skin. It didn't look as if she was wearing lipstick, so he figured her pouty lips really were the color of roses.

"Hey, Diego." She moved quickly to the back of her car. He appreciated the view as she bent into the trunk, then straightened with a couple of big books in her arms. Books angled protectively against her chest, she smiled.

That smile sent a thrill of something through Diego

that he'd never felt before. He'd seen a lot of action in his time, most of it military, plenty of it sexual. He'd felt plenty of things, but that smile?

That smile made him nervous.

"I was hoping I'd see you," she said, shifting the books in her arms, her fingers playing with the strap of her purse before she slung it over her shoulder.

It wasn't guilt he saw on her face, he realized, leaning his hip against the back fender as he studied her carefully.

It was nerves.

Why?

"You're back early," he noted. When her eyes flashed, he answered before she could ask the question. "Nathan figured you wouldn't be done settling him in until one or two."

"Apparently the guy who runs the Seafarers Camp is a tight ass with a scheduling fetish. He doesn't like parents ruining their children's experience by clinging and crying all over the campers." She rolled her eyes. "He gave an annoying lecture on independence and emotional maturity the minute we got off the ferry. By the time he was finished, Nathan was practically begging me to go home so I didn't make him look like a baby in front of all his new friends."

She blinked her damp eyes. Then she gave Diego a searching look that said she was desperate for reassurance. He had no idea what that feeling was in his chest, but he didn't like the melting sensation or tug of responsibility that came with it.

"I did the right thing, didn't I? Letting him go to camp, not staying until they kicked me out?" She sniffed. "Coming home instead of pitching a tent in the woods where I could watch in secret?"

"You did a good thing," Diego said with a laugh, appreciating the way she joked instead of giving in to the pain she obviously felt.

"Thanks." Her fingers pleated and unpleated the leather strap, her lips pursed as if she wanted to say something but couldn't quite figure out how.

"Were you on your way to somewhere?" she finally asked.

That wasn't what she wanted to know.

"Nope." Diego shoved his hands into his pockets. And waited.

It was his experience that waiting made people nervous. He liked the idea of making Harper Maclean nervous.

At ten seconds she had a small line forming between her brows.

At twenty she shifted from one foot to the other, glanced toward her house, then back at his and bit her lip.

At thirty Diego bit back a smile as that line between her brows slid into a full-fledged frown and her foot was tapping out a beat in those sexy heels.

"Do you have plans then, or were you just standing around out here?" Her gaze traveled from his face to his porch, then back again. "Or were you waiting for someone?"

"Could be I was waiting for you," he admitted in a low tone, wondering if that'd make her turn and run.

It didn't.

"Is that so?"

"It is, indeed."

He moved in a little, crowding her body with his. He liked her there, within touching distance. He liked seeing the pulse race in her throat, liked hearing her breath

catch with a little shake. He expected her to look horrified, or maybe even irritated. But all he was seeing
were those nerves.

Because of Ramsey? Or something else?

"Problem?"

"No. I guess I'm just wondering what you're planning to do now that I'm here."

"Is that what you're wondering?"

He was usually aces at reading women, but this one
was a mystery. He couldn't tell if she was sending mixed
signals or if he was picking up what he wanted to see.

He shot out a breath as his fingers closed around
hers. It was like grabbing a live wire.

Sparks. Heat. Such a charge, his whole body came
to attention.

Her skin was silky soft, her bones delicate enough to
feel fragile in his grip. Her fingernails pressed lightly
into his palm, and he wondered how they'd feel if she
used them during sex.

Was she wild?

If the heat sparking between their bodies was any
indication, she had enough wild in her to handle his
every fantasy.

Wanting more, interested in seeing how she'd react,
he stepped closer. Her eyes widened. She tried to pull
her hand from his, but he wasn't ready to let go. He
rubbed his thumb along her wrist.

She stopped tugging as her breath caught. He could
feel her pulse jump as her hand trembled in his. He liked
how responsive she was. Oh, yeah, he liked it a lot. He
curled his fingers into her palm, brushing, teasing.

She dropped her books on his feet. They bounced
harmlessly off his leather boots, but he still blinked in
surprise at their weight.

"I'm so sorry." She pulled her hand from his and bent down. The move sent her purse swinging off her shoulder so it hit the ground, too.

When Diego kneeled down to help, she jerked to the side, as if to avoid him touching her again. That caused her sunglasses to fly off the top of her head.

"Oh, my God," she muttered, sounding exasperated as he started stacking book on top of book. They were surprisingly heavy, he realized, glancing at one of the oversize hardcovers. He flipped it open to see little pieces of fabric arranged like a waterfall on each page.

Before he could ask, she slipped the book out of his hands.

"I've got them," she said, her words a little too breathless to be insistent.

"Just trying to help." He left her to it, leaning back on his heels to watch her face.

"Thank you," she said quietly. Then she rose. "I don't suppose you could help me with the rest of these?"

Diego followed her gesture to see another pile of books in her trunk.

She was asking him if he'd do more than carry her books.

He'd been around the block with women too many times to not hear that; his instincts were too finely honed to not realize that.

God, first nervous, now hesitant?

She was making him feel all kinds of crazy things he'd never experienced before. The spikes of desire he was okay with. But nerves and hesitancy? What the hell? He'd never been nervous around a woman, never hesitated to go for what he wanted.

Diego considered—for a very brief second—making some excuse so he could refuse her offer. But that meant refusing her request for help, and he simply couldn't do that.

His reasons were personal and had nothing to do with the mission. So he simply gathered up the stack of books from the trunk, shut it with a slap of metal to metal and tilted his head toward the house.

"You want these inside?"

"I do." She nodded and turned toward the house. "I want them inside."

Whew.

Blinking and wondering if she'd actually meant that as a double entendre, Diego had to take a second before he followed her. Even then, he kept a good couple of feet between them as her long legs ate up the distance to the door. Despite her slender hips, she had one hell of a sweetly curved ass going for her.

She let him in, gesturing with her head to the arch to the left of the foyer that he knew led to her office. Diego followed, pretending he hadn't already had a look-see.

But Harper wasn't offering a tour. Instead, she dumped her armful of books onto her desk, dropped her purse right next to them, then turned back to face Diego. Her fingers meshed at her waist for a moment before she crossed back to where he stood.

"Thanks for the help."

"Sure."

He could see the nerves in those eyes again as she moved closer to take the books from him.

"I'd love to show you my appreciation with more than just a thank-you," she offered quietly, her eyes drenched with needs. So many needs that Diego debated turning heel and running.

Answering those needs would cause all sorts of problems. The kind that started with breathy sighs, then got naked and led to all sorts of complications.

That didn't mean he could resist, though.

"Would you now?" His smile spread, slow and wicked. "What'd you have in mind?"

"I was thinking that maybe I could make you something," she murmured.

"Like what?"

The possibilities were very interesting. Could she make him moan? Groan? Come? He was down for all of the above.

As if reading his mind, Harper's eyes flashed with something hot. She pressed her lips together as her gaze meandered down to his chest, over his shoulders, then met his eyes again.

"Dinner. I'll make you dinner." She arched one brow. "Tonight. Interested?"

"Oh, yeah. I'd like to have dinner with you."

"Yeah?" She glanced at her watch. "I do have a client call soon. Then I'll have to run to the store, get a few, um, groceries." Her lashes fluttered. "Is six too late?"

For what? Because while her words said groceries, the look in her eyes said something a whole lot tastier.

"Six is good." Remembering his mother's rules for the rare times they ate at anyone's house, he added, "Can I bring anything?"

Stupid rule, he realized as soon as the words were out. What was he supposed to do? Hop into his rental kitchen and whip up dessert? Like he'd have a clue.

"Wine." Now her smile hinted at plans that went well beyond a friendly dinner.

Even as the warning bells went off, Diego's body responded. Because, damn, she was pure temptation. Trying to shake it off, he calculated the time it'd take to grab a bottle of vino versus her trip to the grocery store. If he played it right, he could finish his search while she was out.

"Wine it is. See you at six."

Mmm, if looks could purr, the one she was giving him would be humming loud and clear. Sexy invitation and enchanting anticipation, all rolled into a pretty blue gaze.

"I can't wait."

And suddenly neither could he.

AS EVENINGS WENT, this one was definitely outside Diego's comfort zone.

Of course, he was a man more at home eating MREs, heating the field rations over a fire pit in the middle of a freezing cold desert surrounded by men who smelled as if they'd been fighting all day long.

So a candlelit dinner at a table covered with a midnight-blue cloth served on fine china wasn't a part of his everyday routine. Throw in simple but perfectly cooked chicken breasts in some sort of herb sauce, rice and, God knows how she made that taste good, broccoli, and Diego was definitely operating blind.

A gorgeous, sexy woman sitting across from him, looking as if she wanted to cover him in chocolate and start nibbling? That he was familiar with.

But it was the last expression he'd figured he'd see on Harper Maclean's face.

He swirled the wine in his glass while he considered the best course of action. He needed to finish his search. Given his orders and the mission's directive, he was cleared to use any means necessary to execute the assignment.

In the past, such means had included killing, destroying or eradicating. Sure, some gave him bad moments from time to time—usually in the middle of the night when his subconscious liked to run replays in the form of nightmares. But he never questioned that the methods were necessary to achieve the objective.

Sharing a naked chocolate feast sounded delicious, and, yeah, doing Harper was a nice fantasy. But the idea of doing either in the name of the mission left a bad taste in his mouth.

Odd moral line, but there ya go.

"Would you like more?" Harper asked, offering the platter with its last piece of chicken.

"I've had three helpings. I should probably stop." He put as much charm into his smile as he could, because it had been a delicious meal. "I'm not used to home-cooked meals. Thank you for a delicious one."

"I'm glad you enjoyed it. It's rare that I get to cook for other people. Especially men." Harper set the platter down, then trailed her fingers along the back of his hand. The move was soft, a barely-there caress that sent a shaft of desire zinging through him, proving that his body didn't give a damn about those moral objections.

Step back, he ordered.

"I'll clear and clean," he offered automatically, both as an excuse to remove himself from her touch, and because he was a man used to the fair disbursement of duties.

"It can wait," she said with the tiniest of shrugs. The move sent her dress sliding, leaving one shoulder bare. "Shall we go into the great room?"

"Great," he quipped, pushing back from the table. She got to her feet at the same time, swaying just a little.

She'd had enough to eat—and more important, to drink—to relax her enough that she might divulge whatever information she knew. He could wind this up tonight, get the hell back to base and deal with this threat like a fighter instead of skulking around like a spy. Anticipation stirred as the call of the familiar beckoned him with unexpected intensity. He wasn't cut out for this crap.

"I'll just bring this, shall I," Harper suggested in a husky tone that sent a tingle down his spine. As she spoke, she lifted the bottle of wine and waved it from side to side. That it was mostly empty occurred to them at the same time. "Oops, not much to bring, is there?"

"No problem," he said. After all, he wanted her relaxed, not comatose. Before he'd finished his refusal, she had a second bottle and a corkscrew in hand.

"We'll bring this instead." Her moves were smooth, her smile easy. But he could see traces of nerves in her eyes.

So she was worried. Time to find out why.

He followed her out of the kitchen. While Harper set their glasses on a low oval table that appeared to be inlaid with stones, Diego looked around the great room. He hadn't gotten this far in his earlier search, so his quick sweep now was twofold. First, to note potential areas of interest to explore later. And second, to check out the space he figured Harper and her kid spent most of their time in.

"I'll get that," he offered as she lifted the corkscrew and bottle. Taking them, he wandered the room as he opened. There were plenty of photos spread over the shelves and decorative tables. Despite being a variety of sizes and shapes, all of the frames were polished redwood. Some were Nathan; some were Nathan and Harper. There was one of Nathan with a group, all wearing Scout uniforms, and a couple of him with another boy his age.

None included Ramsey.

Diego frowned a little as he pulled the cork free. Once again, where were the family photos? The grandparents, the multigenerational group pictures. It was as if Harper and Nathan had only each other. Was that deliberate? Her family was long gone, but what about Ramsey's? They were still alive and kicking. Was Harper one of those anti-the-ex's-family kind of women? Time to find out.

"Wine?" he offered, facing her with the bottle lifted high.

"I'd love some."

With a slow smile that could easily be taken for seductive, Harper slid onto the couch, tucking her feet beneath her so her dress spread like flower petals. She held out her glass.

It only took a glance at the dilated pupils and delicately flushed cheeks to see she was well on her way past enjoying to overindulging. All things considered, getting a woman drunk wasn't the worst interrogative method he'd ever used.

He filled both glasses, although his was only for show, and joined Harper on the sleek leather couch, shoving aside a pair of nubby turquoise pillows.

"How'd you get to be such a good cook?" he asked for lack of a better opening. He felt like such an ass that he decided then and there to tell Savino they needed to add spy craft to their training regime.

"Necessity. I didn't want to raise Nathan on fast food."

And there was his opening. Maybe he was better at this than he'd thought.

"You're a good mom," he complimented. "If I had a kid, I'd want to know he had someone that conscientious in charge. I'll bet Nathan's father appreciates it, too."

As if he'd flipped a switch, Harper's smile dropped, a brow-furrowing frown taking its place.

Yeah. He did suck at this.

"Didn't mean to bring up a sore subject," he lied. "I'm just saying I admire how you're raising him. A nice home, good meals, a cool bike. Everything a boy needs for a good childhood."

"You think?" Her gaze shifted to her wine for a moment; then she shrugged again and met his eyes. "Nathan's a great kid. He makes it easy."

"He's excited about camping. Sounds like he's done it a few times. Does he go with his father?"

"With his…" Her face paled, her lips tightening over whatever words she'd been about to say. She tunneled her fingers through her hair, the shaggy ends falling tidily back in place, then shook her head. "No. I took him camping last year. He's gone once or twice with his best friend, too."

"You went camping?" He couldn't help but grin a little.

"You're surprised?"

"No," he realized, shaking his head. "You're a good mom. Good moms do things they don't like sometimes. Like camping."

"And letting their little boys go to camp for two weeks," she said, wrinkling her nose.

"You didn't want to let him go?" Her shrug wasn't a denial. "So why did you?"

"Because he wanted to. And he needed a chance to grow a little more independent. According to my friend,

Andi, that's important if a boy is going to grow into a strong man."

"But you'll miss him," Diego said, pinpointing the emotions he saw in her eyes.

"I will, but I have a plan to keep it from overwhelming me," she admitted, wetting her lips and looking at him like he was a big bar of creamy chocolate.

"Do you, now?" There he was, feeling nervous again.

"I do, indeed." She leaned closer, so that her breast brushed against his shoulder. "It involves a great deal of wine, a lot of body contact and perhaps a few less pieces of clothing."

"Is that a fact?"

"Indeed." To prove her point, Harper trailed her fingers down the delicate mother-of-pearl buttons of her dress, flipping them open as she went. Each one revealed a little more of the silken skin and satin fabric beneath.

"You're good at this." Too good, he realized when he shifted, trying to find a comfortable position to sit while not giving away just how well her flirting was working.

Of course, another couple inches of interest and hiding would be pointless.

"You really think so?" Her expression was so delighted, he had to smile back. "I wasn't sure if I would be. I wonder what else I'll be good at."

Oh, baby. Images flashed through his mind of flesh, bare and slick with sweat, sliding together. Tongues, teeth and hands teasing, taking. Moans of pleasure, groans of satisfaction. Intense passion, hard need.

All it'd take was a single touch, one more hint that she was willing, and he'd sit up and beg.

God. The woman was killing him.

His orders were to use any means available; those were the terms of this operation.

So there was nothing to stop him from having sex with Harper. The question was whether it'd help or hurt the mission. Beyond distraction, the cost could be high. He tried to calculate it.

What did self-respect go for these days?

"Why weren't you sure?" he asked, playing for time.

"Long story," she said. She tiptoed her fingers along his thigh, each tap moving higher, getting closer to the rock-hard length pressing against his zipper.

Diego wrapped his fingers around hers, then, using their joined hands, gestured toward the wine.

"Pour a drink. Tell me all about it. I like a good story."

It was a risk, he knew. Rejecting a horny woman could bring on hell's fury with a vengeance. But Harper didn't seem to have her ego tucked in her bra, so he figured it was worth the risk.

Still she hesitated. So he pushed.

"Let's call it a bedtime story," he suggested, coating his words with enough heat to stir them both a little closer to that sharp edge of no return. He figured it was worth the risk. If he got the intel, he was closer to getting the job done.

If she got him into bed, well…

There were worse ways to spend an evening.

CHAPTER TEN

EITHER BUYING HER own time or gathering her thoughts, Harper slid her hand from his and leaned toward the couch. She added wine to both glasses, although Diego's was nearly full.

She handed him his and, after a deep drink of her own, settled onto the couch next to him again, thankfully leaving a couple of inches between them. Not enough to put her out of temptation's reach—it might take a few states to do that at this point. But her body wasn't touching his any longer, and that was enough to keep his thoughts clear.

"See, it was like this," she gestured with her now half-empty glass, the pale gold liquid catching the light so it glistened like her hair. "Once upon a time, there was a naive girl who thought she could be better."

"Better than what?" he asked.

She frowned into her glass for a second. "Better than the neighborhoods she'd been raised in, I suppose. Better than everyone expected her to be, for sure. She had big plans, and, being the practical sort, she knew the only person who'd make those plans reality was her. So she worked hard and she scrimped and saved."

So Harper had learned young not to depend on anyone. Was that why she kept Ramsey at a distance? Wanting more, Diego made a show of keeping his expression interested as he knocked back a little wine. As expected, she followed suit.

"She had her life all planned, and plans were a big deal to her since for a long time, they were all she had. But like all fairy-tale characters, tragedy visited her life."

She'd lost her mom. He knew that from the files. What he'd read didn't indicate that Olivia Maclean had qualified as mother of the year, but losing her had to hurt. Especially since Harper, at fifteen, had enough experience with Child Services to be wary of being sucked into the system.

"This naive little girl thought she had a handle on everything. She used that tragedy to her advantage. She got her shot at college—at a future. She was on her way to a better life."

Her words trailed off, her expression filled with a sadness that gave Diego the unfamiliar urge to gather her into his arms and give her a comforting hug.

What the hell? He didn't even know what a comforting hug was. So he stuck with what he was good at. Gathering information.

"Wait a minute—doesn't every good story include something sexy? Every good adult story, I mean."

"Believe me, this one has that," she agreed, her sharp laugh echoed by the snap of her glass on the table when she set it aside. "Throw in seduction by a sophisticated older man, and a girl like that doesn't stand a chance."

He'd seen Ramsey's charm in action. He couldn't imagine it had been less effective when the guy was twenty.

"Oh, don't get me wrong," Harper said when she glanced over and saw his scowl. "That girl, she enjoyed every second of it. Being courted with attention, seduction and sex, it was a powerful, heady time."

"And then you got pregnant," he interrupted, not sure why he was cutting her story short. Except that he really didn't want to hear the details of her and Ramsey doing the dirty deed.

"Look at you—seeing right through my little parable." She gave a self-deprecating roll of her eyes before laughing. "And here I thought I was so subtle."

How did she do that? How did she laugh as if those scars weren't filled with pain?

He'd seen things, done things that ripped at him in the middle of the night. He'd experienced pain; he'd learned to tuck it away and go on.

But that was the job. This was her life.

Her heart.

"I don't regret what happened, not even a little bit. But, bottom line, the last time I was with someone, my world changed." She wet her lips, staring at him with a gaze so soft and wounded that Diego ached for her. "That's the sort of thing that puts a girl off trying, you know?"

He did.

He also knew an emotional trap when he saw it looming in front of him. Between her poignant expression, her sexy body and the sweet vulnerability emanating from her like firelight, she was trouble wrapped in temptation.

Sidestep, his brain screamed. Even as the warning echoed through his head, he found himself reaching out to slide one of those silky strands of hair around his finger.

"I let that girl's story control a lot of my life for a long time. But what if she was wrong, vowing to never have sex again? What if it was simply the wrong time, the wrong guy?"

"You shouldn't throw away years of belief just to prove a point," he advised, although he didn't really believe his own words. "Just like you shouldn't let the past control your decisions."

"So I should do what feels right, now?"

Since the question was accompanied by her hand sliding up his thigh again, he had a really good idea of what she was thinking might feel good.

God, he was tempted. The woman had an innocence that sparked so many unfamiliar feelings in him. It was that unfamiliarity, the uncertainty it engendered, that warned him that temptation could prove more dangerous than he could handle.

He'd kick himself later.

For now, Diego backed away.

"You should wait, make sure whatever you're thinking is the right thing to do." Realizing he still had her hair wrapped tight around his finger, he quickly let go, then tapped her glass. "Decisions should never be made under the influence. Especially big decisions."

"Mmm, good point." Eyes never leaving his, Harper downed the rest of her wine, then leaned forward to set the empty glass on the table. "But since I made my decision before the bottle was open, I suppose I'm fine."

Whoa. That trap he hadn't seen.

HARPER HAD NEVER seduced anyone before. She'd never even considered it.

In her sole relationship, she'd been the one seduced. Her mom had always said that men were only too happy to take what they could get. Nothing Harper had ever seen had convinced her to think differently.

So other than getting multiple forms of birth control—pills, condoms and a spermicide, not that she was paranoid—along with her groceries earlier that evening, she was feeling very clueless about what to do with Diego.

Did she make a few more flirty plays? Strip naked and straddle him? Or take a hint and accept that the man simply wasn't into her?

The few brain cells not swimming in the grape suggested she take the damned hint, already. She'd been hitting on Diego all evening, and he hadn't responded. Keeping at it would only embarrass the both of them.

But he had responded, a tiny voice whispered. She might have put her hormones on ice over the last handful of years, but she recognized interest when it ran its fingers through her hair.

Of course, that tiny voice was backstroking through wine, but she had to figure it knew what it was talking about.

"I'm interested in you," she said, deciding to round the truth out with a little more brazen honesty. "I haven't been attracted to a man in a long time, but I am to you. I'd like to spend some time over the next two weeks exploring that attraction."

As he started shaking his head, she moved closer, pressing herself against him, her hand sliding up and down his arm. The hard, rippling muscles of his shoulder were so arousing that she had to swallow the hot knot of desire in her throat before she could speak again.

She whispered in his ear, "I'd like to do that exploring naked."

"Damn it all to hell," he muttered, his body tensing as if he was about to jump off the couch.

Harper blinked hard to clear the tears suddenly burning in her eyes. But before any could fall, he tunneled his fingers into her hair, angling her head toward his.

"This is a mistake," he warned tightly. "You know that, right?"

Yeah. She probably did. But she didn't want to stop it.

So she stayed silent as he leaned closer.

As those dark, intense eyes locked on hers, he gave her a second—only one—before his mouth took hers. It was like being pulled into a vortex of sensations. His lips were soft, his mouth hard. His teeth scraped, his tongue soothed. The kiss slid from testing to teasing.

Her mind went blank, her body on overload. All she could do was feel. And she felt incredible. Tiny goose bumps of pleasure tingled over her skin. Her nipples tightened, pressing with aching need against the smooth satin of her bra, and desire curled, hot and needy, low in her belly.

When Diego's tongue speared between her lips, past her teeth, luring her into a sensual dance so hot and so intense, Harper's head spun with desire. She didn't know the steps, but he made her feel like an expert, the way he moaned his approval when she slid her tongue over his.

Harper curled her fingers around the rigid hardness of his bicep. She knew she couldn't circle the impressive muscles. But, dammit, she needed something to hold on to.

Breath shaky with need and her body turning into a puddle of sensations, she could only whimper when he slowly pulled his mouth from hers.

She could barely think. She could only stare into those intense, dark eyes, watching and wondering what he was thinking. Wishing he'd kiss her again.

More, she wanted to beg. So much more. But she couldn't find her voice.

Just as well, she realized as a few of her brain cells reengaged. She'd feel like an idiot saying that aloud.

Admitting need aloud.

"Look, that probably wasn't a very good idea."

Well, that cleared her head. Harper blinked away the lust from her vision to study Diego's face. She could see the echo of his words in his eyes.

She frowned. It was one thing for her to have doubts, but she didn't like knowing he had them, too.

"Why not? Unless you're actually in some sort of committed relationship with another person, which would definitely put you off-limits," she conceded with a wave of her hand.

"Of course I'm not. I wouldn't have kissed you if I was," he grumbled, looking so offended that she had to smile. He wasn't the kind of man who'd lie or cheat.

She'd had no idea how sexy that was. How attracted she could be to the idea of honor in a man.

"Are you not attracted to me? Is that why you don't like the idea?" Not exactly a pleasant thought, but she'd rather face the truth now and spend the next two weeks bandaging her ego.

"You're kidding, right? You're hot enough to melt glass, babe. I could be deaf, dumb and blind, and I'd still be attracted to you."

Oh, my.

Those words trembled through Harper's body, stirring delight and passion and the sort of excitement she'd never felt before. The sort that guaranteed more pleasure than she'd ever felt before. The sort that promised more than just orgasms.

And he thought she was going to let it go without a fight?

"Then what's your reason?" She arched her brow at his silence. "I think I deserve to know."

"I'm not a relationship kind of guy," he said. Apology and warning mingled together, overlaying the implacableness of his tone.

"That works. I'm not interested in a relationship." *God forbid.* Having her life turned inside out once was enough.

Apparently Diego wasn't buying that.

"You trying to tell me you're a one-night-stand type of woman?" he scoffed.

No. But given that she didn't know whether telling him that would hurt her chances of getting lost in the naked distraction of his body, she kept her mouth shut.

Instead she slid her finger along that rigid bicep, over the sleeve of his faded black T-shirt, then under it to skim the warm flesh. Wishing she knew what was going on beneath that inscrutable expression of his, Harper shifted her fingers to scrape gently with her nails.

His eyes flashed.

Mmm, that worked.

It worked well enough that he grabbed her hand.

"I'm serious about not being here for a relationship. I've got nothing to offer, including time." In case she didn't get that, he added, "I'll be leaving soon. Could be in a week, no more than two."

From the look on his face, even that long was unlikely.

"I'm not open to more than two." Since honesty had gotten her this far, she figured she might as well keep using it. "If we do this, whatever you want to call it. However hot, however awesome, in two weeks my son is home. Whatever happens—" she wiggled the fingers of her free hand between their bodies "—it ends when Nathan gets home."

"And you're not going to change your mind after a few nights of the best sex you've ever had?" His words were light, but the easy conviction on his face assured her that he wasn't just boasting. "You're not going to want to keep on having it? To see if it's enough to build into something more?"

Something more? Like a relationship? That mythical *Happy Ever After*? She'd long ago given up believing in fairy tales. So it was with complete assurance and a personal vow to never go back on her word that Harper leaned forward to tap her finger against the full temptation of his mouth and make her promise.

"Not even if you're a god in bed, not even if you fall head over heels in love with me." She kept her gaze steady but let slip a hint of a teasing smile.

Then she waited, breath tight. His stare was intense, deep and mysterious as he studied her.

As she wondered how he could be even more appealing like this, with his expression unreadable and his eyes cool, he reached out again. Instead of tangling in her hair this time, his fingers skimmed along her jaw. He cupped it in his hand, leaving his thumb free to rub over her mouth.

It was calloused and just a little rough, a sensual contrast to the soft fullness of her bottom lip.

Harper almost purred.

"So you're looking for, what? A little sexy distraction while your son is away? A diversion to keep you from thinking about missing your kid? No strings, no expectations, just sex?"

She almost said yes.

Actually, with him touching her like that, she was pretty sure she'd say yes to anything. But while she wouldn't let her past make her decisions for her, she wasn't going to ignore its hard-learned lessons, either.

"I do have expectations," she admitted, trembling a little at the sensation of her words vibrating against his thumb. "I expect to be treated with respect and honesty. I won't…can't do less. I can trust you for that, though, can't I?"

Not that she was really worried.

Unable to resist touching, exploring, Harper skimmed her fingers along his chest, reveling in the hard planes rippling beneath the soft cotton.

No. She wasn't worried. Not about this.

If she'd learned nothing over the last eight years, she'd learned to trust her instincts. They said that she could trust Diego.

That he was an honorable man.

DAMN IT ALL TO HELL.

She'd had to push the trust button? Diego wanted to groan his frustration. Why'd she go and do that? Hadn't sexy temptation been enough?

Now, even as Harper's fingers took a teasing walk down his chest, Diego was walking along the edge of danger zone.

He'd walked it often enough in various guises to know the signs. His senses were on full alert. His body tense, adrenaline surging in a dozen directions. His mind blank, clear, waiting to assess the risks, to develop the best strategy to get through the situation with minimal damage.

He wasn't a spy. Special ops weren't maneuvered between the sheets.

But he had his orders.

Stay on her good side, make nice and get as much information as possible.

And he had his body's orders.

Go for the pleasure today because chances were, tomorrow would bring pain.

His mind screamed at him to make his excuses and leave. Every second he stayed played to the odds of him giving in to need, going for pleasure.

Diego fought the internal struggle between those orders, his own clamoring needs and his mind's warnings. Maybe there was some third-date rule that he could invoke here, something that would keep his pants on.

"I want you." Harper's words were a quiet caress that slid under his skin. Her fingers traced a silken path down his bicep, so light they almost tickled his forearm before she meshed them over his. "You can tell me that you don't want me. We can write this off as a nice evening and go back to being temporary neighbors." Her shrug said she'd be fine with that.

But the look in her eyes, the depths of the vulnerability he saw there, said different.

Diego gave up playing the gentleman. It wasn't a familiar role and definitely didn't fit. He'd always been better at being bad.

He turned his hand so their fingers entwined, palm to palm, taking a moment to delight in how delicate her hand was compared with his. Then his eyes met hers.

"I won't lie to you." That didn't mean he'd tell her everything—or anything, really—but he'd never straight-up lie to her face. Something he was starting to think Ramsey had done on a regular basis.

"What will you do to me?"

His smile turned wicked. "Let's find out."

He took her mouth, breathing in her flavor like it was air. Afraid he needed it just as much.

He started by sipping. By dipping his tongue into the well of honey and tasting. Testing.

She was so sweet. Heady. Her tongue swept over his, welcoming him into the dance. Tempting. Her fingers dug into his biceps, gripping as if she were afraid that otherwise she'd fall. Addicting.

Diego took the kiss deeper. His tongue plunged, sweeping through the wet heat of her mouth. His teeth scraped and tugged. She met every move with one of her own.

That she didn't even hesitate was even sexier than the rich flavor coating his tongue. Each time he plunged his tongue into her mouth, she sucked it in deeper. Each time he changed his angle, she did, too.

He cupped her breasts, his palms sliding over the cool fabric of her dress as he weighed their fullness. His blood pounded hard and fast, heading south to fill his throbbing dick with need. His heart pulsed in time with the flexing of his fingers as he gripped her breasts, molding the soft flesh to fill his hands.

Damn, she was delicious.

He shifted, angling so he trapped her body between his and the couch. He took a moment to enjoy the view, her blond hair splayed over the rich leather, that pale skin flushed with desire. Her lips were wet, pouting and bruised from his mouth, and her eyes filled with slumberous need.

Need he was happy to answer.

This time the kiss went wild. Tongues dueled, lips crushed, teeth snapped.

Hard enough to rip through his jeans, his dick throbbed against her thigh. Every move—his and hers—was a lesson in painful pleasure. He pressed harder, wedging his thigh between her legs.

He knew his actions, his voracious need, might scare Harper. A part of him hoped it did.

So he didn't bother tempering the fever of his need. Instead, he took.

He tucked his fingers under the top of her dress, pressing deeper so his knuckles rubbed the hardened nipples. Her gasp was a fast whip of air over his mouth as she arched her back to press her breasts tighter against his teasing fingers.

Damn, she was responsive. Deliciously responsive.

He slid a series of wet kisses over her cheek, along her jaw. He stopped for a brief second to nip at her earlobe before moving on.

Shit.

"No condom," he realized, his words a groan of frustration against her throat. He steeled himself, pressed one hand on either side of her head, then forced himself to push away.

His smile fell somewhere between wicked delight at the sight of her—so tousled and flushed with her eyes filled with desire—and relief. He'd never figured a missing raincoat could save his virtue. So to speak.

Even as he tried to bullshit himself into believing that, he saw the small gold foil packet Harper was holding between her fingers.

"Check you out." The relief faded in a blast of heat, because who the hell cared about virtue when sex was on the line?

"I was den mother to Nathan's Cub Scout troop," she said, her smile wide and soft, a strong contrast to the hot desire in her eyes as they roamed his face. "I was lousy at the camping stuff, but I rocked at being prepared."

"Babe, you might think you're ready." He leaned down, his lips rubbing over hers in a gentle caress before he nipped—just hard enough to make her gasp. "But you have no idea what I'm bringing your way."

He didn't notice her hand leave his waist, but it sure as hell caught his attention when she reached between them to cup it over the throbbing length of his erection.

"I think I know what you're bringing my way." This time it was Harper who nipped at his lip. She soothed the tiny hurt with her tongue. Diego groaned and swore he felt his dick groan right along with him. "And I'm ready. So why don't you give it to me?"

That was all it took.

His brain shut off. Instincts took over—passion-fueled instincts. The kind of instincts that pushed him to grab cloth, to tear it away. The sound of the tearing fabric, of her breathy gasp, was almost as erotic as the view.

Her breasts were full and heavy. Her cream lace bra covered but didn't hide the milky-white flesh or the large raspberry nipples.

For all her sexual energy and welcoming moves, she was damn near innocent. He should remember that. He should take it slow. Ease her into bed with soft moves and sweet words. But as he met her eyes, he knew that wasn't going to happen.

His.

That was his only thought as he took her mouth. The kiss was too hot and much too intense to worry about things like delicate emotions or old-fashioned courting methods.

Hell, no.

He wanted.

She was willing.

He was taking.

His finger slipped under the delicate strap, sliding up and down between the lacy fabric and her silken skin. He took each pass a little lower, each slide bringing his finger closer to that full breast.

He slipped the strap all the way off her shoulder with his teeth, licked his tongue over her flesh.

She was delicious.

Like a man falling off a steep cliff, he grasped for one last toehold on sanity. For all her willingness to get naked, he had the feeling that this first time, they'd better take it to a bed.

He licked his way up her chest, along the side of her throat, took her mouth. As she welcomed his kiss, he scooped her into his arms and straightened. Her fingers teased and scraped along the side of his neck as he headed up the stairs.

He hit the landing, ready to drop and take her there, but he started to turn instead. At the last second, he remembered that he wasn't supposed to know her house this well.

"Bedroom?" he murmured against her mouth.

"That way," she said, tilting her head toward the left. Her eyes were still closed so that her lashes left fringed shadows over the delicate curve of her cheeks.

He deepened the kiss as he carried her down the hall. Wanting to see her, planning to enjoy every nuance, he used his elbows to flick on the light as he stepped over the threshold.

His tongue dipped even deeper, sweeping in slow, seductive swirls. She tasted like heaven, and he'd happily walk his way through hell to continue enjoying her response.

Figuring there was no point in fostering any illusion

that he was a gentleman, or even gentle, Diego gave her a little toss so she bounced on the bed.

She didn't look shocked. Or disappointed. She looked pleased. Her hair splayed out around her head like sunbeams against the rich copper satin of the pillow, and her eyes gleamed with a satisfying mix of passion, appreciation and curiosity.

"Welcome to my lair," she said, her smile much too wicked for a face so innocent.

A small part of him made note, worried over that fact. But most of him was too busy appreciating the view. She made a damned pretty picture laying there, dress gaping open to highlight a pair of luscious breasts and skirt puddled high on her thighs.

Thighs he wanted to get between.

He pressed his palm against her calf, appreciating the muscle tone for a brief second before moving higher. Over her knee, along that tight thigh, to the fabric of her dress where it barely covered the peach-colored lace of her panties.

"I want in," he breathed.

"I'll let you in." Her fingers flicked his nipples, sending a shaft of sharp heat through Diego's body. "Just as soon as I get a look at what you've got."

"Afraid?"

Her laugh was nearly as sexy as the body laid out beneath him.

"Why don't you strip down and show me if I've got anything to be *afraid* of?"

"My pleasure.'

And it would be.

Because the minute he was out of these clothes, he was getting into her.

CHAPTER ELEVEN

OH, BABY.

Harper was lost in the power of the passion coursing through her system, but even that wasn't enough to distract from her appreciation of Diego's body.

Standing at the foot of her bed, his body lit from behind by a soft wash of light and his eyes locked on hers, Diego pulled his T-shirt over his head. It was like watching the sun rise as the faded black fabric slowly peeled away to expose his gold-hued skin. With every inch revealed, her body tightened in anticipation.

She wanted to ask him about the scar. She wanted to lick the tattoos. But mostly she just wanted to enjoy the moment.

The sculpted hardness of his chest was covered with a sprinkling of silken hair with nary a curl that trailed a downy path down his belly. That dark shadow emphasized the chiseled perfection of his six-pack, abs so well muscled, so beautiful, that her fingers itched to trace over them. To see if they were as hard as they looked or if there was softness overlying the steel. The brilliant colors of his tattoo stood in stark contrast to the soft gold of his lower belly.

Diego tossed his shirt aside, the fabric fluttering like a pennant, declaring the games had begun. Then his hands moved to his belt buckle.

Her mouth was desert dry. Harper thought she could

hear the click of her own throat as she tried to swallow. She could hear her heart, roaring in her head. She could hear her breath, coming fast and hot and just a little shaky. She could hear the slide of leather as Diego unhooked his belt, the snick of metal as he unsnapped his jeans.

And, oh yeah, baby, the whisper of fabric over flesh as he shoved the last of his clothing away.

Her eyes widened as her mind tried to accept what she was seeing. He was huge. His penis stood at attention between rippling thighs, the rigid length of him rising from that silken black hair.

Her breath came even faster as she wet her lips, trying to imagine something that big, that thick, hard and full, inside her.

Harper swore she could feel the wet desire trickling down her thighs in anticipation.

"Afraid yet?"

She should be. Oh, yes, she should be.

She didn't know why she wasn't.

Pent-up sexual wildness called out from deep inside her. She knew he'd hear the call, that he'd answer it. That he'd show her everything she'd been missing, everything she'd ever desired. That he'd teach her things she'd never even imagined.

Instead of answering, Harper rose to her knees, her skirt dangling around her legs and her shirt falling open, gaping at her breast.

She didn't watch his face now. Her eyes locked on the impressive length of flesh rising, hard and rigid from the dark thatch of hair between corded thighs.

"So big," she breathed.

Her eyes flashed to meet his for a moment, for

permission. She reached out her hand to brush her fingers—just the tips—over the velvety head.

The man was incredible. Like one of the Greek statues she often commissioned for clients, he was a study of muscular beauty. Of absolute perfection.

Suddenly Harper wanted to hide. The urge to clamp her legs together, yank her dress closed or, at the very least, turn off the light so she could hide the imperfections of her body came over her.

She wanted to blurt out that she was twenty-five and she'd had a baby. She wasn't as perky as she'd once been, and the evidence of her child was there in the silvery marks spanning her belly, her breasts.

She hadn't had sex in more than eight years, and while she didn't think the basics had changed all that much, her lack of experience was bound to show. Buying condoms along with two pounds of chicken, a head of broccoli and fresh ginger had been easy enough. And she'd obviously known what she was doing when she'd flirted with Diego, when she'd maneuvered him into her bed.

But she realized now that she hadn't thought it through. She hadn't undertaken any sex rituals. She hadn't waxed or polished or rubbed enticingly scented oils into her skin. She hadn't even changed into sex clothes.

"Shhh," Diego whispered, tucking his finger under her chin and lifting her face to his. His eyes, so dark and intense, studied her with a care that touched Harper deep inside, beyond the distraction of desire.

"We can simply call this show-and-tell. We can say we both had a good look, enjoyed the view, and let it end at this. It doesn't have to be more."

He was so sweet. She knew he was excited, the rigid

proof of that simple fact was waving right in front of her face. That he wouldn't push, wouldn't insist on satisfaction, simply melted her heart. And just like that, her nerves were gone.

Harper actually heard it in her head, her last defense, crumbling to dust.

"Let's call it do-and-tell, instead," she invited with a teasing smile, falling right back into the fun of sex, the enjoyment of Diego's smile. "Why don't you show me what you've got, gorgeous?"

So he did.

His mouth was hot, his hands wild. He stripped her dress away, her bra and panties flying as his hands raced over skin sensitized to a fever pitch. Harper gasped when his hand worked its way between her thighs, shock and pleasure mingling in a wicked climax. She cried out, her body contracting, her thighs trembling.

How'd he do that? He'd barely touched her, and she was panting and wet and ready to come.

"More," she begged.

She reached down to touch him, to tease him, but he stopped her with the touch of his hand against her wrist.

"Let's do more," he said. His eyes locked on hers, she heard the ripple of foil, knew he was sheathing himself.

Harper shifted, her knees up and heels digging into the mattress, her legs wide in welcome. Diego moved right in. She'd never seen anything—anyone—as impressive as Diego as he poised over her. His skin glowed with a light sheen of sweat, his breath labored in that broad chest.

His erection slid along her wet flesh, teasing the sensitized bud, dipping for just a moment, then pulling out.

"Diego," she groaned.

He plunged. He simply buried himself inside her.

So, so deep inside her.

Harper lost it. Her mind spun into orbit, taking her ability to think with it. Her control shattered into a million pieces, taking with it everything but instinct.

He thrust again.

Hard.

Deep.

Intense.

And she exploded.

Pleasure ripped through her, spiraling out so fast and hard and wild that she couldn't breathe. The orgasm was huge, like a tidal wave, overwhelming and delicious. All she could do was feel.

"Diego," she chanted, his name carrying her moans.

Clamping her thighs tight, her ankles locked behind the small of his back, Harper slammed against Diego in time with his thrusts. Feeling more and more and more as she came again and again.

She didn't know if it was the vehemence of her moves or the sound of her moaning his name, but Diego froze. For just one second, his eyelids flew open, his gaze like a laser staring into hers.

Then he plunged again.

So deep. So hard. So, so good.

She felt the ripples of his orgasm deep in her belly even as his shout reverberated through her body. The sound of it, the feel of it, sent Harper over again.

On the edge of hyperventilating, her hair matted with sweat and her body slick with their juices, Harper simply collapsed with pleasure. As she slid into a fugue of passion, the only thought that made sense, the only word her mind recognized was *when*.

When could they do it again?

Damn him all to hell three times over.

Before his breath had leveled, before his heart rate settled, Diego felt the painful slap of regret. He shouldn't have touched her. If he'd had to touch, he should have stopped before they got naked. He could have given her satisfaction, could have overwhelmed her with enough pleasure.

He could have kept his dick in his damned pants.

But, no…

As remorse pounded at his temples in the same way his body had pounded into Harper's, Diego gathered her into his arms, pulling her tight against him. He tucked her under his chin, rubbing a soothing hand up and down her back. His fingers skimmed the line of her spine, teasing and swirling, until her heartbeat settled and her breath evened.

She didn't sleep, though. Not yet.

He wondered what was going through her head. And hoped like hell she wouldn't tell him.

"Mmm," eventually came her soft murmur.

Diego closed his eyes against his instinctive wince.

"I have to admit, that was impressive." Her soft words were a teasing breath over his skin, warming his heart yet filling him with an icy chill. "Almost godlike."

There was laughter in her words, a teasing that didn't try to make light of the wordless expectation.

Laugh it off, Diego ordered, forcing himself to stay relaxed, not to betray his concern with one twitch of a muscle.

"Are you angling for a relationship now?" he asked making sure his tone was ripe with a cocky sneer.

She laughed aloud this time, but he felt the tiny shudder run through her. He didn't know if it was in reaction to his arrogance, or simply the same reaction he'd seen already whenever a relationship was mentioned.

"I hate to disappoint you, but as good as you are, you're not quite that good." Her tone was strained, but her words rang true enough to relax some of the tension from Diego's spine. "But I wouldn't mind filling the next two weeks with a little more sex like this."

She shifted, angling herself up so she rested her elbow on his chest. The light glowed like a halo behind her, shimmering through the gold strands of her hair, leaving her face too shadowed for him to clearly read her expression.

"I liked it."

Liked?

Diego's brow creased. What the hell did she mean, *like?*

It'd been fucking awesome.

"Liked it enough to spend the next two weeks doing it again?"

"Well…"

She slid upward until she lay over him, both elbows propped on him now. The brush of her body over his was an erotic charge, the effect instantaneous. It didn't matter that he was still damp from her last orgasm; he went rock hard.

"Like I said, I was impressed." She wet her lips; then, with her blue eyes dancing with delight, she wet his, too.

"But I'd be interested in seeing what else you've got."

"Babe, you're lying on every inch of it."

And every inch grew even more when she straightened. She shifted again so that her knees gripped his hips, her hands caressing his shoulders, down his chest. She drew a delicate path over the scar left by a gangbanger's bullet. She skimmed her hand over his belly, tracing lightly over his honor before curling those fingers around his pride.

"I like your tattoos," she murmured. "I like your body even more."

"How much more?"

She held up a foil packet and arched one brow.

As Diego tilted his head, gesturing for her to go ahead, he wondered just how many of those she had and where she was hiding them.

Then her hands were on his dick, sliding down so the latex was a caress of its own. She met his eyes again when she was done.

"You ready to ride?" he asked, his gaze heating as he reached up to cup the weight of her breasts in his hands. He squeezed, then, mimicking her moves, circled his palms over her nipples.

"If you're up for it, of course," she gasped.

With passion-blurred eyes, Diego watched the contrast of his dark fingers against her ivory breasts, the way his skin looked gold against the raspberry-pink nipples.

Only because he knew the coming pleasure would be greater did he release those breasts. He slid his hands down the soft silk of her torso to her slender hips. He gave in to need, reaching around to caress the round globes of her butt before gripping her hips, positioning her body so her hot, wet core teased the tip of his throbbing cock.

"Oh, yeah," she said, her words a breath of laughter. "I'd say you're definitely up for it."

"Let's find out."

With that, he yanked her downward, impaling her on his rigid staff. Pleasure exploded as her body engulfed his. Gripping him, she rode. Each thrust harder, each thrust deeper.

Reveling in the pace she set, content to let her control the rhythm, he released her hips to return his hands to the pleasure of those glorious breasts.

His thumbs worked her nipples, rubbing a teasing friction over the beautifully responsive tips.

Every time she thrust herself down, she added a little twist of her hips, a counterpoint of pleasure.

Every time she thrust, he pinched her nipples between his thumb and forefinger, the gentle pain making her gasp.

Every time she thrust, the tension grew, tightened, intensified.

His body was aflame, hot and needy and so ready to explode.

He watched her face, teasing her higher, wanting to give her more pleasure than she'd even imagined possible. Her breath came in gasps now, each ending on a whimper of pleasure.

He liked that.

But he wanted the pleasure to come in screams. He wanted Harper to come in screams.

He gave up toying, grabbed her hips again. Gripping tight, he used his hold to intensify the moves.

Deeper.

Harder.

Faster.

His own breath came in gasps now. Her cries filled the room. But she didn't scream.

Yet.

Diego reached one hand between their bodies, fondling the wet folds with the same teasing flicks he'd stroked over her nipples.

The effect was instantaneous.

Harper gave another fast gasp.

Her pleasure-glazed eyes closed; her back arched as she came. She let out a scream of ecstasy that triggered Diego's own orgasm, ripping the pleasure from him with almost painful speed. He'd never gone up so fast, or exploded so intensely.

Watching Harper shake back her hair, a few strands wet and gleaming as they stuck to the flushed perfection of her face, he decided he liked it.

As she collapsed against him, fitting too well into his arms, he decided he liked it way too much.

IT COULD HAVE taken minutes; it could have taken hours.

Diego didn't count, and he didn't care.

He simply enjoyed every second of the time as he waited, patiently, to be sure Harper's sleep was deep, her breathing smooth and her body lax. He gave it five more minutes, not for the delight of holding the slick warmth of her nude body against his, he told himself. But to ensure that she didn't wake.

Then he slipped from her bed, tucking the blankets around her so she didn't chill and realize he was gone. He didn't bother with shirt or shoes, but he snagged his jeans on his way out of the room.

He needed to finish searching the downstairs, a room at a time, and clear this house. He figured he'd start with the office tonight, move into the kitchen if he had time.

Ten minutes later, and feeling a little naked without his usual equipment, he cursed suburban ops once more. Instead of night vision, infrared and body armor, he was bare-chested, with a penlight between his teeth and one ear listening for a sexually satisfied woman while he looked through papers. He flipped through the folders from one of the two filing cabinets. The wood felt like silk beneath his fingers, instead of the manila card stock, the file folders looked like watercolor landscapes. Blue water scenes, pastel florals, gold pillars of light.

Damn, the woman was something.

Even her filing was pretty. He spared a brief glance at the closest door he'd pulled open, noting the various boxes lining the shelves. Each stack was color coded, each bin carefully labeled.

Poking through her stuff was truly an education. But not on terrorist activities.

His cryptology training was pretty basic, but he wasn't seeing any hint of code in the decorating descriptions or client files. He carefully read through each one before moving on to the more promising file drawer labeled "Suppliers."

Catalogs, flyers and price charts. Furniture, art, fixtures. Lots of fluff, little of interest and nothing related to the Middle East.

If she was hiding something, she wasn't keeping it neatly filed in her pretty cabinet.

Maybe the computer.

Before he started there, he pulled out the comm he'd tucked into his pocket, fitted it into his ear and tapped it on.

"Electronics available," he murmured.

It took a minute and a half for Lansky to respond, giving Diego plenty of time to wonder how far in the bag his buddy was. Sure, it was after 1:00 a.m., but that was early enough for the guy to have his MacGyver skills on full alert.

"Roger that. Ready at your mark" came the response finally.

The words were clear and sharp, no sign that the

Lieutenant had spent any time in the day's bottle of choice. Maybe Savino had laid down the law.

"You having a cozy break?" Diego joked, reaching around to the back of the twenty-seven-inch screen to power on the machine.

"Some of us don't have times for breaks. Some of us have a job to do" was all the guy said.

Right. Because some of them were what? Sitting around on their asses, ignoring the fact that their entire team, their entire career, was in danger of imploding?

Those facts had been front and center in Diego's mind—or at least back and sideways—throughout the evening, during every moment except those handful of hot, orgasmic ones when he'd been buried inside Harper's welcoming heat.

But those moments were his. He wasn't taking anything from the team by having them. He wasn't compromising the mission, dammit. He was entitled to a life, he was allowed to have feelings—no, not feelings, the hots—he was allowed to have the hots for a woman.

Even as Diego's fist clenched in his lap, even as guilt tore at him, he still wondered what the hell Lansky's problem was.

After grinding his teeth as he waited for the iMac to boot up, Diego hit the browser and typed the code. He took a moment to watch Lansky's remote magic as the arrow moved around the screen.

Without bothering with another word to his teammate with the stick up his ass, Diego got back to work. Scowl still in place, he decided to search the desk while he was there. He went through it one drawer at a time. He checked the undersides; he looked for false bottoms. He pulled apart each pen, seeking anything incriminating.

But he found nothing.

More telling, he found nothing that he could connect to Ramsey.

There was plenty on the personal side in the large side drawer. Accounts payable for the house and the kid's school. Medical records. Even school report cards. Assorted communications between various friends and acquaintances.

But letters, canceled checks, legal papers—hell, even old birthday cards—with Ramsey's name on them? Nada.

If intel hadn't confirmed Nathan Maclean was the guy's kid, Diego wouldn't believe he was or had ever been a part of their lives. Even if he applied Harper's bedtime story to Ramsey, he still couldn't make it all compute. His financial records claimed the guy paid child support, that he sent money at Christmas. There should be a money trail.

But Harper's records didn't reflect any of that.

Diego flipped through the papers neatly stacked in a crystal tray. Notes, to-do lists, penciled sketches of room designs. He paused when he came across one with a phone number, noting the Southern California area code.

"Need a number checked," he murmured after tapping his comm open.

"Reel it off—I'll reel it in."

It took Lansky only a moment to come back with, "Burner cell. God dammit."

Diego gritted his teeth.

God dammit, indeed. People who used throwaway cell phones were usually up to no good.

"Finish the electronics" was all he said.

A burner phone. That she'd left the number laying

out, that she'd even had to write it down, said she was clueless. But clueless didn't negate what might be proof that Harper was involved in something. In what shape or form wasn't entirely clear. But Diego's driving need to find out just intensified.

"What are you going to do?" The question snapped through his ear.

"Contact Savino. Tell him we need to talk."

He couldn't contact his commander himself. Savino's communications were likely being monitored, and Diego didn't have the equipment—or, truth be told, the skill—to bypass whatever NI had in place. Lansky did.

In the meantime, Diego knew what he had to do.

And he'd do it.

He'd up his game to get to the truth. He'd push Harper.

He'd been ordered to keep watch and wait for Ramsey to appear or for Harper to let something slip over the course of friendly conversation.

He'd use his advantage of being in her bed to get her to divulge more.

To get her to tell him everything.

"When the hell are you going to confront her? Make her tell you what she knows?"

His body tight, his mind racing with one furious thought after the other, Diego tried to reel in his emotions, tried to bypass the sense of betrayal.

He'd been so sure about Harper.

But even faced with proof that he might be wrong, he couldn't—he wouldn't—believe she was dirty.

"I need to talk to Savino."

He could feel Lansky's irritation beating at him. Could hear his frustration at the situation. His perception of Diego's failure was coming through loud and clear.

Just as loud were the weighted expectations of the entire team. The men were counting on him to find out the truth. Their reputations—his career—were all on the line.

"Did you pull anything on that burner yet?" he asked.

"Manufactured nineteen months ago in Taiwan, sold three months ago in San Diego. Cash sale."

"That doesn't prove it's connected to Ramsey."

Still, Diego's frowned slid into a scowl. "But it doesn't prove it isn't. Dude, what's the problem? You've been sitting on your ass for days, and this is the first piece of evidence you've found. Now you're trying to dismiss it. What's the deal?"

"How about the truth? Isn't that why I'm here? To figure it out."

"How much figuring can you do when your mind's closed to the very real possibility that the Maclean woman is dirty?"

"How much are you doing when your mind's closed to the very real possibility that Ramsey is ash?" Diego shot back. "What proof have you found?"

"The only thing I've found are big, glaring question marks aimed at the blonde. Financials, contacts, discrepancies. She's got them all."

Even as fury and frustration tangled in his gut, Diego knew that was why he was here.

Harper was the key.

He'd use her to unlock this disaster.

Just as soon as he talked to Savino.

A faint creak overhead sent a warning tickle down the back of his neck.

"Neutral approaching," he murmured into the comm.

"Distract or deploy. I'm in too deep to stop now" came the response.

Diego considered the computer. It didn't have a separate monitor to turn off; putting it to sleep would shut MacGyver down. And leaving the light on in a darkened room would alert Harper that he was investigating her.

He moved quickly, carefully, making sure everything was exactly as it had been. He adjusted the stack of papers to be sure the one with the incriminating phone number was tucked away where he'd found it.

"Can you remotely shut down when you're done?" he asked quietly.

"Affirmative."

Diego waited, but nothing else came through his comm. No stupid jokes, no smart-ass remarks, no clever quips.

That was it, then. Like he didn't know *fuck you* when he heard it wrapped in an affirmative?

Well, fuck Jared right back if he wasn't satisfied with the progress or with Diego's methods. He didn't report to Lansky, and he didn't have to justify his choice to defer to their commander.

He had his orders. He knew his job.

And right now the job was heading his way.

CHAPTER TWELVE

CALLING ON YEARS of training, Diego bottled the anger churning in his gut and tucked it away. He sidled out the office door, pulling it closed behind him with a quiet *snick*. He moved toward the great room, sticking to the shadows as the cut-glass chandelier above the stairs gleamed on.

Grabbing the wineglasses he'd set out as cover for being downstairs, he moved back to the foyer, checking for tells as he went.

After he'd noted it was all clear, he glanced up.

Harper stood at the top of the stairs, wearing only his shirt. The faded black fabric hit her midthigh in vivid contrast against her pale skin, offering a mouthwatering view from his vantage point below. His pulse picked up, his body reacting to the memory of how soft he knew that skin to be, there, just between her thighs.

With a lot of effort, he pulled his eyes higher, appreciating the way the worn cotton molded to her flat belly, highlighted her full breasts.

Tousled hair tumbled around a sleep-flushed face, flowing over a shoulder covered with his tee, the left side temptingly bare by the wide collar.

He knew what that silken shoulder tasted like. He knew what her delicate skin felt like. He knew the feel of those supple thighs wrapped around him, gripping him with sensual strength.

He knew the power of losing himself in her body. Of pounding into that welcoming heat. Of pouring himself into her, making them one.

Damned if he wasn't ready to know it all again.

Even with the changed intel, even with that suspicious phone number still etched in his brain, he wanted her.

Was that because she was the most incredible woman he'd ever met? Or was he simply betraying himself the same way someone had betrayed the team?

"Diego?"

"Hey," he said, keeping his voice as soft as the night.

"Hey," she said back in a voice husky with sleep. "What are you doing?"

Prepared for that question, Diego lifted the two wineglasses in one hand, snagging the open bottle from the waist-high table behind him.

"Round two."

Eyes glistening, a shy smile spread, wide and delighted, over rosy cheeks. She held out one hand, the long fingers beckoning him to join her.

He'd thought she was incredible when he'd watched her poised over his body, daring him to make her come again and again.

How could she be more tempting now?

"Let's go to bed," he suggested when he reached her, lifting those fingers to his mouth to brush a soft kiss over her knuckles. "And after we finish this round, you can tell me another one of your stories."

So THAT'S WHAT great sex was all about.

Harper's body hummed. But now it was with nerves, not passion. She'd have thought a night of soul-slamming, mind-blowing orgasms would wear her out, but Diego had shown her otherwise this morning in the shower.

Now, moving around the familiarity of her kitchen, she felt totally unfamiliar in her own body. She ached in ways she'd forgot were possible. She tingled with pleasure in ways she'd never imagined.

A part of her waited for the weirdness. Shouldn't she feel strange having a man she barely knew sitting in her kitchen wearing just a pair of jeans while she made him a breakfast of bacon and waffles? Of course, given that she'd had the same man sliding into her body wearing nothing but skin while he made her scream with pleasure, maybe it wasn't so strange.

It was awfully complacent, though. Here she was, having her first fling, and there was nary a worry in her mind.

"Did you want juice?" she asked, her focus on the bowl of batter she was stirring.

"This coffee is enough. It's great."

She glanced over to see him lift the cup in a toast and then take a healthy gulp. Gratified, thrilled that he seemed so, well, satisfied, she smiled and flipped on the round Belgian-style waffle maker. She moved to the stove top to turn the bacon, easily avoiding the splatters as it crisped.

"You're good at that," Diego noted.

"At making breakfast?" Tugging the sash of her robe a little tighter, she leaned against the counter to sip her own coffee. "It's Nathan's favorite meal. We love Sunday breakfasts. Waffles or pancakes or an omelet, depending on his mood. Or if we have company."

"Company?" His tone didn't change. His body stayed relaxed with his legs thrust out in front of him, one arm wrapped around the back of the chair while the other lifted his coffee to his lips. But she'd swear that his eyes sharpened.

Why?

A giddy sort of delight curled in her heart. Was that jealousy?

"Company. Like, sometimes Nathan has friends for sleepovers and we do a big *manly* breakfast. Every once in a while Andi stays or comes over early to join us for brunch."

There it was again. That look.

She wasn't good at jealousy games, had never seen any benefit in playing with emotions. But Harper couldn't stop the small smile from working its way over her lips.

"Andi spends a lot of time here. She's my best friend." She tested the waffle maker. Deeming it ready, she gave the batter one more stir.

"Andi's a chick?"

"Andrianna," Harper confirmed absently as she poured batter into the waffle iron. "She's with her family right now in Greece celebrating her grandmother's birthday, but she'll be home in a few days. She's going to want to meet you."

Harper grinned as she imagined Andi's expression when she got a load of Diego and realized that, yes, indeed, Harper had finally done the deed. She'd be so proud. Actually, Harper realized, gauging the pleasure still tingling through her body, she was pretty proud herself.

"A woman like you, I'd think you'd have guys lined up for breakfast."

Lined up? Why? Because she'd been an unwed teenage mother?

Harper's jaw set as tension flashed behind her eyes.

Her reflex was to tell him that breakfast was over and push him out the door. But that wasn't ladylike, definitely wasn't classy. So she'd offer him a damned waffle, then kick him out of her kitchen.

She turned the iron handle with trembling fingers and forced herself to take a deep breath. She didn't have any practice at the morning after. Maybe this was standard. The exchange of sexual history to get to know each other better after getting naked together.

She was tempted to confess that she'd had only a single lover in her entire damned life, and that'd been eight years ago. But it didn't take but a blink to realize that while the fact might tamp down the jealousy, it was probably the sort of thing that freaked a guy out.

She'd initiated sex between them, she told herself. She'd wanted a distraction. So she turned to give Diego a smile. It was chilly, she knew, but hey, it was a smile.

"Just because they line up doesn't mean they get breakfast." She waited a beat. "Or anything else."

"So that means I don't have to share?"

DAMN. WHAT WAS he doing asking dumb-ass questions like that? Not only was that on the standard morning-after blacklist, it was a lousy way to get intel on Ramsey. Ignoring the jealousy knotted in his gut, Diego's mind raced to find the right angle. The one that would garner the information he needed while putting him and Harper back on the right track.

"Do you have an objection to sharing?" Harper asked, her words slow and measured. As if she'd weighed each one carefully before using it.

There it was. A nice, tidy opening to push on the Ramsey issue. Even as he prepared to do just that, Diego realized he was pushing for himself, too.

He needed her. And dammit, he wanted her. Bad. He couldn't remember ever wanting a woman more. But that was secondary. Priority, always, was the mission.

"Maybe that's something we should have talked about before last night. I'm not a sharing kind of guy. So if you've got someone else in your life, a guy in the background or whatever, I'd like to know."

Hell, yeah, he'd like to know.

Harper didn't say anything as she finished plating the waffles. The sweet scent of them crossed the room before she did. He watched her face as she sat, noting the shyness in her eyes, wondering at the color washing her cheeks.

"There's nobody else," she said after a moment. "I haven't wanted there to be. My focus, my priority, is Nathan."

"I get that. I know being a single mom's rough," he said with a nod. "Juggling work, the kid, life itself, I know it's a demand. Especially when a lot of fathers don't pull much weight."

Diego's gut clenched when something flashed across her face. Was she thinking of Ramsey? Did the man add weight to everything she had to juggle? Before he could push for more, she urged the platter of waffles toward him.

"Should I ask how you know so much about being a single mom?" she teased.

"All I know is what I learned from watching my own mom," he admitted, watching Harper's face as he cut into his breakfast. "My father was what you'd call a bad influence. He even tried to pull her into his crappy choices, into his crimes. He had this huge personality, made it really hard for anyone—especially my mom— to say no when he got rolling."

"Did she get pulled in?"

"Maybe peripherally," he admitted, both because it was the truth and because he wanted to keep the parallel going, to build that common ground. "But for the most part, she walked the straight and narrow. She tried to teach me to be a good person. Mostly she just wanted me to grow up to not be like the people around us."

"And was she satisfied that you did?"

"I think she would have been," he admitted as pain slapped at him. The same pain he always felt whenever he thought of his mother being gone. Of what she'd been like, of what she'd faced. Of what she'd missed.

"It sounds like you had a rough upbringing," Harper said quietly, her eyes filled with empathy.

"Rough for my mom, yeah." As much as he liked the admiring look in her eyes, he knew she deserved the truth. "I was probably worse on her than my father was, though. My mom, she was a good woman. She worked hard to give me a good home. But I followed my old man instead. Because it was cooler. Because it was easier."

"What'd you do?"

"I didn't do time like he did." Maybe that was his only saving grace. "I was a gang initiate before I hit puberty, though. I ran on the streets. Hell, I ran the streets. I lived the ugly life."

"What changed?" she asked, leaning toward him. Her expression wasn't disgusted. Instead, she seemed fascinated. "Something obviously changed since you provide security now instead of breaking it."

Provide…oh, yeah. He almost smiled at her take on his cover.

"I got shot." He expected her gaze to shift to his chest, but while sympathy filled those big blue eyes, they stayed locked on his. Damned if that didn't make him want to dig deeper. "Laying there in the hospital, I realized I didn't want to go down that way. I wanted to make a difference. To be more than what I saw growing up. To be more than anyone expected me to be."

"And that led to working for a security firm? Did you ever consider anything else?"

Nope. He'd seen a clip of the SEALs on TV, and that'd been it for him.

"I tried a few things on for size, got some training here and there," he said as he dug into his breakfast. "Security work, it just fit."

"Because you love it?"

"I'm good at it. I like the structure of it. There are protocols and rules, standards that have to be met," he said softly, playing with her fingers as he thought about the structure of the military.

"Is there a bad side to it?" she wondered, pushing her hair back before nibbling on a strawberry. "For instance, I love decorating, but sometimes trying to meet the client's vision is painful. Not everyone has good taste."

She gave an exaggerated eye roll that made him laugh.

"The good side is the bad side, I suppose. It's not a nine-to-five job. It involves a lot of travel and a lot of risk. Which means there's not much room for a relationship." Or more to the point, not many women who'd tolerate taking the backseat like that.

"I'd think that if it's the right woman, the right relationship, how much room there was wouldn't matter. You'd just make it work." Looking suddenly uncomfortable, Harper dropped her gaze to her bowl of berries. She looked sweet with her cheeks all pink like that.

"Maybe." Why did he suddenly hope so? "The training never ends, because the threats always change. So I learn, I adapt, I grow."

And didn't he sound like a total geek? He tried to shrug it off with a self-conscious laugh. "Apparently I obsess, too."

"But that's what makes it work—don't you think? Because you define yourself by your career, or obsess as you say, you continue to push yourself to be the best you can. That's something Nathan and I talk about sometimes when we discuss his favorite superheroes. That it doesn't matter where a person comes from. What matters is what they make of themselves."

Diego wasn't often stumped, but he didn't know what to say to that. Not when so many emotions he couldn't recognize were battering at him.

"It sounds like you'd fit right into one of those chats," she said. Her smile flashed before she leaned forward to brush a kiss over his cheek. It wasn't a sexual move, but Diego felt it deep inside.

Damn.

Now he recognized those emotions. Or at least a few of them. Admiration and gratification, a bashful sort of pride in himself. And something else. Something deeper that he wasn't willing to acknowledge right now.

"You're a lot like my mom," he realized aloud. "You do what it takes to give your kid a good home. You do the right thing because you want him to do the same. What changed was that I figured I'd better live up to what she'd given me."

Her smile flashed again, full of bright surprise, as she spooned fruit from the bowl onto her plate. Diego felt something warm—too warm—in his chest. *Remember what you're here for,* he reminded himself. *Time to shift gears.*

"I suppose I feel a connection with Nathan," he said, choosing what he hoped was the right gear. "For instance, we've got great moms in common."

"And lousy fathers," she murmured, stepping right where he'd hoped she would. "Of course, Brandon didn't stick around long enough to leave an impression like your dad did."

Telling himself the feeling in his gut was triumph and not self-disgust, Diego put on a curious expression.

"Brandon? That's Nathan's father?" he asked, forcing himself to resume eating as if everything were perfectly normal.

After a long moment studying his face as if she were trying to decide if she wanted to discuss a previous lover with the man she'd spent the night melting sheets with, Harper finally lifted her own fork and cut into her single waffle.

"I suppose that's what he'd be called," she said before taking her own bite. Her tone was offhand, but he could see the bitter pain in her eyes. "He wasn't really around long enough to deserve the title."

Always the same song and dance. How many times had he heard guys he served with lamenting one version or another of it? Diego shoved in another forkful of waffle to keep from sighing. He wasn't a fan of Ramsey by any means, but the guy had been in the service when she'd hooked up with him. She had to know he'd be deployed, that he'd be gone a lot.

"Guess it was rough doing the parent thing on your own a lot of the time" was all he said.

"Try all of the time," Harper replied, focused on her strawberries. Her discomfort with the topic was as obvious as her waffles were delicious. "He's never been part of Nathan's life."

What the fuck? "You mean he wasn't around as much as you wanted?"

Her expression closed, Harper grabbed her plate and carried it to the sink.

"He was never around. He's never met Nathan, never seen him. Brandon never had visitation, never spent time with him."

That wasn't right. Ramsey had bragged about his son all the time. He had pictures of the kid, knew where he went to school, everything.

"So what's the deal? You kept him out of your kid's life?"

"Kept him?" Her laugh dripped scorn. "I begged him to be a part of it. But he didn't need the responsibility, didn't want the expense or the commitment and was damned if I'd ruin the trajectory of his perfect life by trying to foist a kid on him."

Shit. "I'm sorry," Diego muttered with a grimace. His gut said she was telling the truth. His stomach tightened with self-disgust at the pain his words clearly caused.

Harper gave him a long look as if trying to see into his soul and decide if he was worthy of forgiving. Then she sighed and gave a tiny shrug that sent her robe in a tempting slide over her chest. Diego's mouth went dry when she sat, the robe draping open over one smooth thigh.

But her words distracted him enough to keep his lust at bay. *Focus on breakfast*, he told himself. He could have dessert later.

"Brandon was my first, and, despite thinking I knew everything there was to know, I was actually pretty naive. You know, knight in shining armor, naive." Laughing a little at herself, she shook her head. "I got over that pretty fast when he decided he didn't want anything to do with the baby, or me once I told him I was pregnant. He handed me a check to deal with the problem, as he called it."

Asshole. That was the only clear word Diego could pull from his racing thoughts as he tried to reconcile what she was saying with the facts as he knew them.

"And when you didn't 'deal' with it?" he asked carefully, not wanting to push her into a painful conversation—or worse, call her a liar—but needing to find the truth. "How'd he take that?"

"I don't know. That was the last time I saw him." Harper shrugged as if it didn't matter. Her eyes were bleak. As he wondered if she knew her hand was shaking as she rubbed it back and forth over the smooth surface of the table, Diego's mind raced, trying to connect all the pieces. With the things Ramsey had said.

"So yeah, to the original question, it was rough at times. But being a parent pushed me to do better, for myself and for Nathan. Because I had a baby, I worked harder to get away from where and how I'd grown up. Wanting to be a good mom means I work harder than I would if it were just me. I wouldn't be where I am, what I am, if not for Nathan. He changed everything. That's one of the reasons it's so important to me that he have the best life I can give him, a happy childhood, every advantage that he'd have had if—"

Suddenly, cheeks bright red, she snapped her teeth together as if trying to bite off the words. "Sorry." Waving her palm in the air as if erasing her words, Harper shook her head. "I sound like an evangelist or one of those born-again vegans. And just a little over the top."

"I'd say you've got every right," Diego observed, making a show of looking around the high-end kitchen.

"It's obvious that your kid means a lot to you. It's just as obvious that you've done right by him."

He didn't doubt her devotion to her son, but the rest? It went against all of the intel. Ramsey's finances had shown child support payments. So either he was lying or Harper was.

And they already knew Ramsey was a liar.

He wanted to push. To find the truth. It wouldn't take much, for all the doubts they had about Ramsey, Harper was a soft touch.

But he couldn't bring himself to interrogate her further. Not when he could see that she was already damaged by Ramsey's actions. All that'd do was open those wounds, soak them in salt.

As a SEAL Diego had long ago learned to juggle any discomfort he felt over some of the more heinous orders he'd sworn to follow.

But right now? This minute? He just couldn't do it.

Instead, he reached out to pull her onto his lap.

"What're you doing?" she asked with a laugh.

"Enjoying dessert."

FOURTEEN HOURS LATER, Diego wondered if a man could become addicted to dessert. The way he was feeling right now, loose and satisfied, he was pretty sure he could keep nibbling at that treat and never have enough.

Time to get his ass to work, he decided. The faster he did, the sooner he'd be out of here and back where he belonged. With that in mind, he settled into his make-shift office in the rental's kitchen and opened up his security system.

Two hours later, he wished he'd stuck with loose and satisfied.

It beat the hell out of frustrated hopelessness.

The encrypted drive Savino had sent contained footage of the mission compiled from spliced-together video he or Lansky must have gotten from the small cameras equipped in each SEAL's helmet.

Seated at the kitchen banquette, surveillance screens open on one monitor, Diego watched the footage for what seemed like the thousandth time on his laptop. Night vision technology gave gritty black-and-white images a green cast, and the footage was spliced together from six different cameras, giving it a shambling jerkiness.

Sort of like watching Frankenstein in combat gear.

Monsters aside, as far as he could see the mission had been solid. He'd watched the footage enough to note the seamless teamwork, the perfect choreography of Operation Hammerhead playing out on the screen.

He watched Prescott and Ramsey infiltrating the low-slung bunker that housed the computer lab. Loudon and Ward were covering them. Diego watched himself go head-to-head with the guard on duty. It was a good fight, a vicious blend of street fighting and martial arts. When a spinning hook kick to the head had put the man down, Diego left him out cold and zip-tied for the cleanup team to deal with.

Two fingers moved into view.

"Hostage in hand," Ward said, his words a murmur through the comm built into their helmets. "Heading to rendezvous point now."

"Electronics?"

"T minus thirty seconds" came Ramsey's reply.

Extraction and electronics had been carefully timed to occur within a minute of each other. Hostage first. The concern wasn't getting him out without sounding an alarm. That was a given. But a civilian couldn't move as easily, as fast, as a SEAL. Since frying the electronics tended to trigger alarms, they carefully timed it so that the hostage was out, covered and moving for the rendezvous point when they blew the electronics.

T minus thirty seconds. A confirmation that Ramsey had installed the electronic virus and it was scheduled to take down the system in thirty seconds. Timed, perfectly, for him to meet the rest of the team at the rendezvous point when it blew, getting them all out at the same time.

Diego watched the team move as one toward the wall. Except Prescott, whose job it was to cover Ramsey. On the screen and in his mind's eye, Diego saw the scene. Saw himself turning toward the wall, watching his men surround the hostage, covering his ascent with the protection of their bodies.

He saw himself look back toward Prescott. He and Ramsey should be making their move.

Saw the man take one step, as if about to run back into the building.

Then Diego watched as the screen exploded. The cameras shook as the team raced. Diego didn't have to close his eyes to remember the heat, the bone-melting intensity of it, as the building gave itself over to the greedy inferno. He shuddered at the memory of Prescott on fire, flames licking their way up his body, engulfing his leg. Heard again the screams, the roaring hunger of the fire as three of them searched for a way into the building, tried to find a way to rescue Ramsey. But the building was gone. Simply blown to hell.

There'd been no way in.

As militant reinforcements started pouring into view like ants scurrying to a picnic it was clear that within moments, there wouldn't have been a way out, either.

With Prescott injured, and Ramsey lost, Diego had made the call to retreat.

It hadn't been an easy choice.

It didn't get any easier to see it on-screen for the hundredth time, either. Nor did it get him any closer to an answer.

Diego pressed his fingers to his eyes, but he couldn't rub away the bone-deep exhaustion. He'd figure it out. He just needed a break. He slapped the monitor closed and pushed to his feet, ignoring the gritty burn in his eyes. A few hours of shut-eye, a workout session or two to clear his head, and he'd go through it all again.

Heroes didn't lie.

Nathan's words came back to haunt him as Diego slipped into bed.

Lies. Even in sleep, Diego frowned.

He jackknifed, sending the too-soft pillow flying out from under his head. Fury pounding almost as hard as his heart, Diego scrubbed his hands over his face.

T minus thirty seconds.

Sonovabitch.

Flopping back on the bed, he threw his arm over his eyes and breathed deep. Long, slow breaths in. Easy, relaxed breaths out. He emptied his mind, regulated his heart rate.

He counted backward from sixty. By the time he'd reached zero, he'd leveled out. Then, and only then, did he replay the thought that'd woken him.

T minus thirty seconds.

He grabbed his phone.

CHAPTER THIRTEEN

SCOWLING, SAVINO STRODE through the smudged glass doors of the truck stop, ignoring the scent of burned coffee, fried grease and overripe bodies. Harder to ignore was the burning in his gut, but only because it was warring with the pain throbbing in his left temple. He was proud of the fact that he'd managed to hold the headache there, in just one spot.

It didn't take long to scan the restaurant. The place boasted only a dozen tables and counter service for four. Most of the tables were empty. Three or four were filled with what looked to be truckers and travelers. And, Savino narrowed his eyes, a gangbanger in disguise.

Shaking his head, he made his way toward the back corner where Torres sat. He wore a black bandanna as a do-rag under a gray hoodie. The denim jacket and wraparound sunglasses added to the badass look. As disguises went, Savino figured it was okay. The dozen or so people in here seemed as if they were too intimidated to look at Torres long enough to actually see him.

But while he appreciated the precaution, that didn't justify this meet.

"What do you think you're doing?" he asked, not bothering to hide his irritation when he reached the table.

"Eating," Diego said, slicing through the stack of fluffy pancakes, then scooping up a forkful. He shoveled the syrup-drenched bite into his mouth, then gestured with his fork. "You outta get some. Place doesn't suck as bad as it looks."

Middle-of-the-night calls to duty didn't usually irritate Savino, but these weren't usual circumstances. His team, his reputation and, yes, the man sitting there slurping up pancakes were all teetering on a razor-sharp edge, and everything he'd seen assured him that the fall was going to be ugly.

"Coffee?"

Giving in, Savino nodded to the pink-clad waitress, then slid into the chair opposite Torres. He sat silently while she filled his cup and handed him a laminated menu, waiting until she wandered back behind the counter before inclining his head.

"You called, said it was important. I assume you have something other than pancakes on your mind."

"Didn't figure you wanted a report over the phone."

He hadn't wanted to get up at one in the morning to drive all this way to get it, either. But he knew Torres wouldn't have contacted him unless he thought it was a solid reason.

Before he could find out what it was, the waitress returned.

"Ya want food?" she asked, pulling a pen from behind her ear and giving Savino an impatient look.

"Whatever he's having is fine."

He waited until she'd clomped back to the kitchen before raising his brows in question.

"You found something on that footage?"

The CIA and NI had gone over it with a fine-tooth comb. A handpicked team of cryptologists watched it forward, backward and sideways. He and Lansky had done all of that and even tried watching it at half speed, double speed and frame by frame.

"T minus thirty seconds."

It wasn't standard terminology, but it wasn't unusual, either.

Savino waited as the waitress set a huge plate in front of him heaped high with pancakes, eggs, bacon and sausage. Realizing he didn't have an appetite, Savino pushed the food toward Torres.

"So?"

"Practice runs, training sessions, every other time, he used the words *mark thirty* to acknowledge the time." Torres knocked back the rest of his coffee, then arched one brow. "Every. Other. Time."

Savino narrowed his eyes.

"It's code," he realized in an icy tone meant to disguise the fury churning in his gut. From the startled look the waitress sent over her shoulder, the effort failed.

"It's code," Torres agreed, shoving one syrup-smeared plate aside as he pulled Savino's toward him. "While it confirms that he's dirty, it also lends credence to the idea that he's alive and in the wind."

"He knew what he was doing."

"He knew exactly what he was doing," Torres confirmed with a scowl as he started digging into Savino's untouched food.

As Savino processed that new piece of information, worked through the steps and stages of who to inform and how to tap into the right resources, he had to shake his head.

"I can't decide if I'm awed or disgusted. How the hell can you eat all of that?"

"Metabolism." Torres gulped down coffee, then

lifted the cup for a refill. "Sitting around suburbia is driving me insane."

Which meant, Savino knew, that Torres was exercising like a madman. That's how he handled stress.

"Lansky's accessed Ramsey's email accounts, his computer files, all of his electronics. So far we've found extensive records on Ms. Maclean, what appears to be surveillance on her and a private investigator's report dating back eight years."

That slowed Torres enough to put down his fork.

"Child support payments?"

"Ms. Maclean's name is on the account the payments are made to, but Lansky hasn't tracked any actual activity on her part."

"Any actual communication between Ramsey and Harper?"

"Nothing we've found."

"He's been stalking her."

Since that was his take on it, Savino inclined his head.

"You might want to hit the grocery store, stock up on pancake mix. I'm sending you right back to suburbia."

Torres wanted to argue. Savino didn't need to be a cryptologist to crack the code written on his lieutenant's face. Fury, frustration and reluctance were easy to read.

"I need you there, watching Ms. Maclean. Stay alert. Get into her house, set up interior surveillance," he ordered quietly. "Obsessive stalking over an eight-year period doesn't go away just because a man's blown himself up."

"She's bait," Torres realized, his frown deepening into a formidable scowl. "You don't think she's dirty. You think Ramsey wants her enough to come and get her."

"What I think doesn't matter." Savino got to his feet

as if Torres hadn't just hit the bull's-eye. "What you think doesn't matter, either. All that matters is the mission. In this case, to pinpoint, flush out and apprehend the hostile."

He could see the arguments on Torres's face and shared the fury.

"Orders are orders, Diego," he said quietly. They both knew that with one word, he'd just made it personal. "I need to know if you can handle them."

Someone back in the kitchen broke a dish. Neither man blinked at the crash or the cussing that followed.

Even as he nodded, Diego looked as if he wanted to argue. Savino didn't blame him. This wasn't a simple mission. It wasn't anything they'd trained for. And it wasn't easy.

But they hadn't signed up for easy.

"MRS. WALCOTT, WELCOME HOME," Harper said, holding open the heavy oak door and waving the woman into her house. She hoped like crazy that they could get this walk-through done as quickly as possible. Once, she'd been happy to devote any time not earmarked for her son on work. But this week all she wanted was to be home in bed doing all sorts of naked things to Diego. With Diego.

"Is it done? Did you finish? I meant to be here an hour ago, but there was a sale. Shoes. Oh, my God, the shoes." The buxom redhead fanned her face as if just thinking about footwear got her hot. Which, Harper supposed, it probably did. "But you finished, right? You're done?"

"As scheduled," Harper said, gesturing toward the archway that led down the hall to, among other things, the basement door. "Let's take a look, shall we?"

Mrs. Walcott teetered down to the basement on her new five-inch stilettos, stopping at the foot of the stairs to clap her hands over her mouth. Harper was pretty sure that was a good thing.

She sure hoped so. This was her first clandestine design job. Mrs. Walcott had been so excited about making it a huge birthday surprise for her husband, she'd come up with code words in case he overheard them speaking and had even bought a prepaid cell phone to hide the calls.

Even though they'd settled on the design a month ago, the woman had called from her secret number at least a dozen times with ideas and changes. Harper still wasn't sure if she was more proud of her skills at diplomacy, her juggling or her actual design.

As the redhead bounced and squealed her delight, Harper settled on pride in her design.

The basement was refurbished and decorated in a 1950s drive-in theme with its red-and-white leather couch that looked like the bench seat of a '57 Chevy, enough chrome to bumper a fleet and a wall of black-lacquer-framed prints of classic cars.

There was an ornate jukebox in one corner of the room, and a sleek bar fitted into the other complete with a milkshake machine.

Not bad, Harper decided with a pleased look. But it wasn't her satisfaction that mattered she reminded herself.

"I hope you like it," she started to say as the other woman stepped farther into the room.

Apparently she did. At least, that's what Harper was taking the happy squeal for. Mrs. Walcott slapped perfectly manicured hands over her mouth to muffle the next squeal, and did a happy, hoppy sort of dance, jumping in place with enough verve to put her bra to the test.

Harper managed not to laugh out loud.

"Oh, my sweetie is going to love this. Just love it. It's perfect, Harper. Now that I see it all finished like this, I can see how right you were to put the pool table down here. I thought it'd be too crowded. But it's perfect. You have such a wonderful eye. Oh, he's going to love it."

"I'm so glad you like it."

Before Harper could say more, Mr. Walcott's voice rang out from upstairs.

"Tiffany?"

"Oh, no," the redhead gasped. She took a deep breath. "I'm down here, sweetie. In the basement. Come on down."

"I'll slip out the side," Harper suggested, snagging her portfolio bag and inching her way toward the door.

"Oh, you don't have to do that. He'll want to thank you." Chewing on her bottom lip, Mrs. Walcott looked around and flapped her hands. "You can explain what everything is. The concept and how it all ties together and stuff."

"You created his dream room," Harper reminded her. "The perfect man cave. He's going to love it. Give it a few days. Then if you or he decide on any changes, just call me."

Harper had her hand on the door when "sweetie," who was built like a bull gone soft in the middle, clopped down the stairs. She took a moment to enjoy Mr. Walcott's delighted surprise at his gift, watching as he lumbered from couch to bar to pool table, exclaiming the perfection of each while his wife bounced and clapped behind him.

They really loved each other, Harper realized. They

were, for all intents and purposes, a complete mismatch. The gruff, overweight, thrice-married banker and the sleek, bubbly trophy wife were completely gone on each other.

With one last look at the cooing couple sighing over the room, while curled into each other's arms, Harper slipped out the ornate side door. Standing on the flagstone side yard of the large house with the sun warm overhead and the ocean a gentle roar in the distance, Harper sighed. The Walcotts were on year ten, and everything she'd heard about them said they were devoted. What was it like to have someone like that? Someone you knew well enough to surprise with the perfect gift, someone who made your happiness paramount?

That was love, wasn't it?

Harper gripped her bag, fingers clenched tight around the leather handle as she tried to catch her breath. She wanted that. She wanted love, the kind that lasted.

She wanted heat and great sex. The soul-baring talks by the fire and easy chats over dinner. Sharing the responsibilities and the dreams, and building them together.

She didn't just want it; she wanted it with Diego.

A chance. A hope. A future.

She puffed out a heavy breath and headed through the lush garden toward her car. She'd clearly overdosed on awesome sex if Sweetie Walcott was inspiring her to think she had a chance at true love.

Time to take it to a cynic and get these crazy thoughts out of her head.

AN HOUR LATER, Harper slid into a padded seat at the posh Beach Inn restaurant. The table overlooked the ocean and was backed by a bank of greenery, giving the illusion of privacy. Crystal and silver gleamed spears of light off the red lily arranged just so in the center of the white linen tablecloth.

"Thanks for meeting me," she said, reaching over to give Andi's hand a squeeze. "Especially your first day home."

"My pleasure," Andi assured her, tossing her dark hair behind her back as she leaned forward with a wicked smile. She'd dressed the part of the society princess today in a silk suit the color of raspberries and heavy gold jewelry. "And since this was your idea, you can pay me back by filling me in on all the naughty details of your sexy affair with the man next door."

"My idea was Maria's," Harper corrected with a laugh, naming the small family restaurant in her price range. "You're the one who insisted on fancy."

"My treat," Andi said, waving that all aside. "The juicy details about your sexy neighbor will be payment enough."

Before Harper could protest, or even decide how much she wanted to share, the waiter was there pouring lemon water and offering seasoned crackers and cheese. By the time he had their order, Andi looked as if she were going to explode with impatience.

"Well?" she prodded as soon as they were alone. "Details, darling. I want to hear everything."

Everything? Harper blew out a breath, trying to separate her jumbled thoughts from the tangle of emotions.

"He's wonderful," she said softly. Seeing the worry flash in Andi's eyes, she added quickly, "The perfect distraction. He's mind-blowing in bed, but more important, he's fun to talk with out of it. He's passionate about fitness, dedicated to his career and seems to care—to really care—about Nathan."

"And Nathan's mom?" Andi asked quietly, her fingers tapping silently on the linen. "It sounds like she's falling hard."

"I'm not falling," Harper said dismissively, hoping her laugh didn't sound as fake to Andi as it did to her. "I'm just enjoying. Wasn't that the point?"

"As long as you enjoy the moment and don't fall into the forever trap."

Harper waited while the waiter served their drinks, an iced tea for her and a champagne cocktail for Andi.

"Which is?" she asked as soon as he'd left.

"Forever is a myth," Andi said, her expression twisting into a sneer. "It's a fairy tale kept alive by romantics and capitalists who make a fortune off selling the impossible."

Once Harper would have agreed. But now she wasn't so sure. Or maybe she just didn't want to think that way anymore.

"Then what's the point of being involved with someone?" Suddenly wishing she'd ordered alcohol, Harper wondered why she hadn't asked these questions before she seduced Diego. "What about love?"

"Between a man and a woman? There's lust and compatibility. Friendship and comfort and passion and affection," Andi listed, gesturing with her drink. "I suppose any one or combination of those elements could be mistakenly called love. But they're not."

"How do you know that?"

"Because there's no such thing as love."

Harper blinked. Well, she'd come looking for a cynic. She'd definitely found one.

"But you believed in love once, didn't you?"

"I believed in Santa Claus, too. But he hasn't left anything under my tree in years, Harper. Myths and fairy tales are pretty things. But they aren't real."

The words were harsh, and the pain in her friend's eyes was real. Her face creased with worry, Andi wrapped her hand around Harper's.

"Is that what you're thinking? That there's more to this guy than a hot, fast ride? Harper, don't be crazy. This is just sex. I'm glad you're having it. You needed to have it. But don't start thinking crazy," Andi chided. "Don't start thinking forever."

"I'm not thinking forever," Harper denied, suddenly terrified to realize she might actually be. "I'm simply out of practice. I've only had one relationship, and we both know how that ended. Maybe I'm just trying to figure out the ground rules. How to go along, how to know when it's right."

"And how to recognize when it's going wrong so you can get out first?" Andi guessed.

Harper considered that while the waiter made a production out of serving their salads. The idea of forever scared her almost as much as it tempted. The only other forever she'd ever believed in was Nathan.

"First off, forget about forever," Andi advised, digging into her steak salad. "Relationships aren't meant to last that long. That's why you need to wring every drop of pleasure out of the time you have. Enjoy the sex. Have a great time. Just don't fall into the trap of believing in love. That sort of thinking will get you in trouble, Harper."

Andi tossed back the last of her champagne cocktail and shook her head. "Trouble," she repeated. "And heartbreak."

Andi's words were still ringing in her head when

Harper got home later that afternoon. That was what she'd wanted, Harper told herself as she rubbed her hands over her chilled arms. That was why she'd come to Andi. Not to validate her feelings, but to have her friend talk her out of them.

She tucked her portfolio into her office and set her shoes on the bottom stair. But as she stepped barefoot into the kitchen, she stopped short.

What was Diego doing in her backyard? Frowning, she crossed the room. Before she reached the door, though, she knew. And almost cried.

He was building Nathan a pitching cage.

Harper let her forehead rest on the cool glass as she watched Diego put it together. Her eyes traveled over the delicious way his dark blue tee stretched tight over broad shoulders before touring on down to appreciate his butt. It was a good one.

Those long, talented fingers handled the wrench with ease, his moves quick and economical as he fastened and tightened and did whatever it was to make the net stretch tautly between the white metal frame. She remembered how those fingers felt traveling over her body, teasing, tempting, driving her crazy.

If he turned his head, she knew her heart would stutter for just a second and her breath would catch in her chest at the sight of his gorgeous face. It had every time he'd looked at her so far, and she didn't expect that to change anytime soon.

But while his body, his sexual prowess and his gorgeous looks were all perfect reasons to revel in their fling, they weren't the reason her heart was stuttering.

No, she realized with a deep sigh. It was because Diego had listened to Nathan, had heard a need her little boy had that she hadn't even realized. And he was out there answering that need. Not to get her into bed—he already had her there.

Diego was doing it just for Nathan.

Harper pressed a hand against the butterflies swarming through her stomach and tried to remember Andi's warning. There was no such thing as love.

That should be a comfort, shouldn't it? After all, she couldn't fall into something that didn't exist.

DIEGO REVELED IN the sweat pouring off his body, focusing his attention on pushing his muscles to their limits. Push-ups, sit-ups, pull-ups, they all kept him focused and helped keep him from going crazy. His thoughts shifted to the sexy woman next door, seeing clients in the safety of her home office.

She was incredible. Breakfast, lunch and dinner, over the last three days she'd entertained him with her clever repartee, her adorable sense of humor and her inescapably delicious body. He couldn't remember ever being so comfortable, or so turned on.

Mostly turned on, he had to admit as he automatically counted rope jumps, even as he thought back to their little pre-lunch entertainment as he'd watched her dress for her client meeting. The woman wore stockings. Real ones, with lacy straps at the top of her thighs.

Diego stopped midjump so the rope slapped on the pavement with a sad *whoosh*, damn near tripping off balance thanks to the erection sucking up half of his blood supply.

He'd never been so grateful to hear his phone buzz.

"Savino," he said in lieu of a greeting.

"Torres," his commander returned. "Find cover."

Diego cast a quick look toward the house next door, then stepped inside his own. He engaged the scrambler, ensuring he wouldn't be overhead by anyone, in person or electronically.

"Covered, sir."

"Report."

Diego wanted to ask why it'd taken three days for Savino to get ahold of him. What the hell had they found out? He'd watched that video a few more times, but so far he hadn't cracked the code. Prescott was the best cryptologist on the team—had Savino brought him in? Could he, given that the man was still lying, burned, in a hospital bed?

Diego wanted to know all of that. He wanted to know the status of the investigation, to know whether the rest of the team had been deployed or if they were sitting around, waiting for him to clear their name. To clear his own.

But he asked nothing.

Instead, he followed orders.

Standing at ease, one hand cupped in the small of his back, chin high, he issued his report. Which was to report that, basically, not a damned thing was going on.

When he finished, he simply waited.

"Continue as you are," the orders finally came.

"As I am? Sitting on my ass, pretending?" he couldn't stop himself from snapping.

"You want to act. To fight. You're an expert at covert ops, you have strong counterintelligence qualifications. But sitting, watching, waiting, it's outside your expertise."

He had that right.

"So you're sending in someone else?"

Even as something ached in his chest, something too close to his heart, relief came, too.

"I can't. Not at this juncture. Everything I'm seeing, everything I've been able to discern, everything I've been able to dig out of NI, points to Ramsey being our guy."

"Ms. Maclean?"

"Financial discrepancies are accounted for. The house is rented from an Andrianna Stamos, who according to what we've dug up, keeps the rent low in response to her divorce settlement. Similar findings on the boy's tuition and a scholarship program the school runs."

"Ramsey's bank account with her name on it?" The account that'd pointed the finger at her in the first place. The whole damned reason Diego was there, watching while a woman he was coming to realize he cared way too much about was used as bait.

"Confirming that the funds deposited to the account came from the militants was easy enough. Tracking the withdrawal was harder. It bounced all over hell and back, but Lansky was finally able to nail it down this morning. The funds were transferred to a numbered account in the Caymans that Lansky's traced to Ramsey and Ramsey alone. There's no evidence that Ms. Maclean is even aware that her name is on that account, let alone has had access to it."

Diego felt a surge of relief, but he knew that not having evidence wasn't enough to clear Harper.

"What about the burner phone number she had in her possession?" He should be out there searching for the answers. He should be finding Ramsey and kicking the guy's ass from here to hell.

"Lansky traced five more calls from that burner to Ms. Maclean's residence, two to her business line with four from that line back to the burner. Hers is the only number the burner dials, and the calls average thirty minutes."

After the fairy tale she'd shared, with everything he'd seen in her house, he knew that while she might talk to her ex once, it'd only be long enough to tell him to get fucked. And that'd be the last call she'd take.

Everything in him, belief, instinct, gut, said she wasn't involved with the guy. But he knew that wasn't proof.

"Her house is clean, no bugs. This must be Ramsey's way of keeping tabs," Diego realized as he paced the kitchen.

"Or keeping in touch," Savino said quietly.

There was a sick kick of betrayal to his gut. Before he could shrug it off and focus on the relief, Savino continued. "He or his partner."

Diego's jaw clenched. *T minus thirty seconds.*

"You broke the code." He'd figured they would if he couldn't.

"It gave Prescott something to do while he's lying in that hospital bed."

Grabbing a can of iced tea from the fridge, Diego uncapped it and waited.

"As we suspected, the code confirmed that he'd transferred the formula and marked the countdown of the explosive's detonation."

The son of a bitch had blown that place himself. As fury rocketed through his system, Diego gulped down the tea and tried to settle his thoughts.

"Lansky dismantled communications in search of a tap or trace. There's no sign that anyone was listening in," Savino said, the words sounding as if he'd bit them off with his teeth.

"So in addition to Ramsey, someone else is dirty."

Diego gave voice to the sick feeling he'd had ever since he'd watched the video.

"Affirmative. But we don't know who he was in league with. Not yet."

It could be another member of Poseidon. It could be one of the SEAL team. It could be one of the support crew.

His vision black with rage, Diego crushed the can and sent it flying into the wall.

"Torres," Savino barked. "Maintain."

Diego took a deep breath. Then another. He focused all of his anger, all of his adrenaline between the fingers of his clenched fist until his mind cleared and his heart rate slowed.

"My orders?"

"Stay the course. This might not be your area of expertise, but that works to our advantage."

Which was Savino's not-so-subtle way of warning him that command, NI, probably the CIA were all interested in his whereabouts.

"Yes, sir."

"Maintain your position. Do not break cover. Do not tip off the friendly, or any potential threat, as to our status. Observe, stay close, be prepared to shelter and defend." Savino's hesitance was a physical thing. "You'll receive a package by special courier within the next two days."

Weapons. Diego pressed his fingers against his eyelids, trying to rub away the pressure's edge.

"Sir, if Ms. Maclean is in danger, shouldn't steps be taken? A safe house, debriefing—"

"Steps have been taken," Savino interrupted. "You."

Shit.

Diego didn't have to monitor his response since Savino had hung up, so he indulged himself in another few minutes of creative cussing. Then he did what he'd been trained to do.

He took a deep breath, grabbed the can off the floor and began cleanup.

It didn't matter what his feelings were. He'd suck it up and do the job.

CHAPTER FOURTEEN

"Mmm, delicious."

"I haven't even started cooking yet." It took only a glance for Harper to realize that Andi wasn't talking about dinner. The other woman was leaning so far into the bay window that all Harper could see was a black ponytail and a denim-covered rear. "Admit it. You only invited yourself to dinner as an excuse to check Diego out."

"Well, I would have hired an investigator, but I figured you'd object."

"You figured right." Harper rolled her eyes at her friend. "You're the one who nudged and nagged at me to do something about my sex life. Quit worrying now that I have."

"I'm not worrying," Andi denied. At Harper's arch look she shrugged. "Okay, only a little."

She turned back to the window, craning her neck to enjoy the view. "But I have to admit, he looks worthy of that smile you're wearing."

Unable to resist, Harper finished adding herbs to the marinade, then hurried across the kitchen to join Andi at the breakfast nook.

Mmm, yeah. Diego was nothing if not incredible.

He was dressed. She knew that, but couldn't say what he was wearing except to note that if he'd been naked she'd be smiling a lot brighter.

All she really saw was the sleek man with skin like gold using the huge oak tree next door to do pull-ups. Something she knew he did on a regular basis—with or without the tree. His muscles looked like they were sculpted from marble, and she knew that they felt just as sleek. The broad shoulders she'd held so tight only hours before when he'd taken her against the wall gave way to a drool-worthy chest—which, yes, she had drooled on. His waist tapered, framing the most amazing six-pack Harper had ever rubbed her naked body over. The dusting of hair accented rather than covered that skin, and his happy trail pointed the way to heaven.

Harper's mouth watered as images of that heaven filled her mind. Memories of how good it had felt to visit there. Anticipation over how soon she'd enjoy it again.

God, he was wonderful.

His arms rippled, sun glinting off his damp skin as he pulled his chin up to touch the branch, released, then did it again. With each pull-up, Harper could feel her belly bunching, contracting, tightening in time with those muscles.

"Very nice," Andi murmured.

She had no idea. Harper didn't say that, though. She simply took one more look before moving back into the kitchen.

"When are you going to introduce us?" Andi wondered, following Harper's lead with a sigh. "He's joining us for dinner, right? Did you tell him that shirts are optional?"

Harper's blood warmed, her thighs trembling a little at the idea of sitting down to dinner across from a shirtless Diego.

"He's not joining us."

Andi laughed and shook her head. "No, seriously. What time is he coming over?"

"Okay, seriously. He's not."

Harper pulled vegetables from the fridge, stacking the choices in her arm as if the perfect zucchini would prevent this from turning into something she couldn't handle.

She'd talked herself out of the crazy idea that she was falling in love with Diego. It was ridiculous. They'd only been sleeping together for a week. And while it'd been an intense week, there was still so much they didn't know about each other. Too much.

Besides, she didn't want a man in her life long term. More important, she knew Diego wasn't looking for more than sex. She'd be setting herself up for heart-break to think otherwise.

"I thought it was better to keep things casual and separate," Harper said as she moved to the sink. "This thing with Diego, it's just for now."

"And when Nathan gets home?"

Harper glanced over her shoulder to give Andi what she hoped was a nonchalant look. The sort a savvy woman used to affairs would offer. Since she was afraid it came off as more of a heartsick grimace, she didn't try to hold it for long.

"When Nathan gets home, life is back to normal." Heartsick or not, that wouldn't change. It wasn't as if great sex was worth turning a life inside out over.

"Okay. But Nathan's not home yet, is he? So why are you keeping the hottie on the other side of the fence?"

"Because you're only just back from your trip and this is our dinner together," Harper said, carrying the fresh veggies to the island, where she'd already laid out the cutting block and knife. "Dinner which you're going to help with. So start cutting."

"Harper." As she started slicing and dicing, Andi searched Harper's face. "Are you okay?"

"Of course. Now instead of obsessing with my sex life, why don't you tell me about your trip?"

"Oh, so you want to talk about my sex life instead?"

Laughing, Harper started on the salad as Andi entertained her with tales of Greece.

By the time the vegetables were chopped and the green leaf torn, she felt as if she'd taken a vacation on a sunny beach.

"You and Nathan should come with me next time," Andi invited.

"Someday." When they could pay their own way.

"In the meantime, I think you should invite your neighbor to join us for dinner. How am I supposed to check him out if he's not here?"

"You don't need to check him out. You need to mind your own business," Harper said, rolling her eyes.

"Fine, be stubborn." With an exaggerated shrug and a look of supreme indifference, Andi set the knife on the cutting board and slid off the stool. "I've finished my contribution to the dinner prep by cutting the vegetables. And your hot lover is still working out. So, if you'll excuse me, I'm going to powder my nose and refine my plot to change your mind."

"Not going to happen."

Harper's smile turned bittersweet as Andi laughed her way down the hall. She might not be able to resist sex with Diego—and why should she? She was young and healthy. He was fun and sweet. And, of course, the sex was mind-blowing.

But it wasn't love. There was no such thing.

And maybe if she told herself that a few million more times, she'd believe it.

Harper clenched her teeth against the snap of pain the thought sent crawling down her spine. Pushing it aside, she added cremini mushrooms and asparagus to a bag, then poured a mixture of olive oil, balsamic vinegar, herbs and garlic over the vegetables, then zipped the bag closed.

Harper gripped the bag of soaking vegetables tightly and shook it to the beat of the soft-playing music.

Adding a little footwork and hip action, she worked her way across the kitchen and back again. As Nickelback listed all the wrong reasons, a movement outside the window caught her eye.

Since Andi hadn't returned and couldn't make a big deal out of it, Harper stepped around the island to see what Diego was doing. She hoped he was still exercising. She hadn't been able to fully appreciate the play of muscles and gleam of sweat over that sleek body with a matchmaking magpie nagging over her shoulder.

Son of a...

She tossed the bag of marinating vegetables on the counter and ran for the door.

HALFWAY THROUGH HIS karate drill, with one eye on the house next door and the sun sliding to bed in a blaze of color, Diego thought back to his call from Savino. The package hadn't arrived yet, and he hadn't received any further information.

It was damned frustrating. He calculated his options, played out the various potential scenarios.

And thought about Harper.

He'd never known anyone like her. Sassy and clever, elegant and sweet.

She was, in her way, as dedicated to her career as he was to his. She studied design magazines as if they were holy scripts, read the newspaper from front to back and kept up with societies' doings. Not for the sake of gossip, she'd told him, but to stay informed for her clientele. Knowing what to talk about and what was off-limits was apparently as important as the difference between rococo and chintz. Since he wasn't sure what either was, he'd taken her word for it.

And she kept walls between them. It had nothing to do with Ramsey and the mission Diego was investigating. And everything, he suspected, to do with Ramsey and Harper's past.

So far, Diego had let it ride. He wasn't a man who sought intimacy. But he found himself wanting it. Beyond sex, which was pretty damned mind-blowingly awesome, he wanted more.

Even though he knew better.

For now, he needed to focus. He'd work out, find his center, move past the guilt that was eating at his gut. Then he'd casually wander over to say hello.

Five minutes later, he had to admit that while he could finish his workout, inner peace was not to be found.

Not with a mouthy brunette yapping at him.

What was the world coming to when a man couldn't get a quiet workout in his backyard while spying on the woman he was sleeping with?

It'd started with a friendly, "Welcome to the neighborhood" from the class act who'd strolled across Harper's backyard as if she were walking the red carpet. His intel was solid. He knew who she was, what she did, even her net worth. But he hadn't been prepared for her babbling. Before he'd even finished his pull-up, she'd started with the questions. If words were bullets, Diego was being peppered with a barrage, and they kept coming, fast and furious.

So far, he'd kept his answers short and his eye on the house in hopes that Harper would come to the rescue. There wasn't much in life that scared Diego, but a matchmaking woman weighing his worth just might make the list.

"The Lowensteins are in Europe for two months. Are you subletting for their entire vacation?"

"Maybe." Wiping the sweat off his forehead with the back of his forearm, Diego wondered if the woman had trained with Special Ops. She had one hell of an interrogation style.

"Maybe? Do you always live so spontaneously?"

He thought of the day in, day out routine and protocol that made up his world in between covert ops and life-risking missions.

"Pretty much."

"So what, exactly, do you do that keeps you living out of a suitcase in such an upscale neighborhood?"

No bullshit here. Diego grinned, starting to enjoy her style. "I'm a security specialist." He waited a beat before asking, "Did you want my credit score?"

"Thanks, but I can get that myself," the brunette said, waving his sarcasm away with an elegant hand covered in diamonds. "Why don't we talk about Harper, instead?"

"Why don't we," he agreed, enjoying the timing as the woman in question slammed her way out her back door.

With a hint of a grimace, the woman turned to watch Harper hightail it across the patio. She looked like spring. Bright and light in a pretty dress that made him think of an ice-cream cone.

"Now you're in for it," Diego said with a laugh, enjoying the way the full skirt swished and swayed, showing flashes of things under the vivid pink.

"You don't know the half of it," the brunette murmured in agreement.

"Andrianna, stop right now," Harper called before she reached them.

"She's so bossy." Andi slanted a look at Harper. "I'd love to know your life story. But Harper has her grumpy face on."

"And why not," Harper muttered under her breath as she reached them. "You said you were powdering your nose. Not poking it in where it doesn't belong."

Diego reached over the stylized wrought iron fence to skim his fingers along Harper's cheek in greeting before focusing on the brunette again.

"You're not afraid of Harper's grumpiness, are you?"

"Well, she is taller than I am, and she has a deep streak of mean," Andi said, dropping her voice to a confiding tone as she leaned one elbow on the fence as if she was settling in for a round of gossip. "You don't want to piss her off."

"Is that a fact?" Brows arched, Diego watched Harper's eyes flash with irritation. She'd crossed her arms over her chest, the move highlighting the swell of her breasts as they rose in creamy temptation above a froth of lace. She wore her hair in a high ponytail that left her face unframed but for a series of small gold balls dangling from her ears.

"True fact," Andi confirmed.

"She does have long legs," Diego agreed, his gaze dropping to what he could see of those legs below her skirt. The color of pale gold, they looked like silk. He knew they'd feel the same.

"And a prurient streak," Andi confided. "She's so weird about nosy friends not minding their own business. I'm sure that's why she didn't invite you to join us for dinner. She's afraid I'll ask all sorts of rude questions and embarrass you, her or both."

"Do you have a standard list of embarrassing questions?" he wondered. He was sure now that Ramsey had never come around, that Andi had never met the man. But that didn't mean she hadn't met others Harper had dated. "Or do you just wing it, depending on who she invites over?"

"She's standing right here," Harper interrupted before Andi could respond. She disguised a laugh as a huff, waved one hand in the air before pointing toward her house. "And she's about to be there. The two of you can go ahead—keep playing."

With that, she spun around. Because he was watching for it this time, Diego caught sight of the opening in her skirt as it swished wide. Damn, she had some great legs. He watched her go, hips swaying and skirt rustling, and rubbed a hand over his stubbled chin. Just how long was it going to take before he could make use of that side-split skirt and get his hands on those legs again?

When she reached the door, Harper called out, "Dinner is in half an hour."

Her gaze met his, and she offered a sweet smile. His body reacted the same as if she'd run her hand up his thigh. Diego didn't get it. A good forty feet separated them, so the smile shouldn't be like a kick of lust.

Yet it was.

He watched even after she went inside, wondering why he didn't feel the same gut-wrenching guilt when he was with her as he did when he wasn't.

It wasn't as if he forgot about his mission, forgot

the stakes, when they were together. He never forgot his duty. But somehow, with her, duty was no longer everything.

"Ahem."

"Yeah?" he responded, watching Harper through the window as she moved around the kitchen.

"I take it you're enjoying the neighborhood, and I don't blame you. There's a lot here to treasure." Andi waited until he met her eyes again before continuing. "Someday I'll have to share the story about another man who lived in this neighborhood. He enjoyed it, too. Unfortunately, he didn't appreciate it. It's a shame what happens when a man fails to value a treasure when it's gifted to him."

Diego tilted his head to one side. Was that a threat?

He played that back twice, just to be sure. Then he laughed. The woman was all of five-foot-nothing and looked like the most she could break was a fingernail.

"Do you often threaten people within five minutes of the first hello?" he asked. Not that he was judging. Not when he tended to do the same thing.

"Threats are so pedestrian," she stated. "Let's just call it friendly advice from someone who cares a great deal about her friend."

"I appreciate friendship."

That was all he'd give her. All he could give her.

Apparently, he realized when she nodded, it was enough.

"So, Harper said dinner in thirty minutes and she's the Queen of Punctual. Are you joining us?"

"Only an idiot would pass up a chance to have dinner with two beautiful women. Especially if the meal includes embarrassing questions."

"Charming." Her smile was approving, but it didn't dim her watchful expression.

"I'll be over in a few minutes. I need to clean up."

He wasn't a vain man, but those words usually earned him an assessing once-over. Andi's eyes never shifted, either from disinterest or loyalty to her friend.

"You do that. I'll stir up a pitcher of something alcoholic. We'll chat."

"Okay by me," he said, grabbing his shirt. No point telling her that whatever her worries were, they had nothing on reality.

Halfway to the house, he stopped and glanced over his shoulder.

"That unappreciative guy, you need me to kick his ass? Or did you already make him pay?"

"You're a sweetheart for offering, but there's no need. Believe me—I left him bleeding," Andi drawled, her smile as satisfied as a cat wrapped in canary feathers.

Diego nodded, sure she'd done just that.

"Five minutes" was all he said.

ANDI WATCHED DIEGO man the barbecue. He had the air of a guy who knew his way around fire. After one look at the vegetables and chicken, he'd grabbed a slab of red meat from his own kitchen and offered to do the honors. With all the prep work done, that left Harper and Andi to lounge with the pitcher of margaritas and enjoy the show.

"Satisfied?" Harper asked.

"Not yet, but you seem to be. Now that I've had an up close and personal, I'll bet he's even better than I'd imagined. Big hands," she explained, holding her own out with fingers splayed wide.

"No comment," Harper said.

But Andi didn't need a comment to know. Her friend's satisfied smile said it all.

"I like it," Andi said at length. "I like seeing you this way."

"Lazing by the pool with a margarita in hand and a full pitcher at my side?"

"Happy."

Harper glowed, an air of satisfaction wrapped around her like a shimmering blanket. But the nerves were there, just beneath the surface. Was it the man causing them? Or something else?

Regretting for a moment that she hadn't run a background check on him before dinner, Andi inclined her head toward the man frowning at the cooking strips of zucchini and mushroom. "I like the way he watches you. Like a starving man about to feast on a buffet of his favorite treats."

Color washed delicately over Harper's cheeks as she shook her head.

"It's just sex," she said, her laugh a poor attempt at sophisticated dismissal.

Andi would give her the sophistication. In everything but men. There, Harper was as innocent as a babe. Worry worked its way down her spine, worry that came dangerously close to remorse.

"Maybe you should slow it down a little," she heard herself murmur. "Maybe you should think it over a little more carefully."

"Fortunately, there isn't a lot of thinking required. With Diego, it's pretty much all about feeling." Harper's smile faded. "What's the problem?"

"You remember what I said, don't you?" Andi tapped her fingers on the arm of her chair. "About myths and fantasies? Don't fall for the myth because of good sex."

"I'm not stupid," Harper snapped. "And it's not good—it's spectacular. Besides, you're the one who's always telling me to let go and enjoy. So I've let go. I'm enjoying."

Diego chose that moment to join them, striding over with a tray of perfectly cooked meat. He smiled at them both, but the look in his eyes was for Harper alone.

"Nathan called this morning," Harper said as they all began dishing up their food. "He is having a great time."

"Now aren't you glad I talked you into sending him?" Andi said, pleased to be proven right.

"You convinced Harper to let Nathan go to camp?" Diego asked, looking like a man who'd just nudged a puzzle piece into place.

"She even paid his way," Harper said with a grateful look that made Andi want to squirm. "She's always doing that sort of thing."

"It's no big deal, and I knew he'd love it." Ignoring Diego's assessing look, Andi shrugged and cut a tiny piece of meat from the sliver she'd allowed herself. As Harper described the phone call and her son's adventures, Andi watched the man watch her friend.

He was attentive. He listened more than he talked, but his sense of humor was apparent in his sly and dry comments. He had a quiet intensity, which was a great match for Harper's smooth polish.

He seemed genuine. More, he seemed to be totally into Harper.

Still, something about him nagged at her.

It couldn't hurt to get a quick rundown on him. Harper didn't have to know, and Andi would feel better confirming he was who he said he was. Of course, she'd married Matt knowing that he was who he said, and look where that got her.

Still…

A movement next door caught her eye.

Oh, my. Talk about hot. The night's shadows couldn't dim the bright golden-boy looks.

"A friend of yours?" She tilted her head toward the neighboring yard, hoping Diego would invite the man over. He was gorgeous.

But Diego didn't appear too excited to see him. It was like watching a door slam shut. His expression blanked, his voice neutralized and his body language closed.

"Excuse me." With that and a nod, Diego rose, striding toward his yard without a backward look.

"Hmm," Andi said, angling a look at Harper, who only shrugged.

"Whoever the man is, he doesn't seem excited to see him," Harper murmured, too quietly for the words to carry over the night air.

"Do you think he'll invite him over? Better yet, should we?"

"If Diego wants him to join us, he'll handle the invitation." Still, Harper hurried inside to fetch another place setting.

Andi stayed where she was, eyeing the newcomer. As boyishly handsome as a teenage girl's fantasy, his body the sort that only a woman could truly appreciate. Lean muscle spoke of strength; his bright smile promised charm.

Mmm, yeah. She could enjoy getting to know him. A lot better.

Best of all, she wouldn't need that background check now. She'd just get all the information she wanted out of Diego's friend.

CHAPTER FIFTEEN

"WHAT THE HELL are you doing here?"

"Savino told you to expect a delivery." Lansky slapped both hands to his chest, then threw them out. "I'm it. Grateful?"

"To see you?" Diego sucked his breath in through his teeth but managed to keep his smile in place. Despite the guy's lousy attitude lately, he really was glad to see him. He and Lansky had served together, hung out together, been friends for a decade. He was a brother.

But the timing? That he wasn't so crazy about.

"We're heading in?" Diego asked in a neutral tone. His expression didn't change, nor did the casual tone of his body language.

That was training. Because while he wasn't sure what he was, he knew it sure as hell wasn't neutral.

Because he wasn't ready to leave Harper.

"Nope. I'm here as backup," Lansky said casually, snagging a bottle of water from the fridge. He toasted Diego with it before chugging. "We broke through another layer of Ramsey's security. The guy's obsessed with your girlfriend over there. He's got enough files on her and the kid to put him in the stalker hall of fame."

The perfectly done steak churned in Diego's gut.

"Savino thinks he's coming for her?"

"You know Savino. He didn't mention his actual

thoughts to me. He just said to get my ass up here and play backup."

"Has Ramsey's partner been identified?"

"Negative. Which is why you and I are currently on recon and regroup. The Kahuna is dodging, said he needs backup. In the meantime, we can't neutralize what hasn't been identified. So we're on containment until replacements arrive."

"Who's the replacement team?"

"Whoever Savino clears," Lansky said as if it wasn't a big deal that most of the team was under suspicion.

But they both knew it was a huge deal. A career-breaking, betrayal-making, life-ruining deal.

"When's next contact?"

"Three days."

So that's how long they had before Savino figured out who was dirty, who'd betrayed team and country, who'd screwed them all over and left them hanging out to dry. Or he'd turn it over to Naval Investigation.

One way or another, in three days he'd be back on base, back on regular duty, back to his regular life.

And saying goodbye to Harper.

"Three days?" he said, staring out the window.

Well, if that was all he had…

"C'mon. I'll introduce you to Andi."

THE MEN RETURNED, both looking at Harper with a laser-sharp focus that made Andi nervous.

What the hell was going on? Whatever it was, it was trouble.

How much was her responsibility, Andi wondered. If she hadn't nagged Harper to break her sexual drought, would trouble be strolling into the backyard looking like pure temptation? The sort of temptation that could hurt a woman. Then again, Andi argued with herself, Harper was a grown woman who had every right to explore her sexuality and enjoy her life.

Still, if Harper got hurt, it was all Diego's fault.

But Andi wouldn't—couldn't—idly sit by and let it happen.

Her fingers tapping time to the muted music coming from inside the house, Andi nibbled at her bottom lip, her gaze shifting from man to man. She wouldn't get anything more from Diego than she already had. He'd been tough enough before, but it was as if he'd wrapped himself in a sheet of implacableness.

But the cutie?

Andi studied him as Diego made the introductions, keeping her smile artless, her eyes guileless. Easy enough to do, she'd had years of practice hiding behind both. But her mind raced.

These weren't just ordinary guys. They both had a little too much testosterone going on. There was something military about them, with their short haircuts, ripped bodies and powerful bearing. The way they spoke, the way they moved, right down to their gestures, were coordinated. As if they'd spent a great deal of time together.

But for all their ease with each other, there was an underlying anger. For all Jared's casual attitude, he had an almost imperceptible air of deference toward Diego.

Oh, yeah, something was going on.

Time to find out just exactly what that something was.

"Welcome back, gentlemen," she greeted them, curling her legs under her and making a show of looking comfortable. "Ready for dessert?"

"Haven't had dinner yet," Jared said with a grin. He

patted his flat belly. "Could use some red meat and a drink."

Diego was a couple of steps ahead of him, using the barbecue fork to spear the second huge steak that he'd left resting next to the grill. He wordlessly tossed it onto the plate Harper had fetched before dropping himself into the chair he'd vacated when his friend arrived.

"Looks great," Jared said, lifting the slab of meat with his fork and grinning when its weight bent the tines. "Really great. Thanks."

And that was that.

The visitor dug into his red meat. Diego sat, scowling. And other than offering her surprise dinner guest vegetables and bread, which he refused, and fetching his beer, which he downed in a couple of gulps, Harper was silent.

Andi gave it five minutes, but that was as long as her patience held out.

"So, Jared, tell me all about yourself."

"Not much to tell, ma'am." His smile was pure charm. "Just a good ol' boy from a small town in Montana. Got two sisters still there. But me? I don't do so well with snow. So I hightailed it to a warmer climate."

"Did you do a lot of comparison shopping before you chose California?"

With the expertise of a woman raised to be a society hostess, Andi used flirtatious charm to subtly grill the guy. But he was good. While she and Jared chatted, Harper murmured something to Diego that turned his scowl into a smile. He shook it off with a simple turn of his head, but it was as if that simple reconnection had opened the door, reminding them both of something sexy.

Andi's concern still nagged at her. Her uneasiness

didn't stop the sexual heat from sparking between her and Jared, though. As it had all evening, a simple look, the presence of friendly banter, they were sending out waves of desire hot enough to drive a devout monk in search of a party girl.

Andi figured that she could either ignore those sparks or use them to her advantage. She decided to use them, of course.

So while Harper looked at Diego like she wanted to coat him with chocolate and lick him clean and Diego pretended that he wasn't interested, Andi moved her chair a little closer to Jared's.

"And you work with Diego?" she asked, adding a teasing skim of her finger over his forearm. Both because she wanted to fluster him into saying more and because it was fun.

"Yes, ma'am. We do work together. In security." He pointed his fork at his friend. "What's it been, man? Six years now?"

"Then you must have all sorts of juicy details." Andi slanted a look at Diego. "Your friend is frustratingly unforthcoming about himself."

"You want dirt, I'm your guy." Nodding his head toward Harper in thanks for the meal, Jared tossed his napkin on his empty plate. He nudged it forward with his elbows as he rested them on the table. "Problem is, I can't dish what ain't there."

"Oh, please. Everyone has something juicy to tell."

"You'd think so, wouldn't you?" Jared's tone was amused, but there was something in his face that said she'd better back off. Whether because he wasn't about to betray his friend or because he simply didn't think she could handle the truth wasn't clear.

Diego didn't seem concerned.

"Andi," Harper murmured, giving Diego an apologetic look. "Stop."

Andi debated for all of a second before demurring to her friend's request. Well, that and to the knowledge that she wasn't going to get anything worthwhile out of Jared while Diego was sitting right there.

So she changed tactics. She morphed into the chatty social butterfly most of society thought she was. Easily drawing the men into conversation, she bounced the discussion from sightseeing in California to snow in Montana to skiing in Switzerland.

A half hour later, her ploy was working. Harper and Diego had gone inside under the guise of KP, as Diego called it. Added to that, Jared seemed to have lost that defensive edge she'd noticed when he'd first sat down.

Instead, she noted with a smile, he was playing her just as tightly as she was playing him.

"So you and Harper, you've been friends a long time?"

"Not quite as long as you and Diego."

"She seems like a nice lady." But the look he slanted toward the house said he wasn't so sure. "Diego mentioned she has a kid. What about the father? Is he the type to stake claim? Gonna burst in here in a jealous rage, or start a pissing match because she's otherwise occupied?"

Ahh, wasn't that sweet. He was worried about his friend getting his heart crushed.

Her distrust melting a little, Andi rubbed a soothing hand over the back of his. "The only male in Harper's life is her son," she assured him. "At least, he was until she met Diego."

"That's probably worse," Jared remarked, opening another beer. "She's a pretty lady. I've never known a guy with a pretty ex who didn't harbor at least a little jealousy."

"Not Harper's ex. Firstly, because the scum-sucking pig deserted her before the babe had even formed in her belly." Andi's teeth snapped off the words but couldn't do much to dim her fury at any man who'd leave the mother of his unborn child like that. "He never met his son, never offered support of any kind."

"No way. None at all?"

"Absolutely none." She shrugged when Jared gave a skeptical shake of his head. "And, of course, the guy is dead. Believe me—he won't be any trouble."

"Sounds like Diego's in the clear then," Jared decided with a hard-to-read look in his eyes. "Maybe we should get out of their way, give them a little time alone while we get to know each other better."

"Should we?" Andi asked with a flirtatious look.

Jared's smile turned unexpectedly wicked. Then he gave her a look, long, intense and interested.

"I know this great place. Good drinks, great music. You dance?"

Was he asking her out? No, he was asking her to bed. The Boy Scout features might fool some women but not Andi. She might have been living without sex since her divorce, but she easily recognized a proposition when it winked at her.

An unfamiliar quiver of nerves did a fast hustle through her belly. Enjoying that as much as the attraction, Andi slowly nodded.

"I'm a great dancer," she promised. "But before we decide on the music, why don't we dish that dirt? Tell me about Diego."

Jared pursed his lips while studying her face, then finished off his beer. Always a good hostess, Andi automatically rose to get another from the small outdoor fridge Harper had stocked before dinner.

Apparently that gave Jared enough time to decide how he wanted to respond, because he had that distance in his eyes again. Who knew detachment could be so sexy?

"Diego is a good man. A little stubborn, a little narrow in his focus sometimes, but he's good. That's about the best compliment I can give."

"Good in what way?"

"Good in that he's a man who sees the right path, who does the right thing. Even when others question, he acts. Even when others doubt, he perseveres."

Impressed with anyone who could inspire another man to wax poetic, Andi's gaze shifted toward the window. Diego had Harper backed up against a wall, his hands braced on either side so she was barely visible.

Sexy.

"That sounds like business," she mused, noting that Diego's stance had shifted and he now trailed one hand down Harper's cheek in what looked like a gentle caress.

Sweet.

"Business, sure. Usually he's aces there." Jared emptied the beer. "Usually."

He added his empty bottle to the others on the table, then shrugged as if trying to shake off whatever worry had inspired that "usually."

"But always pulling aces could get boring, right? Gotta have a few challenges now and then to keep things interesting," he said.

Andi didn't like the sound of that. "And whatever is challenging him?"

Jared's eyes stayed clear; his smile didn't shift. But

she saw something there that made her breath catch in her throat. "Why don't we hit that club, do some dancing?" he suggested before she could figure out what it was.

Heat flared, swirled, tempted.

Andi knew there was something bad about this good-looking man. He clung to secrecy the way her father clung to his financial portfolio. He talked in double-speak with the skill of a politician while smiling like a choirboy.

Lips pursed, her eyes trailed over the tidy line of empty bottles. And he drank like a frat boy, yet showed no sign of inebriation.

She wasn't a stupid woman. All of that should put him off-limits. Yet Andi found herself holding out her hand in invitation.

"I know the perfect place."

DIEGO WOKE, HIS face buried in the soft scent of Harper's hair and his arms filled with the delight of her curves. She hummed against his chest, stretching so her body slid over his like silk. She was such a study of contrasts. Soft and sweet, sharply sexy.

She made him feel…so much.

Too damned much.

"I don't understand," he murmured.

"Don't understand what?"

"How a woman as amazing as you would end up involved with a man like—" Realizing what he'd been about to reveal, Diego bit down on the words and took a breath before shifting gears. "A man like Nathan's father. He took advantage of you, Harper. He used you. Hurt you. Hurt Nathan."

"And it's over," she said dismissively, pushing out

of his arms. He let her go when he saw the expression on her face. Frustration battled anger, but under it was shame bordering on self-disgust. "Look, whatever else he did, Brandon gave me the most precious gift of my life. Nathan. How could I hate him?"

Because he'd left her, alone and pregnant and broke? Because at twenty-two, he should have known better than to screw around with a seventeen-year-old?

Because the fucker had kept tabs on her, using the kid he'd abandoned as a ploy to con the men he served with before screwing them over, injuring one and committing treason?

"Diego?"

"What?" It wasn't until he'd blinked a couple of times to clear the fury from his vision that he realized his hands were fisted on the sheets, his face tight with the need to pound them into a man who was, in some people's opinion, dead.

"Let it go," she said softly. Either unaffected by or simply ignoring the violence emanating from him, she lay down again. Her thigh pressed against his, her eyes as gentle as the hand she laid against his cheek.

"I realize you're angry on my behalf. That you're the sort of man with a strong sense of right and wrong. But I'm okay with the way things turned out. I'm happy with the results. I have Nathan."

From her expression, he knew she'd made her peace with that. He'd seen that same look on his mom's face. Pain, resignation and an odd sort of gratitude because the worthless jerk had given her a son to love.

He'd thought it was crap then. He thought it was crap now.

Diego scrubbed his hand over his hair and, for her sake, tried to let the anger go. But it wouldn't budge.

The best he could do was set it aside and deal with it later.

He had other things to deal with now. Most important was getting that look of doubt out of her eyes.

She deserved better than Ramsey.

Hell, she deserved better than him.

Something he was pretty sure she'd agree with in a day or so. Diego pushed off the bed, needing to dissipate the sudden tension ripping through his body.

"Diego? What's wrong?"

"Just trying to figure out what to do."

"About what?"

Everything. Every damned thing. "Look, I care about you. A lot. More than I'd figured I could." He threw up a hand when she started to rise. He needed to get this out before she touched him or he'd distract them both with sex. "But my career, it saved my life. It pulled me out of an ugly place. It's been my whole world for my entire adult life. It's who I am."

Afraid he was about to apologize, knowing he probably should, Diego blew out a breath.

"Do you get what I'm saying?" he asked, grimacing.

"Of course I understand what you're saying," Harper assured him, crossing over to take his hand. "It's the same for me. I mean, Nathan changed my life. Because of him, I became who I am now, I pursued the career I did, and to a huge degree it defines who I am."

She did get it. He hoped she still got it in a few days. He didn't figure there was a chance in hell that she would, but he could still hope.

"You wanna take a ride today?" Diego skimmed the back of his finger over her face, tracing the sharp edge of her cheekbone before sliding his thumb along her bottom lip. "We can cruise down the coast, hit the beach, take it easy. Just get away."

He saw the answer in her eyes. Before she could put the refusal into words, he tucked his finger under her chin to lift her mouth to his. A brush of the lips, a slow slide of the tongue.

"Oh, my," she breathed, shakily enough to give his ego a nice, long stroke. Since his ego wasn't the only thing wanting to be stroked, Diego pulled her tight against his growing erection. Her eyes blurred, and she gave a little hip swivel that sent the blood careening out of his brain, right down to his dick.

Oh, yeah. This was all the distraction he needed.

"No, wait. No." Before he could stop her, Harper yanked herself out of his arms and hurried to the other side of the room. She threw out her palm and shook her head before he could grab her back. "I can't."

"Take it from me, babe. You can. You really can."

"I'm glad you think so." Her eyes lit with delight as she gave a breathless laugh, shoving her hair off her face. He didn't need a stop sign to see that her no was firm. "But still…"

Her words trailed off into a sigh as her eyes narrowed.

"What's up?" He had the urge to shove his hands into his pockets, but given that he was bare-assed naked and she'd already dry-docked the idea of sex, he didn't figure it for a smart idea.

"I wouldn't mind taking the ride, but today's Saturday," she said slowly, sounding like she hadn't decided if she was going to tell him what was up or not.

"You said you weren't working this weekend, didn't you? So you've got something else to do? No problem." Diego looked around, then snagged his jeans off the floor.

What a dumb ass. Had he thought that he'd sweep her away, give her a romantic day to remember? Prove to them both that he could hold his own romancing a classy woman like Harper Maclean? Hell, he wouldn't know romance if it bit him on the ass.

Too pissed at himself to risk the zipper, Diego left the pants loose as he hunted around for his shirt.

He'd use the time to toss the house and see what he could find. Dig through the drawers, tap into her computer again. Might as well top off sleeping with the objective by pawing through her privacy. Bottom line, despite everything she'd said, she was still their only link to Ramsey. Stupid move or not, that was why he was here.

He looked around for his shirt, freezing when he saw it dangling from Harper's finger.

"Are you okay?" she asked, her eyes intent on his face.

"Yeah, fine." When he reached for his shirt, she pulled it away. Figuring he already felt like enough of an ass, he didn't make a play for it. Instead, because they were there this time, he shoved his hands into the front pockets of his jeans. "Why? What's up?"

"Today is Parents' Day at camp," she said, sounding excited. "They do a tour, a demonstration and lunch, even."

"Oh."

"I know it probably doesn't sound like much. It'll probably take most of the day. Nathan says I'm not the camping type." The rush of words was filled with doubt and a sort of apology that made him feel like a jerk. "But

I have to go. I miss him like crazy, and this is the only visitation before camp ends next week."

Diego offered the only apology he could under the circumstances. He stepped in, crowding her up against the dresser as he scooped his fingers through her bed-tousled hair. His eyes locked on hers, he rubbed a soft kiss over her lips.

"You're a great mom. The kid's gonna get a kick out of showing you all the fun he's having." He leaned in again, this time letting the kiss heat to a nice simmer. His tongue teased along the seam of her lips but didn't delve deeper. He ended with a scrape of his teeth over the cushioned softness, then lifted his head. "I can be around when you get back."

He didn't bother to detail what he'd be around for. From the way her gaze shifted past his shoulder to the bed before meeting his again with a look, hot interest made it clear that she could fill in those details just fine herself.

"Um, yeah, that'd be good," she murmured. Then she shook her head as if tossing off distraction. "Unless maybe you'd like to spend the day with me."

Shit. Shit, damn, hell.

Diego knew he should stay here. He should assess the situation, make sure her house was secure before he left for good. He should spend this last day ensuring her safety instead of romancing a woman he had no future with.

"I KNOW IT's not very romantic. Or probably very exciting. But we could spend the day together this way. And Nathan would love to see you," Harper said, trying to slow her rush of words. She wrinkled her nose, mocking the nervous burst.

All her years of building a sophisticated shell seemed stripped away, leaving her bare but for the emotions rippling through her. "What do you say? Want to spend the day with me? No big deal if you don't want to," she added quickly, seeing the frown forming and the look of hesitation in his eyes.

"I should stay here," he said in a tone that implied he didn't want to. "I've got some things I should do."

Harper bit her lip. As her mind warned her to let it go, she found herself sliding her foot along the length of his leg.

"I know it's not quite the day you were thinking of. But you're welcome to join me anyway." She paused to run her tongue over her bottom lip, reveling in the way Diego's eyes followed the move. "Parents' Day only lasts until three. Maybe we could take an evening bike ride."

"What time do we leave?" he asked with a wicked smile, his fingers dancing over her hips and down to cup her butt, tucking under her cheeks to lift her against his burgeoning erection.

Heat curled in her belly, wet pooled between her legs as Harper rubbed against him. Oh, man, what was she doing? Her breath shook, even as her heart trembled at the look in his eyes. He was so sweet. So supportive. And, oh my God, so sexy.

Nathan might not realize what it would mean when she brought Diego with her to a family-focused event. There was absolutely no way he'd clue in that his mom was sleeping with a man he considered a rival of Han Solo on his list of cool people.

And nobody else would care.

Except Harper. She'd care. She'd know what it meant to bring a man to Parents' Day. She'd have to face how deep her feelings must be if she were to open that part of her life to someone, to Diego.

The only thing she wasn't sure of was how much she was risking. Just a piece of her heart? Or all of it?

Ready to take a chance, Harper pressed both hands against the rigidly cut muscles of his chest, skimming upward. Teasing. Delighting.

It could be a mistake. But all Harper could do was listen to her heart. After all, what were the chances that it'd steer her wrong twice in a lifetime?

"Oh, I'd say we have time for at least two more orgasms before we leave," she murmured with a sigh of pleasure.

CHAPTER SIXTEEN

OH, BABY.

She liked riding a Harley.

Lips carefully closed over her teeth—she'd heard enough bug jokes to be careful—Harper smiled as the power, the rhythm, the intensity roaring between her thighs reminded her of Diego.

The erotic charge was intense, maybe because she was still oversensitive from their morning bout of lovemaking. *Bouts*, she corrected herself with a sigh as she watched a pair of sailboats disappear from view.

They'd made love when they woke, again after they'd decided to spend the day together, once in the shower, then he'd taken her one more time—one crazy, shocking time against the wall before they'd walked out the door. She'd still had her purse across her body and her boots on her feet when he'd plunged into her ready heat.

Harper trembled at the memory and wrapped her arms tighter around his waist. Taking a break from the view, she rested her cheek against his back. His leather jacket was warm in comparison to the chilly air sweeping over them.

The view driving up the coast was like something out of a movie reel. Blue oceans, bluer skies and so much green between as they moved from coast to mountain to coast again.

Mmm, this was good. A new experience, a sexy man

and a ride to see her son. A contented pleasure filled Harper, making her think that she could get used to this sort of thing.

So it was with regret that she eventually swung her leg off the bike once Diego parked in the ferry lot.

"Whoa." She grabbed him when her legs, thrumming from the ride, went lax from thigh to ankle.

"Careful." Grinning, Diego wrapped one arm around her while he removed his helmet with the other. "Take a second. It's like getting your sea legs."

Tugging her helmet off, Harper laughed. "It's fabulous. I had no idea."

Like hers, his eyes were shielded by sunglasses. But she could feel the answering heat, knew he was just as affected as she was.

There was so much power in that.

Harper leaned into him, letting her breasts press against his chest. She liked the pressure, even through the jacket's layers of leather.

She knew he was looking at her mouth. She could practically feel his eyes caressing her lips. She wet them, hoping to lure him into doing just that.

One hand shifted from her hair to slide her glasses free. She should feel vulnerable. Naked.

Instead she felt powerful.

His eyes still shielded by mirrored glasses, he leaned in, using the earpiece of her own glasses to tilt her face a little higher.

Then his mouth took hers.

The kiss was sweet. A slide of his damp lips across hers, the skim of his hot tongue. Gentle, soothing. And so, so exciting. *Mmm, yeah.* So much power.

She felt as if she'd never get enough.

But, as he lifted his head away, she felt a frown crease her brow. "Diego…"

"I know, I know. We're just friends." She didn't need to see his eyes to know he was rolling them. His tone made that perfectly clear. "If you don't want Nathan to know we're more than neighbors, I'll refrain from jumping you on the rock-climbing wall."

Her mind suddenly filled with the image of her foyer wall, the one she'd been pressed face-first against while he sent her screaming over the edge of ecstasy.

"Maybe we have rock-climbing walls close to home," she murmured, making him grin.

She unzipped his leather jacket so she could splay her hands over his chest, then brushed a kiss over his down-turned lips.

"I appreciate you coming with me," she said softly against his mouth. "I know Nathan will be happy to see you."

For a moment, Diego looked as if he wanted to say something. His eyes were pained. He opened his mouth, then kissed her instead. A hot, intense thrust of his tongue that sent her swirling into turbulent need and aching want.

"We'd better go or we'll miss the ferry," he said when he lifted his head.

Because it was a beautiful, balmy Saturday, they had to wend their way through the crowded marina. The ferry, which hauled tourists and made multiple stops in addition to the little island where the Seafarers camped, was no different. It took them five minutes to find an empty bench on the top level where they could sit together.

The air was cold on the top deck. She warmed herself by leaning into the shelter of Diego's arms.

She couldn't wait to see Nathan. She knew he was happy and that he was having fun. But the couple of phone conversations over the last week weren't enough. Anticipation danced through her system, making her want to jump up and run to the rail to gauge the distance to the island. She checked the clock on the far wall as her fingers danced a rat-a-tat over her thigh.

"Just a few more minutes." Diego perfectly read her restlessness.

The anticipation turned to warmth. He knew her so well. Probably too well, she realized. How was it possible that it was almost sexier—and definitely scarier—than the lust?

Before she could dwell on it, the small leather purse she wore strapped across her body vibrated. Harper shifted out of Diego's arms to check her cell phone.

She'd brought her private cell. When she'd opened her own business, she'd gotten a separate cell phone, not wanting to use the same number as her personal line. But she'd left her work phone home, on her dresser. Something she rarely did, usually only holidays or special outings with Nathan. That she'd done so today, to be with Diego, was something to worry about later.

Harper glanced at the screen and frowned when she saw that the same number had called ten minutes ago. She must not have heard it over the bike's engine. She started to tuck the phone away.

Diego grabbed her hand.

"Answer it."

"But I don't recognize the number." And she didn't feel like explaining that one of Brandon's grieving BFFs had been calling the house and had probably switched to her cell in his attempt to glom on to any connection—however perceived—to his lost friend.

"So?"

"So, too late," she said, relieved when it stopped ringing and the screen blanked. "They'll leave a message."

As if mocking her, it immediately rang again. Stress jabbed with sharp fingers along the back of her neck. Harper wanted to throw the phone back in her bag and return to the romance of the ride, but Diego looked grumpy, so she answered.

"Hello?"

"I'm trying to reach Ms. Maclean."

Harper sighed. She didn't recognize the voice, but with the wind blowing and the sound of the ferry's engine filling the air, that didn't mean it wasn't that Dane guy again.

"This isn't a good time."

"Ms. Maclean, I'm calling about Nathan."

"Nathan?" She frowned. "Who's calling?"

"Ms. Maclean, there's been an incident."

"With Nathan?" Had he done something? He never caused trouble at school; she never got calls for misbehavior. "Did something happen?"

"Ms. Maclean, this incident needs to be discussed in person. I see your name is on the list of attending parents for Parents' Day. What time will you arrive?"

Worry starting to take on the sharp edges of dread, she looked at Diego. Whether it was the expression on her face, or whether he simply had that take-charge thing down pat, he took the phone from her suddenly trembling hand, pressed speaker and held it flat between them.

"Who is this?"

The phone crackled like papers wrinkling; then the man on the other end cleared his throat.

"This is Bob Marin, Seafarers Adventure Camp director. As I told Ms. Maclean, there's been an incident. Her presence is required at the campground as soon as possible."

The world took a fast spin as Harper's blood dropped into her toes. She gripped Diego's hand, squeezing tight as if it were her only anchor to the world.

"What happened?"

"That's better explained in person."

Harper wanted to grab the phone and demand that he quit dancing around and tell her what the hell was going on. But all she could do was stare at Diego.

His expression as hard as granite, Diego wrapped his hand around hers. He glanced at the clock on the ferry wall.

"We're five minutes out. Meet us at the dock."

"I'd prefer that Ms. Maclean come to the office. This is better discussed in private."

"Meet us at the dock," Diego repeated adamantly before hitting the off button.

Harper had no idea what was going on. But she was sure that the director would be at the dock.

"Why wouldn't he tell me what happened? Nathan must be hurt—why didn't the man tell me how hurt? He could have broken a bone. What if he fell and has a concussion? Or cut himself and lost a lot of blood." Her voice rose with each word as she imagined her baby hurt, broken and bleeding.

She stood, pacing the small area between the wooden bench and the protective wall of the ferry. She gripped her fingers together, then pushed them through her hair, then gripped them again. She craned her head to look toward the front of the ferry, trying to see if the island was in sight. All she could see was water. Her breath lodged in her chest. So much water.

"First things first," Diego advised in a tone so calm that half her panic simply melted away. "And right now you need to chill out."

Harper spun around, ready to get in his face and tell him just what he could do with his first thing. "Chill out?" she repeated, the words forced through her teeth.

"Yeah, chill out. Put a cap on whatever you've got brewing there and have a little faith that everything is okay." He studied her face, then grimaced. "Or just pretend to have faith. Whatever."

"I do have faith. I have faith that this was a mistake. I shouldn't have let him go to camp. He's only seven. I should have kept him home, where he'd be safe."

"And when he was ten? Would you keep him home then? What about fourteen? Eighteen?"

Maybe.

"Look, the kid's a pistol. He's smart, he's courageous. He's probably having the time of his life. Getting hurt at adventure camp? For a boy, that's like earning the big daddy of all merit badges. If you go in there wailing worry and leading with drama, you're going to embarrass him."

Her jaw dropped.

"Embarrass…"

"I know you're thinking about Nathan right now as your little boy. And to you, he is. But he's also a guy. This situation, going to camp, handling an injury, it's a proving ground. Don't take that away from him by flying in there with your momma face on and making him look like a pansy."

He was right. The worry would never go away. But that was her problem. Not Nathan's. Harper dropped onto the seat next to Diego.

"Atta girl."

In contrast to his unyielding expression, the hand he skimmed over her hair was gently soothing. Harper wanted to curl into the comfort of his touch, to fold herself into his arms.

"Harper?"

"I'm fine," she said with a smile. It was probably a little shaky around the edges, but it must have been enough since he gave a nod of approval.

Then, as if he'd read her mind—or maybe just the hope in her heart—he pulled her onto his lap.

"Just practicing for later."

Harper tried to relax. She told herself that everything would be okay.

But as the ferry approached the island, she held on to Diego's hand like a lifeline.

FIVE MINUTES LATER, that lifeline was all that was holding her upright as the camp director's words buzzed around her head like an angry swarm of wasps.

She stared into the face of the aging surfer, with his closely shorn blond hair, fishing shorts and blue Seafarer Adventures tee, trying to take in his words.

"We've notified the authorities, and they're on their way." The network of lines etched on Bob Marin's face deepened as he finally met Harper's eyes. "I'm sorry, Ms. Maclean. We've checked and double-checked everywhere since his absence was reported an hour ago. There's no question that Nathan is missing."

Harper attempted to repeat the word *missing*, but no sound came out.

She looked beyond the man, her gaze flying over the faces of his counselors, the camp's security team. There was no comfort in their worried expressions.

"Who reported his absence? Who saw him last and

where? What is the extent of the search so far, and who is in charge?"

It took her a moment to realize that those demands and that tone of absolute authority came from Diego.

Within minutes, he'd organized the counselors into search groups, issued orders that all of the campers and guests be held in one area, the ferry closed to departures and that the director take them to his office.

The crowd dispersed, some in tears, others looking glad to have something to do. Leaving only Harper, Diego and the man in charge of her son's safety.

"The authorities are on their way, they'll handle this. I assure you, we don't need another person trying to take charge." His feet planted on the wood dock, Marin scowled, looking at his clipboard as if searching for something there that gave Diego permission to call the shots.

"Mr. Torres works in security. And he cares about my son." Harper got in Marin's face with a look of ice-cold fury. "You will listen to him. You will do everything he, and the police, direct you to do in order to get my son back. Or I will have a team of high-priced lawyers here faster than you can belt out the opening lines to 'Kumbaya.'"

Either worry about a missing child or worry about being sued overrode his clipboard protocols, because the harried lines on Marin's face deepened as he tucked his collection of rules under one arm. With a sharp nod, he marched them through the trees, along the sun-dappled path toward the cabin she knew to be his office.

It was as if that show of strength was all she had. Harper sat in the rickety chair in Marin's office, her arms wrapped around herself and her mind blank.

Diego continued to snap out orders, this time through

the phone line. Words like *perimeter control*, *air support* and *search logistics* filtered through the buzzing whiz of panic spinning through Harper's head. Air eked through the knot in her chest, one painful breath at a time.

It could have been a few minutes. It could have been a few hours.

Harper had no idea how much time passed. She only knew her son wasn't there, hadn't been found. And other than running around this forsaken island screaming at the top of her lungs there was nothing she could do.

Except hold on to the fact that Diego was in command.

He'd find Nathan.

Finally, something pulled at Harper's attention. She blinked, clearing the tears from her eyes to look around.

The room was wall-to-wall testosterone.

Eight men stood facing the desk, listening to Diego snap orders. Her swollen gaze moved from one to the other, a tiny spark of awareness starting to poke its way through the pain in her head.

Who were these men?

Not policemen or FBI. They'd come and gone, offering no comfort or information other than, based on a sighting of an unauthorized boat seen leaving at the estimated time of his disappearance, Nathan had been abducted.

Diego had said he'd take care of everything. Her gaze landed on Jared. Maybe these guys were from the security company he worked for?

Then a man caught her attention as he walked past the window. Like the police, he wore a uniform. But his was a crisp khaki. Like the government official who'd asked so many questions, he wore dark glasses and an air of power. But her throat closed up when she saw the small silver insignia on his collar. She recognized that insignia.

Shock faded as reality slapped her upside the head. These men were Navy. They were Special Ops.

Had they served with Brandon? Why had nobody said anything to her?

Harper couldn't breathe.

The pain squeezing her heart was so tight, the terror smothering her thoughts was so intense, that her entire world had narrowed to two simple facts.

One, someone had stolen her son.

And, two, Diego had lied to her. He must have.

She buried her face in her hands, trying to squeeze feeling back into her numb flesh.

This had something to do with Brandon. There were too many coincidences for it not to. The letter informing her that Brandon was dead, Diego suddenly showing up in her life, now her son missing and the Navy stepping in to handle the search. Somehow they were all tied together.

Tears leaked through her fingers, soaking the denim of her jeans. She didn't know how long she sat there, didn't listen to the talk surrounding her.

But she recognized the soothing hand brushing over her hair. She knew the scent so well that she wordlessly threw herself into the comforting arms without question.

"I know, sweetie," Andi murmured, the words choked, the petite frame shaking with her tears. "I'm here. It'll be okay. Somehow, we'll make it okay."

Harper's mind cleared. The blinding terror, the miserable pain, even the niggling hint of anger, they were gone.

"How'd you know?"

Andi handed her a handkerchief with fingers shaking so hard, the lace fluttered. She waited for Harper to wipe her face, to dab her eyes; then she tilted her head toward the reception area where the men had gone. Through the open door, Harper could see half a dozen men, two of which were Diego and Jared.

"He spent the night at my place," Andi said, gesturing toward Jared. "When he got the call about this, he apparently decided I'd be useful here, so he brought me along."

"I'm glad you came." She gripped her friend's hand tight, offering as much comfort as she took. "I need you. Need someone I can trust."

"They're not security, are they?" Andi murmured, her icy gaze tagging Jared and Diego.

"No. Navy. But apparently they didn't lie about working together."

"I didn't lie about a lot of things."

As one, the women turned their heads.

Diego looked from Harper to Andi, then back again. They stared right back. After a moment, he scowled and rubbed his hand over his hair, looking like he wanted to punch something.

Good. So did she.

"We need to talk."

Suddenly her tiny niggle of anger exploded, expanding to mammoth proportions. She grabbed the anger. She needed the anger. It was all she had to keep the terrible pressure at bay, to stop that looming black hole of heart-wrenching misery from swallowing her whole.

"We don't have anything to talk about."

His expression didn't change. One brow arched over those intense eyes, he simply stared.

A part of her wondered what he was thinking. The rest of her didn't care.

"We need to talk," he said again.

"We have nothing to talk about. Not a single thing," Harper snapped. "Unless you'd like to try the truth for a change?"

Diego didn't flinch. Instead, he angled his head as if he figured she had the right to her anger.

How fucking generous of him.

WELL, THIS HAD gone FUBAR insanely fast.

Diego drew in a long breath. He could feel Savino's stare at his back. He could see the accusation in Andi's glare. He could hear the betrayal in Harper's voice.

None of that touched on the fury ripping through his skull. He'd fucked up. Their intel had failed; the team had taken another hit.

And Harper paid. Harper and Nathan.

Because his gut clenched with unfamiliar anxiety, Diego shoved all thought of the young boy aside. The guilt, the worry, he'd deal with them later.

Right now, he had his orders.

Contain and control.

"We need to talk," he told Harper again, tilting his head toward the door. He'd prefer privacy.

For a moment, Harper looked as if she'd refused. Then, after giving Andi's shoulder a reassuring squeeze, she swept from the room with the grace and dignity of a princess mowing through peasants.

With a wary eye and brief thanks that he'd been there when she'd dressed and so knew she didn't have any weapons tucked away, Diego stayed one step behind Harper as she made her way outside.

He had minimal experience soothing angry women. He'd never cared enough about one to have to.

And now that he did, what had he done? He'd fucked up her life. How did he apologize, make up for everything?

All of that flashed through his mind in the half minute it took them to walk through his men, out the door and into the shrub-lined dirt clearing just outside the cabin.

He watched Harper pace from one log-hewn bench to another. Back, forth.

He wanted to find some way to make it up to her. The lies, the deception. The fact that they hadn't anticipated this sort of move from Ramsey.

He knew he should regret the week he'd spent in Harper's bed, but he couldn't quite get there.

When he thought of Nathan, he had intense feelings of pain, regret, a horrible sort of fear he'd never experienced in his gut. What was that poor kid going through?

Did he know who'd grabbed him? Even if Harper had told him who his father was, Ramsey was a stranger. A murderous, treasonous stranger with the US Navy gunning for him.

A desperate man.

Diego resisted the need to pound on something. On someone.

Before he'd managed to fully yank in control, Harper finished her pacing and strode up to him.

Standing close enough that their boots almost touched, her face a study of fury that made his seem like a temper tantrum and the wind dancing through her hair, she stared.

She'd be hell at interrogation. He held out for ten seconds. He blinked at thirty. Discomfort hit at sixty. He kept his chin high and his expression blank.

Shit. "Look, I know what you're going to say."

With a furious growl, Harper jabbed one finger into his chest. "You owe me."

Diego blinked. Okay, he hadn't known that was what she was going to say.

"I beg your pardon?"

"Diego…" She lifted her brows. "Is that your actual name?"

"Diego Torres," he confirmed. She jabbed again. "Lieutenant Diego Torres."

"Navy?"

He nodded.

"Yeah. You're Navy," she said, her words close to a hiss and so disgusted she might have been calling him a gangbanging thief. She'd have been right about that, too.

"You're a SEAL like Brandon, aren't you? Special Ops. Super training, secret missions. All powerful, like you're a big deal.

"You targeted me. You moved in next door to me, you hit on me, you kept tabs on me. You had a reason."

Technically, she'd hit on him. But Diego didn't figure this was the time to point that out. Not when it was the only part of that accusation he could respond to.

"You owe me," she said again.

"I do." He couldn't deny it. Nor did he figure he could ever pay her back enough to make up for what she was going through right now.

"You're going to get my son back."

"I am."

She didn't even blink at his fierce vow. Her expression of loathing didn't change in the slightest.

"Wherever you go to find him, whatever you find, you're taking me with you."

No. No way. A thousand arguments filled his head. A million reasons, logistical to practical to reasonable, ricocheted through his mind.

He didn't have to look back toward the cabin to know that Savino was watching through the window. He didn't have to check with his commander to know her demand would be refused outright. With good reason.

There was no room for emotion on an operation such as this.

Sentiment biased judgment, limited decisions. Civilians had no place in a manhunt. Mothers had no place on a mission.

Diego watched Harper's face as those blue eyes narrowed in cold challenge and one brow arched as if she were daring him to try to refuse her.

Dammit. "Fine."

"What?"

Well, at least that'd made her blink. "I said fine. You want in—you're in." He crossed his arms over his chest, giving her his most intimidating stare. The one that made petty officers cringe.

She simply mirrored his stance. Crossing her arms over her chest, she tilted her head to one side so the blond strands blanketed her shoulder.

"You think I'm lying?" he asked.

"I know you lie."

CHAPTER SEVENTEEN

HARPER STEPPED INTO the camp director's office, this time fueled by fury instead of terror. Oh, the fear was still there. But she held on to the anger like a lifeline, grateful for something—anything—that'd keep her from falling to pieces again.

The room was full, some of the men in uniform, most not. It looked as if they'd been called in unexpectedly, which seemed odd. She knew next to nothing about the military—deliberately knew next to nothing—but she'd think they would use ones who were already on duty. Her gaze cut from one man to the other, wondering if any of them was Brandon's good buddy, Adams.

Then her eyes landed on the uniformed man who'd tipped her off that they were Navy. Although he stood at the far end of the room, behind the desk, he was the center of everything.

His hair was short, black like Diego's. But that and the military bearing was where the resemblance ended. Rather than dusky gold like Diego, this man's skin was pale, and while his eyes appeared black, too, on closer inspection she realized they were a deep, dark blue. A few inches taller, he had a sleeker build, subtler muscles. And an arrogant tilt to his chin that said not only was he in charge; he planned to stay that way.

"Harper, this is Commander Savino."

She didn't acknowledge Diego's introduction.

"Where's Andi?"

"Ms. Stamos has stepped outside."

Been taken outside, more likely.

"I want her here." Needed her there.

The man Diego had introduced as Savino didn't say a word. All it took was an inclination of his head and Harper sensed movement behind her, heard footsteps. Still, she didn't sit, didn't say anything until she heard Andi's lighter steps hurrying into the room.

"I'm here, sweetie," her friend said, wrapping her in tight arms.

"Nathan," Harper murmured, breaking for just a second as she gave Andi a desperate look.

"I'll call my father. I'll get investigators. Real security people." Andi aimed an angry look at the men in the room. "We'll get Nathan back."

"Please, ladies, have a seat."

They both glared at Savino.

His expression didn't change as he swept a hand toward the chairs in front of the desk. They looked as rickety as Harper's nerves, but she wanted this over with.

She sat, perched on the edge of the chair. After a moment, Andi followed suit.

"Thank you." Savino slanted a quick glance at Andi, then put his entire focus on Harper. His eyes were direct and assessing as he lifted a sheaf of papers, the small recording device that rested on top didn't shift.

"Ms. Maclean, I know you've already spoken with the local authorities and the FBI and I've studied the interviews. I won't waste your time covering the same ground."

"Good. Because I have questions of my own."

"That's reasonable." He nodded. "Why don't we call this an exchange of information? I'll begin, shall I? The sooner I can gather all of the specifics I need, the sooner I can deploy my men to retrieve your son."

"You make it sound so simple. As if that's all it'll take to get Nathan back. I've answered hundreds of questions already. Why isn't he here?"

"It's not a matter of asking questions—it's a matter of asking the right questions." He paused as if letting that sink in, then offered a hint of a smile. "And, ma'am? As well intentioned as the locals and FBI officials are, they're not SEALs."

As if that was all it took, Harper thought with a mirthless laugh. "Fine. Go ahead and ask. The ferry leaves in twenty minutes. I'll give you ten of those to ask whatever you need and to explain yourself to me. Then I'm getting Nathan's belongings and going home."

The man simply arched his brow.

"The FBI said that's where I should be. If someone—" she swallowed hard to get past the terror in her throat "—kidnapped him, they'll likely contact me there. So I'm going home."

"That's a solid plan," Savino agreed. "But you won't need to concern yourself with the ferry. We'll provide transportation at your convenience."

Harper considered telling the quiet man just exactly where he could put his transportation. Before she could, Andi squeezed her hand.

"What do you need to know?" Harper asked instead.

"Would your son recognize his birth father if he saw him? And if so, would he willingly go anywhere with him?"

"Brandon's dead."

"Please, answer the question anyway."

Harper's stomach tightened, her heart racing so fast her breath was shoved into her throat. The other authorities had asked about Nathan's father, but as soon as she'd said he was dead, they'd dropped that line of query.

What did Savino know?

"What does Nathan's abduction have to do with Brandon? Is he why Diego and Jared wormed their way into my neighborhood, lied to my face and pretended to be something they weren't?"

"I command SEAL Team 7. Lieutenants Torres and Lansky report to me. As did Lieutenant Ramsey." When she only stared, he continued. "I'd like to apologize for my team for the invasion of your privacy and the necessary deception employed in carrying out this mission."

She clenched her hands together to keep from wincing. It wasn't like she hadn't seen that coming. Not when she realized that these guys were with the Navy. Was this that brotherhood thing Brandon's SEAL friend had spoken of? Just another example of how these guys stuck together, even when one of them was dead.

"The only SEAL I've known up until now was skilled at lies and betrayal," she said, her eyes sliding toward Diego, who stood at the side of the room with his hands clasped behind his back and his eyes locked on her. "Apparently that's the norm."

She looked away before Diego could respond. Because if Brandon's connection to the SEALs was somehow useful, if his brothers-in-arms could be helpful, could bring Nathan back to her, she'd take whatever she could get.

She wanted to scream. She wanted to throw things and break things and pitch a hideous fit. But none of that would get her son back.

"What do the SEALs have to do with Nathan?" she challenged, her eyes shifting to Diego for a brief moment. "I'm sure you're aware that other than biology, Mr. Ramsey had no part in my son's life."

"Yes, ma'am. On the surface that's correct."

He arched a brow toward someone behind her in unspoken command. Harper knew before he joined Savino that it was Diego.

He was still wearing the jeans and leather jacket from earlier. Then they'd given him that irresistible bad-boy appeal. Now he was all military. Harper told herself she could wonder about that later, how with just the slightest change in stance and shift of his chin made such a difference.

"While nobody doubts the truth of Ramsey's abandonment of you and Nathan, his lack of parental responsibility or his…" Diego's words trailed off for a second as if he had to resist the urge to spit. "For all his disregard for his legal and moral obligations, he was still very informed of your and Nathan's lives."

A shiver of trepidation trickled down Harper's spine. "What do you mean?"

"He carried photos of the two of you. Some, we've been able to discern, were copied from your computer. Whether in person or by remote is undetermined." He gave that a moment to sink in. "A search of his computer turned up files on both you and Nathan. Health records, grades, even an application to a specific military academy that was open to enrolling Nathan when he reaches thirteen."

"That doesn't make sense." Harper shook her head, but that only made the thoughts spin faster. She pressed her hand to her temple.

"That son of a bitch," Andi hissed. "He was planning to take Nathan, wasn't he? He didn't bother sticking around for his birth, never paid a cent for his upbringing, but as soon as Nathan was old enough that scum-sucking pig was going to slap the Ramsey label on him and ship him off to be his legacy."

"No," Harper denied, shaking her head at Andi. "That's not possible." *Please.* Her breath knotted in her throat, her fingers numb as she tried to grasp her hands together. It couldn't be possible.

"My father would do it," Andi pointed out, her words all the more powerful for how quiet they were. Harper wanted to claim that Brandon wasn't a misogynistic Greek tycoon with power issues. Except, to her knowledge, the only thing different was nationality.

Still, Harper's gaze sought Diego's. "He couldn't." She silently begged him to say no. "Could he?"

His grimace was infinitesimal, so small that she didn't think anyone who didn't know his face intimately would see it. But she did. And it broke a small piece of her heart.

"With the right plan, the right lawyers, he could have tried." Diego lifted one hand. "He'd had a solid field of groundwork laid. He had the ego, the arrogance and the funds to make that sort of play."

She thought back to her sad little comment about being grateful to Brandon, and she remembered the look on Diego's face. She'd thought it was a hint of jealousy and had been flattered.

Now she knew it was pity.

"Ms. Maclean, would your son recognize his birth father if he saw him?" Savino asked again, waiting until she met his eyes before continuing. "If he did, would he voluntarily leave camp with him?"

"No." She had to stop and swallow twice before she could get any more words past the knot of misery in her throat. "He wouldn't recognize him. And he'd never go with him. He was angry when Brandon died. Not because he was dead, but because his death put him in our lives."

She wet her lips, staring at her fingers for a moment before lifting her gaze again.

"He's young, but Nathan has a very strong sense of right and wrong, a code of honor. His way of dealing with Brandon's abandonment was to pretend he didn't exist." Probably because that'd been her way of dealing with it. "Added to that, he'd never leave camp. Not when he knew I was coming today. Not when he knew he'd see me."

She remembered how brave he'd sounded during their last phone call, how proud he'd been to sleep without his night-light. She'd heard the longing for home in his voice, and for her in the way he'd told her that he loved her before he said goodbye.

She couldn't take it anymore.

All of the bottled emotions, the terror and pain and confusion exploded. Harper lost it.

The tears burst, ripping from her in miserable pain that shredded her into tiny pieces. With her composure destroyed, her heart crumbled. She sank into Andi's comforting arms but found no comfort. She sobbed on her friend's shoulder but found no release.

She was simply finished.

Harper didn't recall the end of the meeting. She didn't remember much after a doctor was called in with medication to keep the hysterics at bay. She had a vague impression of barked commands and soothing hands, of the thumping throb of a helicopter and the quiet hum of a powerful car engine.

And the soft oblivion of her own bed.

DIEGO PLANTED HIMSELF in their temporary command center, as they'd deemed Harper's office, leaving the door open and his view of the stairs unobstructed. Even as he worked, reading the intel Savino had provided and sketching out various attack options, he watched.

She'd been up there since last night. Had she slept? Did she hate him?

He calculated various extraction scenarios and wondered if it'd be easier to hate himself. He'd hurt her, and in the process, he'd destroyed them. Why hadn't he realized how much he needed there to be a them until it was too late?

Diego gripped the tablet he was working on with one hand, rubbing the other over his brow in hopes of relieving the pressure there. He'd caught an hour of sleep when Savino had ordered him to stand down at 4am, but worry had him right back at the desk now that the sun was rising.

A sound caught his attention.

"Son of a bitch," he murmured when he saw who walked in the front door.

"Torres." Light brown hair longer than usual, pretty-boy features tighter than usual, Lieutenant Elijah Prescott stepped into the room with a frown.

More relieved than he'd admit aloud—and more worried than he'd admit inside at the sight of Prescott's limp—Diego strode forward to offer his hand.

"Damned if it's not good to see you, man."

"Suck circumstances." Prescott's smile was pained as he glanced around the room, with its pretty antiques and soft fabrics. "Sweet digs."

"Beats the hell out of the hospital?" It was as much question as statement.

"I'd had enough. I checked myself out."

Diego inspected his teammate. The brown bomber jacket and baggy jeans hid the burns on his body, but from the way Prescott was favoring his left side, they were still tender. A rippling scar angled from his squared chin, along his jawline toward one ear, but it wasn't angry as it'd been several weeks ago. There was pain in his eyes, but no blur to indicate he was taking anything for it.

He shouldn't be here. He had months of rehab ahead. But fit to serve or not, Diego knew that Prescott was there to serve. "You sure you're up for this?"

"No big. It's not like I'm on duty" was all Prescott said. "Doesn't look like anyone else is, either. Officially."

Because making this an official investigation meant NI would step in. Take over. Push them out.

And Diego would be damned if he was going anywhere before Nathan was home in his mother's arms.

"Ramsey's confirmed as our hostile?"

"You tell me," Diego invited, since Prescott's specialty was cryptology. Lansky was the computer whiz, but Prescott oversaw cyberwarfare. He was the team's go-to expert for deciphering communications, for understanding the signals that Lansky unearthed. Added to that, the guy spoke, like, eight languages—there wasn't a whole lot that got past him.

"I've gone over our records, as well as the information Lansky hacked from NI. My analysis is that while the initial codes were sent prior to the explosion, there was a brief period after the first detonation where another message was sent."

"You know what it said?"

"I'm out." Prescott gave that a moment to sink in before leveling what Diego could see was going to be a major blow. "The message was crafted to look like it was going to one of the team. It bounced a few times, though."

Diego could see the same shock of betrayal in Prescott's eyes that he felt in his heart. Could hear the same disgusted fury in Prescott's voice that he felt in his gut.

"You've confirmed with Savino that Ramsey is our hostile. That he set us up? Can you prove it to NI?"

"You betcha."

"And his partner?"

Prescott slowly shook his head.

"Lansky traced the rental of a power cruiser and a Humvee to one of the various bank accounts linked to Ramsey." Trying to push past the frustration, Diego rubbed his thumb over his forehead. "Whether it was Ramsey or his as-yet-unidentified partner is the question."

"You guys think he stole his own kid?"

"His own is a misnomer," Diego snapped. "He's never met the kid, never showed any responsibility for him. At this point, he's stroking his ego while putting a child in jeopardy."

Prescott's jaw tightened, his pale eyes dimming for a moment as his gaze dropped to the floor. Diego knew the guy's history, knew that this had to bring history to the forefront, slapping at him with the memory of losing his own son.

"The kid is the priority," Diego said quietly, as close as he could come to reassuring his friend. He held out the electronic tablet he'd been studying, Savino's preferred method of communicating during missions. "We'll have him home before the weekend is over."

"Let's hope," Prescott murmured after a moment. Then, with a heavy sigh and on pained steps, he crossed over to take the tablet. "Nathan Maclean, age seven. Risk?"

"Minimal."

"Minimal?" Harper repeated, her quiet words not hiding the disgust in her tone. "You call someone kidnapping my son minimal?"

They turned toward the woman who'd appeared in the doorway.

"Harper Maclean, this is Lieutenant Prescott."

"Ma'am."

Diego scanned her face, noting the dark circles and deep grooves. For all that she'd rested, it obviously hadn't been restful.

"You should get more sleep."

"You should go to hell."

"Already have my room booked," he assured her, taking her arm to guide her to a curvy little couch by the window. If she wouldn't sleep, she could at least sit.

"Keep your hands to yourself." Yanking her arm free, Harper glared with the fury of a she-wolf about to spring. "I don't want you touching me."

"Harper, you need to sit down."

"Diego, you need to kiss ass."

Prescott, with the tact born of brotherhood, simply stood there enjoying the show. Diego pointed toward the exit, but the Lieutenant just grinned and leaned against the desk.

Since Diego couldn't justify kicking an injured man's ass, he did the next best thing. He ignored him and focused on Harper. "You want to be updated?" Ignoring her frustrated expression, he pointed to the couch. "Sit."

"I could spend a lot of energy hating you," she said in an ill-tempered mutter as she dropped onto the couch.

Good. He wanted that energy. As long as she had it

for him, there was a chance he could change it to something else. He'd figure out what later, after he'd brought her son home.

"We know that Nathan was taken off the island by boat. We know what direction he was taken in." Diego wanted to promise that he'd be home soon. But he couldn't. Not because his training told him not to. But because he couldn't bring himself to raise her hopes any more.

"It's been less than twenty-four hours. We'll get him back soon" was the best he could offer.

"Why is my house filled with men?" She flicked a glance toward Prescott, then back to Diego. "Are they all your kind?"

"Heterosexual Hispanic hunks?" The only smile that got was from Prescott. "They're Poseidon."

He waved away Prescott's move of protest. He'd been cleared to give her that much.

"We're an elite team within the SEALs, led by Savino." Her expression didn't change, but Prescott did grab a chair. "Ramsey wasn't one of us."

"Bet he hated that."

He arched one brow in agreement.

"We've made a lot of progress since last night."

"Minimal?" she snapped, referring to his previous comment.

"I said the risk was minimal, meaning that we don't believe Nathan is in danger."

"Because you think Brandon has him." Her tone was as resigned as the expression on her face. "I thought your kind pronounced him dead."

"Not officially," Diego said. "Bureaucratic red tape keeps the door open until an official determination can be made."

A frown tightened her brow, her eyes blurring for just a moment as she were trying to remember something.

"Torres."

Blinking away his frustration at the interruption, Diego turned. "What?"

"Three possibilities locked."

Jared looked past him to give Harper a tentative smile. She gave him a nod in response, which was friendlier than anything she'd offered Diego.

"What's that mean? Three possibilities?" Harper glanced from Jared to Diego to Prescott. "Have you found my son?"

"Have you found Nathan?" She repeated when nobody responded.

"Gentlemen," Diego murmured. This time, Prescott took the hint—or order—and hobbled toward the door, where Jared waited. Once they'd cleared the room, Diego took a breath and made a choice.

He crossed to Harper but didn't sit. He knew she didn't want him to. He could see she'd rather he went straight to hell, but he didn't do that, either. Instead he waited.

Until she leaned back on the couch and met his eyes.

Until she let out the angry breath he could see she was holding.

Until he heard the foyer clear and knew they were alone.

Until he knew that what he was about to do was the right thing. The one thing he could live with. No matter the outcome.

"That I was under orders is a poor excuse, but it is the truth." He met her glare with a nod. "As bad as I feel about that, as much as I regret it, there are still things that I can't tell you. Things that are classified. Top secret."

She simply crossed her arms over her chest and one leg over the other, her foot bouncing with irritation. The disdain in her expression didn't change.

Crap. Diego rubbed a hand over his hair and wished he could do anything other than what he knew he had to. But there was no other option.

So he sucked it up and told himself to take it like a man.

"I'm sorry," he muttered.

That got her attention.

Harper's gaze shifted to meet his for a brief moment before she looked away again.

"I *was* under orders, and this is a matter of national security," he continued. "But I let it go too far."

"You mean your orders don't usually include sex."

Diego rocked back on the heels of his boots and considered.

She wasn't going to forgive easily. That was okay. He didn't need life to be easy. He did need to do the right thing, though.

"I'm going to Northern California in less than an hour."

Her foot froze.

"Brandon's parents live there." She wet her lips. "Do you think they have Nathan?"

"No," he said honestly. The team had the house under surveillance and there'd been no sign of Ramsey or of Nathan. "But I think they might have key information that could help us find Nathan, and help resolve this mission's objective."

"Which one is your priority?" she wondered quietly, her eyes drenched with pain.

"Nathan," he heard himself say.

Civilians were always a priority. But for all of Diego's life, his reputation, then his career, had been the most important thing.

Not anymore.

"Come with me."

"What?"

"Come with me. I'm flying in and out of Alameda. It's what? An hour from there to where Ramsey's parents live. We'll be back tonight."

He shouldn't take her.

It was against regulations.

She shouldn't go.

The FBI had made it clear that her best place was here at the house in case a call came in or Nathan was found.

But Diego reached out and skimmed his hand, light as air, over the stress-induced tangles of her hair.

"Come with me."

CHAPTER EIGHTEEN

She had to put it away.

The heart-wrenching terror and the soul-crushing sense of betrayal had to be set aside. She couldn't think about Diego's betrayal. She couldn't ask herself what Brandon had done, or she'd curl up and start crying again. And Nathan? Harper pressed her knuckles against her mouth to keep from sobbing. She couldn't think about that, couldn't let herself think about it or she'd start screaming and never stop.

So for now, until she'd dealt with what had to be dealt with, she'd put it away.

Harper stared out the window of the Silverado 3500HD, watching the green hills of Oakland give way. Apparently SEALs didn't bother with rentals. They simply borrowed whatever they wanted from other guys on base, in this case, a big daddy of a diesel truck.

With every mile they were farther from her home. With every mile they were closer to her past. She'd never personally driven this road, had left before she'd got her driver's license, but she recognized the entrance to the Caldecott tunnel.

She watched the walls of the tunnel slide by, noting the gray cement. There had been an explosion in this one years before she was born, but it still wasn't retiled or pretty like the others. She'd always wondered if that meant this one was bad luck.

It wasn't until Diego asked if she was okay that she realized her fists were clenched around Nathan's baseball. She didn't even remember taking it from her purse.

"You were next door watching me, you got to know me, got to know Nathan because of Brandon," she said, voicing the realization that'd played through her head over and over in those foggy hours the night before.

"Yes."

Harper would have laughed at the matter-of-fact simplicity of his response, but she couldn't find the energy.

"Is it because you think I have something to do with whatever Brandon did?" She didn't ask what it was. Since Savino had used the term *treasonous activity*, she knew they wouldn't tell her.

"It was a possibility that had to be looked into. The way Ramsey talked about you gave credence to the suspicion. And—"

"And, what?" she prompted when he snapped his mouth shut.

"The phone calls, the burner phone. They added weight to the idea," he finally said, slanting her a quick look.

"Burner phone?" This time, Harper did manage a laugh. It was rusty and painful, but it was still a glimmer of humor. "Mrs. Wolcott. A client who wanted to surprise her husband with a renovated and decorated man cave for his birthday. She went a little over the top in her attempt to keep it secret."

"Ah."

"That's it?" she asked with a frown. "No further explanation, no apology. Just an *ah*."

"Would you accept an apology if I made it?"

"No," Harper realized as her shoulders drooped.

She tried to find the fury. The sense of betrayal.

But she was so empty inside that nothing was coming through. Nothing except...

"Do you think he's alive?" she asked, the question barely more than a whisper. "Brandon, I mean."

"Do you think he could do this? Stalk you and your son. Fake his own death. Steal Nathan. Put you through this sort of terror."

"You make it all sound horrific. Like I should say no. Like I should deny that the man who fathered my son was capable of such repugnant behavior."

"Is he?"

Harper stared out the window, watching the hills turn even greener, the buildings farther apart, the houses on the hills fancier.

"Growing up, it was just me and my mom. She tried. She had two jobs, sometimes three, but we never had much money. Food stamps, state help. She worked so much that she was hardly ever around. It was like an ugly circle with no way out." She'd never told anyone that. Not even Andi knew how bad her childhood had been.

"What happened?"

"She got sick. Cancer." She wiped her cheeks dry, but the tears kept falling. "Then she died, and I was alone."

"How old were you?"

Ancient. "Fifteen. Old enough to think I was so smart, dodging the authorities and flying under the radar to avoid child services. I figured I'd learn from my mother's example, so I stayed in school. Even though I was working two jobs, I aced my classes, snagged a scholarship." She gave a watery little laugh that mocked that naive girl. "Then all of a sudden, there he was. Brandon was my knight in shining armor. Or, rather, in a Navy uniform. He strode into the restaurant where I worked as a hostess and swept me off my feet. He made me believe in magic. In happy-ever-afters."

"I can see that." When she frowned at him, Diego shrugged but didn't take his eyes off the road. "He had that boy-next-door thing going on."

"I'd like to say I didn't realize he was rich, that it didn't matter to me one way or the other." She heard the GPS's warning to take the next exit, knew her past was a blink away. "I did care, though. I wanted a better life. I wanted out of poverty."

"Nothing wrong with that."

That's what she'd told herself at the time. But she could think of so many things wrong with it right now.

"And then I got pregnant," she said quietly as Diego pulled off the freeway.

She waited until he'd stopped at the red light, until his eyes met hers.

"I didn't get pregnant on purpose. I was terrified when I realized that I had more than a flu bug. But I was sure Brandon would be thrilled." God, she had been stupid.

"I take it he wasn't."

Harper wasn't sure if she was glad or not when, instead of continuing on his way, Diego pulled into a nearby parking lot.

"Want all the dirty details before we arrive there? That's what you've been trying to get from me since we met, right?" she asked, not ashamed at the bitterness of her words.

"Your life is in turmoil because of the actions of one man. Your world had been violated, your trust betrayed. As much as you resent the intrusion, maybe even hate the people involved, you're depending on a team of elite SEALs to put your world to rights." He paused as if waiting for her to confirm or deny, but Harper could only frown. "That's on a personal level. Imagine the threat on a global level and instead of one person being betrayed, it's an entire country."

Betraying one's country? Harper's chest hurt with the effort to push air through the cracks of pain.

Diego was talking about treason. That was the word for it, wasn't it?

She tried to swallow but couldn't as she remembered how for so many years she'd thought she had no feelings for Brandon, had believed that he was completely irrelevant to her life. Only to have the past thrown in her face with his supposed death.

Then, just as she'd found a way to make her peace with his abrupt reentrance to her life—and to force the reality of him into Nathan's world for the first time—she had to accept the possibility that he was not only alive but he'd outright stolen her child from under her.

Now they were asking her to accept that the father of her child was capable of such a heinous act? Harper had to clench her teeth tightly together to keep from screaming in horror.

"Do you think he's really alive?" she was finally able to ask again.

Diego put the truck into gear. Before he pulled into traffic, she caught the expression in his eyes. If possible, it made her feel even worse.

That look, the pained betrayal, told her that Brandon being alive was a possibility that hurt Diego even more than it hurt her. Brandon had been a part of her world for three months and out of her world for almost a decade. But Diego had served beside him. He'd worked with him, trusted him, put his life on the line next to him.

"You want him to be dead," she realized.

"I wish I could say I did," Diego admitted quietly. "I believe he deserves to be. But as ugly as things are if he's alive, they're uglier if he's dead."

Harper's breath shook, her stomach churning so miserably that she spent the next minute worrying that she was going to be hideously sick all over some poor stranger's truck. She'd already figured that whatever Brandon had done, it was bad.

But it must be worse. A million times worse.

Harper closed her eyes, trying as hard as she could to shove it all aside before she slid past nausea and right into hysteria. She couldn't think about that now. She couldn't worry about how horrible Brandon was.

Not when he had her son. *Focus on something else*, she told herself. *Focus on the task ahead.* On facing her past. On confronting her own personal demon.

A demon who'd shaped the direction of her life, whose existence had influenced the woman she'd become more than anyone else in Harper's world.

Traffic was a nasty snarl through Danville but neither of them spoke again. Not until they passed the Blackhawk Country Club gates when Harper reached down for her purse.

She pulled a small black bag out of her leather tote, choosing her makeup tools as carefully as she imagined Diego chose his weapons.

She blotted and dabbed, hiding the signs of tears and disguising the dark circles under her eyes.

"Primping in case we run into your ex?"

"Hardly." She'd be damned if she'd confront that demon looking anything less than her best. Still, she paused in the act of repairing her eyeliner long enough to frown at Diego. Then Harper pressed her lips together and confessed. "If we see Brandon, I expect you to beat the hell out of him."

Focused on smudging the dark gray pencil under her lashes, she didn't see his reaction. But his snicker was loud and clear.

"What's the paint for, then?"

"A preemptive attempt to salve my ego," she admitted as she slicked on a rich berry-hued lipstick. Since checking her image in her hand mirror wasn't enough, she pulled down the visor for a better view. All she saw was a scared girl. A girl too poor, too weak, too pathetic to stand a chance.

"Who're you afraid of?" Diego asked.

Brandon. Alive or not, he'd still proved he could hurt her, that he could impact her life. He'd turned her world upside down and showed her that he could still hurt her.

The Ramseys. Like Brandon, they provided a threat that, despite everything she'd done, everything she'd built her life into, could still destroy her heart.

She was even afraid of Diego.

He'd made her feel. He'd made her hope. And now he'd broken her heart. And she was pretty sure he wasn't finished yet.

"Harper?"

She leaned her head back against the headrest and closed her eyes.

"When I told him I was pregnant, Brandon warned me to get rid of the baby. He didn't want it, and he said there was no way his parents would let me keep it. He promised me that if they knew there was another Ramsey on the way, they'd take it from me. And that they'd make sure I had no part of the child's life. After all, I was in no way suitable to raise their grandchild."

"The Ramseys never knew about Nathan?"

"I let Brandon think I was going to a clinic to have the pregnancy terminated," she admitted, swallowing back bile inspired by the words. "I let him think there was no way I'd give up college, no way I'd let a baby stand in the way of the amazing future I had planned."

"Seems to me you created a damned good future. One that's totally on par with whatever the Ramseys could offer." It was obvious that he didn't know where she'd come from and just how far a trip it was to hit that part.

"I'm not their equal." She never had been. How could she be?

"C'mon. You've got a fancy career working for the rich and famous. You live in an exclusive, upscale neighborhood with a guard at the gate. And you've raised a great kid, who, despite private schools and fancy camps, is down-to-earth and fun to be around."

"Thank you." Harper was surprised enough to open her eyes. She didn't turn her head, but she did slide a glance toward Diego. "Be that as it may, thanks to Brandon, thanks to you, now in order to find my son I'm going to see the very people who could take him away from me."

"Nope."

She did turn her head now. She had to, to shake it in confusion. "What do you mean, nope?"

"Nope, that isn't happening." His words were so matter-of-fact, so absolutely sure, that Harper had to believe him. "There are two things you need to focus on right now. First, if the Ramseys have Nathan, they already know he exists. Second, it doesn't mean a damned thing what they want. They aren't getting it."

"You said it yourself," she said, reminding him of that ugly discussion about Brandon's plans for Nathan's future. "They can file for custody. They have the money, the connections, to get whatever they want. If Brandon is dead, they've lost their heir apparent. If he's a criminal, you'll put him in jail. Either way, they'll know about Nathan. They'll try to turn him into one of them."

Diego snorted as he pulled up to the guardhouse at the gated community. He flashed something to the man on duty, waited while the guy made a call, then nodded his thanks when they were cleared through. It wasn't until he was headed into the luxurious neighborhood that he spoke again. By then, Harper's nerves were wound so tight, she could barely listen.

"It'd be awfully hard to turn a sweet, honest kid with a strong conscience into a spoiled, selfish, narcissistic asshole with delusions of grandeur," he pointed out.

She wanted to believe him. But the Ramseys? They had skills.

"Wouldn't matter if they wanted him or not, though. The Ramseys, they're going to have to get through Poseidon to keep Nathan." She assumed he meant his Special Ops team, and not the sea god. "More specifically, they'll have to go through me. And nobody gets through me."

He stopped the truck then, killing the engine and leaning one arm on the steering wheel as he turned to give her an assuring look.

Harper stared into his face. The hard planes, unforgiving lines and implacable expression. There was so much strength there. So much power.

For a moment, she looked past him to the mansion that she'd never been allowed inside, with its white pillars and wide front steps flanked by perfectly tended garden beds of bleeding pastels. Then her eyes met Diego's again.

He'd lied to her. He'd used her.

But he was her anchor.

So she grabbed hold.

Unsnapping her seat belt with the flick of a finger, she leaned closer. Her eyes never left his as she wrapped one hand around the back of his neck and pulled his head down to meet her mouth.

She felt his smile against her lips but ignored the amusement. As their tongues danced, she breathed in his strength. She drew in his power. She held tight to his implacable obstinacy.

"Thanks," she breathed as she pulled away. "I needed that."

"IT'S GOING TO be fine." He flicked a look over his shoulder at the mansion, frowning at the idea of a real man coming from a house that looked like an imitation palace. "This visit is strictly recon. The chances of Ramsey or your son being here are slim to none."

Her eyes narrowed.

"Then why are we here?"

"I told you. Reconnaissance. We're scoping the mother, assessing the situation. Ramsey lied about a lot of things. His relationship with you. His involvement with Nathan. His father's influence—although that's debatable since his old man was pretty high on the totem pole before he was sent up the river for fraud." He grinned when her jaw drop. "Yeah. MacGyver discovered that instead of Mr. High-Powered Investment Banker, the elder Ramsey is doing time for engineering some skeezy Ponzi scheme that bilked thousands of rich people out of millions of dollars."

Harper shook her head in confusion. He waited for the questions to explode, possibly even a defense of her son's genetic pool. He'd seen it plenty of times. People got weird about relatives in prison. Not in his world—being able to claim blood behind bars was a badge of honor in the gangs. But in her glorified world? That her little boy carried the blood of a con—if a sneaky white-collar criminal counted—had to grate deep.

"Who is MacGyver?" was all she asked, though, making Diego frown.

"Lieutenant Jared Lansky, call sign MacGyver."

"Call signs. Those are like nicknames, right?" When he nodded, she asked, "What's yours?"

"Mine?" He didn't know why the question made him uncomfortable. It wasn't as if she'd asked his designator or last deployment assignment. "El Gato."

"The cat?" Despite the gravity in her eyes, her lips twitched and her gaze skimmed over his body as light as a tickle. "Is that because you cat around?"

"That, or I move with speed and grace, pouncing when others are unaware, never giving up until my curiosity has been satisfied." As soon as the words were out, he felt like an ass. Call signs, they held as much ribbing as reality. It was one thing to joke about with the guys, but he didn't want Harper thinking he was an egotistical jerk. "Let's go."

She laid her hand on his before he could pull the keys from the ignition.

"It's a compliment, isn't it? That your teammates believe you're tenacious and talented."

"It's a fact. I won't give up until I've done what I set out to do. I won't stop until I put Nathan back in your arms." The vow was quietly made, but that didn't hide the steadfast resolution of his words.

"Two days ago I'd have believed anything you told me," she said, her words just as quiet as his.

"And now?"

Harper simply stared, her blue eyes shadowed. After a long, gut-clenching second, she shrugged.

"Why am I here? You don't need me for, what do you call it? Recon."

"Impressions." He grabbed and pocketed the keys, then stepped out of the truck, rounding it to open her door before she'd gathered her purse. "And it got you out of the house. If you'd stayed there, you'd have worried yourself sick."

Her expression more closed than he'd thought her capable, Harper slid out of the truck but didn't say a word. He watched with interest as she shook the wrinkles out her jacket before pulling it on. With a couple of quick moves she'd cuffed the sleeves to show the sassy gray-and-white-striped lining. She stepped out of her casual rubber flip-flops, sliding her feet into gunmetal spike-heeled pumps.

And that's all it took, he realized, to turn her simple jeans and black tee into a classy outfit that fit right in with this upscale neighborhood.

The rich really were different.

"Armor ready?"

Her smile was like lightning, flashing fast, intense, then gone.

He hated the pain in her eyes. He hated his part in putting it there. But he knew it wasn't going to simply go away. Not until Nathan was home. Maybe not even then.

Leaving the truck parked at the base of the curved driveway and sticking out like a sore thumb, Diego let Harper lead the way up the flagstone path.

"Nice place," he murmured under his breath. Feeling her tension ratchet higher beneath the fingers he'd pressed against her back, he added, "If you like penis palaces."

"What?" She snorted with surprise and laughter but shook her head as if she didn't understand the reference.

"You know, some guys compensate for a tiny dick with a fancy car with a big-ass engine and loud exhaust. Like people are going to see the flash and figure the rest of the package is just as impressive." He rolled his eyes, gesturing toward the fancy house. "People will look at this place and think, hey, the guy might have a crap personality and is a total ass-hat of a human. But this house, it proves he's got some redeeming quality."

"And a man with an already impressive penis?" she asked, giving him a look from under her lashes that said she had a very good memory. "Isn't he always trying to prove that he's worthy of his size?"

"Nah." Diego grinned. "That guy is just looking to find the right fit. A woman who can handle him? Finding her ain't easy."

Harder still was keeping her once he'd found her. But he didn't tell Harper that. Instead, Diego held out his hand when they reached the wide marble steps skirting the ornate double doors.

Harper stared at his hand for a long moment, then into his eyes as if she was making a huge decision. He didn't realize how much tension he was holding until it eased away as she tucked her fingers into his.

Then, as she often did, she shocked him with her teasing smile. Tilting her head to one side, she asked, "And if he finds that perfect fit?"

He was sure she wasn't asking for a commitment—not from him. Still, he couldn't help his response.

He pressed his thumb on the coat of arms doorbell, then took a deep breath and met her gaze.

"He hopes she can handle a guy who wears a uniform for a living."

Before either of them could process that response, the door swung open.

"May I help you?"

Eyeing the dour-faced mortician, Diego decided he had to be a servant. The Ramseys wouldn't allow someone that ugly to be a relative.

"We're here to see Mrs. Ramsey."

"Mrs. Ramsey is not available at this time. Perhaps you'd care to leave a message?"

"You the butler? Or the answering machine?"

"Neither, sir. I am the house manager."

"Right. Maybe you could manage to make Mrs. Ramsey available, then." Diego didn't wait for another one of the guy's polite brush-offs. "It's in regard to her son."

The prune face puckered even more for a second, which apparently was good because he pulled the door open wide and swept them inside with one skinny arm.

"Please, wait in the downstairs parlor."

He led them to a room directly across from the door, waving them inside before disappearing. Whether it was a power play, a bid to buy time or because she was stashing her grandson in a closet, it took Christine Ramsey a good ten minutes to join them.

Which was plenty of time for Diego and Harper to get over their shock at the downstairs parlor.

"It's like a monument. Or maybe an altar," Harper whispered after she'd walked the room once. Every surface was covered with some semblance of Brandon Ramsey's greatness. Photos of him in uniform, in digies, in combat gear. Framed newspaper articles, matted commendations, a display of medals. The room was spotless, as if dust were too intimidated to try to settle there. But Diego could tell that the memorabilia had stood for a long time. Long enough to cast protective shadows on the sun-bleached wood.

This wasn't for show. Harper was right. It was a monument, and it'd been here long before the Ramseys got word that their only son was dead.

"It's a little much," she said, looking at Diego after she'd gone around a second time. "Isn't it?"

"Way too much," he agreed. Like, nauseatingly too much. Bordering on obsessive, leaning toward fanatical. Even for a parent, this room was serious overkill. Was this why Ramsey had been such an egomaniac? Did this sort of worship breed narcissism? Or had the man's ego simply demanded worship?

They both heard the sound of high heels snapping across marble and turned toward the door. A woman paused there as if allowing them the privilege of enjoying the view. Posing, one hand resting on the door frame and the other on her hip, she was the epitome of her son. Not a blond hair out of place, her eyes were ice blue and her features perfect. Thanks to great genetics or a talented sculptor, she didn't look old enough to be Ramsey's mom.

"You have word on my son?" Looking down her nose at them, the woman's gaze shifted briefly to Harper before she focused on Diego as if he were the only other person in the room. "Are you here to tell me there's been a mistake? Brandon is alive, yes?"

"What sort of mistake are you expecting, ma'am?"

"The mistake in which some idiot claimed that Brandon could be dead. You're with the Navy, correct?" Without waiting for an answer, she moved into the room, staring up at the portrait hanging over the fireplace. Almost life-size, Ramsey smirked down at them. "He couldn't be captured. He's too good. But there must be an explanation. I'll admit, I expected someone to contact me sooner, but I realize the government has its own timetable."

"That it does," Diego agreed, giving her the space to keep talking.

"My son is a decorated officer, a highly skilled SEAL who leads men in top secret missions. He's honored by admirals, admired by all who serve with him." She made a ladylike look of scorn. "The very idea of him dying on a routine mission is ridiculous."

"To my knowledge, the circumstances surrounding Lieutenant Ramsey's supposed death are still under investigation," he said, going for honesty. Not out of virtue, but because he figured it'd piss her off.

He was right.

Her face convulsed, mouth working in bitter lines but no words coming out. Finally, the woman harrumphed and fast marched her way toward the door.

"Mrs. Ramsey..." Whatever Harper had planned to ask, she let it go when the woman speared her with an icy look.

"My son is not dead. I would know if I'd lost my only child, if the last Ramsey were gone." Despite the poignancy of her words, there was nothing soft in her frigid demeanor.

He could feel Harper's tension, saw her body jerk as if recovering from a blow. Diego shifted toward the center of the room to keep the woman's attention on him and give Harper time to compose herself.

"Ma'am, if your son were alive, where might he be? Does he have someone he'd stay with or a place he'd go?" Diego asked politely. "We'd like to settle this matter as much as you would. Telling us anything that could help track him down would help."

"If he wanted you to know where he is, then you would." And with that, Mrs. Ramsey gestured toward the door. "We're done here. I want my son home. Don't contact me again unless you're here to tell me where I can reunite with Brandon."

Diego nodded, and when Harper looked as if she were going to protest—or finish whatever she'd been trying to say—he took her arm.

"Thank you for your time," he said quietly, moving past the woman without releasing his hold on Harper.

The mortician was waiting at the door, swinging it wide as if to hurry them out. They didn't speak until it had closed behind them and they were on their way down the driveway.

"Well, she was a delight, wasn't she?" Diego muttered.

"Nathan has her chin." Looking like she was fighting the urge to cry, Harper took a deep breath and glanced back once before continuing walking. "I didn't want to see a resemblance. But it's there."

"That's all that was there, though."

"What do you mean?" She stopped and shook her head as if throwing off the fear that had kept her so quiet. "We should have asked more questions. Should have pushed harder. What if she knows where he has Nathan?"

Diego took her by the arm.

"She doesn't."

"How do you know? You didn't even ask about Nathan."

It wasn't easy to pull a woman down a sloping driveway and make it look like a casual stroll. But Diego thought he managed okay.

"No reason to do either." He waited until they'd

reached the truck before letting go of Harper. Once there, he kept his voice low.

"You saw that shrine. She worships her only begotten son. If she really thought he was alive, she'd have behaved differently. She's telling herself he is, but she was looking for reassurance. And if she knew he had a son, there would be evidence. A mini-throne, signs that she'd moved photos out, filled in the blanks." He shook his head, pulling a face as he retrieved the keys. "Could be because Ramsey doesn't trust her—could be he simply doesn't need her. But she's not involved. I didn't think she would be, but now we know for sure."

"Why?" she asked.

"Why what?" He studied her face, taking note of those penetrating eyes and their wounded depths. He realized he couldn't bullshit her. "I told you. Recon. It had to be checked out. She's the closest living relative, unless he's holing up at the prison where his old man plays golf. She's his safety net."

Harper simply waited.

Giving her points for interrogative skills, Diego shrugged. "You needed something to do." He eyed the edgy nerves on her face, the way her fingers clenched and unclenched. She still did. "You want to drive?"

Harper blinked her surprise. "You'll let me? I thought guys got their dicks in a knot over giving women that kind of power."

"My dick likes it when you're on top."

She was either so emotionally drained that she'd lost her ability to hold the anger. Or that'd actually been funny.

Either way, he was glad it made Harper laugh.

CHAPTER NINETEEN

HARPER FIGURED IT was easier to let Diego do the driving.

Not out of any worry about his equipment. She knew, up close and personal, that it could withstand any number of challenges.

But there was simply too much conflict going on between her head and her heart, in her thoughts and her fears. It was easier to sit back in the passenger seat and rest her head against the cool glass of the window while she tried to sort through it all.

She loved her son. Adored him. She found herself pulling his baseball out of her bag and rolling it between her palms. Feeling that worn leather against her skin seemed to bring Nathan a little closer.

But even now, knowing he was in danger, facing the possibility of losing him—of never seeing him again— she couldn't imagine building him a shrine.

What did being raised with that sort of unhealthy obsession do? Was that why Brandon was—or had been— so sure of himself? So absolutely positive that he was right, that he was best? She'd always thought he was just a selfish jerk. But if he'd done…well, whatever it was that he'd done that was so dangerous that a team of SEALs was dogging him, he'd gone beyond arrogance.

However he'd been raised, however he'd been trained, he'd chosen his path. He'd decided that he was beyond the law, that he was smarter than the military and more important than world peace.

She'd always told herself that DNA didn't matter, that it made no difference who Nathan's biological father was. But boy had she been proven wrong. It mattered.

Harper blinked, actually surprised when she saw the tears falling on her hand, sliding over the grimy leather of the ball.

She'd been wrong.

Now she had to figure out how she was going to make it up to Nathan. How she was going to fix her son's world once he was back in hers. She had to believe that he'd be back. That Diego and his men would find Nathan so she could make it up to him.

Lost in the pain of her thoughts, it wasn't until Harper's stomach growled that she remembered that she hadn't eaten in hours. For the first time since Diego had started the truck and pulled away from the Ramsey mansion, she paid attention to where they were.

Which turned out to be no place she wanted to be.

"Why are we going this way?" Tension gripped her belly as she scowled at the familiar highway with its sloping hills and congested traffic. "I thought we were flying right back to Santa Barbara."

"Quick side trip. Call it a roundabout route to the air base."

She wanted to ask why, but she was afraid she already knew the answer.

When Diego got off Highway 4, Harper was so tightly wound as he wended his way down familiar streets, she was afraid she was going to throw up. As she tried to keep from screaming, she noted that the streets weren't any prettier now than they'd been when she was a kid.

"There's an address here that Lansky found in Ramsey's computer files. It was buried pretty deep, hidden under a few layers. I figure it's worth checking out to see what he was hiding."

But it wasn't Brandon's secret hidden on these streets. Harper tried to swallow the bile rising in her throat. Her eyes burned as she imagined the look in his when he realized the truth. His admiration, his attraction, even his perception of her, they were about to be blown to teeny tiny pieces, showing Diego just how fake she was.

Harper wiped the tear that trickled down her cheek and mourned the loss of Diego's vision of her. It shouldn't matter, since he wasn't who she'd thought he was, either. But finding out the sexy security guy was actually a big-time hero was one thing. Finding out the elegantly classy woman living in the fancy estate was really a cheap loser from a scummy neighborhood? It wasn't the same.

Just ego, she assured herself. It wasn't as if she'd actually fell for the guy like she'd thought.

And if Harper had learned nothing the last couple of days, it was that she didn't get to choose what she could face or avoid. So when Diego stopped in front of a building that appeared to be held together by dirt as much as mortar, Harper could only sigh.

"Why would he keep track of this place?" she wondered, so quietly it was almost a thought. "He never even visited. Not once that I know of."

"You know the significance of this address?" He gestured toward the dirty apartment building, with its dead lawn and sad bushes, the paint scarred here and there with darker patches where the landlord had tried to disguise graffiti. There was a parking lot to one side, half-empty but for a handful of run-down cars—two of which rested on cinder blocks.

On one corner was a QuickMart, on the other the high school. Trash, plastic bags and fluttering paper waved through metal fencing surrounding the school like pennants, but Harper had no desire to celebrate.

"You won't find Brandon here," she said. "But if he was tracking Nathan all these years, he probably started with this address."

"Why?"

"In case I ran here, brought my baby here. More likely, because I'd used this as my address for a few years, even after I'd left." At Diego's questioning look, she grimaced. "I didn't think Brandon would come looking or bother trying to keep track of me. Why would he? He'd dumped me and didn't want the baby. He believed I was getting an abortion. But I was a little paranoid after he threatened me with his parents, so I used this as my official address for a couple of years."

"You lived here?"

Despite her mortification, Harper's lips twitched at the shock in his tone.

"I grew up here," she murmured, noting the fresh graffiti that hadn't been cleaned off the walls of the high school. She pointed. "I graduated from that school. Three other girls were pregnant our senior year, but they dropped out."

"You didn't?"

"Too stubborn. And I had a baby coming. I didn't think I could give him much of a life if I didn't even have a high school degree."

"I'm impressed."

She glanced at him in puzzlement. How was that possible? There was nothing impressive about this place.

The air itself stank with misery and pessimism. The few people on the street looked toward them with expressions of suspicion, hate or both.

"Nobody would believe you came from here," he explained.

She wished she could say she was proud to look around this sad neighborhood and know how far she'd come. But as always, all she felt was shame at how she'd began.

"You won't find Brandon here," she said again. "Nor anything connected to him. So can we go?"

Before she gave up all hope.

DIEGO NOTED THE drug deal going down on the corner, the two girls—looked like preteens—hooking at the far end of the high school yard and a couple of brave flowers growing in the window box of a house whose paint peeled like onion skin.

He hadn't thought Harper could surprise him again. He'd been wrong.

He hadn't thought the two of them had more common ground than great sex and a connection to Ramsey.

Apparently he'd been wrong about that, too.

It looked like they had their beginnings in common, too. What did it say about him that he found pleasure in that? Maybe it was the idea that she might understand. That she might see him a little clearer. Someday.

After he brought her son back to her.

He glanced at the clock on the dashboard and slid the truck into gear. She was right. They had other things to do.

"Once the kid is home, remind me to show you where I grew up," he couldn't help but say as he pulled away from the curb. "In the meantime, you hungry?"

He took her murmur as agreement and pulled into the first drive-through he saw. Since she appeared ready to drop, he opted to keep driving while he choked down a couple of burgers. She only managed half of hers, along with a scant few fries, but he figured that was pretty good, all things considered.

For the most part, the rest of the drive back to the air base was made in silence. Per Savino's directive, a cargo plane was waiting, fueled and cleared for flight. All Diego had to do was drop off the truck keys before they boarded.

Harper had wrapped herself in a cocoon of silence, her expression exhausted, her demeanor defeated. It was all Diego could do not to pound his fists into the wall of the plane. He'd brought her along to give her a focus outside her misery. For all the damned good it had done.

Since it was just the two of them and the pilot on board, Diego gestured Harper into the body of the plane, pausing briefly to speak with the pilot to confirm take-off and conditions. Then, using the privacy, he took a moment to text the team for updates.

Nothing. Not a fucking thing had changed.

He gave in to the need to grind his teeth, then sucked it up and put on the poker face. His only concern for the next forty minutes of travel time was Harper's state of mind.

When he stepped into the bay, he found her curled up on one of the benches that ran the length of the cargo hold, her head resting on that giant purse of hers and her feet bare.

"I just need to close my eyes for a few minutes," she said, stating the obvious since they were already closed. "I'll get up and put a seat belt on at takeoff time."

"Mmm-hmm."

His shoulders heavy with worry, he slid an anchor strap around her, belting her in where she was. A few minutes later the plane took off.

"There's no word on Nathan, is there," she asked without opening her eyes. Her words were so heavy with despondence that Diego couldn't stop himself from brushing a hand softly over her cheek, hoping to offer even the smallest amount of comfort.

"The team is working on it," he promised. "We're almost there."

"Almost?"

"MacGyver's working on it." He'd broken through Ramsey's encryption; Prescott had worked a little decoding magic. They had an electronic signature verifying that Ramsey was behind the sale of the formula. They'd pulled together enough data for NI to deem the team was in the clear and the CIA to be told to get off Poseidon's ass.

Savino hadn't sounded sure, though. Whether because he didn't think NI was going to let go of their vendetta against Poseidon, or because it wasn't enough to shut this down, Diego wasn't sure. Bottom line, they didn't have a location. They didn't have the kid.

Guilt a misery in his gut, Diego watched the emotions play over Harper's face. He hated what he'd done to her. And there wasn't a damned thing he could do to fix it. Not yet. Not until they caught that break and found Nathan. But maybe for just a moment he could give her a tiny break from the worry.

With that in mind, he took her mouth. When she didn't pull away he took the kiss deeper.

Slow. Oh, so seductively slow, he swept his tongue along her lips, sipping gently before sliding between the seam and engaging her in a sweet dance.

Her fingers gripped tight, digging erotically into his flesh, making him want, making him desperate.

But this wasn't about him.

Harper's hum of approval worked at his resolve, but Diego reminded himself that he wasn't controlled by his dick. No matter how insistent it was.

He found the hem of her shirt, reveling in the warm skin beneath. He traced a pattern up the silken delight of her waist, circling until he reached the lace of her bra. He teased her nipple where it pressed tight against the fabric, flicking his thumb over the rough design of the lace.

"More," she murmured against his mouth. "Give me more. Make me forget."

Oh, yeah. He intensified the kiss. His tongue stabbed, teeth scraped. He gripped her breasts, working those delicious nipples between his fingers.

Her hands pressed, fingers dancing over his shoulders, down his arms and back up to cup his head. She gripped his hair and arched her back.

He took the hint and worked his kisses across the soft planes of her cheek, along her chin and down her delicate throat.

Impatient, he shoved her shirt out of the way, tugging the lace down to expose the berry tip of one breast to his tongue. He laved it softly, round and round the rosy edges, feeling her body tighten with each circle. When her fingers gripped his biceps, nails digging into his flesh, he sucked.

Hard.

She cried out as her hips arched. The rumble of the aircraft muffled any noise she might make.

Filling his mouth with her deliciousness, he tweaked the opposite breast even as his free hand teased and

swirled a path over her belly. He made quick work of
the button on her jeans, shoving her pants down so he
could dip his fingers into her wet heat.

That's what he wanted. What he needed.

Her.

Wet, wanting, ready.

He dipped, swirled the tip of his finger around the
sensitive bud between her thighs, then dipped again.
Her breath came faster, panting little mewls of need.

His mouth followed the path his hand had took, his
lips leaving a hot trail down her torso, over her belly.
Between her legs.

His tongue slid along her pouting, swollen clitoris.
She gasped. His teeth gently tugged. She moaned.

Her hands gripped, trying to pull him up. Trying
to angle him back up, to move him over her body. He
wanted that. He wanted in.

They had the time, at least twenty more minutes in
the air.

They had privacy, this ride had no autopilot option.

But Diego had a point to make. "This is for you,
babe."

She mumbled a breathy protest, but his mouth was
too busy to respond. The rest of her comments came in
the form of escalating whimpers and gasping breaths.

He swirled his tongue around the rim of her core,
fingers tweaking, pinching. When he felt the tension
ripple through her, when her back arched high, her heels
digging into the bench so she could press tighter against
him...

That's when his tongue plunged.

Deep inside. Again and again.

Until she exploded over his tongue, into his mouth,
through his being.

But once wasn't enough. So he sent her up again.

Even as he swallowed her addicting juices, his teeth and tongue worked. He slid his hands up her body to cup her breasts, fingers tugging and tweaking in time with his teasing tongue.

This time she came with a scream.

God, he loved that sound.

Because he knew he was afraid he could stay here all day making her repeat it, he reluctantly shifted out from between her thighs. He couldn't let go, though.

He had to hold her. Had to pull her tight into his arms and hang on, to feel the quivering aftershocks of pleasure ripple through her.

"Why?" she finally mumbled, the words almost lost against his chest.

"You needed it."

He grinned when he felt her laugh. *Good.* She needed that, too.

"I don't want to lose this," he confessed, surprised to hear his thoughts put into words.

"Lose what?" Her eyes still heavy with pleasure, she looked up to meet his gaze. "The sex? That's supposed to be over. Whether it was over yesterday or next week, it wasn't supposed to last."

"It wasn't just sex." He scowled. "Don't cheapen what we had by pretending that's all it was."

As soon as the words were out, he wanted them back. What the hell was wrong with him, spouting crazy talk like that? What was next? Shoe shopping and braiding each other's hair?

"Isn't that supposed to be my line?" she asked, her words as wary as the knot in Diego's belly. "Are you going to ask if I still respect you next?"

He had to grin, appreciating her mouth even though

he was frustrated that she wasn't playing the game the way most women would.

"There ya go," he said. "Keeping the spirit alive."

"Is that a SEAL saying?"

She pushed her hair off her face, then took a deep breath and wiped her fingers under her eyes as if tidying that makeup she'd so carefully applied. "Brandon's friend said the same thing."

"What friend?"

"One of you." She leaned back enough to flick a hand toward Diego as if he was the embodiment of whatever she was talking about. "One of your Navy teammates. A SEAL, I guess."

"Which friend?" Diego's body, already tense with need and edgy with unfulfilled desire, stiffened. "One of the guys you met yesterday?"

"I guess he was there, but we didn't formally meet." Her shrug was more a slide of her body against his than an answer. He harnessed his impatience as Harper hummed, then leaned back to tug, button and adjust her clothing. His mind was racing too fast to slow down and appreciate the view.

"But that's when you heard it? Yesterday?"

The orgasm apparently draining the last of her reserves, Harper lay back again, her legs curled up and hands folded beneath her cheek.

"Not yesterday. Before," she murmured as her lashes fluttered down. "Sympathies. He sent a letter saying he was sorry that Nathan lost his father, that we should keep Brandon's spirit alive."

He hadn't found a letter in her house.

He hadn't found evidence of any thing to do with Ramsey. Not a single thing.

Trying to harness his impatience, he waited. But

Harper was drifting, exhaustion pulling her deeper into its clutches.

"Harper!" Grabbing her by the shoulders, he gave her a single shake. She mumbled something, sighed, then snuggled her chin into his wrist.

Dammit. Feeling like enough of an ass to be glad there was nobody else on this flight, Diego huffed, then leaned down to get her attention the only way he knew how.

He pressed his mouth to hers.

Her lips opened, welcoming him to the damp warmth of her kiss. Their tongues tangled in a hypnotically sensual slide.

"Again?" she murmured. Her lashes fluttered open, her eyes filled with a dusky, sleepy passion.

"What's the name?" he asked, ignoring that passion. "The name of the friend who sent the letter?"

"Hmm?" Harper blinked the sleep away, looking as if she were trying to find her thoughts. "The friend? Dane, something."

Shit. Damn, shit, damn. Diego grabbed his cell phone.

"Adams, Petty Officer Dane Adams, contacted you?" he asked, wanting to confirm facts before he called the team to action.

"Yes, that's his name." His tension obviously getting through, she pushed herself into a sitting position. "He's the one who sent me notification of Brandon's death. He sent a box to Nathan and a letter. Called once to reminisce. It was sad, in a way."

"What did the letter say? And what was in the box?"

"That Brandon was a hero and a good friend. He said the box held some medals and some of Brandon's stuff. He figured Nathan should have it." She wet her lips, her brow furrowed with worry. "We never went through the box. Nathan didn't want to and I was just as happy to go back to pretending Brandon didn't exist."

"Where's the box? The stuff he sent? I never saw anything connected to Ramsey at your place."

He didn't say that he'd searched her house. From the dawning anger on her face, he didn't have to.

"This guy thinks Brandon is dead. Just like you did." She took a deep breath. "Isn't he one of your guys?"

"He's one of the support team. He's Ramsey's wingman. His best friend." Even as Diego confirmed that, he was texting instructions, contacting Savino, putting the team on alert. He wanted them ready to move as soon as the plane set down.

While he sent the messages, he watched Harper. She knew this was a break. He could see the knowledge on her face, the worry in her eyes. And, unfortunately, the self-blame. He couldn't do much about the latter.

"We don't know that Adams is involved," he told her.

"You aren't acting as if you think he isn't."

"Do you remember anything about the box? Where you put it? What you did with the letter? What'd he say in the call?"

"We only spoke for a couple of minutes. He seemed upset that I wasn't going to let him meet Nathan, that I had no interest in sharing stories about Brandon." She met his gaze for a long moment, then shrugged. "I shredded the letter into confetti because it made me cry."

"And the box?"

"I didn't go through the box, but the letter said that it held medals and papers and stuff, things he figured Nathan should have. He wanted Nathan to know what a hero his father was." Her laugh was a puff of air, humorless and filled with pain.

"Some hero, right?" she said, her head falling back against the metal bulkhead.

"Where is it?"

"I don't know. I was so distracted with Nathan going to camp, so enamored with you, that I honestly forgot about it. All I know was that Nathan didn't want it. He believes in real heroes. To Nathan, Brandon didn't qualify."

LIKE A CAT, Andi curled in the comfortable corner of Harper's kitchen banquette, watching the show. Nerves ran through her, sharp, edgy and demanding, so it was all she could do to stay still.

But still she remained. Because she saw more that way. Andi's eyes shifted from here to there, her fingers tapping on the table while her mind raced.

She'd heard of the SEALs. Who hadn't? But these guys seemed like more.

She'd never watched a military operation, so it was hard to know if this was normal. The Navy had taken over Harper's house. Two men had commandeered Harper's office, one of whom looked like he was about to drop dead. The other simply looked pissed. Jared, or MacGyver as his buddies were calling him, seemed to be everywhere. The office, upstairs, downstairs and next door. Where, she supposed, they were still playing covert games, since some of the men moved between this house and the one next door through the backyards instead of the front door. Poor Nathan. He was such a brave little boy but he must be scared. Andi caught her bottom lip between her teeth, biting down until she was sure she'd battled back the tears.

Of course, Jared chose that moment to walk in.

"You okay?"

Giving herself a second to dab her finger under her eyes and take a fortifying breath, Andi pulled on her most regal expression.

"Fine, thank you." She pointed through the window toward the house next door. "So what's the deal? Does your kind hide out of habit? Or do you need a reason for sneaking around?"

Jared bared his teeth in a smile of sorts, then, as if dismissing her, walked over to the fridge. But Andi could see the awareness in his eyes, the discomfort in his stiff carriage and, unfortunately, the worry in the set of his chin.

"We're not spies. We don't hide. We don't sneak."

And you don't look so good, she thought. But she kept that opinion to herself. Andi pursed her lips and looked a little closer.

He wrenched off the cap of a bottle of water, chugging it dry, then twisting the plastic into a knot. His face was drawn, skin pale and those pretty blue eyes of his were bloodshot. With worry, she decided, noting the furrowed brow and creases etching his forehead.

No. He didn't look good.

"It must be rough," she stated, toasting him with her own water, hers being in an etched blue glass with a tasty sprig of mint. "Being called out on such ugly behavior. Tell me, did you get in trouble for carelessly letting a little boy be abducted? Or, like lying, is that just business as usual in your world?"

"No more than being judgmental and bitchy is business as usual for you."

"Touché," Andi said with a twist of her lips, pretending that his words hadn't cut.

But with a hint of the sensitivity she'd found so attractive only recently, he sighed. He rubbed both hands over his face, then gave her an apologetic look.

"I'm sorry. That was rude. It's been a rough few days. A rough couple of months, truth be told." He rested his hand on the back of a chair, waited as if for permission.

Andi tilted her head, figuring he'd take that whichever way he wanted. Apparently what he wanted was to sit because he pulled out the chair, and joined her.

"Let's clear the air, okay."

"Be my guest."

"I don't use sex. I seek it out. I enjoy it. Hell, I amass it if I can. But I don't use it." His expression a study in frustration, he tilted his chair forward, leaning his elbows on the table and pushing his face toward hers. "I didn't use you."

Andi wet her lips. Desire shimmered in her belly, hot and wanting.

"Please, you are a professional liar," she replied with a breathy laugh. "Am I supposed to believe the other night meant anything to you?"

"Did it mean anything to you?" he countered.

She didn't know. As much as she wanted to say it had meant nothing, as much as she wished it had meant the world, she simply didn't know.

"Truth be told, I'm a professional naval officer. I specialize in computer ops." Jared snagged the water, toasting her with her own glass. "And you're a professional socialite. What does that have to do with what happened?"

"To do with lies? Probably nothing, I suppose." Andi called on all those socialite skills to keep her voice even and her expression bland.

"Look, we see ugly stuff. We do ugly stuff. But we

never do it for personal gain or for individual profit. We do it to serve our country."

Jared shrugged as if that's just the way it was, but Andi could tell from the expression in his eyes that it mattered to him.

A part of her wanted to wrap her arms around him and cuddle him close, to soothe that wounded little boy. But like he said, he was deeply enmeshed in ugly stuff. And his priority would always be serving his country.

As if his words weren't proof enough, a buzzing sounded. He pulled out his cell phone—the tech was so intricate it appeared as if it could control a space satellite. His frown flashed.

"What?" she asked.

"We need to find a box."

"What box?"

"Ad—someone sent Nathan a box," he told her, correcting whatever he'd originally planned to say. "We have to find it."

Andi looked around the kitchen as if whatever it was would jump out at her.

"Does Harper know where it is?"

"If she did, I'd have said we need to get it. Not find it."

"Didn't your kind already do a thorough search?" she mocked. But gently, since she couldn't seem to hold her anger against him.

"Torres said he searched, but it seems he was a little too distracted to be thorough." Andi could see the frustrated pain in his eyes, in the hand he swept over his face.

"Do you resent him falling in love?"

"Does that word make you feel better?"

God, no. She had no faith in the idea of love. Andi

only shrugged. And she was grateful when, instead of saying more, Jared got to his feet.

"We need to find it. The box, or whatever was in it." He looked around as if baffled where to begin his search.

"Did you know I lived here for two years?" She rose, sliding her feet into the delicate leather of her sandals before crossing the kitchen. She started with the built-in desk, opening one drawer after the other, sorting papers as she went. She only made it to the third before her light was blocked by Jared's shadow.

"What are you doing?"

"Looking." She arched her brow. "Weren't those your orders? Your superior told you to find the box."

"First, they were my orders. Second, Torres isn't my superior. Third, a box is a contained cardboard form, not a bunch of scattered papers."

She pursed her lips, wondering if she liked this side of him. The totally sober side.

"First, orders are orders as far as I can tell. Second, my impression from the man who is your superior was that Diego is in charge of this mission, which makes him the boss of you. And third, you guys are idiots."

His grab wasn't unexpected, but Andi didn't sidestep. Instead she used the move to pull him closer, enjoying the feel of her body rubbing against his. She liked the way the heat flashed, almost as strong as the irritation darkening his eyes.

"You want to try me again?" she murmured, her gaze sliding over his mouth. "Want to see what it's like now that I know what you are?"

"You want to try *me* again?" If there'd been any more cynicism in his tone, it would have dropped on her bare toes. "You like the idea of doing it with a SEAL? Got a thing for a guy in uniform?"

Andi's laugh was pure disdain. Luckily he didn't know that the heat in her belly was pure desire. A fact she planned to keep to herself until she'd decided what she wanted to do about it. She wasn't about to reward Jared's bullshit with hot sex.

But she really did want that hot sex.

Then Jared backed her up against the wall, his hands flat on either side of her head. His body angled into hers, heating, tempting, but not touching.

Not quite.

He'd take her if she let him. He'd pull her to the floor or drag her upstairs. He'd make her scream with pleasure.

If she let him.

Andi knew it was up to her. She hated that he was forcing her to choose. Forcing her to take responsibility. But this was Harper they were talking about.

This was Nathan.

For them, Andi shifted away, ducking under Jared's arm with a shrug. "Harper didn't put the box away, and she didn't unpack it. She set it aside to go through with Nathan. If Harper doesn't know where it is, if Diego searched the house and didn't see it, it's because Nathan did something with it."

Frustration flashed in his eyes for a brief moment. He frowned at the desk, then looked around the kitchen.

"Then let's think like a kid. Let's find it."

CHAPTER TWENTY

"You think Adams is in on it with Ramsey?" Diego asked the minute he walked into their Temp HQ. "Or is he behind it?"

"That's what we have to find out," Lansky said.

Diego grimaced, his face a study of frustration. "Did Savino head back to base already?"

"Ten minutes ago," Prescott confirmed. "He's pissed. Adams is supposed to be SIQ but nobody can find him. Savino's ordered the MPs to start a search in case Adams went out for Pepto Bismol or something."

"Sick in quarters, my ass," Lansky muttered, his fingers flying over the computer keyboard. "That'll be AWOL if they don't find him by the time Savino gets there."

"Did you find anything in that box of crap he sent Nathan?" Diego asked next, starting his own sift through the contents spread over the desk. It was like a shrine-in-a-box. Same feel, different size as what he'd seen at Ramsey's mother's house. "You found this in the coat closet?"

"Found it in a duffle belonging to some kid named Jeremy," Lansky confirmed. "We went through it piece by piece. Didn't see any encryption, no coded messages, nothing."

Impatience was a ripple in the air, easily identified and mutually felt by all the men in the room.

Fifteen minutes later, Diego had to admit he wasn't finding anything, either. Frustration wrapped so tight it felt like it was squeezing him dry, he started pulling the photos out of the album sleeves, arranging and re-arranging them on the desk.

"Where is this place? The place on the lake. There are a few shots of Ramsey and Adams here. Do either of them own lakeside property?"

"Neither of them appear to own any property under their real names," Lansky said. Even as he shook his head, he pulled up their files again to double check.

"They aren't all taken on the same trip. These are over a few years' time." Diego glanced at Prescott, who was sprawled in one of Harper's fancy office chairs, looking as if his full attention was on the sketch he was drawing. But Diego knew he was hearing every word. "You hung out with them. Do you have any idea where this is?"

Prescott tossed aside the pad and pencil, the image of an evil genie with Ramsey's head landing faceup on the couch next to him. It took him a lot longer than it should have to push to his feet, his movements pain-ful to watch as he tried to work past the stiffness of his muscles and the lack of cooperation from his injured leg. Diego didn't let his concern show, though. He sim-ply stood there, expressionless, waiting for Prescott to take the photo.

"I never went camping with Adams or Ramsey, never went anywhere off base with them." His face anguished, either from his injury or facing the ugly facts. "I thought we were friends. But I guess not."

Diego debated various options to soothe or comfort. But soothing and comforting weren't his job. Finding the traitor and saving the kid were. And his gut said that this lakeside locale was key to doing just that.

"Do a deeper property search," he ordered. "Try variations on their names, on family names, businesses under the same. It'll be a combination," he concluded. "Use the same parameters to search financials."

Both men got to work.

Diego watched as Prescott and Lansky went to work, fingers dueling as they hacked, decrypted and fought their way through various levels of electronics and security.

Getting a headache watching the monitors flash from screen to screen to screen, Diego went back to pacing and thinking about where Ramsey would take Nathan. Could he get the kid out of the country without a passport? How hard would that be to forge?

Diego drilled his fingertips into his forehead, wishing he could dig through the pain and find the damned answers.

"Hold a second," Diego said, lifting one hand as the idea hit him. "Add Nathan's name into the mix. Nathan Alexander."

They'd never thought to look into the kid. They'd never thought someone would use a child. They should have. He should have. "Got him," Prescott muttered five minutes later. "There's the motherfucker."

Lansky leaned over to peer at the screen, then gave a sharp nod and went to work on his own keyboard as Diego hurried across the room.

"What've you got?"

"Lakeside property on Castaic Lake owned by Alexander Michaels. Alexander being Nathan's middle name, Michael being Adams' mother's maiden name," Prescott explained before jabbing his finger at his screen. "Look, Zillow photos show the same house, even."

"And here we go, I'm pulling financials," Lansky crowed. "Holy shit. There's over a million dollars in this account alone and there are at least two others in the Caymans that I haven't accessed yet."

"I've got an email address," Prescott said. A second later, he added, "And I've accessed the account."

As Prescott started reading through emails for clues, Lansky made a choking sound. "Holy shit," he breathed. "Look at these deposits. He's gotta have been selling military information for years."

"They," Prescott corrected, tapping a finger on his own screen to show a series of emails between Ramsey and Adams. "Their communications are coded, it'll take me a while to break them all. But I'm going with *they*. As in, they were in it together."

"We've nailed them," Lansky said, slapping his hand on the desk. "Nailed their asses to the wall."

"This'll clear Poseidon," Prescott said, letting out a heavy breath that Diego recognized as the same relief he felt himself. "Unless one of us is listed in here, it'll clear our names."

"Nailing asses and clearing our names aren't the priority right now. Retrieving the child is the priority," Diego pointed out, his muscles tight as adrenaline surged. Priority or not, he was so totally ready to kick ass.

"We need to let Savino know." Lansky pushed away from the desk. "We need to hand this over to NI."

"Savino hasn't answered my last two texts and digging through NI's red tape will take too long," Diego snapped. "The hostage in question is a little boy, and he's in danger."

Diego grabbed the computer tablet with its real estate listing and handed it to Prescott. "Are you finding any other properties besides this one?"

"Not yet." Prescott scanned the property listing again, then went to work pulling up maps and aerials of Castaic Lake and the surrounding area. "I'd guess this is probably the one."

"You'd guess?" Could they rely on guessing at this point?

"It's remote enough to defend, close enough to the kid's camp to afford minimal risk." When Diego arched one brow, Elijah puffed out a breath. "Even if it's Ramsey, whoever grabbed that kid, he's a stranger to the boy. Unless he incapacitated the child, his options are minimal."

A gasp sounded, alerting the three men that they weren't alone. They winced as one as a slight figure with blond hair spun away.

His eyes locked on the back of Harper's head as she ran up the stairs. Diego made a decision. "I'm going in," he murmured.

"You're crazy."

"Are you willing to put all our asses on the line? We all know that NI isn't going to stop breathing down our necks. The team is in serious trouble. Even if this clears Poseidon, someone wants us disbanded." Prescott looked as if he wanted to punch something, but he managed to keep his words even. "Savino is down there trying to salvage your rep, but if you go vigilante, he's wasting his breath."

"A kid's life is at stake." If Diego had to pay with his career to put Nathan back in his mother's arms, then so be it.

"He knows our playbook."

Yeah. If it was Ramsey, he'd even written part of it. If it was Adams, well, the guy had worked plenty of the team's missions besides that last one. He'd served as part of the support crew for years, had trained with them, had studied them.

"Whoever it is, he knows SEAL Team 7's playbook," Diego corrected meticulously. "We're Poseidon."

"Splitting hairs."

"Hairs are all we've got."

"You're not waiting for Savino? Not waiting for the rest of the team?"

Diego shifted through the crap they'd piled on Harper's desk until he found the photo of Nathan she'd brought them. He held it high.

"Do you think we have time?" He slapped the photo in the other man's hand. "Are you willing to gamble on that?"

"Are you willing to gamble with your career? With your freedom? The brig ain't a picnic, Kitty Cat."

"A boy's life is at stake," Diego said again, heading for the door. He had one thing to do, and then he was leaving. "If it makes you feel better, wait here. Get a hold of Savino, wait for his arrival, fill him in, run backup."

Their silence followed him up the stairs, but he couldn't worry about that. His plate was already too full. Diego paused in the doorway of Harper's bedroom but didn't step over the threshold. He knew he wasn't welcome.

Just as he knew it had been her downstairs, listening. That she'd heard enough to judge and find him guilty. Of what didn't matter.

He stood, shoulders back and chin high, trying to pretend he didn't hate watching the woman he loved—

yes, dammit, loved—rip the sheets from the bed they'd lain in as if she could tear away the reality of their being together you.

"What do you need, Diego?"

Noting the ice dripping off her words, he was sure she wanted to rip him out of her life. He couldn't blame her, but just in case her reasons were a little different than he was figuring, he'd like to know why.

Diego knew he could tiptoe around it; he could try to assuage it. Or if he were smart he'd ignore it, finish the mission, and get on with his damned life.

"Why are you so pissed?" he asked, confronting it instead.

"Pissed?" Holding the sheet against her chest as if protecting her heart, Harper widened her eyes in exaggerated surprise. "What could I have to be pissed about?"

"A lot of things, I'm sure." But when she'd let him bare her to his mouth, let him drive her to a gasping orgasm earlier that afternoon, he'd pretty much thought they'd settled most of them. "Why don't you tell me exactly which one you're working on right now?"

"You're leaving, aren't you?"

Was she worried about him? Going to miss him? A spark lit in Diego's chest. Maybe hope, maybe heart. He wasn't sure.

"In about ten minutes." He clenched his teeth, but couldn't stop himself from offering what he shouldn't— a promise. "I'll bring him back. I'll get your son."

He wasn't going to tell her what desperate men did when confronted with deeds like kidnapping or treason. She didn't need to know that the men they were going after were likely armed and unquestionably dangerous. They'd already committed treason, their lives were on the line and they were trained to kill.

Diego swallowed hard against the tiny kernel of fear that'd lodged in his throat. "I'm going to get Nathan. Because he's important. To you. To me."

"I was bait! I was just a means to an end for you. A way to get to Brandon. And you thought I was part of it!" Before he could respond, Harper threw her arms wide, then wrapped them tight around her again. "You used me."

Her eyes were defeated, filled with so many layers of betrayal that Diego knew that even if he devoted years to the task, he'd never heal them all.

But he had to try.

"At first, you were a part of the mission. Intel indicated that you were involved." Diego shoved his hands in his pockets. God, he'd never felt so useless. "At first. Not now. At first, doing my job was my priority. Now you and Nathan are."

And that scared the hell out of him. Apparently it didn't impress her, though, because she only shrugged.

"How can I convince you?"

"It doesn't matter." She sighed, a shaky, tear-filled sound. "I just want my son back. I want him safe, here in my arms where I can hold him. Then he and I can try to rebuild our world."

"And me? Do I have a place in that world?"

It didn't matter. He could see the answer on her face. In the way she smoothed the fresh sheet over the bed, tucking it tight under the mattress as if keeping even air from sliding between.

And Diego knew. Harper had room for only one person in her world.

Nathan.

So he'd better get him back for her.

No matter what the cost.

HARPER WANTED TO be glad Diego was gone. He'd lied to her; he'd used her. He'd come much too close to breaking her heart.

But a part of her wanted to beg him to stay. Because despite everything he'd done, he was her only hope right now. The only person she believed could bring Nathan home.

She wanted to chase him down the hall and out the door. She wanted to beg him to be safe. To take care.

But she *was* afraid. Diego was going to save Nathan. But at what cost? And what if he didn't?

She clenched her teeth against the fear. But it came anyway. She fought it, ignored it, pushed past it.

Until she couldn't.

Andi found her there, curled in a ball on her freshly made bed. "Hey, sweetie."

Harper didn't move.

"Mission Rescue is in effect," Andi told her. Harper felt her weight settle on the bed just a moment before a soothing hand rubbed her shoulder. "They'll bring Nathan home."

Harper managed a nod.

"I listened from the kitchen to Jared and their friend Elijah. The one who's hurt. He's supposed to still be in the hospital, recovering from whatever Brandon did." Andi's hand kept rubbing a soothing pattern and her voice didn't change, but Harper knew her friend was mad, could feel the anger emanating off her. "The three of them, Jared, the hurt guy and your lover, are acting against orders. Apparently they're supposed to sit around and wait for a bunch of paper pushers before they do anything."

Harper simply blinked. Andi had never been big on waiting or in believing in orders.

"In a prime junior high moment, I heard Jared tell

Elijah that Diego had it bad for you. That he'd gone off the deep end, way past sex and into being crazy about you." Andi patted Harper's back. "He's risking his life for you. He's risking his career for you. He'd stick around if you wanted."

If she wanted. She was so miserably, irrevocably, sick in love with the man that she almost hated herself. But that didn't mean she knew what she wanted.

Harper sat up slowly, giving herself a moment to settle her swirling head and her spinning emotions. She took a deep breath and met Andi's dark eyes. "Would you? Could you get past Jared's career? These guys are SEALs, Andi. Could you live with the doubt, the uncertainty and the danger? Would it be worth the fear, the unknowing?"

Even as she reeled off the drawbacks, listing all the rationales and reasons to think twice, she knew Andi's answer. It was written all over that exotic face.

Harper wiped at the tears sliding down her cheeks before swinging her feet off the side of the bed. She knew what she had to do next.

She didn't know what she'd do last, though.

"Where are you going?"

Harper paused in the act of lacing up her boots to look at her friend. "Do you believe Diego will come back with Nathan?" she asked in lieu of an answer.

"Absolutely."

Grabbing on to that assurance with a heart too desperate to consider otherwise, Harper nodded.

"Then I'm going to get Nathan his kitten."

NATHAN CURLED UP in the corner of the bed, his pillow clutched in one hand and the other fisted tight. In case he had to hit someone.

He missed camp and all the fun he'd been having. He'd liked hiking, and it had been cool to learn about boats and sleeping under the stars.

He missed Jeremy. They'd had a blast listening to ghost stories around the campfire and whispering into the night, reliving their adventures and talking about home.

Those talks with Jeremy had kept the homesickness at bay, had kept Nathan focused on the adventure. Jeremy had cried that first night because he missed his mom. Nathan had told him he understood.

But he hadn't cried himself. Percy Jackson hadn't cried when the Minotaur crushed his mom into gold dust, Nathan told himself. He'd see his mom in just a few days, he'd figured. She'd visit on Parents' Day and give him big enough hugs to get him through until it was time to go home.

He'd been excited. And proud.

Then the man had come.

His mouth wet with salty tears, Nathan curled tighter, his knees drawn up to his chest and his eyes squished shut.

The man had grabbed him right out of his cot, had pulled him into the woods and onto a boat. He hadn't even let him get his stuff.

Not his cell phone, with the GPS tracking his mom thought he didn't know was on there.

Not his jeans or his backpack, with the little notes of paper with his address and phone number written in case he lost his pants or something.

He didn't have anything. Not even his baseball.

Now he was cold and he was hungry. Now he missed his mom so much, he couldn't stop the crying.

Nathan buried his face in the pillow, his hand pressed

over his head. He didn't know where he was. He didn't know how long he'd been gone.

And he didn't know who that man was.

As if his thoughts had sent out an alert, footsteps sounded down the hall. Each one sent a deep thrill of terror down Nathan's spine, constricting like a rubber band in his belly until it was so tight it nearly snapped when the shadow fell over the room.

Nathan scrunched his eyelids closed, trying to look like he was asleep.

"Hey, Nate, how ya doing?" The steps came closer. "You awake yet? You should get up. You need to eat. Then we've got things to do."

Nathan's breath locked in his chest.

"Nate? C'mon. Let's go."

Grinding his teeth together, Nathan debated for a few seconds. Then he slowly turned over. He glared, but the light came from the hallway, so he couldn't make out the man's face.

"My name isn't Nate. It's Nathan."

"Okay, sure." The guy said it in that grown-up, let's-humor-the-little-kid sort of way. When he flipped on the dim light next to the bed, he had a friendly smile. But his eyes were scary. Not mean.

Afraid.

Nathan didn't figure anything that made a big guy like that afraid would prove to be good for him. But he knew better than to let the man see that he was worried. Heroes never showed stuff like that.

"You hungry, kid?"

Even though his stomach wanted to grumble, Nathan frowned and shook his head. Diego called him kid and it was kinda cool. He didn't like the way this man said it.

"You have to eat." The guy stepped over to the window, lifted the shade and peered around as if checking to see if anyone was outside. "I made sandwiches. Way better than rations, let me tell ya."

Still checking the window, the guy tossed a plastic-wrapped sandwich onto the bed.

"Eat."

Nathan slowly sat up, rubbing his hand over his face and hoping it didn't show that he'd cried.

"Who are you?"

"Me? I'm Dane. Dane Adams. Your dad and I are pals. Best pals."

"I don't have a dad."

The man's face screwed up into a tight look that made Nathan's stomach hurt again.

"I know they told you that your dad is dead, but he's not. There's just stuff going down. He has to lay low for a while, but he's alive." The man's smile flashed. "Believe me, kid. Your dad is alive."

"I don't have a dad," Nathan screamed before the man could say more. Fists tight, he glared. "The guy who made me walked out. He never visited. He never helped with money or anything. My mom raised me by herself. She's all I need."

"You're mad—I get it." The man smiled like he was a friend, but something ugly flashed in his eyes. Something that made Nathan's stomach hurt. "But sometimes a guy's got to do the hard things because he's trying to be a hero. Sometimes he's got to walk away from the people who matter, but that doesn't mean he doesn't care. That doesn't mean he isn't taking care of them."

"A hero does the right thing," Nathan said stubbornly, shoving the uneaten sandwich away. "Maybe he has to leave to do it, but he doesn't ignore the people he leaves behind."

"You're too young to understand" came the easy dismissal. "You don't know what a hero really is. How could you, being raised by just a woman."

Nathan wanted to yell that his mom wasn't just a woman. And she never did that. She never blew him off or treated him like a baby who was too stupid to understand things. She either explained whatever it was or she said he'd understand when he was older.

Nathan wasn't stupid. He could see how much smaller than the guy he was. He couldn't defend himself. He couldn't fight his way out of this. And until he found an opening, he couldn't run.

DRESSED IN PLAIN CLOTHES, armed to the teeth, Diego stared at the small house set back in the hills surrounding Castaic Lake. A cabin, really, but not isolated like he'd expected. He supposed that was smart. There was appeal in a remote location. But the team was trained to avoid civilian casualties, so one man had a better chance when surrounded by the potential of collateral damage.

"You should wait here, Rembrandt," he told Prescott without looking around. "Monitor communications—try Savino again."

"Want me to do a coffee run, too? Maybe play secretary?"

"Nah." Knowing it was what his teammate wanted, Diego did turn now, giving Prescott a once-over. "You'd make a crappy secretary. You don't have the legs for it."

He saw Lansky's wince out the corner of his eye, but Prescott only smiled and angled out his damaged leg.

"Yeah. I guess skirts are out for me. That leaves MacGyver. His face is pretty enough."

"Not as pretty as Kitty Cat's here."

And that was all Diego needed to know the men had

his back. That they were, for all that'd happened, still a team. A brotherhood.

"Let's do this," he said, jerking his chin toward their goal. The small house had no growth around it, no trees or bushes to disguise their approach. The sun was low, but darkness was still at least four hours away. Too long to wait when a boy's life was at stake.

"Options?" he asked quietly, more than willing to hear a better one than his. But his friends stood, one on each side of him, and kept their silence.

"Our priority is to extract the hostage. Without equipment, we can't tell if Adams is in there alone or if he's got backup with him," Lansky pointed out. "Without intel, we don't know if he's working alone, or if our suspicions are correct and he's following Ramsey's lead."

"You're stalling," Prescott said.

"He always repeats the obvious when he's trying to do something noble." Diego didn't need to look over to know that Jared's words were accompanied by a roll of his eyes. "Next, he'll point out that if we hold back, the report won't show us disobeying orders. He thinks he's covering our butts."

"Big boys don't need diapers." With that, Prescott pulled a jammer from the pocket of his bomber jacket and aimed toward the cabin. "All tech in a half-mile radius is down for the next five minutes. Computers, alarm systems, cellphones are jammed. Let's rock and roll, gentlemen."

Since force was out and stealth not possible, they went with what they did best.

Balls-out cockiness.

They strode up to the house nearest the cabin as if

they were expected guests, knocking loud enough to alert the entire neighborhood of their arrival.

"Hey, gorgeous," Jared said as soon as a pretty redhead answered. "Is Mary here?"

While Jared worked his charms at distraction, Prescott fiddled with his cell phone. As soon as he got the tech wizard's nod, Diego slid along the blind side of the cabin, working his way toward the back.

He had to time it just right, waiting for a count of ten to give Prescott time to create a diversion. Diego crossed the distance in a low sprint, his ears tuned to any hint of jeopardy. Not for himself but for the boy. All was silent.

He rounded the back of the cabin, pressed his ear to the window. When he heard nothing but silence, he moved to the back door. The plan was to wait for the two men to join him, but Diego silently picked the lock and slipped inside alone.

Not out of heroism or because he didn't trust his men. But he'd gotten them into this. Whatever the risk, it was his to take. Whatever the payment, it was his to make.

The back of the cabin was unprotected, a small kitchen with a sink holding a single glass, a rickety stove and the quiet hum of a sickly green fridge. Pressed against the far wall, Diego angled his eyes around the doorway to check the next room.

Empty but for a sleeping bag thrown over a sagging brown couch, a table holding a laptop and a nice arsenal of weapons. He counted four rifles, two semiautos and a Glock cozied up next to a rusty hunting knife.

Somebody believed in being prepared.

Diego checked his SIG but didn't bother to pull the knife from his belt or the backup Glock from his ankle holster.

There was prepared.

And there was simply damned good.

He and his men? They were damned good.

NATHAN WAS SCARED.

He hadn't heard anything, but the man had. In a flash, the guy pulled a gun out from somewhere as he moved from the window to the bedroom door. Nathan's gaze locked on the gun. It wasn't anything like the ones in the movies. This one was ugly and shiny and mean.

The man's face tightened, his eyes narrow as he peered around the corner. Nathan wanted to yell out a warning. He wanted to let whoever was coming know he was here, to scream for them to get him out, to keep him safe.

But he didn't know who was out there.

"I want my mom," he sobbed, no longer able to hide from the ugly monster's teeth and claws that made up his fear. "I want to go home."

"You are home, Nate. Now shut up until your dad gets here to rescue us."

He didn't have a dad, Nathan wanted to shout.

And he was pretty sure whoever was out there would rescue him. Hoping, praying, crossing all his fingers using the wishes of every birthday and Christmas rolled in one, Nathan dropped to the floor to roll under the bed.

He'd hide. He'd wait. The good guys would come. They had to.

A SHOT RANG OUT.

Nathan threw his hands over his head, biting back a scream.

The good guys sounded scary.

He heard a grunt, it sounded like the guy who'd brought him here. He waited for more, for another gunshot. But there was a thud and what sounded like something heavy sliding down the wall.

Then nothing.

Terror spun in circles, swirling like a pinwheel in a windstorm, making Nathan's head hurt and his stomach rebel. He wanted to cry out, but he couldn't find his voice. He wanted to run, but he was afraid to leave the safety under the bed.

A pair of boots, black and polished, stepped into the room. His throat clicked as he tried to swallow the bubble of fear, as he tried to burrow silently back farther against the wall.

Those big feet stepped closer.

Nathan pressed himself as flat as he could to the wall and squeezed his eyes shut tight. He felt the mattress shift, weight bearing down so it almost touched his head.

"Hey, kid. I figure you've been missing this."

Nathan knew that voice. His lips trembled at the sound, at what it meant. The fear that'd tied knots in his belly loosened enough that he felt safe enough to peel open one eye.

His heart stopped. Both eyes flew open and he couldn't keep the gasp of surprise quiet.

His baseball.

He was safe!

Nathan scrambled out from under the bed as fast as he could, his eyes wide and his heart racing. "Diego. You came. You saved me."

Nathan threw himself into the man's arms and held on as if his life depended on it. He didn't care that he was crying all over a man he admired like none other.

He didn't care that his words were a blubbering mess, impossible to understand.

Diego was here.

Diego had saved him.

Everything was okay. It was really okay.

"Hey, kid. It's good to see you, too." Diego's words finally penetrated enough that Nathan released his stranglehold so Diego could lift his chin and inspect his face.

"You okay, kid?"

Nathan tried to look toward the door, but Diego was too big to see around. Still, he saw the shadow on the floor.

And he knew.

"Is he…" Nathan wet his lips and tried to swallow past the rock that was caught in his throat. "Did you—"

"Don't worry about him." Diego snagged his chin between two fingers and lifted Nathan's face so their eyes met. "Was there anyone else here?"

Despite his comfort in the arms of his rescuer, a spark of fear chilled its way down Nathan's back.

"Just him. He talked like someone was coming, but he was mad when nobody did. He kept talking about that guy." His mouth bitter, Nathan had to swallow the nasty taste before he could finish. "The one he called my dad."

"He's not going to bother you. Nobody's going to bother you," Diego promised. "You're okay."

Looking up at the man he'd thought would be a cool hero, Nathan wanted to admit that he'd been scared. He felt like he should confess that he'd cried. But even as Diego patted him down for injuries, Nathan knew he didn't have to.

Diego already knew.

"You're a SEAL, aren't you? Like that guy wanted to be. But you're a real hero."

"I'm a real SEAL, sure. I don't know about the rest, though." Diego's smile was the same as it'd been the first time Nathan saw him. Amused, kind and just a little weirded out. Nathan liked that smile. "I do know we should get you out of here, though."

"I want..." The words choked in Nathan's throat. His eyes slid to the floor again, there just behind Diego. He swallowed hard, then met Diego's eyes again.

"Anything you want, kid. You name it—I'll get it."

"My mom," the boy murmured as he buried his head into the curve of Diego's neck. He breathed in the man's scent and felt safe. "I want my mom."

"You got it, kid." Diego's words were a warm blanket of comfort, wrapping tight around Nathan. Making him feel safe. "Let's get you home."

CHAPTER TWENTY-ONE

HARPER WATCHED THE chilly expression on Commander Nic Savino's face as he stood in her great room, hands clasped behind his back and his attention on the window that faced the street.

She, on the other hand, paced. She strode from one end of the room to the other, fluffing pillows and adjusting trinkets as she went. With every pass, she studied the scowling SEAL team leader.

"You're sure Nathan's okay?" she asked for the fifth time since he'd walked in the door with news that Diego had apprehended the kidnapper and retrieved her son.

"The operation was a success. The hostile has been apprehended and the boy safely extracted from danger." He slanted her a patient look. And, for the fifth time, said, "Your son is fine."

Even as she told herself to believe him, Harper fought the nerves dancing down her spine.

It was only when, hands still clasped behind his back and his face inscrutable, Savino turned toward her that Harper realized that it wasn't Nathan she was nervous about.

She knew her son was safe. Diego had him. And he'd promised to bring him home.

It was Diego she was worried about.

How much trouble was he in? She almost asked

aloud, but Savino tilted his head before she could get the words out.

"There were mistakes made in this operation. Will you file a complaint?"

"What?" Baffled, Harper shook her head. "Against who? Brandon, for lying and scheming and, apparently, doing something heinous enough to put an entire SEAL team, possibly our entire country, in danger? Or this Adams guy, who has, according to you, been apprehended?"

"Torres, for misleading you. Myself, for ordering him to do just that." He paused for a moment as if debating, then added, "The Navy, for not taking a decisive stand on Lieutenant Ramsey's life or death, and as such, opening the door to just this sort of incident."

He sounded like a lawyer. Someone who chased accident victims down the hospital corridor, trying to con them into becoming a client.

But somewhere in the last few hours, Harper had decided that she wasn't going to be a victim. And she wasn't looking to extract a pound of flesh from anyone. Not the Navy, not Savino. Not even Diego.

She *had* blamed him. She pressed her hand through her hair, tugging at the ends as if it'd help relieve some of the pressure her thoughts were causing.

She'd blamed Diego for lying to her. For deceiving her and making her think he was just another guy.

She'd blamed him for spying on her, for searching her house and for having sex with her without telling her why he was really there.

For a few brief moments she'd even tried to blame him for Nathan's kidnapping. Of course, that'd simply been a desperate grasp to try to avoid the misery of blaming herself. But, eventually, she'd reasoned that Nathan's abduction wasn't her fault. And it wasn't Diego's.

No. That one was completely Brandon's responsibility.

Which left only one thing.

The one that, if she were honest with herself—which she tried to be whenever possible, was at the core of any blame she held Diego responsible for.

She'd blamed him for being a man she could fall in love with. A man who made her believe in possibilities. Who made her see what it'd be like to be more than content, more than just a mom. He'd made her see what it'd be like to live in a bigger world with huge emotions. He'd shown her what it was to want, to need, to desire. He'd seen where she was from and he'd accepted it. He hadn't been appalled, but impressed.

He'd made her want to be happy. Happy in love.

Was that Diego's fault? Did she blame him for showing her all of that?

Harper swallowed hard, but couldn't dislodge the knot in her throat. "No," she finally said, shaking her head. "I wouldn't complain about anyone."

"Just checking. And for the record, Torres declared your innocence long before the evidence supported his claim." A hint of a smile played over his lips while he gave Harper time to digest that. Before she could respond, he tilted his head a moment before the door slammed open with Nathan's usual entrance. "Your son is home."

Harper was already halfway across the room, running as fast as she could. She flew into the foyer, her feet sliding across the slick marble, but she didn't slow.

Not until she'd wrapped her arms around Nathan, squeezing his small body tight into hers. She held him as close as she could, as if feeling his heart beat against her hand, his breath move over her skin, she'd be sure he was real. That he was really home. Really here.

"Mom, I can't breathe," he mumbled against her shoulder with a choking laugh.

She loosened her hold just enough to look into his face. Running her palm over that smooth skin, she checked for marks as her eyes searched his for pain.

"Are you okay? You're okay," she said, when she saw the look in his eyes—somewhere between relief, impatience and embarrassment. But no fear, no pain, no horror.

He was okay. Her baby was home. Right here, in her arms. And he was okay. Relieved tears clogged her chest as all of the horrifying images she'd tried so hard to lock away flashed through her mind. Ripping at her composure, slicing her heart open.

But she had Nathan back. And none of that was going to happen.

Since she knew he'd hate her crying over him, she pulled him against her again so he wouldn't have to watch.

"You're getting my hair all wet," he said. But she felt the clutch of his small hands holding tight the fabric of her shirt.

Harper gave a wet laugh, shifting so she could look over his head at the men still gathered in the doorway. Elijah and Jared appeared uncomfortable, their bodies poised as if they were going to run at the first opportunity.

Diego looked satisfied. His eyes met hers, his gaze direct and filled with the same relieved pleasure coursing through her own heart.

"Is everything okay?" she asked quietly. "Is it finished?"

Diego hesitated, then gave her a half shrug. She didn't miss the glance he shot over her shoulder and knew he was getting clearance before saying anything.

"Everything is under control."

Under control? That's it? That's all she got?

Her son had been abducted. She'd spent the last forty-eight hours in terror. She'd been lied to, deceived, spied on and—yes, it was a questionable point, but she had climaxed under false pretenses.

And all he'd say was that *everything was under control*?

She waited for the anger, and for a second wondered why it wasn't there.

Then as Diego met her eyes again, she understood.

Saving one small boy, chasing down bad guys, that wasn't his job. Diego was a warrior, a fighter. A man who spent his life battling to protect hers and others like hers. He did the hard job, the impossible job, the scary job. He fought the ugly fights, he waged the incomprehensible battles. He was one of the very best Special Operatives in the US military. He was a SEAL.

He'd spent his entire adult life working at being the best. He'd endured more than she could comprehend to make himself the best. He'd trained, served and studied with the sole purpose of becoming one of the elite.

And he'd put all of that on the line to bring her son home. How could she be mad at a man who risked his all to give her back hers?

"Brandon?" she murmured, having to at least ask that. She didn't know if Diego would tell her, but she had to ask. Wanted to know if he was actually alive.

"Nobody was in the cabin except Nathan and Adams.

I saw no sign that Adams was working with anyone but himself."

Harper searched his face, but she didn't see anything to make her think he wasn't telling the truth. Of course, he was so hard to read, she didn't see evidence of the opposite, either.

It simply came down to trust, she realized. Did she trust him?

"Mom, you don't have to let go or anything, but I am kinda hungry."

"Hungry, are you?" Laughing a little, Harper's gaze traced her son's face. "There's someone who'd like to see you before we have lunch."

"Andi?" Nathan looked around, his smile lighting with joy when he saw his honorary aunt in the doorway. "Andi! I had an adventure. Wanna hear about it?"

"I do, sweetie," Andi said with a smile at odds with her tear-choked voice. "I want to hear everything."

"Andi has something of yours." Harper gestured for Andi to bring the kitten. But instead of handing it over, her friend simply walked closer with it still hidden behind her back.

"What's she got? I know it's not my baseball. Diego brought me that." Nathan's smile was like sunshine, shining bright, as he lifted his ball in thanks. "Isn't he the best, Mom? He is, isn't he?"

Andi arched her brows at Harper as if daring her to answer *that* question. Calling on years of practice, Harper ignored her way to a graceful sidestep.

"I suppose this isn't as cool as your baseball, but I hope you won't mind taking care of it anyway." With her back to Andi, Harper reached behind so her friend could put the bundle into her hand. "It's one of those questionable gifts, I suppose. The kind that requires responsibility, takes work."

Wrinkling his nose, Nathan put on his best *it's okay* face.

Harper shifted her hand to her front so she could show him the gift. She could feel Andi hovering behind, felt the kitten squirm out a yawn in her hand. She could sense Diego's anticipation and Savino's curiosity.

But her eyes were locked on her son's face.

His mouth dropped. Nathan reached out one finger, but pulled it back as if he were afraid to touch and find out it wasn't real.

"That's a kitten. It's really a kitten?"

"It is a kitten." Not sure why, Harper glanced at Diego. "He's little and needs care. For the rest of his life, you'll be responsible for him. He'll look to you, depend on you. He'll love you."

Diego's eyes flashed, dark with understanding. He lifted one hand, in agreement or refusal she didn't know. Before she could ask, before he could say, Nathan cupped his hands under the kitten.

"Is this because of that guy?" he asked, his eyes narrow with suspicion even as he cuddled the furry bundle under his chin. "Did you get me a kitten because you're upset that I was gone?"

Leave it to Nathan to pick an act to pieces. He was so like her that all Harper could do was laugh.

"Yes," she admitted, her eyes meeting Diego's again. "I'd thought a kitten was too big a responsibility, that you weren't ready for it yet. I was afraid it would be too much."

She slowly stood. Even as she felt Andi's support at her back and Savino's hulking presence moving toward the door, she watched Diego.

"I was afraid of a lot of things," she confessed. "But I was wrong."

"TORRES."

Harper's words echoing through his head, a million questions sounding right behind them, Diego watched as Andi herded Harper and Nathan toward the kitchen. He wanted to follow. He wanted a moment, or ten, alone with Harper. To ask her what she'd meant. To try to assuage some of that worry about Ramsey. To make sure she was okay.

"Torres," Savino ordered again.

Allowing only a breath for regret, Diego turned to face his commanding officer.

"Yes, sir."

Savino angled his head toward the door. "Debriefing. Let's go."

"Back to base?" Diego looked in the direction Harper had gone. Could he at least say goodbye?

"Temporary base," Savino said. "Since I'm still paying a sick amount of rent on that house next door, we might as well use it."

Savino paused. "Unless you need a minute to deal with...things?"

Diego wanted that minute. He wanted to check on Nathan. To see if he was okay. To see how he was handling his homecoming and meet that cat of his.

He wanted to say something to Harper. To tell her he'd be back, that they'd talk. To find out if she cared.

But she didn't want him here. She might say differently now, out of gratitude. But that's not what she'd said before.

So, after a deep breath and one last look around, he shook his head and followed his leader out the door.

SAVINO STUDIED HIS MEN.

The setting might be a little out of place, with the

fancy wallpaper and rich leather couches flanking a competition class pool table. And the gentle sound of kids playing outside the window was odd to a man used to the sharp retort of gunfire.

But the three men dressed in civilian clothes and sporting their own competition class attitudes were as familiar as his face in a mirror.

In jeans and a beat-up leather jacket, his face unshaven, Diego's stance screamed frustration, despite the fact that he stood at attention, feet planted wide, hands clasped behind his back and his gaze aimed straight ahead.

Lansky's chinos and tee were preppy perfect and his face clean shaven, as usual. But his eyes were shadowed, and there was no hint of his typical amiable ease.

His hair grown out from its usual military cut so it fell in curls over his brow, Prescott was clearly in pain. His face was pinched, his eyes sharp and his body swaying just a little as he held at parade rest.

"So, gentlemen. It appears we have a situation," Savino said after a half dozen or so minutes of tense silence. He'd needed every second of them to reel in his anger and adjust his priorities. "The question is what we do about it."

Being smart men, nobody said anything.

"While the three of you were off on your personal mission, I made it a point to read through the various emails you accessed." His expression as cold as his tone—because, dammit, they hadn't gotten his authorization for that mission—Savino looked from man to man. "While I've ascertained Adams's motive to be simple greed based on my cursory analysis, determining the extent of Ramsey's motive will require someone with a psych degree."

Hands clasped behind his back, Savino strode in front of his men from the one on the left, past the one in the middle to the one on the right. Sometimes silence was a more effective chastisement than words.

"Adams claims that he was spending time with the Maclean boy because he wanted to visit with his friend's child. He swears he was working alone. But he didn't access the funds. At the time they were tapped, he was in an underwater training program under the command of Captain Jarrett." In other words, he couldn't get cell or satellite transmission under a thousand feet of waves.

"Adams would say anything to cover for Ramsey," Prescott said quietly, his eyes bitter. "But if he was working on his own, he had the skills to make sure he was covered."

"Adams was a dumb ass in love with the wrong guy." They all looked over at Lansky's comment. "But that's not the real issue, is it?"

"Of course not," Prescott agreed, his eyes shadowed. "The question is still whether Ramsey is alive or not."

"The priority of the moment is whether Poseidon has been cleared of suspicion." Savino looked from one man to the other. "Adams and Ramsey's culpability is fact and has been proven. There is no evidence of any further involvement by anyone on the team, any of the support staff or anyone within Poseidon."

That sounded good. Unfortunately these men were smart enough to realize it sounded a little too good. So, again, none of them said a word. They simply waited. Savino didn't make them wait long.

"Did we contain the threat? Or did we simply curtail one element?" Savino took a breath, his fingers tapping a quick tune on the pool table before he shrugged. "The CIA has closed their case and, although they're protesting the breach of protocol in Adam's apprehension, NI *says* they're satisfied."

But Savino wasn't. Clearly his men knew it. Each of them showed their frustration in their own way.

Torres gritted his teeth.

Lansky beat a fist on the desk.

And Prescott swore.

"This is bullshit." The Lieutenant emphasized his feelings by kicking a chair across the room. The delicate wood splintered into an explosion of toothpicks, but nobody even raised a brow.

"Could be bullshit," Savino agreed calmly. "Or it could be something deeper. We won't know, though, until we dig in and see what we see."

"So the investigation is ongoing?" Torres asked.

"The investigation is ongoing," Savino agreed. "It's also now deemed SAP for Poseidon only."

SAP. Special Access Program. Which meant that the CIA and NI might have cleared this issue, but someone pretty high in the pecking order was still watching. And, for better or worse, willing to keep Poseidon, but not the rest of the team, on the inside of the information loop.

"And our status?"

Yes, they'd saved the kid. And, yes, they'd brought down the hostile, exposing one—or two—of their own.

But they'd disobeyed orders. And they'd ignored protocol. And the ends didn't always justify the means. Not in the military. Not even for SEALs.

Savino knew they were waiting to see how hard he'd slap them down. He knew in the back of their minds, they were wondering if they were still on the team.

Torres's expression didn't change, but Savino could see the misery his friend felt. Torres thought he'd lost the woman and now he was wondering if he'd lost his career, too.

Savino's gaze traveled from one man to the next, his expression impossible to read.

"As far as Admiral Cree is concerned, you were under orders." He waited, letting that sink in, watching the top layer of tension leave his men. "As far as I'm concerned, we have work to do."

He gestured to Lansky's laptop and the tablet, indicating the research they'd used to chase down Adams.

"What do you want us to do?" Torres asked.

"Prescott and I will get started here." Savino tilted his head toward the house next door. "The two of you are on damage control."

Despite the stress pounding through him and the gravity of everything they still faced, the look he offered both Torres and Lansky was abject pity.

"Good luck."

ALL IN ALL, the debriefing was pretty quick. But it was still a lot longer than Diego had wanted to be away from Harper. Not when he knew this was probably the last time she'd want to see him.

"Gentlemen," Andi greeted as she opened the door. But her eyes were all for Jared. "All the details settled?"

"Pretty much."

"And the man who calls himself Nathan's father? Did you find out if he's alive?"

"That's not something we can talk about," Jared said as they stepped into the foyer. He flashed Andi the smile that Diego had seen smooth his way so many times. "How about we go get a drink, though, and see what else we have to talk about."

"Does that mean you don't plan to fill us in on the

details of the man who could be an ongoing danger to Nathan and possibly to Harper?"

"Need to know, babe." Jared's expression was confident. "Don't worry about it. We've got everything covered."

And just like that, Andi's face closed up. It was like watching a curtain come down. A lead curtain. Heavy, solid and unassailable.

Diego would have winced in sympathy, but he didn't know if Jared realized he'd been shut out.

"Harper's in the kitchen," Andi said. And then, without another word but in clear dismissal, she stepped out the door, closing it behind her with a sharp snap.

"What the…" Jared looked like a kid who'd bit into a plastic cookie. Totally confused, ripped off and worried that his treat was gone for good.

He made for the door, but Diego laid a hand on his shoulder before he reached the knob.

"You go after her now, you're making a commitment to open more than just that front door."

Jared froze. His face went blank except for the flash of terror in those baby blues.

Diego rolled his eyes. He felt for his friend. He really did. But he had his own heartbreak to deal with right now.

"We'll get drinks later," he promised with a consoling slap on the shoulder before he headed for the kitchen.

Mimicking Jared, he froze in the doorway. But not because he was afraid of committing. Because he didn't think she would.

He observed Harper as she watched Nathan play with the kitten in the great room. His giggles came through the doorway, filling the air with joy, making Diego smile, too. Who could resist resilience like that?

"How much did Nathan see, with everything he went through," she wondered softly, making it clear she knew he was there even though she didn't take her eyes off her son as he dragged a feather on a stick for his kitten. "How does he deal with it? And more important, how long before he forgets?"

"I was with him when Nathan was debriefed. He wasn't abused. He wasn't exposed to violence, or even made aware of Ramsey's suspected crimes." Diego wanted to assure her that there wasn't anything to worry about. But he was through lying to her. "He'll have a lot to deal with. Abduction will leave its mark. But he'll get all the help he needs to get through it. Counseling for both of you, defense training so he feels safer in the future."

Diego listed the options he'd researched, the services and support he'd got Savino to guarantee. As he wound down, he hesitated. Then, because he had to be honest, he reluctantly added, "It'll all help. But he'll never forget."

He could hear her breath shake all the way across the room. After Harper pressed her hand through her hair, she rested it against the window for a brief moment. Then her eyes locked on his as she moved toward him. She stopped just a foot away.

Close enough for him to reach out and touch, yet still as far as the moon.

"Will you help him?"

"What?"

"I know the services, the programs that Savino offered will help. Counseling and learning to protect himself, I want that and I know Nathan will, too. But he's going to need more."

"Whatever you want, I'll get it for him."

Her gaze dropped to the floor, but not before he saw the tears fill her eyes. She blinked them away, though, so when she looked up her expression was clear.

"I know you can't share anything confidential and I know you won't share more than a little boy should hear." She stepped closer still. Only a hairbreadth away. "But will you be there for him? When you can, will you be there so he can talk to you, so he can understand that good men, that heroes, behave a certain way."

God. It was like taking a sudden fist to the gut. Shock rocked his system, chasing away his breath, sending his thoughts reeling.

She thought he was a hero? "You don't blame me?" he asked.

Her smile flashed, her eyes soft and sweet for just a moment before her expression turned serious. "I blame Brandon. I blame Adams. I blame the bad guys who did whatever it is that Brandon was involved in." Her brow creased for a moment before she sighed. "But I don't blame you. I don't blame your team. I don't blame your job."

No pat on the back, no commendation, no medal had ever felt as good as hearing those words.

"You'd let me stay in touch with Nathan? To visit him once in a while? After this is done, you won't see me as a reminder of what he's been through?"

"I'd see you as a reminder of what got him through it. He'll see you as his hero."

He shook his head. Again, all he could think was, *God.*

"Did Nathan tell you what he named the kitten?"

Good.

Subject changes were good. It saved him having to tell her all the reasons he wasn't a hero.

"No." He glanced into the great room and smiled. The kid was stretched out on the floor now, a little ball of gray fluff cuddled in his arms. Both of them were fast asleep. "I did meet the little fur ball and saw the kid's victory dance. Quite a feat, being able to kick that high while cuddling a cat, by the way. But I didn't get its name."

"Nathan is a boy who loves his heroes. Movie heroes, book heroes and now real heroes." Harper stepped into the doorway of the great room, her arms crossed over her chest. "He ran through all of the names a few times before he narrowed it down to just one that seemed to fit."

Diego eyed the kitten, and, even as his heart warmed, he hoped like hell it wouldn't be bearing his name.

"And?"

"And he's calling the kitten Poseidon." Her lips twitching at Diego's arch look, Harper shrugged. "He doesn't see anything at odds with a cat being named for the God of water."

"God of the sea," Diego corrected automatically. "He named that cat after us?"

"After your team."

"We'll have to make it our mascot. The guys'll love that." His smile slowly faded, his eyes tracing Harper's features as if simply by looking he could commit her face to memory. "What about you?"

"Do I see you as a hero?" she asked, whether for clarification or simply to tease. "Or will I let you see me again?"

Either.

Both.

He remembered the look of desperation he'd seen in Jared's eyes. The willingness to do almost anything to keep the girl.

Almost.

"I'm tempted to let you think I'm a hero if it gets me what I want. But I figure there've been enough lies, too much deception already."

Her eyes searched his face, but her expression didn't change. "What is it, exactly, that you want, then?"

"You."

HE WANTED HER. Enough to fight to keep her? A fierce sort of joy took hold in Harper's heart.

"You liked the sex," she murmured, skimming her hand up the length of his arm from wrist to shoulder. Then, because it felt so good, she slid it right back down again.

"*Like* is a mild word," he corrected her. "It doesn't come close to what I felt with you."

Harper's heart raced. Her body screamed at her to go for it. To jump at the chance. She wanted this. More time. And, yes, more sex.

But mostly the time to get to know Diego better. To let him get to know her better. To see if he'd stick around after the initial flash of hot sex was over.

"As good as it is between us, though, it's not enough," he said.

Disappointment cast a shadow over the hope that'd been building in her heart. "What do you mean?"

"We're compatible in bed. We're hell on wheels in

bed," he clarified. "In bed, in the shower, in the air and against the wall. We're damned good together."

"But?"

"Well, I know you said it wouldn't matter. But." He drew in a deep breath that seemed to take the very air from Harper's lungs, too. "I've fallen head over heels in love with you. So even though you aren't angling to build this into more, I am."

Her heart shook as her mind flashed back to their first night together.

He was in love with her. And he wanted more.

Oh, God. He loved her and wanted more. The words played over and over through Harper's head. A part of her wanted to climb into his arms, curl up and purr. But she couldn't get past the snarling fear in her belly.

"We had fun, Diego. Great sex. Good times. But it's different now. It's not just me. I'm not a single woman. I have priorities…" she said. His scowl stopped the rest of her words before they left her lips.

"Get real. You think I don't care about that kid? I'd step away if my being around hurt him, if I was a reminder. A source of PTSD. But you closed that door when you said my involvement wouldn't hurt him." His scowl softened for a moment as he looked at Nathan, cruising through his happy dreams with his kitten. "I care about that kid too much to let you shut me out of his life. Not even if you and I are done."

That self-assured arrogance was exactly what she wanted to hear. It was the perfect fit for the last piece of the puzzle that made up the image in her mind of the life she wanted. The life she hadn't let herself dream about until Diego.

He stepped closer, his fingers cupping her chin, tilting her face higher so he could stare into her eyes.

"So, here's the thing. I am head over heels in love with you."

Her heart jumped again, pleasure pouring through her.

"But I'm a SEAL."

Harper blinked, frowning as that pleasure changed to confusion. "What does that have to do with anything? I already know you're a SEAL."

"I told you once that I wasn't open to a relationship and never would be. I changed my mind." And he didn't exactly look thrilled about it. "But I won't, I refuse to, change being a SEAL. You've seen for yourself the risks that go with that, and I won't lie. Kidnapping an innocent kid, it sucks, but it's nothing compared to what we usually face."

Harper nodded, her heart pounding faster, this time with fear. He'd never be a safe man to love. "You live a dangerous life," she acknowledged.

"I'm one of the best. I'm trained by the best. I'm good now—I'll be better tomorrow. It's what I do."

Desire, always present when Diego was around, curled hotter in her belly. God, that arrogance was sexy. "So why is that a problem?" she asked, trying to focus on the matter at hand and not on jumping him. "Do you think I'm afraid? That I can't handle the reality of what you do? That I can't accept the secrets that you keep?"

She should be insulted by either option. But she wasn't. She'd almost seen her worst nightmare come true. She knew what it was like to live with the terror of losing her heart.

"Hell, no. I think you're the bravest woman I know. You have a strength that humbles me. Enough strength to face what I do, and to accept not knowing the details." He shook his head and gave a low laugh. "It really isn't an issue with you? My being a SEAL?"

"No more than my being a mom who is an interior decorator is an issue for you."

She saw the kiss coming a heartbeat before he took her mouth. It was a heady, wild dance that sent passion spiking through her system with its needy edges and tugging demands. Harper pressed tight against his body, wanting his strength, reveling in his power.

"So?" he asked, his words low and husky when he lifted his head.

Harper could only stare as her mind swirled on the delighted waves of pleasure. It took a few moments for his word to sink in, but she still didn't get the question.

"So, what?"

"So what are you going to do about me being head over heels in love with you?"

Suddenly she felt as if her whole world was shining a little brighter. "Well, you are a god in bed," she admitted, sliding her palms up the hard breadth of his chest and reveling in the fact that this didn't have to be the last time. "And you're a true hero, even if you don't want to believe you are. Added to that, you make me feel pretty amazing."

"And?"

"And, as good as you make me feel, that's probably not enough." Harper pressed her palm against his stubbled cheek, delighting in the rough contrast of his strength and her softness. "But when you add the fact that Nathan adores you, and I love you, then things get a little more complicated."

His eyes lit up, but he didn't smile. Not yet.

"And?"

"And…" Harper rubbed her lips against Diego's and tried not to cry at the intensity of her feelings. "I guess I'd better keep you."

Diego's arms wrapped tight around her, pulling her close to the hard warmth of his body. "I guess that makes me a winner."

* * * * *

Look for the next exciting SEAL Brotherhood Novel featuring Lieutenant Elijah Prescott, when CALL TO ENGAGE goes on sale in July 2017.

And for more from New York Times *bestselling author Tawny Weber look for a sexy SEAL story on sale in June 2017 from Harlequin Blaze.*

Read on for a special
SEAL Brotherhood Novella
bonus prequel
from Tawny Weber

NIGHT MANEUVERS

CHAPTER ONE

"AND THAT, MY FRIENDS, is how it's done."

With a cocky grin and a cockier salute, Chief Petty Officer Aaron Ward flipped his empty shot glass into the air, caught it upside down and placed it with the others on the tower already stacked on the table.

Across from him, blurry eyed with a slack expression, his opponent reached for his shot of tequila. He overshot the distance by a few inches and lost his balance. With the speed and dexterity they were known for, one of the SEALs on the team opposite Aaron slid a chair under his wavering teammate.

"Concede?" Elijah Prescott asked from his position at the head of the table. Deemed the fairest of them all by most of the personnel at Coronado Naval Base, the majority of SEAL Team 7 and the entirety of Poseidon, the lieutenant was their usual go-to referee.

Half the bodies in the Officers Club surrounded the table, forming a wall of testosterone with a random nod to estrogen sprinkled here and there. There wasn't much that offered more off-duty entertainment than the friendly rivalry between SEAL Team 7 and Poseidon. Although, as plenty had pointed out, every member of Poseidon was on SEAL Team 7 themselves.

The brass deemed the healthy competition to be beneficial, and a lot of the sailors on base who weren't in Special Forces saw it as inspiration. The SEALs, those who were and those who weren't Poseidon, saw it as just one more way to train.

That was what they did.

They trained to be the best.

There was a lot to be said for being the best.

With that in mind, Prescott reached over to tap the still-untouched tequila shot and asked again, "Concede or not? Time, it is a-wasting."

Petty Officer Brett "Chug-a-Lug" Samson tried to reach for the glass again, but only managed to lift his hand about three inches before his eyes rolled back. Laughter rang through the low-roofed building as the man slid off his chair, into a puddle under the table.

Prescott bent at the waist to peer at Samson, then rose to his full six feet two inches. He made a show of pointing both hands toward Aaron.

"The winner and still reigning champion, Team Poseidon," Prescott declared with a wicked grin. "That's twelve face-offs out of twelve."

"And that, my friends, proves that there is nothing that we're not the best at." The room exploded in groans and applause as Aaron took his bow.

"Bullshit," someone muttered. Aaron glanced at Mike Borden, noting the guy's face was a study of frustration. "There's got to be something."

"Well, Lieutenant, let's see," Jared Lansky mused from his spot at the bottle-laden table next to the jukebox. With an arrogant tip of his beer, he leaned back so the chair rested at that perfect tipping point on its rear legs. "That's pool, track and poker. We've nailed rock climbing, para-targeting and a dance off. Beer guzzling, weight lifting, sharpshooting, the trivia trifecta and now tequila shots. What else did we beat everyone at? Oh, yeah, who could eat the most pizzas. What's next on the list?"

"How about a bake off?" someone called from the other side of the room.

"Got that covered. Powers grew up in the restaurant biz, did his first tour as a culinary specialist on a sub. He can cook the hell out of anything from five-alarm chili to turducken to oh-la-la éclairs."

Mixed in with joking recommendations of just exactly what should be done with turducken were suggestions of which arena they should compete in next. While that raged around him, Aaron took a seat. He figured he did it with a lot more grace than Samson had, but with far too many shots of tequila swimming in his head, he couldn't be sure.

While the debate raged on, Diego Torres snagged the deck of cards, shuffled and dealt four hands of poker. He tossed a twenty into the center of the table, snapped up one of the hands of cards and waited for three others to pony up. Aaron debated for a few seconds, considered his chances of winning in his condition, then dug some cash out of his pocket. A pair of tens and two more twenties joined the one on the table, with Aaron, Prescott and Lansky snagging hands at random.

"Bet's to you, Bulldog," Torres said after a glance at his cards.

Aaron eyed the hand of crap he'd pulled, shot a quick glance at the other three faces and, reading exactly what he'd expect on them—nothing—tossed another twenty in the pile. He might have a lousy hand, but he'd won with worse.

"And that, my friends, is how you win," he murmured four minutes later as he laid down three ladies and a pair of aces.

Lansky tossed his cards onto the table and shook his head.

"You're on a roll, Bulldog. Me? My luck is sucking big-time tonight," he muttered. "I should ditch this and head for Olive Oyl's. Good-looking women, loud music. Just the ticket."

"Not like you'd have any better luck with women, Lansky. At least, not the way I hear it," Brandon Ramsey said from his spot at the next table. The image of relaxation, the tall blond lieutenant had propped his four-legged wooden chair to recline against the wall and leaned back with his head resting in his hands and one booted foot propped on the other knee. "Can't say as I've seen you step up for any of these competitions, either. Twelve men on Poseidon and, what? Seven of you have done all the heavy lifting. Gotta wonder what that says about your qualification process."

"Haven't you been beaten enough yet, Ramsey?" Torres asked, not taking his eyes off his cards. "You really want to battle wits with MacGyver here? He'll fry your ass."

Not even a gallon of tequila could dull the senses to the waves of hostility bouncing between the tables. Before it could explode into anything more than a few hard glares and cursing, a man moved between the tables.

"Now that you mention it, Ramsey, I haven't stepped up to compete myself. Do you think my qualifications might be lacking?" Lieutenant Commander Nic Savino stood like an avenging angel for his team. Spiked black hair, obsidian eyes and sharp features echoed the blade-sharp edge in his voice.

"No, sir. Of course not," Ramsey said, his words as conciliatory as his smile.

"I didn't think so."

Aaron grinned at Savino's tone. The man had one hell of a way with the verbal eye roll.

"Gentlemen, if you've finished playing, we have a matter to discuss."

As one, the seven members of Poseidon who were in the room came to attention. They didn't stand, they didn't salute, but all of them gave Savino one hundred percent of their focus. Everyone in listening distance quieted, all wanting to hear as much of the discussion as possible.

Savino had that effect.

As ranking member of Poseidon under Savino, Torres took the lead.

"Sir?" he asked, his voice lightly accented with the same hint of Mexico apparent in his dark features. The sharp spikes of barbed wire and the base of a trident were visible beneath the rolled edge of his shirtsleeve. A gang tattoo, Aaron knew. One Diego had changed to represent his service after he'd joined the SEALs. What the man hadn't changed, though, was his devotion to brotherhood. His belief in the sanctity of the team. And the strongest handle on temper Aaron had ever seen.

"Word just came down. There's a new civilian public affairs specialist. She has a hankering to create a special campaign to celebrate the SEALs' fifty-fifth birthday. A big splash outlining the SEALs' achievements over the years, their skills and renown. In our interest, she wants to do a PR piece highlighting Poseidon."

Mutters and derisive laughter skittered around the room. While the SEALs had gotten a lot of press over the past few years—movies, books, write-ups—as a whole, the men preferred their oath of anonymity. They didn't fight for fame, they fought for their country.

"We don't want PR and we do all of our liaising on

the field of battle," Torres pointed out, tapping his cards on the table.

"That's what I said." Savino nodded. "That preference was noted and dismissed. Orders are to comply with the interview."

The mutters took on an angry edge. Public relations, publicity, public forms of attention, they were all against the motto most of these men lived by.

"'I do not advertise the nature of my work, nor seek recognition for my actions,'" Aaron muttered, quoting the SEAL ethos.

"I agree." The moment Savino lifted his hand, the room quieted. Settled. "But we've all been given unappetizing orders before. We all know how to swallow our objections, to move past any issues and do the job we're assigned to do."

"Some versions of unappetizing are uglier than others," Lansky said, rat-a-tat-tatting his hands on the table in a nervous staccato.

"Only the ones we're not trained for," Prescott reminded him. "Which, let's face it, this would qualify for. Nobody on the team worked in PA. We're warriors. Not puppets."

"I'll do it," Ramsey offered, his pretty-boy smile flashing with movie-star glam.

"There ya go. Let Hollywood do it." Aaron figured he'd be good at it. The guy had the looks, charm and a mile-deep line of bullshit that'd easily bury a reporter.

"Yeah, be sure they take photos, too. Ramsey needs something else to add to his personal scrapbook," Prescott joked without lifting his eyes from the sketch pad he'd been doodling on since the contest had ended. Within seconds, he tore off the sheet he'd drawn on and tossed it onto the middle of the table. The paper fluttered down to cover the pile of bills that made up the current poker pot, with Ramsey's face grinning off the page in charcoal.

The quick sketch showed the SEAL posing in shorts and combat boots, his T-shirt covered with medals and arms lifted to show bulging biceps. His pretty-boy features were exaggerated, the smile gleaming with tiny stars. At his feet were a series of bowing figures, a couple with notepads and pen and the others with cameras.

"Rock on, Rembrandt," Ramsey said, snagging the sketch and laughing. "You captured my best side."

"Best side is the one you sit on," Lansky muttered, tossing his cards on the table. "Weren't you listening? This PR expert is looking for someone in Poseidon. That ain't you, Ramsey."

Ramsey's smile didn't change, but his eyes went ice-cold. It wasn't news that the guy was having trouble adjusting. Used to being the shining star of every force he'd served on, Ramsey didn't much like that Poseidon's rep was almost on par with DEVGRU. Poseidon was made up exclusively of twelve men who'd come out of BUD/S class together a decade ago. All twelve served among SEAL Team 7's various platoons, putting in extra training, extra studying, extra time together in their off hours with a single goal. To be the very best. Their mission was known only to them, their focus broad and well defined. Ramsay had no part in all this.

"Doesn't matter what they're looking for. SEALs are SEALs and SEALs don't want publicity," Torres said, tossing his cards on top of Lansky's and scowling before Ramsey could respond. "Neither does Poseidon."

There was a second of silence as if everyone was waiting to see Savino's reaction to Torres's response. When he said nothing, the men exploded. Protests, complaints, dissection and criticism foamed through the crowd like an overshaken beer.

Through it all, Savino stood, listening. When the litany quieted to a mutter here or there, Savino nodded, his elegant features calm. Aaron knew a lot of people thought calm and cold were the only expressions the man had. Poseidon knew better, of course. But their leader's mythical reputation added to the team's mythical reputation, so nobody bothered to correct it.

"Objections acknowledged and, for what it's worth, I agree." As he spoke, Savino pulled a Leatherman knife out of his pocket, slit an inch off the bottom of one of the straws, then gathered them all together. "But our views are irrelevant in the matter. Word came down and it came down from Admiral Cree. Apparently this person has enough pull and knows which strings to tug. They want the article to focus on Poseidon. They want to talk to one of the team. We've been ordered to cooperate."

With that, he held out a hand filled with eight straws, one for each, including their leader. Nobody grimaced, none of them said a word. They knew the drill. Starting with the man on Savino's left, each took their turn tugging a small red-and-white-striped cylinder from the lieutenant commander's hand. This was as much a ritual as the mantra they recited before each mission.

Savino met the eyes of each of the seven men who were Poseidon as they pulled their straw. The others who made up the twelve-man team were deployed elsewhere, off the hook for this particular venture. If they'd been there, he'd have looked them right in the eye, too. Savino never sent a man on a mission he wouldn't take himself, and he reminded each of them with his direct and honest gaze.

When it came to his turn, Aaron contemplated the

three straws remaining, figured the odds, went with the one in the middle.

And frowned at the short straw.

Shit.

He'd rather be sent into a terrorist cell wearing neon. It'd beat the hell out of dealing with a clueless journalist with more enthusiasm than smarts.

"Congratulations, Bulldog. Looks like you're our PR patsy." With a slap on the back, Savino grinned. "You'll meet Ms. Radisson tomorrow, nineteen hundred at Olive Oyl's."

Shit, again.

A clueless female journalist.

Could it get any worse?

CHAPTER TWO

THIS WAS SO GREAT.

Her foot bouncing to the beat of the band's pretty decent rendition of "Brown Sugar," Bryanna Radisson had to force herself to stay in her seat. There was so much to see here. So much to do. And she was a woman who embraced seeing as much as she could see and doing as much as she could do. What better way to enjoy life than to live it to the fullest, after all?

And talk about enjoyable.

She surveyed the bar, loving the clever name. Olive Oyl's. Who knew a small seaside bar would have such an eclectic variety of patrons. Grizzled, unshaven fishermen types bellied up to the bar next to sleek businessmen with their ties loosened and their shined-like-glass shoes. There was a guy in the corner playing a handheld game one-handed, using the other to alternately lift his beer to his mouth or shove his glasses back into place. A trio of women argued good-naturedly in the corner, and Bryanna swore she even saw one guy in cowboy boots dancing with a woman in a dress that looked like a watercolor.

She could write a whole series of articles based on this bar alone. Relaxation options for the average sailor, base-community relations, a visitor's drinking guide. The possibilities were endless.

It was a great example of local color, a glimpse at the

type of people who lived and served in Coronado. The small resort town was nestled between the cool waters of the Pacific and the San Diego Bay and sported that casual beachside glamour she loved. The gorgeous area housed both the Naval Amphibious Base and the Naval Air Station, which meant there were a plethora of military hotties to ogle.

Especially SEALs.

Bryanna shifted in her seat, halfway out of it as she angled a look toward the back room. This was reputed to be a SEAL bar, and she'd heard that back room was where they hung out. She'd grown up on the fringes of the Navy, paying just enough attention to know a petty officer outranked an ensign, that *Bravo Zulu* meant "well done" and that a pollywog was a sailor who'd never crossed the equator.

Nobody had been more surprised than she when she'd decided to take her journalism degree, with a minor in marketing, and apply for a job as a public affairs specialist, civilian, for the Navy. But she'd been at loose ends and dissatisfied with the jobs she'd tried out and had always wanted a chance to live in California. So when her uncle had mentioned the position, she'd jumped at it. And, in her inimitable way, got it.

In her usual gung ho fashion, she was determined to make it a huge success. Bryanna firmly believed in the power of thoughts, and since she had so many, she figured that meant she had a lot of power to make her dreams come true.

Her smile widened as the waitress stopped at her table, a glass-covered ship's wheel. Bryanna took a second to admire her modified sailor suit—double-button-front white jeans and a navy shirt with red and white stripes—then smiled.

"Great lemonade, Lila," she complimented, admiring the redhead's sassy sweep of side bangs. "I love your hair. I wish I could pull off that style."

Lila blinked, either at the compliment or over Bryanna remembering her name.

"Thanks. I like yours, too. I suppose you get compared to a fortune-teller all the time with those long, dark curls."

"Usually when I ask someone to cross my palm with silver," Bryanna said, waving one hand mysteriously over the other with a wicked smile. "You must love working here. It looks like a shopping spree at Hunks R Us in Navy uniforms."

She waited for the other woman's laughter to fade before leaning closer.

"I hear the bar counts a lot of SEALs among its clientele. I'd think that'd make this a great place to work. You must have some fun stories, hmm?" Elbow on the table, Bryanna planted her chin on her fist and gave the waitress her patented "sharesies" smile. The one that invited whoever she was talking with to spill everything to her welcoming ears.

Whether she was well trained or simply disinclined to gossip, Lila only offered a shrug.

"Can I bring you anything else?" She tapped a laminated anchor-shaped menu on the middle of the table. "The red-pepper hummus is seriously delish, or if you're in the mood for something heavier, the sliders are good tonight."

"Hmm, I'm meeting someone, so it'd probably be smarter to wait and see what their preference is." Bryanna glanced at her watch, then at the menu, then shrugged. Ordering would give her another chance to chat with Lila. She was sure that, sooner or later, she could convince the woman to share a story or three. "But he's late, so why not? Let's do the hummus. And another of these fabulous lemonades."

"Five minutes," Lila promised with a smile before hurrying off.

After a brief thought as to whether her appointment would actually be here by then, Bryanna leaned back in her chair to enjoy the view and the music.

And saw him.

Wow.

Just… Wow.

Bryanna pursed her lips and blew out a long, slow whistle of appreciation. The man was gorgeous. *Tall, dark and handsome* didn't do justice to the power of his looks, the strength of his build or the intensity of his expression.

Simple jeans and a tee did nothing to detract from his power. She was sure he'd command the same attention in a three-piece suit or a Navy uniform. That he was Navy went without saying. From his shorn hair to the way he carried himself, he shouted military. Powerful military.

Was this Chief Petty Officer Ward? she wondered.

Oh please, oh please, oh please, let it be, she chanted under her breath. Her imagination soared at the idea of spending time with this man. Anything from interviewing him to licking her way over his body to having his baby appealed at the moment.

Bryanna was a firm believer in love at first sight. So much so that she'd spent most of her adult life hoping to experience it. As a deep sigh of longing swelled in her chest, all she could think was wow, this would be the perfect guy to experience it with.

With every step he took, the man got better looking.

As he drew closer, Bryanna searched. But she couldn't see a single flaw to keep her lust in check.

Yowza.

His short, spiked hair was the color of polished oak and his skin a dusky gold, as if he'd spent the weekend on the beach. His body… Oh, his body. Broad shoulders were hugged close by the soft blue cotton of his long-sleeved tee. The shirt molded to a muscular chest, tapering down his slender waist to tuck into jeans draped over tight hips and strong thighs. The glint of a chain around his neck and the smooth leather of his watchband finished the look.

She suddenly felt overdressed in her black pencil skirt with its ruffled hem and high slit at the calf and her white silk blouse. But when she'd picked out her outfit, she'd been thinking about business. Not about finding her perfect man.

Mr. Perfect, or Officer Perfect in this case, tapped the waitress on the shoulder. Her stomach did a little dance of delight when Lila gestured toward Bryanna, then it slid into her toes as the man smiled his thanks. Oh, God. What a smile. His entire face lit up.

Despite sudden, rarely felt nerves, Bryanna got to her feet as he headed her way.

She could see the interest in his eyes, hot admiration that made her want to preen with delight. More, it made her want to reciprocate. She'd like to skim her hand over those biceps, to squeeze tight and find out if they were as hard, as solid, as they appeared. Was his skin warm or cool? Smooth or work-roughened? There were so many questions running through her head that she had to take a second to sort them out.

Some, the sexy ones that involved wondering how he looked naked, she set aside.

For now.

Others, a multitude of others that revolved around her assignment, her career, her goal, those she forced herself to bring front and center. It helped to picture her uncle's face, that formidable glare of his heavy with expectations. With that, and a deep breath, she was ready.

Thankfully, Bryanna prided herself on her ability to multitask. So she figured she might find a way to pull a few of those sexier thoughts to the forefront while she worked through the rest. If she found the right opportunity.

In the meantime, she had a job to do.

"Ms. Radisson?"

"Hi, yes. I'm Bryanna. Bryanna Radisson. You must be Aaron, right? Chief Petty Officer Ward? We're going to talk about all things Navy, SEALs and Poseidon, right?"

His smile didn't shift, and she could still see the interest in his eyes. But something in his expression told her that he didn't want to talk about any of those things. Not because he'd rather discuss the two of them getting naked together—although she was pretty sure he'd be happy to converse about that at length. But because he didn't want anything to do with her project.

Why? Bryanna's easy smile slipped a little. Didn't he think she was qualified?

People tended to judge her by her beauty, sultry and exotic, and her personality, bubbly and outgoing. It was rare that anybody bothered to look beyond the sexy packaging or friendly chatter to realize that she was also savvy, smart and ambitious.

Bryanna never bothered wasting time blaming them. Why, when she could use their shortsightedness to her advantage? Not that she figured it'd be an issue with this man, she decided, her smile widening as she slid her hand into his.

Her breath caught in her chest, hot and tight. Need coiled in her belly with edgy fingers, wanting more, desiring satisfaction. If he could stir this much heat with simply a touch of their hands, what would happen if they got closer? Nakeder?

Bryanna felt her smile turn sultry as she gave him a flirtatious once-over.

"You are Aaron Ward, right? I admire—"

"Chief Petty Officer, or simply Chief Ward, actually," he interrupted in a deep voice that did justice to that deliciously broad chest. "That's my rating, or rank if that's easier. In the Navy, we're addressed by our rank."

Oh. It wasn't the words, so much as the tone that sent a spiral of disappointment curling through Bryanna's belly. He was one of those. Well, she'd dealt with misogynistic chauvinists plenty of times before. Especially in the Navy. Sometimes she wondered if it was an enlistment requirement. It was probably too much to believe that such a gorgeous face and mouthwatering build would come with an open mind, too.

No big deal. She was here to gather information that'd help her write her article, Bryanna reminded herself. Not to score a hunky new hottie for her very own boy toy.

With that firmly in the forefront of her mind, she set aside her disappointment and slipped her hand from his, putting a little distance between her and temptation. Sitting again, she smoothed the snug fabric of her skirt over her knees and offered him the smile she used for pushy salespeople and head-patting repairmen. The one that oozed ice-cold pity.

"Hmm, chief petty officer, did you say? That'd be an E-7 rating, one of the higher ranks an enlisted man can achieve in the Navy, right? Until they instituted the senior chief and master chief ranks in the late '50s, of course." She sipped her frozen lemonade and arched one brow. "Added to that, you're a SEAL, which affords you the rating of Special Warfare Operator. Assigned to Coronado Naval Base, you serve primarily with SEAL Team 7, which is comprised of six platoons and is deployed worldwide."

"You did your homework." He pulled out the chair opposite hers and sat. But instead of looking impressed, or cowed—which had been her real goal—he smiled. And sent that spiral of heat swirling through Bryanna's belly again.

Ignore it, she told herself. *Pretend he's cross-eyed, pockmarked and sin-ugly.*

"No, that wasn't homework, that was simple knowledge," she corrected precisely. "A basic understanding of Naval ratings, duty assignments and deployment structure should be a necessary component of the position as a public affairs specialist, don't you think?"

"I agree. Unfortunately, those basic qualifications don't always make the cut when it comes to some things." Before she could take offense, he smiled and leaned one elbow on the table. "I'm glad to see that's not true in your case. So, Ms. Bryanna Radisson. Why don't you tell me all about yourself?"

Uh-oh. Bryanna blinked as the full wattage of his smile flashed. Like the sun, it was warm and inviting, with just a hint of danger.

Heroic, sexy *and* charming?

If the man had a brain, she was in serious trouble.

CHAPTER THREE

WITH HER TUMBLE of curls and those fringed doe eyes, Aaron figured the brunette could be taken for cute. But the wicked arch of her brows, those razor-sharp cheekbones and lips that rested in a sultry pout shifted cute into damned sexy.

From what he could see, her body matched the promise of that.

Damn, she was one hell of a package.

Aaron had thought he'd use calm persuasion, a little charm and maybe even resort to flirtation if he had to. He'd planned to use facts and numbers, duty and allegiance, the safety of the troops and, if that failed, intimidation.

Charm wasn't something he had to call on very often, but like any of the rest of the weapons in his arsenal, he knew how to use it when necessary. And it seemed to be necessary right now.

Aaron had expected smart, although he'd hoped for not. He'd figured she'd be pushy and arrogant, while complacent would have been easier. He'd been ready for a certain amount of self-interested zeal, while a civic-minded openness would have been welcome.

What he hadn't prepared for was hot.

Hot, sexy and appealing.

Bryanna Radisson was all of that and more.

After an hour, he knew her to be smart, charming,

savvy and clever with the quips. Another hour of side-stepping her subtle attempts to lead the conversation to the military and he realized she had a good-natured dedication to duty that he admired almost as much as he did the sexy sweep of her lashes over those huge dark eyes. She had an exotic look she tried to contain with ladylike clothes but those wild curls and lush curves spoke to him louder than her sedate outfit.

He knew they were here for a specific reason, but as Lila brought drink after drink, hummus then sliders followed by a molten cake, Aaron continuously shifted the conversation. Finding out as much as he could about her while keeping her off balance, he figured. What he found was an intriguing amount of common ground with an enticing woman he wanted to know better.

A woman he wanted. A great deal.

"C'mon, Aaron, let's talk Navy." Bryanna leaned forward, her smile washing a hint of delight over him. "You're a member of Poseidon, a decorated SEAL. I have facts and details, but I'd really like the human factor so I can craft the perfect presentation. I'll put into words and images the romance and power of your calling."

"I'd rather hear more about living in Hawaii. I served there for a few months when I first joined the Navy. Have you lived there your entire life?"

Bryanna huffed a little breath, but smiled her resignation at his subject change.

"I lived there since I was ten, and love it. I'm a little homesick already, to be honest. I'm sure I'll feel more settled once I find a place and all my stuff arrives. Car, clothes, that sort of thing. We can talk more about that, compare our Hawaiian adventures and you can tell me the best places to visit here in Southern California.

Later. After we finish this business," she chided in a tone of gentle stubbornness.

As clear as footsteps in wet sand, Aaron could see his missteps, his mistakes. Time to switch tactics.

He knew that he should go for intimidation. He should pull out the facts, lay out the truths of why the work the SEALs did, why their training, their methodology, their strategies needed to remain classified. Not only were men's lives on the line, but the safety of their nation, of other nations, depended on their work being kept top secret.

But he couldn't quite bring himself to get ugly with Bryanna. He wanted her to see his better side. He wanted to laugh with her. To enjoy her. Damned if he didn't want to get naked and see how well they fit together. And that wasn't going to happen if he went on the offensive.

"Want to dance?"

"We're supposed to be discussing the talents of the Special Forces," she reminded him.

"Dancing might be one of my talents," he pointed out with a teasing smile. "You want to find out?"

"Mmm, okay." Her smile widened, dark eyes sparkling with anticipation. "I have to admit, I'd like to see if you've got moves."

"But?" he asked, giving voice to her unspoken word.

"But, much as I'd enjoy finding out if our rhythms match, I'm a little concerned with your reluctance to discuss your work with Poseidon."

But not angry, he noted, starting to enjoy himself. Most women he knew leaned toward pissed when they thought a guy was coming at them with an ulterior motive. But Bryanna simply appeared amused.

"We've talked for a good two hours. How do you call that reluctance?"

"We talked about music. We talked about movies and traveling and our mutual love affair with NASCAR," she said, tiptoeing her fingers over the back of his hand. "We've talked about your dedication to fitness and various foods that aid in building muscle. We've even discussed the myriad of Navy bases over the world. But you seem uncomfortable discussing Poseidon."

Aaron wasn't a stupid man. While her tone had been friendly and her easy smile hadn't changed, he was a SEAL. Expertly trained to recognize traps, extensively skilled at maneuvering around them, exquisitely adept at strategizing his way toward his goal. And his goal was to distract her from the idea of writing about Poseidon until Savino could convince the admiral to deem their team off-limits.

So he knew better than offering a simple answer.

Instead, he angled his head to the side, gave her a considering look, then shrugged.

"I can't think of any reason to be uncomfortable. This is a great bar, the food and drinks are good, the band decent. You've got a job you're planning to do, I have an assignment I'm going to conclude." Granted, his assignment was to keep her off their backs and dim as to the reality of Poseidon. But she didn't know that. "So...? You know how to dance? I'm up for showing you a few steps if you don't."

"You'll show me..."

"A few steps. I'm a damned good dancer."

Those big brown eyes held his for a long heartbeat, then Bryanna angled her head toward the dance floor.

"Let's see if I can keep up with you."

"Excellent." He pushed to his feet, held out one hand.

Those sultry eyes slid from his toward his hand, then back again. He liked the sassy way she arched one brow, as if asking what the hell he thought he was doing. He figured they'd both find out, eventually.

"Finally," he said as her fingers slipped into his. "I've been wanting to get my hands on you all night."

Her laugh rolled over him as her hand tightened around his. As he led her through the crowd to the postage-stamp excuse of a dance floor, he appreciated that the strength in her grip belied her fragile slenderness. Good. He'd do his duty either way, but he'd feel kinda bad about rolling over a delicate blossom.

He'd still do it, of course.

But, yeah, he'd feel bad.

He caught the gleam of calculation in her eyes as she shifted into his arms. Despite the high heels she wore, she was a tiny thing, her profusion of dark curls barely reaching his shoulder.

Enjoying the way the crowd buffeted their bodies closer together, Aaron released her hand to shift both of his to her hips. Their moves matched, their beat in sync with each other as they smoothly slid into the dance.

Nice.

Very nice.

The band shifted into a reasonable version of "Patience," giving Aaron his next maneuver. He slid his hands up those hips and skimmed his fingers lightly along her slender waist to pull her closer.

Warm. She radiated heat. The kind that tingled and tempted. The kind that reached inside him and touched in a way he hadn't expected. A way he wasn't sure how he wanted to handle. Yet.

"You are good," she commented. The interest in her eyes was vivid and strong.

"I get even better."

"Is that a fact?" Her hips rubbed against his now, sliding, teasing. Her breasts were warm against his chest, pressing and tempting with every step.

"That, sweetheart, is a promise."

Her smile turned as slumberous as the gleam of desire in her eyes.

Guess he'd found the perfect way to distract her from their little interrogation-slash-interview.

It wasn't tidy, and some might not consider it honorable. But he had his orders.

Aaron always followed orders. Even when they didn't sit comfortably with his moral center. His call sign wasn't Bulldog because of his pretty face. He'd earned that nickname through sheer, stubborn persistence and a refusal to ever give up.

He did that by focusing on the end goal, on the reason behind the orders. On the purpose at hand. And, usually, by finding something redeeming in the action. Or, in this case, the distraction.

With that in mind, Aaron curled his fingers over the delicious softness of Bryanna's hips and held her even tighter. Tight enough that their thighs brushed together as they moved. Sliding from side to side, rubbing in tempting friction that mimicked, that invited.

He slowed his steps, added a little hip bump to the dance. Nothing subtle. This obviously called for a more direct approach.

As her eyes blurred, desire shimmering in the dark depths, Aaron smiled.

He did like naked distractions.

"I'd love to get you somewhere private," he murmured against the soft silk of her hair. Breathing deep the scent of coconut and...was that passionflower?

Aaron reveled in the need throbbing, hot and hard, through his body. He liked desire. It was clean. It was simple. "Alone, just the two of us."

"Why do I doubt we'll get much talking done if it's just the two of us? Alone. Someplace…private," she asked, her dark eyes flashing with heat and interest.

"We'd talk. Among other things." His fingers skimmed up, then down, the center of her back, sliding along the delicate slenderness of her spine. She arched just a little at his touch, her breasts rubbing over his chest, sending spears of desire into his gut, spiraling out through all his senses.

"Other things?" she repeated breathlessly, wetting her lips. "What other things, exactly?"

Aaron's fingers twined through her curls, the ones that floated loose and sexy down the side of her neck. He felt her shiver as if it were moving through his own body. He liked that. His gaze dropped to her lips, the wet fullness of them tempting him to taste.

He slid one hand between their bodies, skimming his knuckles up her side, along the graceful length of her throat, then tucking them beneath her chin to lift her mouth for his.

God, how he wanted a taste of her.

"Other things, like getting to know each other better," he said just before his lips took hers.

His tongue dipped into her sweetness, sipping at the rich flavor, delighting in the wet heat of her mouth. He felt her heart beating against the back of his hand where it now rested on her chest. Her taste and his senses, so delicious he knew that he had to have more. So, so much more.

But not here. Not on a public dance floor. He slowly, reluctantly lifted his mouth from hers. Aaron waited for Bryanna to open her eyes, for her gaze to meet his again. Then he smiled.

"We'd get to know each other much, much better."

He waited, moving gently to the beat of the band's rendition of "Patience."

Finally, the waiting paid off when she smiled and tilted her head.

"Let's go."

CHAPTER FOUR

BRYANNA WAS A woman who prided herself on living life to the fullest. The fullest, however, had never included leaving a bar with a man she'd just met with the intention of having wild sex.

But she figured life must have put the sexiest, most intriguing, overwhelmingly compelling man she'd ever met in her path for just that reason, since that was where they were heading.

Wild sex.

Bryanna was as open to and interested in sex as she was everything else in life. But she'd never felt anything like this. Such a hot, intense, demanding need that wouldn't let her turn away. Not until she'd experienced what Aaron could give her, had enjoyed everything he could do to her. From the second she'd seen him in the bar, she'd wanted him.

And now she'd have him.

Unabashedly watching Aaron as he drove the car she'd rented, she wet her lips and wondered. How good was he? His kiss had been off the charts. What did that say for the rest?

"Second thoughts?" he asked.

She should be having them. His tone made it clear he wouldn't hold it against her if she did. But Bryanna didn't have room in her head for second thoughts. Not when there was so much speculating going on.

"Not second thoughts. More like interesting fantasies," she teased.

"Fantasies, huh? You've heard the rumors, right?" He shifted his eyes from the road to give her a sweeping look that had Bryanna's stomach tightening and her thighs trembling.

"Rumors?" Cursing her breathlessness, she wet her lips again and blew out a long, silent breath.

"Yeah. SEALs are rumored to be the best, to be the strongest, the biggest. We are bigger, better and harder than all the rest." He flashed her a smile that made her want to wiggle in her seat to relieve some of the hot pressure building between her thighs. "We last longer, too."

Her intellect peeked through the desire long enough to remind her that she was supposed to be getting an interview with this guy. But when Aaron smiled at her, every thought fell from her head. Every thought that didn't include sex, that was.

"Is it true?" She almost came just thinking about it. "The rumor, is it based on fact?"

"We're going to find out," he promised, reaching over to grasp her hand with his. Not taking his eyes off the road, he lifted her fingers to his mouth and nibbled gently. She gasped when he slid his tongue down her index finger and almost moaned out loud when he scraped his teeth over her palm.

God.

From that point forward, Bryanna didn't remember the drive to her hotel. She was barely aware of the elevator ride or pulling the room key from her purse. Her entire focus was on the man standing next to her.

"Nice room," he decided as he strode through the space. He tweaked the curtains, checked her view. He stepped into the bathroom for a fast glance, flipped the light on, then pulled the door almost closed.

Why was he waiting? Why didn't he kiss her? She wanted to feel his hands on her again. Needed to feel those lips, to taste his mouth.

He moved to her desk, picked up her heavy copy of *The Bluejacket's Manual*, running his fingers along the words etched in gold on the spine of the navy binding. Afraid he'd flip it open and start reading up on Naval history and customs, she stepped forward.

"I thought you brought me back here to seduce me."

His smile flashed as he met her eyes. He tossed the book onto the desk without another glance, but didn't move other than to lean back, cross one ankle over the other and his arms over his chest.

"I thought we came back to have that little chat you wanted in private."

Bryanna knew what he was doing then. He was giving her an out. The chance to stick with business without feeling like a tease. Despite their coming here, to her hotel room for hot, wild sex, he'd let her out of it without saying a word. Without a hint of pressure or guilt.

God. It made her want him even more.

"Why don't we start with seduction," she suggested, her body humming with need as she began flicking open her blouse buttons one by one. "Then we can get to the chat."

HELL, YEAH.

Already hard, ready to get harder, Aaron watched with admiring eyes as the silky fabric of Bryanna's blouse gaped open. Her skin gleamed in the soft light as she shrugged it off, the fabric sliding away to reveal full breasts cupped in the temptation of a black satin bra. She was long lines, her torso slender pouring into a tiny waist. Her skirt's wide waistband rode low on her hips, revealing the tiny red jewel gleaming from her belly button.

Aaron's mouth went dry, blood rushing through his head so fast, so hard, it sounded like the ocean's roaring demand. A demand he'd made it his life's calling to answer. He wanted to touch her. Needed to taste her. But knowing the power of timing, and truly curious to see what she'd do next, he forced himself to stay where he was.

He did, however, strip his long-sleeved tee over his head and toss it aside.

"Just evening things out," he said with a grin when she lifted a curious brow.

"I like a man who believes in equality." As if testing his commitment to that, her hands skimmed down the flat planes of her stomach to the waistband of her skirt.

Mimicking her move, Aaron hooked his fingers under his belt buckle and slid the heavy canvas from its metal clasp without taking his eyes from hers.

A smile playing over those full lips, Bryanna made quick work of the hook and zipper on the side of her skirt. She held the black fabric against her hip so it wouldn't join her blouse on the floor, then waited.

His turn.

Knowing they'd only be in the way, Aaron skipped ahead to his boots. Without taking his eyes from hers, he leaned against the desk and lifted one foot, then the other, to untie the laces, then toed off the stiff leather. A sweep of one foot shoved the boots aside.

Already hard enough that the pressure was forcing his zipper down, Aaron shifted to concrete when she slid her tongue over her bottom lip so the wetness glistened. She didn't kick her shoes away, though. Instead, she let her skirt drop.

Leaving her standing there in panties that were no more than a tiny scrap of black satin to match her bra. And her shoes. His mouth went dry as his gaze traveled the length of well-toned legs, long thighs and delicately chiseled calves to her feet encased in slim red straps of leather and spiked heels.

Was there anything sexier than a practically naked woman in high heels? He'd seen his share—enough to figure the answer to that was a resounding *hell, no*. But never in his life had he seen a woman as sexy as Bryanna. And never had he been affected by one so strongly.

Done playing, ready to get down to the real action, Aaron made quick work of his jeans, kicking them, his socks and boxers out of his way so he could move freely across the room.

"Whoa, hold up," Bryanna said, gesturing for him to stop. Her eyes danced with delight as they roamed over his nude form, then she gave a soft hum. "I need a second to appreciate this view."

"Appreciate later," he suggested with a laugh.

Two steps was all it took to put his hands on her. To touch that soft skin, to feel her warmth. His fingers curled over her waist as he pulled her against the hard, needy length of his body. Her scent wrapped around him, that floral-drenched coconut that made him think of the hot tropics, a moonlit beach and the pounding surf.

His mouth took hers. Those lips gave way and her tongue wrapped around his in welcome.

Needs and wants battled.

He wanted to shove her against the wall and drive

himself into the pleasure of her lush body. He wanted to lose himself in her, to experience every drop of pleasure she'd give.

But he needed to make sure she felt more. That the pleasure he gave her was beyond anything she'd ever experienced before.

Needs, in this case, overwhelmed wants. So Aaron slowed down. He harnessed his own driving desire and set out to tease and torment, to delight and worship.

"Do you do this often?" she asked in a breathy tone.

"Sweetheart, I promise, I do it often enough to make sure you don't have any complaints," he teased, his fingers skimming down the delicious fullness of her breast. Barely contained by the black silk of her bra, her flesh was like gold.

A sailor through and through, he knew the lure of gold. The temptation of treasure. With her black curls tumbling around that lovely face and a smile that spoke of a million secrets, he realized she might be the most alluring temptation he'd ever seen.

He slid one strap down her shoulder, then the other. The fabric held tight for a moment, then dropped away, taking his breath with it.

Holy hell, she was gorgeous.

Berry-pink nipples tilted upward, as if begging him to take them into his mouth. To sip. To taste. To devour. So he did.

He touched, his thumbs circling, fingers pinching. He bit, teeth working those tender nubs to a fever pitch. He pressed her back onto the bed, slipped those tiny panties from Bryanna's slender hips and gave a deep sigh of appreciation.

"Gorgeous," he breathed. "You're so damned gorgeous."

Her hair spread over the blankets in black silken coils, Bryanna gave him a long, slumberous look.

"Do you want me?"

His eyes traveled up those golden legs, one bent at the knee and the other wrapped around his thigh. He took in the glistening curls between her thighs, waiting and beckoning. Her waist was so slender, her torso so delicate as it opened to breasts lush enough to lose himself in forever. And that face. God, what a face. Her eyes were hooded, inviting, and her mouth wet and waiting.

"I've never wanted anyone more than I want you," he confessed. Her eyes widened but he didn't give her time to think.

Pausing only long enough to slip a condom from his wallet—like Boy Scouts, SEALs were always prepared—Aaron ranged himself over her sweet body.

Eyes locked on hers, Aaron sipped from her lips, sliding his hands up and down, then into her delicate folds. Testing and teasing, he took as much pleasure from the passion fogging her eyes as he did the feel of her beneath him. Finally, feeling her tense, he took a moment for the condom, then slid the hard, aching length of his cock into her wet passage.

One slow inch at a time.

Her hands raced over him, nails scraping gently as she tried to urge him on, tried to tempt him to go faster, to hurry them both over the edge of pleasure.

"My pace," he said between his teeth, holding tight to control as he watched her lose hers. "My pace, your pleasure."

His pace. Her pleasure.

He chanted the words with each thrust, delighting in the heat as she gripped tight to his throbbing cock. One hand braced on the mattress beside her head, he shifted the other between their bodies, cupping her breast, squeezing. Delighting. His fingers tweaked, teased, tugged.

Her body tightened, arched like a bow, her breath coming in gasps. She was so damned delicious to watch as she went over that first edge. Aaron reveled in her climax, even as he shifted to send her up again.

BRYANNA WAS PRETTY sure this was what heaven felt like. Even as the orgasm shot through her, exploding in tiny prisms of pleasure, her body went up again. He felt so good, so big and hard and, God, amazing, as he slid into her. She wrapped her ankles tight behind his back, meeting each thrust with her own.

Suddenly she was airborne, her body flying, her stomach plummeting as he flipped positions so she rose over him, staring down at him. Her thighs straddled his hips, his hands gripped hers as he guided her down, impaling her on the hard length of his cock still nestled inside her.

Bryanna shuddered at the power of it. She could feel him slide along every inch of her, pleasuring her a centimeter at a time. When he'd filled her, when he'd reached her very core, he paused, his fingers digging into her flesh.

Her eyes fluttered open, her mind struggling to clear enough to focus on his face. His features were taut, pulled tight with desire. His eyes were intent on hers, narrow and hot.

He waited.

For what?

Her body trembled, her chest tense with the need to scream her pleasure. To demand more.

That was what he was waiting for, she realized.

For her to take more.

Bryanna moved. Bracing her knees on the mattress, she slowly rose, moaning with pleasure at the feel of him sliding along the wet depths of her channel. Gripping his shoulders, her fingers digging tight, she slid back down, crying out this time at the intensity of it all.

His hands slid up her body, caressing her waist, teasing her skin until he reached her breasts. Fingers spread, hands cupped, his thumbs worked her aching nipples into a frenzy of pleasure.

Bryanna went wild.

She plunged. She gyrated. She took.

She came. Over and over again.

Feeling as if her chest were going to explode, the breath coming fast and furious, Bryanna tried to find a sane thought. Or, hell, even an insane one. But her mind wouldn't work, couldn't focus. The sensations were too strong. Too powerful.

Like Aaron's hands.

Hard and demanding, he pushed her to her limits and beyond. Even when her body felt it could take no more, he showed her how wrong she was. Proved how much more pleasure there was to be had.

"Now," she begged, panting out the word with desperate need. "Please, now."

"You want me?"

"Yes," she gasped. "Yes, yes, yes."

She chanted the word, still chanting as he flipped their positions again, gripped her hips as he rose to his knees. He lifted her butt high to meet his body. He pressed the hard tip of his erection against her throbbing wetness.

He plunged.

Bryanna's chants became keening demand, her fingers digging into the rigid hardness of his biceps, gripping tight as she met each thrust with one of her own.

The world exploded.

Pleasure burst in starlight, flashing shards of passion against her closed eyes. Even as she cried out, she felt Aaron's body tighten. His body tensed. His breath caught.

And he came on a guttural cry that sent her flying again on that trembling cloud of delight.

Love. That one word floated through the pleasure swimming in Bryanna's mind, filling her senses. Love.

CHAPTER FIVE

AARON WAS IN TROUBLE.

His head was spinning in about twenty different directions while his body did a slow loop the opposite way.

What the hell?

This wasn't the usual "oh, yeah, it feels good to have sex" pleasure. This was beyond anything he'd ever felt. Anything he'd even imagined.

Damn.

Aaron had made enough mistakes in his life to recognize one when it was draped over him, naked flesh still damp enough to slide along his in a tempting reminder with every breath.

His assignment was to eliminate the threat to Poseidon—in this case, the focus Bryanna wanted to spotlight on the team. Or, if that wasn't feasible, to mitigate the damage.

As he slowed his breath, aiming for calm reason instead of frenzied passion, he wondered if overwhelming sexual satisfaction mitigated or exacerbated. He'd thought his training covered every contingency, but maybe not. He couldn't call this a mistake. Not when the rhythm of Bryanna's heart beating against his chest made him feel whole in a way he'd never experienced before.

But Aaron had taken an oath when he'd become a

SEAL, he'd made a vow as a member of Poseidon. To be loyal to Team and Country, and to earn the privilege of his trident every day. Loyalty to that privilege meant his team, his mission, came first.

Before everything.

Even himself.

"You're tensing up," Bryanna murmured, her lips testing his resolve as they caressed his chest with every word. "Isn't it a little soon to go again?"

Aaron's laugh was a puff of air.

"Yeah, I might need a few extra minutes before round two."

Unless round two was what it took to convince her not to write that article. Then hey, he was a SEAL. He'd get up for it.

"So why do you feel as if you're preparing for something?" Bryanna angled onto her elbows to give him a searching look. Her eyes were dreamy, her hair draped like a curtain on either side of her face. Her smile was hesitant, her lips swollen and inviting.

"I guess we have a few things to talk about," he said, carefully setting her aside. If his hands lingered to enjoy the softness of her skin, he didn't figure that was a crime. Not when his chances of touching her after their chat were slim and none.

"Talk, hmm?" Proving that she was more than a gorgeous face and a smoking-hot body, Bryanna's eyes turned shrewd as she moved into a sitting position, wrapping herself in the sheet as she did. "Sounds serious. Are you married?"

Even though her words were casual, he could hear the tension spiking through her tone.

"What? No way. I wouldn't… We wouldn't have… That'd be…" Realizing he sounded like an idiot, Aaron took a second to swallow the outraged shock. He gave himself another to take a calming breath, then leaned back against the headboard. Finally, he figured he'd pulled it together enough to respond in a way that took control of the situation—without sounding like an idiot. "No. I'm not married. Nor am I engaged or dating. I'm not involved with anyone or anything except my career."

"Ahh." She wrapped the sheet tighter, tucking one loose end between her breasts to hold the fabric in place. That, or to drive him crazy since all that did was emphasize the fact that she had excellent breasts, the shape of her nipples shadowed against the fabric. Thanks to his decision to have this conversation, he was missing out on them.

But what choice did he have? He knew he had to settle the issue of why they'd met before he could take her again. So he'd settle it. Fast.

His gaze dropped to those breasts again. His hardening cock throbbing in time with the pounding of his heart.

Focus.

His focus was almost as legendary as his stubbornness, he reminded himself.

"I take it that it's careers you'd like to discuss," she guessed, pushing her hair off her face and twitching her shoulders back. And, somehow, managed to portray the same charming dignity she had when dressed in her earlier version of a power suit. "Mine, yours and ours?"

"Sure." He liked the sound of that. "So tell me, why PR?"

More to the point, why Poseidon. He left that unspoken, though, figuring his path to that particular question would depend on how the rest of the conversation went. As Savino had suggested, he'd feel her out first.

Conversationally, that was.

He already knew exactly how she felt in his hands. Against his body. Surrounding him. God, delicious.

Bryanna's expression was careful as she studied his face, her eyes searching.

"Why public relations?" Her shrug was like a shimmer of gold. "I guess it's because I really like people. Finding ways to bring them together. And I love showing things in their best light. Sharing facts in a way that makes it clear to anyone interested just how great something is."

Proof positive just how good she was at it, since Aaron almost nodded before he realized that was quite a pretty spin she'd just offered.

"For instance, the SEALs' fifty-fifth birthday event. I believe it's important to focus on what a difference this force makes in the world, to highlight why they're not only the pride of the Navy, but should be the pride of the country, of the world, for that matter." Bryanna shifted, drawing her knees and wrapping her arms around the sheet-covered flesh. Enthusiasm filled her voice, shone bright on her pretty face. "Some things deserve more attention, you know? Because that attention brings them the honor they've earned, it helps people appreciate how lucky they are because of forces like the SEALs."

"Okay. I don't disagree with most of that." Except the attention part.

"Which is why I want the special sidebar on Poseidon," she continued, ignoring his unspoken words. "To show the type of men who make up the SEALs. That intensity of dedication that doesn't simply accept being the best, but pushes beyond."

God. Was it harder to push her aside realizing she

understood than it'd been when he'd figured she was clueless?

"Being a SEAL, a Special Operative, it's a damned big deal." Aaron tried to find a way to explain the most important part of his life. "It's hard work. A lot of hard work to get there, to stay there. The training doesn't end in BUD/S. It's ongoing. Every single day, training the body, training the mind, training the spirit, even."

Rapt, her attention focused like a laser on his face, Bryanna nodded encouragingly. So encouragingly that Aaron found himself saying more.

"Poseidon started with an idea, a concept of taking the best to the next level. That twelve men banding to-gether could all graduate BUD/S was impressive in and of itself considering the average class size is two hun-dred with barely twenty percent earning their trident. That we all did speaks to the focus, the dedication and power, of our concept." Lost in the past, Aaron's gaze blurred as he focused on the pain they'd endured, the costs they'd paid. "SEAL teams are known for their cohesive nature, for their brotherhood. But Poseidon? We're known for being one. Every action we take, it's unified. Every career choice we make, it's integrated into the vision of the whole."

He shook his head, wishing he could as easily shake loose the fervor of his belief in what Poseidon did.

"We've endured, we've suffered and sacrificed for the team. For our purpose. Because of that, we bring power to the SEALs, to our teams. They are stronger because of us. They are better because of us. Some of them, they are pissed because of us." He gave a hint of a laugh and shrugged.

"This is wonderful information," Bryanna said, her words as bright as her smile. "I wish I'd written it down, or recorded it. I want to use those exact words, the power of them, in my article. I want to bring that passion to the readers, so they understand how important this is."

Aaron's head rocked back as if she'd punched him.

It suddenly hit him with the painful impact of a belly flop. She'd got more information out of him in the past five minutes than he'd ever told anyone. More than he'd intended—or been given permission—to share.

She'd used him.

Sonofabitch.

Her body was still wet from their lovemaking. He could smell himself on her, could still feel the sensation of her body surrounding him. Gripping tight, milking him dry.

And she was conducting her interview. Gathering intel, facts and insights so she could work up a fancy promotion using him, using his team, using Poseidon.

"You're still writing that piece?"

A tell-all exposé on the workings of Poseidon as a Happy Birthday to the SEALs. Damn it.

Bryanna blinked, her eyes shaded by lush lashes for a moment before her brows drew together.

"Did you think I wasn't? Isn't that why we were here?"

No.

They were here for sex.

Great sex.

Mind-blowing sex.

The best freaking sex of their goddamn lives.

And she'd turned it into a part of the interview.

Furious, his mind spinning in the face of betrayal, Aaron shoved out of the bed.

"And you thought, what?" Bryanna rose into a sitting position, one hand pressing the sheet to her breast. "That a fast pass to a wild ride on your amazing body would change my mind? You actually believe that I'd risk my career? That an orgasm would somehow tempt me to ignore my assignment?"

Her voice rose with each word. Her body, too. By the time she spat out that last one, she was on her knees with one hand fisted on her bare hip and the other clenching the sheet. The fabric dripped off her lush nipples, skimming those golden breasts before pouring like a waterfall down her body.

Sparks of fury flashed from narrowed eyes, color rose under burnished skin. Passion—whatever its form—intensified everything about her.

Aaron was pissed. Seriously pissed. But not even copious amounts of righteous anger could keep him from noting how amazingly hot she was. And realizing, somewhere in the back of his head, that if things were different, he could seriously fall for her.

He was pretty damned grateful that things weren't different. And because they weren't...

"Four."

"I beg your pardon?" Scowling, she shoved at the tangled curls pouring over her furiously flushed cheek.

"That ride netted you four orgasms. Not one."

He told himself it was entertaining to watch her mouth open, then shut, then open again as she tried to come up with a pithy response. He used her confusion to snag his jeans and yank them on.

"You counted?" she finally managed, making it sound like an accusation. "Do you need those numbers to add to the tally notched on your anchor?"

Color him offended.

"Credit me with a little class. Do I look like a green

ensign on his first tour? I'm a chief petty officer in the United States Navy with a dozen years of service to my name. I'm part of the SEAL brotherhood. A member of Team Poseidon. I don't need notches," Aaron snapped. "I've proved myself a hundred times over, sweetheart."

With that, he yanked his zipper closed. And had to bite back a yelp. He'd almost caught his goods in the metal teeth.

Realizing how close he was to losing his cool—among other things—Aaron took a deep breath. Maybe he couldn't look at Bryanna's gorgeous body and not have a reaction, but there was no point in damaging himself in the process.

And maybe he couldn't stop her from moving forward with her plan to write that article of hers. So he'd have to find a way to mitigate any damage.

"Look, I know you have a job to do. But for just a second, consider how your job will impede mine. Ask yourself if fancy words, bells and whistles will help the Navy's purpose, or if it'll hurt the men who put their lives on the line."

"Oh, please, don't be so dramatic." Bryanna waved his words away with the flick of her hand. "The Navy isn't going to let me use confidential intelligence or personnel secrets to promote the SEALs' birthday. This isn't an exposé. It's promotion."

"Too much information is already out there under the guise of the public's right to know. Plenty of details, much of it bordering on confidential, has already been spilled in the name of personal glory or individual agendas. When is enough enough?" he countered. "The SEALs aren't a tool to be used by Public Affairs, and Poseidon isn't a recruiting tool."

"You should trust me to do my job."

Ignoring the hurt in her voice, Aaron shook his head.

"Impossible when the world's trust depends on me doing mine."

"I take it our evening of fun and games is over." Wrapping the sheet around that lush body, Bryanna climbed out of bed. She snagged Aaron's T-shirt from the blankets tangled at her feet and threw it at his head. She looked as if she were going to scream when the fabric fluttered to the floor halfway there.

He shouldn't want to laugh.

But he did.

Not sure what that said about him, the situation or Bryanna, Aaron simply hooked the shirt in one finger and pulled it over his head. His anger seemed to be gone, but he wasn't crazy about the feeling of loss left in its place.

"You want to go another round, try for five in one ride, you give me a call," Aaron suggested as he walked out the door. He had to close it behind him, had to get the hell out, before he did something he'd hate himself for. Before he begged.

BRYANNA STARED AT the closed door for an entire minute before she could get her mind to accept what had happened.

She'd gone from the best night of her career to the best sex of her life to… What?

Sitting naked in a messy hotel bed. Feeling as if her heart was breaking.

Ridiculous, she told herself, trying to comb her fingers through her tangled mess of hair. She'd have to be in love for her heart to break, and that wasn't possible.

She'd only met Aaron six hours ago. Nobody fell in love in less than six hours.

They'd barely talked. She didn't know anything about his past, didn't even know his favorite color or if he liked pineapple. She had no clue if they had an inch of common ground, if there was a single thing between them to build a future on.

She didn't even know if he wanted a future.

For all she knew, Aaron Ward was a dog. A man who saw sex like most saw water. Something that quenched a thirst, one glass the same as another. But she remembered the way he'd waited, how he'd given her a graceful option out when they'd first come into the hotel room. How he'd put her needs first. And the way he'd spoken of his career, how he'd sounded when he explained what Poseidon meant to him.

Aaron Ward was a good man. A noble man.

She wanted him for her man.

It wasn't until she found herself wrapped around the pillow, its soft cushion hugged to her chest, that she realized she was crying. It wasn't as if she'd never thought love had a cost. She'd always believed that good things, important things, had to be earned. But love at the expense of her career? One dream for another?

Bryanna knuckled away a tear, then sighed and let her head fall back onto the pillow. Aaron's scent enveloped her. She turned her face into the pillow and breathed deep.

This was why. Because it felt good. What was between her and Aaron, it felt right. And if she didn't believe her heart when it told her those things, what good was believing in anything?

It was pointless to just lie there pouting like a three-year-old on time-out, Bryanna decided. So she forced herself to sit up and, heaving a deep sigh, slid to her feet. She tidied the sheets, scooped the comforter off the floor to drape over the foot of the bed and gathered the pillows. Wrinkling her nose at what she'd squished into an unrecognizable shape, she plumped the pillow back into a rectangle and, after breathing in Aaron's scent once again, added it to the others.

There. One thing set to rights. Now for the rest.

She started with a hot shower and a strong talking-to.

By the time she'd dried off and slid into the cozy comfort of her favorite flannel sleep pants and tank, she'd found a hint of her customary optimism.

She wasn't going to pretend the night away, nor was she going to give up on climbing an important rung in her career ladder. And while it would be smarter to accept that she and Aaron weren't meant to be and to chalk tonight up to just one of those things—one that included the most amazing sex of her life—Bryanna wasn't ready to do that, either.

So, as she always did when she wanted something, she decided to find a way to make it happen.

One way or the other, dammit.

CHAPTER SIX

IT WASN'T UNTIL Aaron stormed into the parking lot that he realized he didn't have transport. His bike was still at Olive Oyl's. They'd driven from the bar to the hotel in Bryanna's rental car.

His cell phone weighed heavy in his pocket. He knew he could call any of his teammates for a ride. He debated for all of five seconds, then started walking south. He gauged it at maybe a mile to the base. Practically a stroll in the moonlight.

He could use the time to review the situation, to consider his options and to figure out how the hell to complete his mission.

His orders were to cooperate with Bryanna's little journalism project. The unspoken mission was to curtail her tell-all venture. The team was counting on him.

Picking it up to a fast march, Aaron sucked in a disgusted breath through clenched teeth.

He'd never failed a mission before—spoken or unspoken. He'd never let his teammates down. In the ten years they'd served together, he'd never performed in a less than exemplary manner. He had the goddamn assessment reports to prove it.

But now?

With the team's anonymity, their purpose on the line?

He'd blown it.

Totally.

Completely.

And for what?

A woman.

An amazing woman.

One with a smile that lit his heart and eyes that, when she looked at him, made him feel like a hero. A woman with a body that sent him straight into hormonal heaven and a laugh that made him grin. And that brain. When he set aside her plan to write about Poseidon, he could really dig that brain. The woman could talk about anything, seemed to know a little something about everything.

Granted, they'd only talked for a few hours, but Aaron was willing to bet that he'd feel the same way after a few months, a few years. Hell, a few decades.

Not that he had a few decades—or even a few minutes—to test the idea. He'd blown it, pure and simple. For himself and for the team.

And with that thought, the litany started all over again. By the time Aaron had walked the mile back to base, he had a serious headache brewing, a strong craving for a shot of whiskey and a few hours of quiet to figure his way out of this mess.

But as he walked through base, still alive and active at midnight, and into his barracks, he realized the whiskey and quiet were out of reach and that the headache wasn't going anywhere.

"I see you guys made yourselves at home," he greeted, letting the front door slam as he stepped over Lansky's body where the man had stretched across the floor. "Don't you all have your own racks to bunk on?"

"You had beer," Prescott said from his usual spot on the couch, his booted feet propped on the coffee table and his sketch pad angled on his lap. "Not a vegetable to be found, though. Just potato chips. All that junk food is going to kill you someday, Bulldog."

"Gotta die of something," Aaron muttered as he side-stepped Torres, who as usual was exercising, this time in the form of sit-ups. The man had a serious workout fetish.

"But we won't die today. Unless it's from embarrassment," Lansky said, his fingers flying over his keyboard in some game or another. "Speaking of, did you manage to maintain our blessed anonymity?"

"I didn't give her the Poseidon roster, if that's what you're asking." Stalling for time, Aaron headed for the kitchen and more killer junk food. He'd decided on his march from the hotel to follow protocol, which meant reporting to Savino first. Granted, as mission leader—and the entire mission force—he could fill the team in at his discretion.

Bottom line, he didn't want to. Not until he'd figured out a workable contingency to rescue this operation.

"Did you guys eat everything in here?" he asked from the kitchen, frowning as he yanked open one cabinet door after another.

"Everything we could find."

"So when's the article coming out?" Lansky prodded, his tone pure glee, as if he knew that Aaron had failed and thought it hilarious.

"About the same time as your personality transplant. We're hoping for human this time," Aaron shot back. Frustration tight as a coiled spring, he continued his search for something—anything—to eat. "As for the mission, I'm not finished yet."

"You mean you couldn't talk her out of it," Prescott said without rancor.

"Didn't think you'd be able to pull the plug completely," Torres said, spacing each word between pull-ups. "Not after Savino sussed out her connection."

"Connection?" Aaron asked from the depths of the kitchen cabinet. Hadn't he hidden a bag of Doritos behind the spare paper towels?

"Yeah. Savino pitched the blackout on Poseidon to Admiral Cree and got shot down. Turns out our inclusion in this little project was made at the specific request of Admiral Granger. The new gal's uncle."

"Admiral's niece would not only have high connections, but a high bullshit threshold," Lansky mused.

Admiral's niece? Aaron pulled his head, and his scowl, from the cabinet to stare at his teammates.

"She's what?"

"Actually, you should ask *she's who*," Prescott corrected absently, not looking up from the sketch pad he was working on.

Aaron stared from man to man, but didn't detect any concern. Prescott was lost in his drawing. Lansky lay on the floor with his laptop angled high against his thighs, playing online poker. Torres, now doing one-handed push-ups, was the only one expending any energy.

"Rembrandt's right. It'd be *who*, not *what*. The who is Bryanna Radisson, niece of Admiral Granger, HQ Pearl Harbor, temporarily assigned to Coronado. I'd imagine they're close, since she lived on Oahu until she went to U of H, Honolulu, for her degree in journalism." Lansky slid Aaron a wicked look and raised one brow. "That'd make her a real professional, Bulldog. One with credentials to go with her family ties."

"What ties?"

"Admiral Granger's niece," Torres grunted as he shifted to one-armed pull-ups. "Who, from the hickey on your neck, is just as hot as she is connected."

Shit. Damn. Sonofabitch.

His head aching from the realization that he'd not only blown it, he'd blown it all to hell, Aaron resisted the urge to slap his hand on his neck and asked, "How does me having a hickey translate into her being hot?"

"You don't do any other kind. You might have charmed her, tried to persuade her, bribed or even threatened," Prescott said, finally looking up long enough to point a finger at Aaron. "But sex? Brother, you only do that with the hotties."

Shit. He didn't know which was worse. Failing to convince the woman to drop the article, or having his team know he'd slept with her in the attempt and *still* failed?

"You should get a beer," Lansky suggested.

"I don't want a beer."

"I meant for me." The man closed his laptop and rolled onto his back, clasping his hands behind his head and giving Aaron a smile. "An alcoholic beverage would make a round of Adventures with a Bait Bunny go down nicely."

"She's not a bait bunny," Aaron snapped.

But he'd treated her like one, hadn't he? He'd used her interest in his status as a SEAL to lure her into bed with no intention of offering her anything back but a good ride and a couple of screaming orgasms to cement his rep as a hot stud deserving that revered status.

God, he sucked.

Then, like an RPG upside the head, it hit him.

"Bryanna is Admiral Granger's niece? As in, he's the string she pulled to get this interview op?"

"That'd be an affirmative."

Aaron had taken a hit to the chest once that'd knocked him back ten feet and, despite his protective gear, had left him bruised and breathless. He felt about the same way now.

"I think I'll take that beer," he muttered, grabbing one from the fridge and, ignoring Lansky's outstretched hand, dropping onto the couch next to Prescott.

"I knew I was going in blind with no intel on the target, but I'd figured the angles. I thought a little judicious use of charm or guilt, whichever seemed like it'd have the strongest effect, would put an end to this article."

"Makes sense to me," Torres said, dropping to the floor to sit, knees raised and arms resting there as he gave his complete attention. "And the results?"

"I screwed up," Aaron admitted, hating the churning in his gut but knowing no other way to deal with his teammates than full honesty. "I got carried away. I was blown away. She's like nobody I've ever met. I thought I could handle her, overwhelm her. I was wrong."

"A lot of women have the power to knock a man back on his ass under the right circumstances," Prescott said quietly, not looking up from his drawing.

They all ignored Lansky's interjection of "Naked circumstances."

"But the right woman? She'll boggle a man's brain while she sends his body straight to heaven and make him grateful for every second. The right woman makes everything matter. Makes everything brighter. Even the bad things."

Prescott was a man with intimate knowledge of the bad things. His pain filled the room, wrapping around them all like a blanket.

Aaron shot a quick look at Lansky, then Torres. He saw the same sympathy in their eyes he knew showed in his own.

They'd all been there when Prescott got married—

the newly formed Team Poseidon had stood as witnesses, all eleven of them. They'd celebrated the birth of his son, mourned the loss of young life to circumstances beyond all control. As a team, they'd drank themselves into oblivion when Prescott's wife called it quits.

It'd been like watching a man get his heart ripped from his chest.

Aaron grimaced, searching for something—anything—to say that'd offer support. But none of them— not even Lansky, a guy known for his serious lack of tact—said a word.

Finally, Prescott glanced up from his drawing and looked from face to face.

"Sorry. Didn't mean to dredge up the past. Just wanted to point out that sometimes the choice seems wrong. But if the woman is right, there really wasn't any choice to begin with."

"Like Bulldog would know if the woman was right after a few drinks and a roll between the sheets?" Lansky laughed. "It's not that simple and it doesn't happen that fast."

"It can be, and it does," Aaron said softly. "Doesn't make it easy. It's no excuse for not completing my mission, though."

"Yet," Prescott corrected, tearing off his drawing and tossing it over so it fluttered onto Aaron's lap. Grinning up from the page was Aaron's own face, little hearts circling his head as he stood at a crossroad next to a signpost claiming one direction as Right, the other as Wrong. "You'll figure it out."

"We'll help. We're Poseidon, brother," Torres said, getting to his feet and offering Aaron a swat to the back that would have felled a smaller man. "Whatever we're in, we're in it together. Like always."

CHAPTER SEVEN

STEPPING INTO THE pristine luxury of 1500 Ocean, the signature restaurant of the plush Hotel del Coronado, Bryanna gave her name to the hostess before looking around. It reminded her of a beach with its light, airy colors and an ocean view that looked close enough to touch just beyond the wall of windows.

Quite a contrast to Olive Oyl's. She was pretty sure she wouldn't see any grizzled sailors in here, she thought as she followed the hostess through the dining room toward a garden table overlooking the water.

"Hello, Uncle. Don't you look handsome," she greeted as the large, uniformed man pushed away from the table as they approached. He was all sailor, but there was definitely nothing grizzled about Uncle Martin.

But it wasn't the two hundred twenty pounds spread over a six-two frame that made him seem imposing. It was the air of power that radiated from him, power that conveyed this was a man who could handle anything. One who could overcome everything. Under it all was an edge of danger, sharp and cutting.

Aaron had that same intensity, she realized as her smile trembled a little at the edges.

"Little Bryanna," he said, wrapping her in a hug. It was like being enveloped by a bear that smelled of Brut cologne. Warm, comfortable and just a tiny bit claustrophobic. "Glad to see you. How're you settling in? Like

California so far? How's your mother? I spoke with her, and your father of course, in our monthly call last week. Tried to talk me into trying that MouthTime thing."

"FaceTime?" Bryanna deciphered as she settled into the chair he pulled out. "Mom and Dad are hooked on it."

They spent the salad course chatting about family, catching up on news and sharing stories of their recent visits. By the time the main course was served, prawns for Bryanna and duck for the admiral, he'd deemed the preliminaries satisfied and allowed the discussion to move on to Bryanna's assignment.

"So?" he prodded, knife in one hand, fork in the other and mouth half-full. "The article you're writing. How's it coming? Will you do the family proud? Did you bring your first draft?"

Used to her uncle's sometimes short, gruff sentences, Bryanna shifted her smile from family-friendly to congenial-business. In other words, she pulled on a layer of bullshit. She hoped it was thick enough to fool her uncle.

"Why don't I give it to you after dinner? You can take it back to your office, read it later. I'm sure it defies protocol to read at the table," she said, trying a joking tone.

"Nonsense." Still eating with one hand, he held out the other.

Bryanna had a brief urge to snag the last prawn from her plate and run as fast as her Jimmy Choos would carry her. But she'd never been a wimp and she didn't see any point in learning that skill now. Not even to win love at first sight.

So she pulled the pages she'd spent most of the night

and all of the day on from her bag and, despite her reluctance to let go, handed them over.

She kept her eyes on her plate as he read, marshaling her arguments as she pushed her rice into geometric shapes. She hadn't changed her focus because Aaron objected to the centerpiece of her campaign. She wasn't the type to sublimate her own needs, her own strengths or, heck, even her style choices in order to get someone else's approval.

Bryanna would never change herself for someone else. That wasn't what she'd done at all. But when her uncle laid the pages on the table between them, she took a quick drink of water to cool the heat in her throat as he tapped an impatient beat over them.

"Well…?"

She didn't have to ask what he was questioning.

"I've been rethinking the scope of this project and this is a representation of that idea. I think it'd be stronger if we take a wider focus so as to incorporate the entirety of the base functions. I'll do a sidebar on the SEALs, of course, but it might be better to take that as a general overview instead of sensationalizing their function." Bryanna ended on an upbeat note, trying to infuse her words with as much finality as she could. After all, this was her job. She was the one putting together the campaign proposal. It was her vision driving the program and she could adjust it if she wanted to.

It only took one look at her uncle's face to see that she wasn't bullshitting him nearly as well as she'd been bullshitting herself. But good ole Uncle Martin, proving he was as much politician as tactician, kept right on smiling.

"Well, now, there's a thought. Nice and simple, easy, even. Something an ensign with basic English skills could manage, of course, but nothing says a civilian needs to bring more to the table than our own personnel. One of the things I admire about you, Bryanna, is the high standard you set for yourself and how well you've lived up to it."

"There's a lot to be said for dipping in toes before taking a deep-sea dive," Bryanna pointed out. She carefully set her fork and knife down, using all of her energy to keep her smile from shaking clear off her face.

"There is, indeed. And there's a place in the world for people who settle for a dip. That place is not the Navy. Do you think we became a world power by taking the easy road? Do you think the Navy SEALs became one of the strongest forces in the known world by trying to please everyone?"

Bryanna shook her head. "I think they've become the best because of their determination, their training and their dedication to their oath. That oath includes something about not seeking recognition or advertising their actions. One of the things they specialize in is covert operations. *Covert* means secret, stealth."

"Very true." Looking unimpressed by her impassioned words, the admiral simply gestured with his fork for her to continue. "And Poseidon?"

"Part of Poseidon's power is their brotherhood. These men are possibly the most cohesive fighting force in the world. Every aspect of their lives is devoted to their team, their mission."

"Indeed. And the details of their overall team mission are known only to these twelve men. And, perhaps, to Admiral Cree, who leads them," her uncle pointed out. "That adds to their air of exclusivity. But their prestige as an elite force does make some people nervous."

Bryanna narrowed her eyes, wondering if there was a message in the admiral's words.

"Their excellence is cause for envy," she agreed. "Like every other element of their training, they go bigger. They cross-train so each man on the team holds multiple ratings. They push harder so each man excels in every aspect of their training. And every single man in Poseidon takes the very core values of the SEALs to heart as a way of life. Especially the value of silence." She knew the awe she felt for that level of dedication rang with evangelical fervor in her voice, but she couldn't help it. Didn't want to, either.

"Excellent summary," her uncle said after a moment. "Isn't that what you're here to share? That standard of excellence?"

He dabbed his mouth with the white linen napkin, then tossed it over his spotless plate.

"Even if it's at the expense of someone else? Do you think that publicity, that funding, takes priority over the anonymity of the teams? Isn't one of the key components to the cohesive power of the team the very fact that they are unrecognized as individuals?"

"All true. Every word of it's fact, Bryanna. And if you can't spin that information in such a way as to protect that anonymity and still promote our forces, your father paid too much for your fancy education. You've been hired to do a job, young lady. To build a campaign around the SEALs' birthday, to create a celebration worthy of their name. One way or the other, you'll do it," he ordered as he got to his feet. "This issue will be settled tomorrow. My office, oh-nine-hundred. You'll bring the campaign you intend to present to Public Affairs after you've defended it to Poseidon and earned their approval."

Oh, boy. Her hand pressed to her stomach, where the rich, buttery prawns did war with nervous butterflies, Bryanna took a deep breath. It looked as if she had one night to make some decisions, and to rewrite the article.

"Will Aaron... I mean, Chief Ward be there?"

"And his commander." Uncle Martin arched one bushy white brow. "You afraid of a little skirmish?"

"Of course not."

That'd be silly.

She was afraid of having her heart broken.

"YOU READY?"

"As I'll ever be." Slanting a look at Savino, Aaron took off his cap, slapped it against his thigh, then put it back on his head. "This is my responsibility. Whatever happens, it's on me. The team will pay enough with the notoriety. Nobody should have to pay with anything else."

"Your official orders were to offer assistance," Savino reminded him with a shrug.

"And the unofficial plan was to stop her," Aaron pointed out. "To prevent this article from making a mockery of Poseidon, more to keep the brotherhood where it belongs. On the down low."

"My unofficial plan was to get Cree to black out our involvement," Savino reminded him. "No plan survives first contact."

Aaron shifted his feet at the paraphrasing of the oft-quoted SEAL saying before routinely responding with "There are two ways to do something. The right way. And again."

Still, Aaron hesitated. He'd worked plenty of missions that carried a heavy cost. He'd spent plenty of sleepless nights mourning collateral damage. But he'd never considered that the cost and damage might impact what he suspected could be the most important relationship in his life.

"The admiral is waiting," Savino said quietly.

"Oh, yeah. The admiral. That'd be Bryanna's uncle."

"Pretty sure he won't keelhaul you for seducing his pretty niece." With that and one of his rare, teasing grins, Savino clapped his hand on Aaron's shoulder for a brief moment, then yanked the door open and waved his teammate inside. "But just in case, we'll keep that on the QT."

"Well, there's reassurance for you," Aaron muttered as he entered the admiral's antechamber. He stood with Savino while the ensign at the desk announced their presence. Without fanfare, they were escorted into Admiral Granger's office.

Shoulder to shoulder, Aaron and Savino stood at attention. They didn't look left, they didn't look right. They simply waited.

But Aaron knew she was there.

He breathed in the coconut-infused floral scent of her. He heard the gentle catch of her breath as he stepped through the door. Most of all, he felt her, the sensual energy that seemed to spike the very air with passion's call.

A call he knew he'd hear for the rest of his life.

"Gentlemen," Admiral Granger greeted in a voice that boomed like cannon fire. "At ease."

As one, both men shifted to a wide stance, their hands clasped behind their backs and their eyes on the admiral.

"Bryanna Radisson, this is one of the Navy's best officers, a highly decorated SEAL and the leader of

Poseidon. Lieutenant Commander Nic Savino, our newest public affairs specialist, Ms. Bryanna Radisson."

"Ma'am."

"Chief Petty Officer Ward, I understand that the two
of you have already met."

Aaron thanked his training for keeping his face expressionless and tried not to think of keelhauling.

"As you both know, Ms. Radisson will be launch-
ing a powerful public-relations campaign built on the
concept of celebrating the fifty-fifth birthday of the
Navy SEALs. Part of that campaign will touch on the
unique role Poseidon plays in the SEAL structure." The
admiral outlined the scope, goals and advantages of
the campaign. With every word, the knot in Aaron's
gut tightened. She'd pulled plenty of information about
Poseidon. Their history, their numbers, the extent of
their training.

"The SEALs are the pride of the Navy," Admiral
Granger continued in that gruff tone. "This campaign
will make them a beacon that will draw likely candi-
dates to the team. The best, the strongest, the most able,
they'll all clamor to serve."

Aaron wanted to point out that they already clamored
plenty. He saw right there on the chart Bryanna had included in her presentation that she'd noted the BUD/S
attrition rate of eighty percent, her notes stressing the
fact that even the best weren't always good enough.

"Now," the admiral harrumphed. "I'm satisfied with
the direction of this campaign. But Ms. Radisson is
rather particular about how it's to be presented. She
wants Poseidon's input and, ultimately, approval. With
that said, Chief Ward, you'll work directly with her to
ensure this information cloaks the anonymity of the
team and holds true to their vow to avoid recognition."

"Because of the exclusivity and power of Poseidon," Bryanna interjected, "I feel it must be addressed with delicacy to avoid problems with the other SEALs as well as ensure continued cooperation and support from the Navy's echelon."

She got it. She understood the threat of what she was doing. Aaron blinked. His heart raced. Even as he re-traced the words, he wanted to give a loud huzzah of triumph. He wanted to grab hold of Bryanna and swing her into his arms, to strip her down to that silky skin and show her just how grateful he was.

But the man staring at him was not only his supe-rior officer, he was the uncle of the woman Aaron was currently visualizing naked.

"I want this settled before eleven-hundred hours. With that in mind, the two of you can use my office to discuss the matter," Admiral Granger said, giving them both a nod. "Savino, with me."

Aaron saw his commander's grin out of the corner of his eye. Knew it was Savino's mark of approval. For some, it wouldn't matter. But to Aaron, it was every-thing. Poseidon, the brotherhood, they were more than his brothers, more than his team. They were his friends, his backup, his family.

Something he'd failed to tell Bryanna before.

But maybe he'd just been given a shot at something almost as rare as the perfect woman.

A second chance.

Now to make damn sure he made the most of it.

CHAPTER EIGHT

"I'm sorry," Aaron said as soon as the door closed behind his superior officers. "Perhaps I should have talked this out instead of *walking* out."

"Perhaps?" Bryanna asked. Obviously at home in her uncle's office in a way that Aaron wasn't, she hitched her hip onto the polished cherrywood desk and crossed one leg over the other. The move hiked the soft blue fabric of her skirt to show a mouthwatering expanse of golden thigh.

Knowing how tempting she was, and how fast that temptation could lure him off track, Aaron forced his eyes to stay on her face. Which was tempting enough.

"The promise of Poseidon having approval over anything that bears our name has a lot of merit. So, yes, perhaps." He tried to read her expression but couldn't tell what she was thinking behind those big, dark eyes. "Why didn't you mention this before?"

"Because I hadn't thought of it before," she admitted, lifting her hands in the air. "When I started this, I saw a job, an opportunity to do something important for a cause I strongly believed in. What I didn't see was the need for someone looking over my shoulder or seeking feedback on my words or style choices."

"And you see the need now?"

"No," Bryanna replied with a laugh. "But something my uncle said sparked a thought. That thought didn't change my plans for the SEAL birthday celebration, or for the various publications and developmental outlines I've drafted."

Aaron wanted to ask her how she was doing. He wanted to know how she'd slept after he left. If her uncle had given her a rough time and what sort of relationship they had. What he really wanted to ask was if she'd thought about him and what those thoughts were. He wanted to know if she wanted him and what it'd take to be with her again. He was desperate to find out if they had a shot at a future and how that possibility would work out.

But his focus had to be his duty. His attention had to be on the mission at hand. He couldn't let his team, or himself, down again by getting distracted.

"What did he say and what did it change?" he made himself ask instead of any of the other questions poised on the tip of his tongue.

For the first time since he'd looked at her, Bryanna glanced away. Her gaze cut to her hands twisting around each other in her lap. Then, with a small frown creased between her brows, she met his eyes again.

"He mentioned the perception of exclusivity and prestige that Poseidon holds and how nervous it makes people." Pulling her lower lip between her teeth, she worried it for a moment as she studied him. "Poseidon is powerful. Strong and focused and nearly invisible. That has to engender not only nerves, but also envy and perhaps fear in others."

Aaron shrugged. "We don't brag, we don't apologize. We are what we are. If what we are causes the enemy to fear, all the better. If what we are causes our competitors to strive harder, good for them." He relaxed enough to rub one hand over his forehead and tried to find the words to make her understand. "But our focus is on our duty, on our mission. Bragging about our training, advertising who we are, negates what we do. Bragging comes from ego, and there's no room for ego on our missions."

"I think I understand that."

She couldn't. Aaron shook his head, but before he could say more, before he could figure out what more to say, she lifted one hand.

"Perhaps," she said, stressing the word in a way that did more to shut him up than the expression on her face, "perhaps you could read what I've written."

Bryanna reached behind her for a paper from the admiral's desk. Aaron noticed her hand was trembling a little as she held it out.

Aaron took it, his frown deepening as he read her outline. Then, a thorough man, he read it again to search for traps or loopholes before glancing at her again.

Looked like he hadn't needed to try so hard to find the right words.

Once again, he should have trusted her.

"You ran this by the admiral?"

"I ran it by Captain Taylor of Public Affairs, who is in charge of the campaign." Bryanna pursed her lips as she nodded at the pages. "Apparently his approval was all that was necessary to convince the admiral that this was the best route."

"You're leaving Poseidon out of the campaign except for this brief mention here?" He pointed to the sidenote where she'd outlined the entirety of how Poseidon was to be included.

"That'd be it. That's why the admiral wanted Team Poseidon's approval. I don't think he believes you'll be satisfied to be referred to as briefly and simply as 'among the SEALs, those who strive to be elite.'"

Aaron's heart pounded loud enough to ring in his ears as he shook his head in wonder.

Damned if he hadn't found a woman as important to

him as his career. One who, if her insights so far were any indication, would understand his devotion to his country, to his team. Understand and accept.

Now that he'd found her, he'd have to get to work at keeping her.

With that in mind, Aaron offered a smile—a charming one, dammit—and tilted his head toward the door.

"Why don't you tell me what led you to make this choice. Then we'll meet with the admiral. After that, I'm off duty. We can go somewhere. Get a drink. Talk about what comes next."

BRYANNA FELT AS if she was teetering on the edge of a precarious cliff and one move to either side would send her plummeting. Which way led to happiness was the question, though.

"Why?" she asked, buying time. A hundred responses flew through Bryanna's mind, but none could keep up with the nerves fluttering in her belly.

Ever since that night, she'd tried to convince herself that her reaction to Aaron was pure romance. That she'd been so caught up in the idea of love at first sight that she'd built him up in her mind. That she'd made him more handsome, more heroic, more intriguing than he really was. Turned out she'd underplayed those traits in her attempt to get over him.

Turned out he was even sexier than she remembered, too.

"Bryanna?" he prompted.

"It seemed like the right thing to do," she said with a shrug. When he gave her an arch look, complete with that little smile that made her want to confess her every secret, Bryanna couldn't stop herself from continuing.

"My career is important. To me, because it's a reflection of who I am, of what I believe in. That's vital. But I also believe that if I do my job right, I'll make a difference. For the Navy, for this base, for the personnel who serve." She tried a deep breath, hoping it'd ease the intensity throbbing in her voice. "I'm not interested in flirting with fame or fortune. I have no intention of compromising my beliefs for sensationalism. I simply want to do my part to serve my country. To share the importance of what we do, to use the power of that to attract new recruits and to solicit funds so the team never has to do without."

Bryanna's face heated at the surprise on Aaron's face. She was a woman gifted with words. On paper, that was. Paper she could revise, rewrite, perfect. Speaking, though, made her feel weird. Her stomach tightened, her flesh chilled, then warmed, then, as if the changing temperatures had shrunk it, stretched too tight over her bones.

"Stop staring at me," she muttered, rubbing her damp palms over the delicate cotton of her skirt.

"I like staring at you. You're hot. Appealing, gorgeous, built. You're passionate, you're smart, you're dedicated. All of that makes for pretty damned sexy."

"You can't kiss me here," she protested, leaning backward in shock. "It's an admiral's office. Isn't that like church to you guys?"

Aaron's laugh filled the room, filled her heart.

"We should go, then."

"Go where?"

"Somewhere that I can kiss you."

Oh, yeah. Bryanna was already on her feet before she remembered that they had a few other things to discuss before they got to the kissing.

"Did you sleep with me to keep me from writing that

article?" She knew the answer in her heart, but some questions had to be asked anyway.

"Did you sleep with me to get more information and insights into Poseidon so you could better write that article?" he countered.

"I guess the answer to both of those is no."

"Good guess. Maybe we should discuss the real answers, though."

Bryanna wasn't sure she was ready for that. This volleying words back and forth, it was a sort of verbal foreplay. Sexy and fun, without any intimate truths to turn it into something more serious.

But the look on Aaron's face, pure stubborn determination, told her that the time had come for truths, intimate and otherwise.

Still, she lifted her chin and said nothing.

"Since I'm the one with all that training facing the terrifying depths of the unknown, why don't I start," Aaron offered, his words hinting at the laughter dancing in his eyes. "I have very strong, probably inappropriate feelings for you."

What was he feeling? But she couldn't ask. Not yet.

"Why inappropriate?" she heard herself wondering instead.

"We only met a couple of days ago, so the timing is probably inappropriate. We haven't even spent an entire day together, so thinking I know everything I need to is probably inappropriate." His gaze didn't leave hers as he shrugged. "And I believed, until just a few minutes ago, that we came from opposing sides of a line that has defined my career. That has formed the focus of my life."

"Those are all important reasons and, yes, all inappropriate." Pressing her lips together to keep them from trembling, Bryanna managed to smile. "Does it make a difference knowing we're on the same side of that line?"

"I don't think it'd matter," he admitted. "What I feel for you is bigger than anything I've felt for another. What I want from you is more than I've ever thought I could have with a woman."

Oh, God. Bryanna was so crazy about him that she could barely think. She wanted to dance in place, she wanted to run from the room and shout her joy up and down the halls. But she wanted to be sure, first.

"And now?" she asked. "What do you think now?"

"Now I want to see where this goes," he admitted. "I feel something for you. I know one night together, a little research on each other and a confrontation in the sanctity of an admiral's office isn't a lot to base a relationship on. But I'm a man who lives on the edge. And that edge teaches you to appreciate the moments. To see life-changing potential and embrace any shot at happiness."

Bryanna's heart leaped in her chest as she struggled to hold back tears of delight. It was as if he'd peeked into her dreams, gathered them up and gift wrapped them all in bright, shiny paper and glittery ribbons.

"You think we have a shot at happiness?"

"I think we have a shot at whatever we want to make this. What do you think?"

Bryanna's stomach clenched. Not with fear this time, but with anticipation. Nerves ran under her skin, tingling little shimmers of delight. She was so ready to see what they could shoot for.

"I have a confession," she admitted quietly, shifting her gaze to her hands for a second to gather her thoughts.

"You're married?"

She gave a breathless laugh.

"Nothing like that."

Obviously willing to risk the higher powers' wrath, Aaron moved forward, stopping inches away, and took her hands in his. His scent wrapped around her, the earthy warmth overplayed by ocean air. The heat from his body seemed to envelop her, to pull her in so she felt as if he'd embraced her with only the touch of his fingers.

"I believe in the power of thought and in making dreams come true. I believe in happy-ever-after. I believe in love at first sight." She bit her lip to keep from saying more and waited. Simply waited.

When Aaron didn't stare in horror or run for the door, the bands around her heart eased. When his face slowly widened into a grin of delight, her heart raced. When he reached out to take her hand and lift it high, brushing his lips in a soft caress over her knuckles, her heart melted.

"Love at first sight, is it?"

"I believe in the possibility of it," she said softly.

"Turns out, love at first sight is something I believe in, too." With her hand still tight in his, he said, "Now that I've seen you."

* * * * *

SPECIAL EXCERPT FROM

◆ HARLEQUIN®

Blaze®

Regan Macintosh doesn't trust Jamie Quinn's roguish charm, but her resolve to keep the sexy stranger away is starting to wane…and if she's not careful, their hungry passion could make them both lose control.

Read on for a sneak preview of
THE MIGHTY QUINNS: JAMIE,
the latest book in Kate Hoffmann's beloved series
THE MIGHTY QUINNS.

Regan walked out into the chilly night air. A shiver skittered down her spine, but she wasn't sure it was because of the cold or due to being in such close proximity to Jamie. Her footsteps echoed softly on the wood deck, and when she reached the railing, Regan spread her hands out on the rough wood and sighed.

She heard the door open behind her and she held her breath, counting his steps as he approached. She shivered again, but this time her teeth chattered.

A moment later she felt the warmth of his jacket surrounding her. He'd pulled his jacket open and he stood behind her, his arms wrapped around her chest, her back pressed against his warm body.

"Better?"

It was better. But it was also more frightening. And more exhilarating. And more confusing. And yet it seemed perfectly natural. "I should probably get to bed," Regan said. "I can't afford to fall asleep at work tomorrow."

He slowly turned her around in his arms until she faced him. His lips were dangerously close to hers, so close she could feel the warmth of his breath on her cheek.

"I know you still don't trust me, but you're attracted to me. I'm attracted to you, too. I want to kiss you," he whispered. "Why don't we just see where this goes?"

"I think that might be a mistake," she replied.

"Then I guess we'll leave it for another time," he said. "Good night, Regan." With that he turned and walked off the deck.

Her heart slammed in her chest and she realized how close she'd come to surrender. He was right; she was attracted to him. She had wanted to kiss him. She'd been thinking about it all night. But in the end common sense won out.

Regan slowly smiled. She was strong enough. She *could* control her emotions when he touched her. Though he still was dangerous, he was just an ordinary guy. And if she could call the shots, maybe she could let something happen between them.

Maybe he'd ask to kiss her again tomorrow. Maybe then she'd say yes.

Don't miss
THE MIGHTY QUINNS: JAMIE
by Kate Hoffmann, available in February 2017
wherever Harlequin® Blaze® books and ebooks are sold.

www.Harlequin.com

Copyright © 2017 by Kate A. Hoffmann

HBEXP0117

New York Times bestselling author

LORI FOSTER

returns with an explosive new series featuring
sexy bodyguards who will do anything to protect
the ones they love.

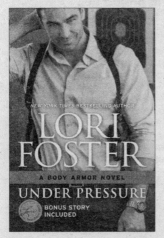

He can protect anything except his heart

Leese Phelps's road hasn't been an
easy one, but it's brought him to
the perfect job—working for the
elite Body Armor security agency.
And what his newest assignment
lacks in size, she makes up for in fire
and backbone. But being drawn to
Catalina Nicholson is a dangerous
complication, especially since the
very man who hired Leese could
be who's threatening her.

What Catalina knows could get
her killed. But who'd believe the
sordid truth about her powerful
stepfather? Beyond Leese's ripped body and brooding gaze is a man of
impeccable honor. He's the last person she expects to trust—and the
first who's ever made her feel safe. And he's the only one who can help
her expose a deadly secret, if they can just stay alive long enough…

Pick up the first story in the **Body Armor** series today!

Be sure to connect with us at:

Harlequin.com/Newsletters
Facebook.com/HarlequinBooks
Twitter.com/HQNBooks

HQN™

www.HQNBooks.com

PHLF993R

Private security gets a whole lot more personal and provocative in *The Protectors*, a sexy new series by *New York Times* bestselling author

BRENDA JACKSON

Strong enough to protect her.
Bold enough to love her.

When good girl Margo Connelly becomes Lamar "Striker" Jennings's latest assignment, she knows she's in trouble. And not just because he's been hired to protect her from an underworld criminal. The reformed bad boy's appeal is breaching all her defenses, and as the threats against her increase, Margo isn't sure which is more dangerous: the gangster targeting her, or the far too alluring protector tempting her to let loose.

Though Striker's now living on the right side of the law, he's convinced his troubled past keeps Margo out of his league. But physical chemistry explodes into full-blown passion when they go on the run together. Surrendering to desire could be a deadly distraction—or finally prove that he's the only man qualified to keep her safe, and win her love.

Available January 31!

Order your copy today.

Be sure to connect with us at:

Harlequin.com/Newsletters
Facebook.com/HarlequinBooks
Twitter.com/HQNBooks

www.HQNBooks.com

PHBRJ000